ALL WE HAVE
TO BELIEVE IN

Jeffrey J. Lousteau

All We Have To Believe In

Published by The Conrad Press in the United Kingdom 2020

Tel: +44(0)1227 472 874
www.theconradpress.com
info@theconradpress.com

ISBN 978-1-913567-21-7

Cover: Palace of Fine Arts, San Francisco - Bernard Maybeck, Architect; image adapted from photograph collection of 1915 Panama-Pacific Exposition; History Center - San Francisco Public Library

Typesetting and cover composed by: Charlotte Mouncey, www.bookstyle.co.uk

The Conrad Press logo was designed by Maria Priestley.

Printed and bound in Great Britain by Clays Ltd, Elcograf S.p.A.

To E,
who made this possible

The winds out of the west land blow,
My friends have breathed them there;
Warm with the blood of lads I know
Comes east the sighing air.

from Stanza XXXVIII - *A Shropshire Lad*
A.E. Housman

PART ONE

Chapter 1

May 1919

He would remember it as a night gone terribly wrong – suspended in disbelief, then reaching for her sprawled unconscious at his feet, another casualty, one more innocent unprepared for the truth. What had she done to deserve it? For that matter, what had any of them done to deserve it? Clear answers would elude him, however, leaving only a nagging feeling of complicity…

The evening had begun with such promise, the world seemingly reborn as a sea breeze and the smell of jasmine filled the air with a sense of anticipation. From trolleys, touring cars, and horse-drawn carriages, guests had alighted at the Lombard Gate to the sounds of a stirring military tune in the distance. Ladies in diaphanous gowns were born along on the arms of men, a courtly procession on gravel paths lit by Japanese lanterns, culminating in a rose garden forecourt to the Parthenon, as re-imagined in Columbia River Basin timber. White-gloved Marines stood at attention before the backlit colonnade, red, white, and blue bunting ran along the entablature, and a banner below the pediment read "Welcome Home Boys!"

'Look, Edward,' Constance exclaimed, 'it's simply magnificent!'

'Grand,' he said distractedly as they paused before the edifice that four years earlier had been the Oregon Pavilion for the Panama-Pacific Exposition. 'I used to see it from my barracks,' he remarked, '—hovering out there in the fog, just like my dreams of a classical education...'

'Oh, but you're a hero now – you've helped win the peace!' Constance said, prompting them on through the rose garden and passed the marine band.

Tall and rail-thin, his overseas cap covering a receding hairline, Edward Dooley knew he was no hero; he'd managed to survive, that was all. Delivered from the trenches the previous autumn and told he was free to pick up his life where he'd left off, he'd grown wary by the time the ferry pulled up to the docks of San Francisco two weeks ago. Tearful reunions with family and friends since then, a host of accolades, and an exuberant parade down Market Street had left him unsettled. It was all happening so fast – there was no time for reflection, for taking stock. But knowing that after this Victory Ball he could put away his uniform for good, he had resolved to push his doldrums aside and make the most of the evening.

Sensing this in his silence, Constance squeezed his arm. 'Let's enjoy ourselves tonight, shall we, Edward? Let's be glad it's finally over, and that you're home safe and sound...'

If he felt more guilty than fortunate to have made it home with merely a knee injury, he also knew that everybody had been through trauma of some sort lately – whether the war or the influenza epidemic – and the last thing he wanted was to feel like an outsider. With his sweetheart caught up in the festive atmosphere and looking so pretty in her new indigo gown, Edward guided her into the stream of guests climbing the steps at the base of the pavilion.

At the top landing they had just taken up a spot beside a column to look out for his parents when Constance noticed a group of civilians at the great doors nodding to them deferentially. Holding her clutch in her gloved hands, she nudged Edward with her elbow. 'See how grateful everyone is for your service!' she said, before returning a happy wave.

Edward looked on benignly a moment. Though the gulf between his experience overseas and what people at home wanted to believe disturbed him, the evening's promise of catharsis buoyed his spirits. Placing his arm around her shoulder, he said, 'It's good to be home.'

Constance looked up at him, her blue eyes sparkling. 'Oh, let's go inside, Edward!' she said excitedly, turning to the great doors, 'Your parents will find us somehow!'

The mood in the hall was boisterous, the music of a popular minstrel band nearly drowned out by laughter and shouted conversations. Society ladies in heavy silk gowns and dowagers in somber wool suits lingered at the coat check, passing judgment on the young women who were gathered like exotic birds at the edge of the dance floor, eagerly awaiting the opening ceremony. Patriotic deprivations were a distant memory now, so eager were they to preview their stylish hats and slim-line chiffon frocks – Georgette crepe for Constance, with a light blue taffeta sash and matching bonnet. Such festive colors were offset by military men in olive drab uniforms, business leaders and public officials in black tie. Smoke from cigars and cigarettes rose with the laughter, high above the bunting, balloons, and crystal chandeliers, swirling around the golden eagle atop the proscenium arch.

Edward didn't recognize many other soldiers – most men from his regiment, the 362nd, were already back in their home-towns across the Pacific Northwest. Steering Constance through the commotion, they made their way to the hospitality station at the north end of the hall, where they were relieved to link up with her brother as planned.

'It's a miracle we could find each other in this bedlam!' Morgan shouted as he shook Edward's hand and kissed his sister on the cheek.

'I had no idea it would be such a big deal,' Edward yelled back. 'I doubt the boys of the San Francisco corps have ever been assembled together in one room!'

Plucking two glasses of punch from the bar and handing them to Edward, Morgan said with a wink, 'These are the ones who made it back…'

Morgan Doherty had been a classmate of Edward's at Sacred Heart, the Christian Brothers high school where the aspiring merchant class of Irish ancestry sent their sons. Quick-witted but slight of stature, he'd taken to Edward immediately for what he mistook as aloofness (in fact, Edward had been shy, but with two older brothers he'd earned a pass with schoolyard bullies.) Despite differences in their stations, they'd become fast friends – they enjoyed discussing their favorite books, going to the pictures together, and afterward ambling through the lobbies of the city's opulent hotels. Edward came to know Constance, four years Morgan's junior and then under the tutelage of the nuns at Convent of the Blessed Sacrament, by spending many happy afternoons at the Doherty's genteel home.

Now seeing her delighted by all the pageantry, Edward grew nostalgic. Though he'd been compelled to quit high school after his family's business foundered, he was touched when Morgan had vowed not to let their friendship lapse; as for Constance, she'd looked up to Edward all the more for his sense of responsibility. The three had been inseparable at the Panama-Pacific Exposition, ending each day in the Court of the Universe, where Morgan, then in college, would recite poetry by the fountain and ignore their snickering. Reunited once again, Edward's blue-grey eyes twinkled as the three of them took in the splendor of the Victory Ball.

'Look – there's Mayor Rolph!' Constance called out as a spotlight streaked across the dance floor, catching up to a dapper man in a top hat making his way to the stage. The musicians lurched from a ragtime number to a military drum roll as the Presidio Commandant, an officious, bespectacled man, tried in vain to call the crowd to order.

When a measure of decorum had descended over the gathering, the beaming mayor declared, 'It is my honor to stand here on behalf of this great city…the Queen of the Pacific that was nearly vanquished just thirteen years ago…to recognize America's ascendance in world affairs…and welcome home our heroic sons of San Francisco – I promise to be brief…'

The crowd erupted in delirious cheers, and as Mayor Rolph bowed to the military brass assembled on stage to his right, Morgan quipped, 'I don't recall Sunny Jim ever being brief.' Constance giggled, while Edward surveyed the crowd, looking for his parents.

Holding his right hand aloft until the cheering had subsided, the mayor then proclaimed in his melodious baritone, 'We bade you valiant men in uniform bon voyage when you set off for France…part of a vast army of deliverance whose deeds in the face of a relentless foe…turned the tide of battle…' here he brought his fist down to the podium for emphasis, 'and made as certain as fate the overwhelming victory won by Allied arms!'

A great roar rose up and shouts of 'Hear! Hear!' echoed in the rafters as the mayor waved majestically to the crowd.

After the army chaplain had invoked God's blessing, the Mayor and the Commandant turned to the gigantic American Flag that formed the backdrop to the stage and tried leading the crowd in the Pledge of Allegiance. But with their backs to the audience the effort faltered, and to keep the ceremony from unraveling altogether the Mayor quickly returned to the podium to present the Commandant with a proclamation from the city's Board of Supervisors. Much of the exchange was drowned out by the chatter filling the hall, just as Edward spotted his mother, tall and imperious with a shock of white hair, coming through the crowd with his father in tow.

'We can only hope things were more orderly overseas,' Honora said dryly by way of greeting her son. She wore a grey wool suit with a high-waisted skirt, a cameo brooch on her white batiste blouse, and a black bonnet with a spray of heavy silk flowers better suited to a funeral. Edward's father, James, red-faced and stooped, wore his Sunday best and took his son's hand in both of his while mouthing his hellos to the Dohertys.

Alert to the pent-up enthusiasm in the hall, the Mayor hastily declared the Victory Ball officially underway, whereupon the band launched into a raucous rendition of the "12th Street Rag". With hundreds of giddy young couples spilling onto the dance floor, Constance handed her bonnet to Morgan and excitedly dragged Edward into the throng, where despite his bum knee he did his best to get in step with the music.

'Given the occasion, you'd think she could summon a happier disposition,' Edward said looking back to his parents, whose reaction to the rambunctious scene was a study in contrast. Honora appeared to disapprove, as she often did in large settings where she couldn't dominate the atmosphere, while James seemed to have slipped her spell and looked positively jovial in Morgan's company.

'Your parents must be so proud of you, Edward,' Constance ventured, '—the only one of their sons to ship off to the crusades.'

Edward let the remark pass, though he considered euphemisms like "crusades" and "noble cause" a way of sidestepping any mention of the horrors he'd experienced. 'Too bad my brothers didn't come tonight,' he said, guiding Constance deeper into the crowd. 'Colm wouldn't give the 30th Regiment the satisfaction, and Walter thinks that because he was stationed here, the party isn't for him.' Drawing Constance close, he went on, 'Anyhow, it's hard to tell whether she's proud of me or simply glad I'll be gainfully employed again as of next week.'

Her cheek against his chest, Constance said, 'She'll have to accept that things are changing, Edward, and your brothers will have to start carrying their fair share of the load.' He said nothing as the tune came to an end and a slow number started up. They danced in silence a minute before she added, 'We have our own future to consider, after all…'

That their relationship had begun in friendship was important to Edward. Early on, they'd enjoyed a good-natured rivalry in board games and tennis, and would place nickel bets before a Chaplin picture to see who could maintain a straight face longer. She considered him very knowledgeable and enjoyed listening to him describe whatever he happened to be reading; in turn, he liked to make her laugh by comically reciting from Gibbons' *History of the Decline and Fall of the Roman Empire*, which was prominently displayed in the Doherty's bookcase. As she grew older, Edward was pleased when she'd ask his opinion about something – the choice of which handbag went with a certain outfit, a piano piece by Beethoven compared to one by Mozart, whether it was the Austro-Hungarians or the Germans who were to blame for the war in Europe. By the time she started high school the two were so well paired that no one was surprised when she asked him to her winter formal. Now, comforted by her familiar scent and swaying to "One Fleeting Hour" as they had many times before, Edward could almost imagine the past two years as having been a no more than a dream – that it made perfect sense to marry Constance, start a family, and embark on a prosperous career.

But everything was different now. He'd seen men suffer and die, men he'd gotten to know, here one minute, blown to bits the next. Doubts that she'd ever understand him, that he wasn't the man for her, left him conflicted, wondering whether he could admit what needed to be said. He was reminded of a firefight in Belgium during the final week of the war. A member of his squad had gone down and in the heat of the moment Private Miller had confronted the Lieutenant – *You rushed it, Foster, you know damn well!* It was the right thing to say at the wrong time, but Miller didn't give a damn; despite the consequences of insubordination, he'd stood his ground, and Edward had admired him for it.

Only now, as much as Edward wished he could confide his doubts to Constance, his sense of duty as a gentleman got the better of him and he held his tongue. The more they danced, the more disappointed he felt in himself, however, and the more resentful of Constance he became, until suddenly he blurted over her shoulder, 'Tell me something, Con, you'd say overcoming adversity makes a person stronger, right?'

'Sure, I suppose so,' she replied.

Steering her around until they were face to face again, he abruptly stopped dancing, and said, 'Well, I've only just gotten back, see, and with all that's happened you can understand why I don't want to rush things, can't you?'

Embarrassed that others were beginning to stare, Constance pressed her head against his shoulder and resumed the dance. She didn't doubt that his war experience must have been terrible, but couldn't he see that it hadn't been easy for her, either, what with the constant uncertainty over his well-being, all the sacrifices on the home front, fighting the horrible flu epidemic? While she'd known him to be moody at times, he'd always managed to snap out of it – but since his return he seemed to be completely preoccupied with himself.

Suddenly bothered by the scratchy wool of his uniform, she pulled away. "I'm not the one rushing things, Edward," she said curtly, '– seeing as how we're practically *engaged* now…'

Edward blanched at the memory of his boorish behavior on their seaside outing a week ago, but before he could respond Constance was pulling him along on a jaunty new number.

He was soon winded, lost in the crowd, a kaleidoscope of searing images flashing through his mind – foreign faces, wagon wheels caked with mud, great geysers of dirt and severed limbs, ramshackle railcars clattering by – and he could hear Constance saying, 'We're not getting any younger, you know…' Blinking hard, he focused on her mouth, on the words, 'You do love me, Edward, don't you? Tell me you love me.'

'I do, Con, sure I do,' he managed to say, gasping for air, but with his knee aching and beads of sweat forming on his forehead, it was all he could do to grab her hand and pull her through the crowd to the edge of the dance floor.

Chapter 2

When he'd pulled himself together, Edward peered over the heads of other bystanders to find his parents. Eventually he spotted his mother by her white hair and saw that she was speaking rather insistently with their former neighbors, the Rileys, which struck Edward as tactless given that their only son had been killed in action. Turning to Constance, he said, 'It's hot as Hades here – let's get some punch…'

They were sipping refreshments at the hospitality station when Constance caught sight of her brother beckoning from a nearby café table. Calling this to Edward's attention, they made their way over and plopped down in the chairs Morgan had been holding for them.

'This just beats all, doesn't it, Morgan?' Constance declared, fanning herself with a program. 'I don't think I've ever seen so many people dancing!'

'Some bash alright,' he said, opening his cigarette case to Edward. 'Who'd have thought tonight would be warm enough for gossamer gowns and blossomy bonnets?'

'Gossamer gowns and blossomy bonnets!' Constance repeated with a little laugh, as she removed her silk gloves one finger at a time. 'Morgan, how poetic!'

Morgan was never more alive than at a party. To Edward's amazement, even if his friend were ill he would come to life like a marionette as soon as he entered a room full of happy people. He seemed to draw electricity from them and return it ten-fold, a one-man dynamo capable of ingratiating himself with perfect strangers simply by telling a funny story or tickling out a tune on a piano. Now as Edward leaned into the cigarette lighter his friend held open for him, he noticed a wink from brother to sister and cringed at the thought of Morgan reprising the recitation by moonlight he'd made the last night of the Panama-Pacific Fair.

'No, Morgan, *please!*' Edward cried in mock distress, 'Not *A Shropshire Lad!*' Not "Wake: the silver dusk returning; up the beach of darkness brims!"'

Morgan offered a sly grin as he pulled a well-worn copy of Housman's ode from his breast pocket, and fending off Edward's attempt to snatch the little book, he found the tabbed section he was looking for and addressed his sister first:

> *OH see how thick the goldcup flowers*
> *Are lying in field and lane,*
> *With dandelions to tell the hours*
> *That never are told again.*
> *Oh may I squire you round the meads*
> *And pick you posies gay?*
> *—'Twill do no harm to take my arm.*
> *'You may, young man, you may.*

Constance sighed wistfully and Edward acquiesced with a smile. In fairness, Morgan's delivery had improved greatly over the course of his college career, and Edward raised his eyebrows expectantly as the next stanza was addressed to him:

Ah, spring was sent for lass and lad,
'Tis now the blood runs gold,
And man and maid had best be glad
Before the world is old.
What flowers to-day may flower to-morrow,
But never as good as new.
—Suppose I wound my arm right round—
'Tis true, young man, 'tis true.'

With a mischievous smile, Morgan snapped the little book shut, held up his punch glass, and declared, 'To lovebirds in springtime!'

Constance looked adoringly at her brother and nestled up to Edward, who bit his lip and shook his head in resignation. 'Ya done good, Billy,' he said in a southern accent, '—why, yer a reglar sophisti-cat!'

Morgan chuckled at the reference to the Will Rogers vaudeville routine they'd seen as schoolboys, and mimicking Rogers to his sidekick, replied, 'Why, thank ya, Buck!' As he tucked away his Housman while Constance and Edward took in the festivities, he remarked, 'Edward, did you happen to see what The Cowboy Philosopher had to say about the Peace Conference? He figures Republicans don't want this League of Nations thing to pass 'cause they're jealous the Democrats got to run this last war and they want to run one of their own!'

Edward smirked. His mother, who came from a long line of Boston Democrats, sometimes made snide comments within the Dooley household about Morgan's father being an ardent Republican. Unaware of this – and with Will Rogers' flare for sarcasm – Constance now asserted that Roosevelt had made

21

the war with Spain a romp, after all.

'Ah, a pity the Ol' Rough Rider left us this year…' Morgan observed with a sigh.

Edward rolled his eyes, prompting a grin from Morgan, before conceding, 'It does seem Southern Democrats would just as soon have Wilson eat his fourteen points…'

'Oh, those Dixie Democrats!' Constance exclaimed, parroting her father, 'They think the Confederacy was the best thing going…' Folding her gloves into her clutch, she added, 'You never did think much of southern hospitality, did you Morgan?'

'True enough, sis,' he replied. He'd worked in army logistics back in Washington during the war and had been promoted to captain at the end. Now, looking sharp in his campaign hat and serge tunic, he said, 'Give me New York or Philadelphia any day.'

Edward said nothing. He'd never been to Philadelphia, and his time in New York had amounted to strolling up the Great White Way one afternoon with some army buddies before shipping off to France. (It was the return trip ten months later that he'd never forget – how quiet everyone got when the Statue of Liberty came into view again.)

Constance was enthralled by all the dazzling frocks and head-dresses, the officers so dashing with their Sam Browne belts, the gusto of the civilian band – this was not the staid military affair she'd feared. She was soon engaged in conversation with a girl at the next table about a silk slip they'd seen on someone, which, in turn, led to a spirited discussion about the judicious use of Valencienne lace. Meanwhile, Morgan was going on about the timeliness of post-war factory conversions, when out of the corner of his eye Edward spotted a stream of army nurses wheeling disabled veterans to a secluded area at the right of the stage.

When Morgan realized Edward was no longer listening, he looked to see what was going on, then leaning over, said, 'I'm afraid those are the boys who only made it halfway home...'

Edward glowered at his friend (there were times when his cleverness went too far), and they looked on in silence for a moment before Edward, his eyes still fixed on the scene, said, 'Most of the wounded from the 362nd are still in St. Nazaire until they're strong enough for the trip home. Those fellows are from which outfits?'

Duly admonished, Morgan replied, 'The 30th Infantry and the 143rd Artillery – most got back in late January.' He removed a flask from his breast pocket and fortified his punch, then offered some to Edward, who accepted.

As they sipped their drinks, Edward surveyed the wounded veterans, some on crutches, most in wheelchairs. Men who'd suffered head injuries wore enormous bandages, and a few who'd evidently been blinded cocked their heads at odd angles to make out the music. 'Know any of them?' Edward asked.

Morgan began to raise his arm to point, then thought better of it. With a nod, he said, 'As a matter of fact, that's Jimmy Fitzsimmons over there...' indicating the young man in a wheelchair who was larger than the others around him. 'Remember? Quite the ballplayer back in the day – pretty bad off now, though, I'm afraid...'

Fitzsimmons had been an upper classman when Edward and Morgan entered Sacred Heart, a stand-out baseball player who'd made a name for himself in local exhibition games before eventually signing with the San Francisco Seals. After leaving high school Edward had relied on Morgan to keep him informed of noteworthy alums, and the two of them sometimes took in a Seals game at Big Rec just to see Fitzsimmons play. They followed the team faithfully in 1915, the year the team won the Pacific Coast League pennant.

Edward nodded to confirm that he'd spotted Fitzsimmons, but also by way of resolving something in himself. 'I'd like to go see him, Morgan,' he said, getting to his feet, '—to pay my respects.' His friend looked at him, startled, then slowly rose from his chair.

'We'll be just a minute, Con,' Edward said, tapping her lightly on the shoulder. By the time she turned Edward had already set off toward the stage, and Morgan quickly held up his hand to indicate she needn't follow. She glanced in Edward's direction, smiled at her brother, then returned to her conversation with the girl at the next table.

Edward's experiences as a soldier had left him finely attuned to the whims of fate: why he'd been spared – and Pitowski, Pereira, and Blanchard from his platoon had not – would haunt him the rest of his life. He'd grown up fearful of his mother's Catholic piety, but doubted that her faith had ever been tested like his was overseas. The circumstances had been so appalling that the very notion of God was impossible to fathom: amid all the senseless violence it seemed folly to attribute his survival to anything other than luck.

Where religion failed him, Edward did find solace in philosophy, however. In his darkest moments he would recall a heady exchange he'd had five years earlier with his younger cousin,

Michael. After discovering they shared an keen interest in Jack London's maritime adventure *The Sea Wolf*, they'd spent an evening passing the book back and forth, reciting passages between the hard-hearted Captain Larsen arguing that life is cheap – *Nature is a spendthrift…In our loins are the possibilities of millions of lives* – and the rejoinders of the young idealist held captive on Larsen's seal-hunting ship – *You have read Darwin misunderstandingly when you conclude that the struggle for existence sanctions your wanton destruction of life.*

'For man is endowed with a *soul*,' Michael had proclaimed, 'and that's what makes him different from other beasts,' prompting Edward to add, 'And by resisting the temptation to do evil, he can win eternal life!' Hunkered down in the trenches, the memory of that episode provided more comfort to Edward than any number of *Our Father's* and *Hail Mary's*. (Later he wondered whether Michael had drawn strength from the same exchange after learning that his older brother, Patrick, had been killed at Saint Mihiel.)

Now as Edward made his way through the maze of café tables, passed other vets reunited with family, friends, and sweethearts, he suspected that each of these men had awful memories of their own which, like him, they felt obliged to keep to themselves. Something was changed in each of them, though – this Edward knew in his gut. What he did not yet know was that the impacts of the war could not be contained, that eventually loved ones would come to feel them, too.

Jimmy Fitzsimmons wasn't necessarily the worst-off of the hundred or so wounded veterans in attendance, but as Edward approached with Morgan he grew apprehensive seeing the magnitude of the young man's injuries. His right arm had been amputated at the shoulder, and his large frame was folded uncomfortably in a wheelchair. The right side of his head and face was sheathed in an elaborate bandage, so he turned his head to listen with his left ear.

'Hi there, Fitz, it's Morgan Doherty!' Morgan boomed with a familiarity he felt entitled to, having visited him at Letterman Hospital several times since January. Fitzsimmons nodded and made a short wave with his scarred left hand.

'I thought you might remember my friend Edward Dooley here,' Morgan went on, '—from our days at Sacred Heart…'

The vet looked up with his left eye. 'Dooley,' he repeated. 'Sure, I remember.'

It was hard for Edward to conceal his astonishment. Burns on the left side of the big man's face hinted horribly at the wreckage beneath the bandages; his lips were purple, and, missing several teeth, he had trouble with s's when he spoke.

'Good to see you again, Fitz,' Edward said, girding himself to awkwardly shake the man's left hand. 'Thank heavens we're home, huh?' he added, with immediate regret.

Morgan started talking about the old days – how stern the Christian Brothers had been, a thrilling double-header the Seals had played against the Oakland Oaks – but Fitz just nodded and Edward was tongue-tied, feeling self-conscious about blocking the view of the festivities for the other veterans in wheelchairs.

Though it troubled Edward that good men like Pitowski and Cousin Patrick were gone, he also felt that they were lucky in a way. Even if all that remained were memories and a few precious photographs, at least they'd be remembered by loved

26

ones as they once had been – full of youth and promise. What troubled Edward were the men who'd returned with something missing, like an arm, a leg, an eye. He was reminded of Corporal Stagby's wounds – 'too damn cruel a fate,' the sergeant had said – knowing that those men would have to live with the manifestation of their sacrifice for the rest of their lives. These were tragic figures, so grievously injured as to be shunted off to the shadows of a Victory Ball. Now it struck Edward that men like Stagby and Fitz weren't heroic simply because of what they'd suffered overseas, but also for what they'd been sentenced to endure at home.

Morgan was going on about Lefty O'Doul pitching for the Yankees now when to Edward's dismay he spotted Constance approaching from the side, looking up at him expectantly as she made her way between the wheelchairs.

'Edward, Gary and Ophelia are asking for you,' she said, drawing near, 'They can't stay long and…Oh!' Caught short by the sight of Fitz, she drew her hand to her mouth. What from across the hall looked to be soldiers on the mend – the gallant warriors she'd read about in the newspapers, making the world safe for democracy – upon closer inspection presented a shocking picture: dozens of amputees and burn victims, many of them lost souls now staring back at her blankly. She stumbled a bit before Edward embraced her about the shoulders.

'Constance, dear,' he said as calmly as he could, 'this is a friend of ours from Sacred Heart, Jimmy Fitzsimmons.' The big man nodded politely but didn't look her in the eye, having grown accustomed to the frightful effect he had on civilians, particularly women.

Anxious to regain her composure, she held out her hand.

'Why yes, of course. How do you do?' she said, then realizing there was no right hand to shake, she became flustered and reflexively pressed her clutch to her stomach.

'I've told you about my sister, Fitz,' Morgan said airily, trying to mask the awkwardness, 'Always the belle of the ball!'

'She's a little peach, alright,' someone in the vicinity said in a distinct southern drawl. Edward glanced around, alarmed, but before he could identify the speaker, he heard the voice again, saying, 'I been waitin' a long time for somma that…'

'Knock it off!' Fitz snarled to someone behind him.

Edward and Morgan looked passed Fitz to a man in a wheelchair with a flushed face and cloudy eyes. One of his legs was missing and he seemed to have suffered a back injury as well for he used a cane to compensate for his poor posture.

'Never mind, Fitz,' Morgan said loudly, 'there's a heckler in every crowd these days.'

The man shot Morgan a foul look, then probed toward Constance with his cane. She recoiled in disgust, and Fitz, clenching the armrest of his wheelchair, made a quarter turn just as Edward stepped forward to cut off the man's view. 'Now listen, friend…' Edward started to say, when he saw an army nurse hastily approaching.

'Minding our manners, Mr. Wilkerson?' she asked brightly, coming up behind the man. She looked as young as many of the wounded veterans but carried herself with a maturity beyond her years. Addressing Edward, she said, 'I'm afraid Mr. Wilkerson here may have gotten a head start on the party so I'm going to fetch him a nice hot cup of coffee.'

'Goddammit, Agnes, it's *Jeb*!' the man growled, 'I keep tellin' ya t' call me Jeb!'

'Okay, Jeb, that's enough,' she said, gripping him by the shoulders and pulling him back into his seat. She came around and glared at him. 'Now you leave these good people alone, hear? I'll be right back.' Turning to leave, she added, 'And it's Angela, remember?'

The man mumbled something and looked down like a forlorn dog. Morgan had steadied Constance on his arm, and the two watched uneasily as Edward tried to smooth things over. 'Our buddy Fitz here was in the 30th Infantry,' he said loudly to Wilkerson. 'Was that your outfit, too?'

The man eyed Edward indifferently, a sulky sag to his lips. At length, he said, 'I'uz in the artillery,' before adding with a snarl, '—backin' up "San Francisco's Own."'

'"Rock of the Marne!"' Morgan called out, quoting the hard-won slogan of the 30th Infantry in hopes of rallying the other vets. Some nodded, but most, including Fitz, didn't respond.

The shabby man grumbled, 'From the looks of it, you two was pushin' papers someplace while we'uz gettin' the shit kicked out of us over there.'

'Actually, *Jeb*,' Morgan said tartly, 'Edward fought with the Powder River boys in the Argonne last September – pushed the Huns back across the Siegfried Line.'

After a moment came the surly reply, 'Ain't his daddy proud...'

'Why we were just talking about southern hospitality, weren't we, Edward?' Morgan said with a twinkle in his eye, turning to be sure the man couldn't miss the captain's insignia on his sleeve. Edward grimaced, but Morgan, focused on the disheveled Southerner, said cheerily, 'I surely do hope you enjoy your stay here in San Francisco!'

Wilkerson eyed Morgan sullenly a moment , then said, 'Go to hell you Yankee faggot…'

Morgan grinned broadly just as the nurse returned with a tray of coffee. The artilleryman petulantly took a gulp of the scorching liquid and started to cough and sputter. Edward was bending down to offer a cup to Fitz when Morgan leaned in to whisper that he would escort Constance back. She was trembling now, and sensing a retreat, Wilkerson wiped his mouth with the back of his hand, and said, 'How 'bout a little squeeze before you go, sweetie pie?'

When he thrust his cane out to block their exit, Constance screamed, whereupon Fitz instinctively swept his left arm through the air and caught the drunken man by the collar as he lurched forward. In the commotion, Edward bobbled the coffee cup and knocked the tray from the nurse's hands, sending it crashing to the floor. When Morgan tried kicking the fallen cane away, Constance clutched Edward for support.

Doubled over on the floor but restrained by Fitz, Wilkerson began to throw up, causing Constance to shriek and jump back, though not enough to spare her silk shoes and the hem of her gown. Other veterans bent forward in their wheelchairs to help drag the sprawled artilleryman away from the stunned trio, while the nurse, already on her knees, pulled a towel from her apron and tried whisking vomit from the lady's dress.

Looking down at this, Constance was overcome by nausea and swayed in Edward's arms. As Fitz struggled to reseat himself, his bandages came askew and she saw that he was missing half his jaw. Her eyes went wide in terror, she began to hyperventilate, and before Edward knew what was happening, she'd slipped his grasp and crumpled to the floor.

Chapter 3

'What in God's name were you thinking, Edward?' Honora said as she took her seat in the front parlor of the Dooley's flat at half passed eleven.

Walter set the tea service down on the sideboard and looked uneasily to his brother. He'd arrived home just as Edward and his parents were returning from the Victory Ball, and noting the tension in the air, he'd made up a late-night refresher while Edward telephoned Morgan to ask after Constance. Now as he poured the tea, Walter started talking about the picture show he'd seen that evening but found that no one was particularly interested. Drawn drapes, dim light from the two table lamps, and the cloying smell of carnations on the mantel only added to the oppressive atmosphere. He handed cups of hot tea to Edward in silence.

'As I've explained, Mother,' Edward said wearily, delivering a cup and saucer to her, 'Morgan and I never intended to put her in an uncomfortable situation. We'd gone over to say hello to Jimmy Fitzsimmons, that's all.' He dropped onto the sofa, upsetting the lace doilies, and added with a sigh, 'Why she came looking for us…Oh, God, what a disaster…'

Honora hastily took a sip of tea. 'Well I think it's simply outrageous – having invalids at a ball! What a ghastly idea! It's little wonder others weren't traumatized as well…' After another sip, 'At a celebration, no less – what foolishness!'

Edward closed his eyes, exhausted. 'They deserved to be there as much as anybody, Mother – probably most of all, as a matter of fact.' He opened his eyes and saw her scowl but went on, 'They weren't bothering anybody – they were as far out of the way as possible.'

'They weren't even ambulatory, so what's the point of their being at a ball?'

'The point *is* that they served honorably, and we should be in their debt...I daresay not many of us would trade places with them.'

'Well said, boyo,' James Dooley offered, raising his teacup to Edward and ignoring his wife's grumbling. 'But don't knock yourself – you'll always be able to say you did your part in the Great War...'

Walter frowned, relieved to be done with his military service. Though two years older than Edward, he'd been sickly as a child, and after barely passing the army physical he'd been stationed at the Presidio for the duration of the war. Colm, the eldest of the three boys, had been drafted as well, but owing to disciplinary problems he never shipped overseas. As with so many things, it had been left to Edward to do the family proud.

'They were rubbing our noses in it,' Honora observed haughtily. 'Someone in charge insisted that those boys be put there on display tonight, and it was tasteless and mean-spirited.'

'What's mean-spirited is keeping them out of sight, Mother,' Edward said in a surprisingly defiant tone, '—that is until some circus impresario starts charging two-bits to see them.' Walter and his father looked at each other uncomfortably.

'Don't be flippant, Edward,' Honora said, her lips tightening, 'No one's calling them freaks. There are modern prosthetic devices those men can use so they can fit in and not draw attention to themselves.'

'Out of sight, out of mind,' muttered Edward.

'I didn't say that!'

'Well, in any case, son,' James interjected, 'your Constance suffered an awful shock tonight. What did Morgan say when you called?'

Edward shook his head dejectedly, and repeated Morgan's one-word summary, '"Overwrought."'

James nodded. 'War's a brutal thing – it's best that women are well away from it…'

'That's true, Father,' Walter said, as if considering this for the first time.

'The nurses aren't,' Edward noted. 'How they cope with the things they see, I can't imagine…'

'That's enough now,' said Honora preemptively. Never one for idle hands, she took her crocheting from the basket beside her chair. 'So, you'll look in on Constance tomorrow, then?'

Edward nodded.

'Picked up your new trousers today, did you? You'll want to look your best on Monday.'

'Yes, Mother.'

'I'm lending Edward my Homburg,' Walter put in, 'and the tie that I bought for—' He stopped short, as if choked by his words, the thought of his cousin gone forever.

'Say it, boy,' Honora insisted, ' *"for Patrick's memorial service."* ' Looking first to her husband, then to Edward, she went on, 'He was killed in the war, Walter. He's dead. That's a plain fact and there's no use dancing 'round it. Death is death – it's too bad, but there it is.'

James shook his head. 'You can be a hard woman, Honora.'

'And you're a soft man, James Dooley,' she retorted, adjusting her spectacles to better see her work. 'Bad things happen in life, that's the way it is…Why my poor friend Brigid and her little Maeve had to be taken by the Spanish Flu is a mystery only God can fathom. A tragedy, yes, but no use dwelling on it because it won't bring 'em back.'

'But there's the grievin', woman.'

Honora pursed her lips. 'You're a professional griever, you are, a first-rate wallower just like your sister, Mildred – the two of you always livin' in a dream world, never facing facts…'

'How'd you manage, Mother?' Edward cut in, 'not knowing what had become of me?

'God knows I've had my share of loss, boy,' she said, expertly wielding her crocheting needles. 'And I was with Mrs. Haggerty when she learned about her Darragh, then the Newmans… and the Rileys, of course. I dreaded the Western Union man, I can tell you…Thankfully Colm and Walter were out of harm's way, but as for you, Edward, I prayed, I prayed mightily. That's what gave me strength.'

She concentrated on her work in silence as James looked over the newspaper and Edward feigned interest in Walter's account of the picture he'd seen. Furtively he regarded his parents, wondering what the future held: so little had changed in the two years he'd been gone.

His brothers had been working in their father's sheet metal business since the great earthquake and fire in '06, but for all the skyscrapers that had gone up, they'd never capitalized on the boom. Though affable enough, Colm had also gained an unfortunate reputation for fecklessness that cost the company some long-standing customers; Walter still kept the books but had recently enrolled in night school at a business college by way of hedging his bets. Edward's two sisters, Katherine and Deirdre, cared for Aunt Mildred, who'd come to live with the family as of Christmas 1917, after the boys had left for the Army. Now in her late twenties, Katherine had inherited her mother's imperious air, which had put off a handful of would-be suitors. By contrast, Edward found Deirdre, now nineteen, to be developing into a winsome young woman.

'We'll go to the nine o'clock mass tomorrow,' Honora announced as she bundled up her knitting, 'then Katherine will get Mildred's liniment while we look in on Old Man McCormick.'

James Dooley closed the paper and rose stiffly from his chair. Walter gathered up the tea service and headed down the hall, while Edward pulled apart the pocket doors that divided the front parlor from the sitting room, his quarters since returning home.

'Got everything you need, boyo?' James asked.

'I do, Father, thanks.' Retrieving his toiletry kit from a hook on the door that connected the sitting room to the hall, he followed in his parents' wake.

'You'll want to slide the pocket doors tight tonight, Edward,' his mother said ahead of him, 'There's no tellin' what time Colm will be gettin' in…'

Edward stopped outside the water closet and said, 'Night,' then watched them disappear into the gloom of the hallway.

Since the earthquake and fire, the Dooleys had been renting the lower two floors of a four-story flat in the Hayes Valley district.

The rooms were strung along a long, narrow hallway like a railcar, with Edward's parents occupying the original dining room at the far end, its swinging door to the kitchen blocked off by a wardrobe. There were three bedrooms upstairs, one for his sisters, one for his brothers, and one for Aunt Mildred, overlooking the rear yard. Below the kitchen was a cellar where Edward would hide as a boy when his parents started bickering.

In an Irish-Catholic household where respectability was prized above all else, Honora's dissatisfaction with the circumstances was a constant refrain. One afternoon in the summer of 1913, with the girls gone to the butcher's and the boys out with their pals, she'd confronted her husband with an ultimatum. Unbeknownst to both of them, however, Edward had stayed behind in the cellar, where he was idly organizing baseball cards when the sound of a skillet slamming against the stove nearly caused him to cry out.

'Oi! James Dooley, you're impossible!' he heard his mother roar. 'You and your stupid ideas! There's no way we're moving into quarters above your sheet metal shop – I'll not have this family living South of Market with the bogtrotters fresh from Cork…I won't have it!'

'Aw, now look, Honora—'

'No, you listen to me,' she cut in fiercely, 'I'm through with yer excuses! For all the construction work around, you only ever manage to get dribs and drabs. We're so deep in debt you leave us no choice – it's up to Edward now, he's all we have left. He'll have to quit the Christian Brothers and go find a proper job…'

Edward cringed in the dank cellar, his eyes wide with alarm. This was inconceivable – surely his brothers, both high school graduates, would turn the family business around!

'But the boys are still learnin' the trade…' he heard his father say.

'Yeah, I've seen,' his mother said caustically. 'Colm's a shiftless wash-out, always involved in some scam or other. And as for Walter, the boy's too scrawny to be crawlin' on roofs – he might have a head for figures but what good's that when yer business is a bust!'

James mumbled something about his health that Edward couldn't make out.

'That's 'cause yer drownin' in drink!' Honora snapped. 'It's useless dependin' on ye – always a rung above destitution we are…It's a disgrace is what it is. A disgrace!'

Edward returned to the sitting room after washing up, closed the door to the hallway and drew the pocket doors to the front parlor shut. From the closet he pulled out his pajamas, a sheet, and a pillow and made up his bed on the narrow bench seat across from the old maple secretary. He stretched out beneath the sheet – he'd been sleeping hot lately, after so many bitter cold nights in France and Belgium – and cradling the back of his head in his hands, he regarded the curious shadows on the ceiling, the play of moonlight on the shiplap siding of the light well.

Though the nightmares came less frequently now, they'd not gone away entirely. The terrible accident on the troop train returned regularly, or would be superseded by the friendly fire incident outside Epinonville; he'd find himself back in he the gruesome battlefields strewn with human flesh, taste the acrid smoke and bile in his throat, gag at the memory of the fetid trenches. To defend against these anxieties, he'd taken to walking miles every day hoping that physical exhaustion would ensure a sound night's sleep. Only now, as the events of evening ran through his mind his pulse quickened, and throwing off the sheet, he returned to the bathroom for a drink of water. Seeing himself in the mirror wearing the same pajamas he'd worn as a teenager, he returned to bed resolved to get a place of his own as soon as possible.

Determined to keep the disturbing images from the ball at bay, Edward trained his thoughts instead on a conversation he'd had earlier in the week with his Aunt Hildie. Though he'd always assumed his mother's incessant criticism had driven his father to drink, only in knowing grief of his own in the war was Edward able to imagine that the bottom might have dropped out for his father before she started nagging him. What Aunt Hildie confided in him during their recent visit had begun to affect how he saw himself.

The story went that James had been sponsored from Cincinnati to San Francisco by a man named McCormick with the promise of construction work; he was apprenticed for a couple of years to a Welsh tinsmith who ended up selling his business to James when he was abruptly called back to Cardiff. His fortunes rising, James brought his sisters out to join him. It was at church one Sunday that James first laid eyes on Honora – recently arrived from Boston and serving as a governess for an up-and-coming Irish family – and supposedly felt a pang of nostalgia hearing her faint brogue even though his own father had thoroughly renounced Ireland.

Not long afterward Hildie married Aidan O'Shea, an enterprising native of County Cork who'd also been sponsored west from Kentucky by McCormick to start a dairy farm north of

San Francisco. When investors lost interest in that venture, by dint of hard work and some financing from McCormick, Aidan eventually managed to parlay his stake in the land into a profitable fruit-growing operation. As a result, the O'Sheas always had an open invitation at Old Man McCormick's (his own children resented his devotion to his hard-working protégés and seldom visited.)

Hildie had come down from Sonoma this week specifically to see Edward now that he was home. Edward was apprehensive when he came into the sunny drawing room of McCormick's sprawling Victorian mansion, however. She'd always been one of the most level-headed people he knew, but given that she'd lost her eldest son in the war he wasn't sure what to expect. Indeed, she looked run-down and her hair was grayer than he remembered.

'Now Edward,' she said, when the maid who had delivered him to the drawing room set down a tea service and withdrew, 'I'll not have you walking on eggshells. What happened to poor Patrick has devastated us, true enough, but this visit is about you, dear boy. I can only imagine what you've been through and I thank the Good Lord that you've been safely returned to us.'

Taken aback by her generous spirit, Edward's eyes welled up immediately. This was the only time during his homecoming he would be so vulnerable, and he gasped to catch his breath while she looked at him solicitously. At length, straining to maintain his composure, he barely managed to whisper, 'It was horrible, Aunt Hildie…just hor—.' She moved to the edge of her chair and placed her hand on his shoulder. With that he broke down and sobbed pitifully, his head in his hands.

'I know, son…I know,' she said.

When he'd composed himself, he told her how sorry he was for her loss, and seeing this in his eyes, she lovingly caressed the side of his face before sitting back in her chair.

Taking up her tea and balancing a shortbread cookie on the edge of the saucer, she said, 'It's your Uncle Aidan I'm worried about, Edward. He's been locked in a terrible melancholy these past six months – he and Pat were so much alike, you know… He's proud of your cousin Michael, in seminary now and all – and of our Cora and Maggie, too, of course – but he and Patrick were cut from the same cloth. Patrick loved the land as much as his father.'

She was lost in thought a moment, then said, 'They're that kind, the kind who see life's meaning in what they can accomplish with their hands – it's all about leaving one's mark, you see. Your Uncle Aidan has poured his heart and soul into the farm, so it grieves him now to think that there won't be another O'Shea to tend it when he's gone.'

The knot in Edward's throat had relented and he sipped his tea. 'But what about you, Aunt Hildie? It must be hard on you, too…'

''Tis,' she allowed, 'but I'll manage.' Raising her index finger to head off any more consoling, she said, 'Now listen, Edward, because there's something I need to tell you. You're not likely to hear it elsewhere and we don't get to see each other that often.' He suddenly looked afraid and she laughed. 'Don't worry! I'm not gonna have you blubbering all afternoon.' She reached for another cookie, adding, 'You were always such a serious one, Edward!'

He smiled with relief but looked puzzled.

'It's just this, dear boy – God be praised that you've come

back to us because you're the reason your father managed to hold on all those years ago…'

Edward watched her gaze out to the magnolia in the garden and braced himself for the full story. She'd once told him that his father had been quite the catch – a gifted tenor with a fondness for romantic poetry – but over the years Edward had overheard talk in hushed tones about a baby sister who'd come between Walter and him.

'He was never the same after Little Mary passed, bless her soul,' Hildie said at length now. 'There was a rumor at the time – more fiction than fact, I'd say – that he'd brought a cold into the house and therefore was the one responsible.' She glanced at Edward. Hildie had never been a fan of her sister-in-law – behind that refined governess air she'd seen an opportunist who'd managed to escape the tenements of Boston. 'Mind you, I know the ordeal was terrible for your mother, especially with three little ones to look after, but then she was never one to dwell on emotions,' and returning her attention to the tree, 'or lay that nasty rumor to rest…'

She went on to explain that Honora's announcement six months after the tragedy that she was pregnant again – this time with Edward – did little to console James. By this point he'd lost two key business accounts to apathy, and within a year the family would be forced to downsize from their rambling Victorian on Harrison Street to a modest York Street rental.

'When you first arrived, Edward, before the move, he was still in a fog, barely putting one foot in front of the other.' Raising her eyebrows, she said with a sigh, 'But then God never gives us more than we can handle…'

After recounting the familiar story about how strangely

41

self-sufficient Edward seemed from the moment he came into the world, she said, 'Years later your father told me that it was only after taking over your nighttime feedings that he managed to turn the corner. He told me,' Aunt Hildie looked Edward straight in the eye, 'that holding you for hours caused his sadness to lift, so consoled was he by your contentment.'

"Consoled by your contentment." The words echoed in Edward's head as he lay there, disoriented now, not sure whether he'd been in bed ten minutes or an hour. Anxious at the prospect of another fitful night's sleep, questions began to nag him:

What chance do I have of getting a place of my own when I've got the family to support?

Why can't Constance see that rushing into marriage now would be a disaster?

How will I ever be able put the war behind me when there are men like Fitz around?

Scratching sounds at the front door startled him and he propped himself up on his elbows. Tilting his head, he tried to make sense of the noise, and when he recognized it as Colm's clumsy attempts to enter the flat, he exhaled in exasperation. He listened as his brother finally got in and pushed the heavy door closed, knocking into the side table in the process.

'Easy there, big fella!' Colm said in full voice. Having evidently caught the porcelain lamp in time, he snickered with relief.

Edward followed the sound of his brother shuffling to the staircase, but when he stopped short and seemed to turn, Edward winced. Falling back on the cushions of the bench seat, he shut his eyes tight, hoping Colm wouldn't barge into the sitting room looking to chat. When after what seemed like an eternity he heard the sound of Colm climbing the stairs, he opened his eyes again and was surprised to find them wet with tears.

Chapter 4

When she awoke, Constance found the sight of the plaster ceiling medallion above her four-post bed reassuring. The tiny ornamental apples, pears and oranges reminded her of summer afternoons at Granddad's farm when the governess would set out lemonade, sugar cookies, and fresh fruit. As Morgan and Cousin Clarence reached for the cookies, Constance would choose the ripest sun-kissed plum, close her eyes and listen for the pop when her teeth penetrated the skin, drawing forth the exotic juice. More than once she'd open her eyes to find the two boys laughing at her, whereupon she would indignantly take up her napkin, dab her chin, and proceed to wipe her sticky fingers one by one.

Now the morning after that ghastly ball the thought of sticky fingers faintly disgusted her. She tried banishing the image of that poor, hideous man from her mind – as for her gown, she never wanted to see it again – and drew the back of her hand against her forehead as though to push it all away. Instead she was reminded of the disastrous seaside outing with Edward nine days earlier: now there were *two* nights she wanted to forget!

She whimpered at the memory of that awful Friday. How carefree she'd felt setting off on a spectacularly clear afternoon with Edward at the wheel of her father's Maxwell, floating down palm-lined Dolores Street, through the Western Addition, and out the length of Geary Boulevard to Lands End. They bought ice cream cones from a concessionaire at the Cliff House, strolled through Sutro Gardens and looked out to the ocean, shimmering like hammered silver in the hour before sunset.

Since returning earlier that week, Edward had described the long journey home but said nothing specific about his war experiences. Constance didn't probe, though she did get emotional recounting the great fear that had been stirred up by the influenza epidemic the previous fall. Now gazing out to the horizon, she was eager to talk about the future.

'Do you think we might live by the ocean someday, Edward?' she asked.

'If you like,' he said, absently twirling a twig between his fingers. 'But let's not get ahead of ourselves, Con,' he added soberly. 'Mr. Breslin's been nice enough to hold a position open for me, though with unemployment on the rise I'm not sure how long the job will last…'

'Now don't worry, I'm sure he has big plans for you.'

Edward tossed the twig aside. 'The thing is,' he said, thrusting his hands into his pockets as they walked, 'I'm not even sure it's what I want to do the rest of my life…'

'Well, I'm still part of your plans, aren't I?' Constance asked, taking his arm. 'We'll work it out together.' He looked over with a broken smile, and she touched his cheek with her gloved hand. 'Come now, Edward, no brooding today, okay? I'm so happy you're finally back!'

But he was out of sorts as they drove down the Great Highway that ran along the coast, going on and on about his mother's harangues and how Colm wasn't bringing in any new contracts. Constance tried steering the conversation to lighter subjects – the seagulls playfully skirting the whitecaps rolling to the shore, McCloskey's Castle on the craggy cliffs above Montara – but nothing could pull Edward out of his funk.

Over what was supposed to be a romantic dinner at a cozy inn in Princeton-by-the-Sea, Constance remarked that her aunt and uncle had found the accommodations there quite lovely, and that perhaps someday they, too, could come for a weekend stay.

'Not on my salary,' Edward said glumly. 'As it is, I can barely afford dinner…'

Constance pursed her lips and picked at her food.

Edward winced. 'Sorry, Con, I'm just having a little trouble settling back in, is all,' he said, patting her hand, then ordering himself another Scotch.

He had two beers with dinner, and though Constance had seen him tipsy before, it had never been quite this bad. Over dessert, he stirred his coffee noisily with a fork, and later, pulling out of the parking lot, he sideswiped a row of mailboxes. Belching from the deep-fried cod he'd eaten, he tried singing "Hello, Hawaii. How Are You?" as he weaved up the coast highway. Twice he veered onto the shoulder before Constance asked him to pull over.

He drove into a clearing and no sooner had he switched off the headlights than they found themselves enveloped by a dome of twinkling stars, immediately reminding Constance of the last night of the Panama-Pacific Fair. It had been well past midnight when they had sauntered over to the north end of the Court of the Universe with Morgan, and with the bay waters lapping the ferry docks below, he'd pulled out his Housman and recited the words,

WAKE: the silver dusk returning
Up the beach of darkness brims,
And the ship of sunrise burning
Strands upon the eastern rims.
Wake: the vaulted shadow shatters,
Trampled to the floor it spanned,
And the tent of night in tatters
Straws the sky-pavilioned land.

That was the night Constance was no longer simply Morgan's little sister. She'd grown fond of Wordsworth and Keats at Blessed Sacrament after all, and whenever Edward accompanied Morgan to recitals or theater productions there, the other girls would remark on how handsome and grown-up Edward was. Wrapped up in his arms that night, Constance felt herself become a young woman when he kissed her under the stars.

Now with the waves glistening in the moonlight at Rockaway Beach, Constance tried bringing Edward back to that memorable night. But he wasn't following her and instead suggested that they retire to the back seat of the Maxwell to cuddle like they used to. She'd always felt safe and secure with him, but now, when he'd returned to the Maxwell after relieving himself behind a sand dune, something was different. After a few minutes, he was no longer talking, and the playfulness had become something else. His kisses were sloppy as he carelessly kneaded her small breasts, and then he started fumbling with his pants.

'No, Edward, please no,' she whispered, but he didn't seem to hear. In fact, he didn't seem fully present, and she had the feeling he might not even know who she was. Breathing hard, he began probing against her dress, and though she tried pushing him off, his weight was too much for her. She was trying to look him in the eye when he suddenly shuddered, gasped, and collapsed against her shoulder. Eventually he pulled away, his hot breath smelling of fish and alcohol as she awkwardly rearranged her dress, her fingers sticky, her eyes wet with tears…

A knock at the door startled her.

'Constance, dear,' her mother said, entering with a breakfast tray, 'I've brought you some tea and toast.' She set the tray on the dresser and peeled back the heavy silk drapes.

'Oh, Mother,' Constance moaned at the late morning glare, 'I have a terrible headache.'

'I know, dear, but this ought to help.'

Mrs. Doherty was petite like Constance and had passed on her wavy red hair as well, though it was her son who'd inherited her fine features. She placed the tray in front of her daughter, who was propping herself up against her pillows, and offering a cup of tea, said, 'You've had a trying night.'

Her mother had turned to pull a chair up to the bed, when Constance took a gulp of the scorching tea which walloped her like an ocean wave. Eyes shut tight in pain, momentarily returned to her recent reverie, she managed to croak the word 'Horrible.'

'Hmmm, yes,' Mrs. Doherty murmured as she sat down on the chair.

Constance blinked her eyes open and returned the cup to the tray unsteadily, then reached for the toast. 'Sometimes I think men are no better than animals,' she said as she nibbled the crust, hoping to settle her stomach.

Mrs. Doherty squeezed her daughter's hand. 'You should never have been subjected to that…'

'It's not like Edward,' Constance continued, waving off the offer of marmalade.

'No, dear…Tell me, had he been drinking?'

'A little bit, maybe. But he was so light-hearted beforehand, it took me by surprise…'

She was beginning to feel better. Constance was grateful for the chance to confide in her mother, because even though she'd graduated high school, she still craved her mother's support and never wanted to disappoint her. 'It was so icky, Mother,' she ventured now, 'Somehow I thought it would be different – the "pinnacle of love," as you would say…'

Clarice Doherty's eyes narrowed. Her daughter had been in shock when Morgan brought her home from the ball the night before, but now, seized by an inkling, Mrs. Doherty said sharply, 'Wait a minute. Is this about you and Edward getting in late a week ago?'

Belatedly aware of the confusion, Constance panicked. Looking down at the bedspread, she said hurriedly, 'I know I should have told you sooner, Mother, but I was so mixed up…'

'He said the two of you had gotten lost and couldn't find a pay phone.'

Constance was having difficulty breathing. 'It's just that… you see, Edward wasn't himself that night…'

'Did he get fresh with you, Constance? Did he take advantage of you?'

Her daughter's downcast eyes filled with tears and she brought her hands to her face.

'Oh, you foolish, foolish girl,' Mrs. Doherty said as she stood up and started pacing the room. 'You never were the brightest girl in the world…And after all the times I've told you—'

'Mother, please don't be angry with me!' Constance cut in, sobbing openly now.

'—that a girl's virtue is all she has. You can't just *throw* it away!'

'I know, Mother, I know! He wasn't himself, I wasn't thinking straight, and it just…it just *happened*! He's been through so much, you can't imagine,' she continued nervously, 'He's all mixed up – but I know he needs me, I do.' She blew her nose into a napkin. 'He was as docile as a lamb afterwards – in fact he was fast asleep when the sheriff came by…'

'The sheriff!'

'A nice man…I told him we had engine trouble, but he was able to get it started again. He gave Edward some coffee from his thermos and then led us back up to the highway…'

Her mother eyed her coolly from the end of the bed. 'Did he ask your names?'

'Oh, no, nothing like that,' Constance assured her. 'No, I told him that Edward was exhausted, just back from the war and all, and the man seemed to understand…'

Mrs. Doherty sighed and shook her head. 'Now you listen to me, Constance,' she said, coming around to clear away the breakfast tray. 'Edward is yours now, do you hear me? He must be made to feel that he owes you…for your *devotion*.'

Constance nodded obediently.

'What we've discussed here is between you and me – understand? We needn't trouble your father with all this…' She brought the breakfast tray to the dresser now, divining a plan to talk to her son Morgan instead. Then she threw open the doors to the closet and started rummaging through a row of dresses, saying, 'Edward telephoned this morning, he feels awful about the ball last night…He'll be calling on you in about an hour so I'm arranging an outfit for you…'

'Oh, no, Mother, I really don't feel up to it,' Constance pleaded.

But Mrs. Doherty ignored her. 'It's important that Edward see you today, Constance – he has to know that he can count on you to be resilient…More importantly, he has certain obligations to you now…' She emerged from the closet with a yellow dress and laid it out on the bed. 'There, that ought to do,' she said. 'Now dry your eyes and I'll go downstairs and tell your father that you're getting ready…'

Chapter 5

Though short of stature, Malcolm Doherty was a proud man. He may not have run in the highest Irish American circles – with the Floods, Phelans, and MacKays – but he *was* among the most prominent men of St. Paul's Parish, a member of the Knights of Columbus as well as the Chamber of Commerce. A vested member of the Ancient Order of Hibernians, he was on the committee charged with sponsoring Eamon de Valera's fundraising trip to San Francisco in July 1919, when the Irish republican was to dedicate a statue to the Irish patriot Robert Emmet.

Malcolm Doherty had come out from Chicago with his brother in 1888, armed with two advantages – his apprenticeship at the Sheboygan Iron and Steel Foundry, which had perfected the art of applying enamel to cast iron, and Hector's experience as a shipping manager with the Union Pacific – that would enable the Doherty brothers to all but corner the market on supplying the latest porcelain fixtures to booming San Francisco. And no neighborhood filled in faster than the Mission District, the destination for Irish immigrants fortunate enough to escape the bowery south of Market Street. The new wood-framed "Victorian" houses and flats featured pediments, bay windows, and ornamental flourishes in elaborate colors – all courtesy of the Sears & Roebuck homebuilders' catalogue. (If families of the Protestant persuasion, living in their masonry mansions atop Nob Hill and Pacific Heights, considered the "painted ladies" outré and vulgar, it mattered little to Malcolm Doherty – he knew even the snobs needed his services.)

He managed to work his way into San Francisco's business and political firmament by being a tireless booster for the Hibernians, recruiting dozens of his brethren in the construction trades as members. By the time war broke out in Europe in 1914, he'd garnered a reputation as a stalwart officer and forward-thinking man who represented the organization well down at The Boxing Bar. He derived great satisfaction explaining the rationale behind the Marquess of Queensberry rules – no small feat where a fondness for brawlers, especially among the émigrés, was pronounced – arguing that a judicious expenditure of energy prolonged one's longevity. He employed this axiom whenever he counseled new members on building their businesses to ensure the long-term security of their families.

A week ago he was holding court on this very subject following the Hibernians' monthly meeting in the back room of The Boxing Bar. It was tight quarters with twenty men crammed around a conference table, the walls covered with framed photographs of famous pugilists, cigar smoke tucked up against the ceiling like spun wool. Doherty had just compared boxing to a waltz, when to his dismay one of his protégés said that he'd seen the "Fight of the Century" between Jeffries and Johnson in Reno nine years before. Brendan Ahern was a hard-working pipefitter from Kilkenny who'd come to California by way of Prince Edward Island and Salt Lake City. He wasn't one of the brash upstarts who rubbed the old guard the wrong way, and his remark might have washed over had it not been uttered in the presence of several powerful men, including the head of the Market Street Railway and the Chief of Police.

'We don't talk about darkies here,' fire department captain Bern Driscoll said succinctly.

'Especially one running from the law,' Police Chief White added for good measure, referring to Jack Johnson fleeing the country after a 1913 conviction for violating the Mann Act.

'I only mentioned it to say that his uppercut—'

'Now look, Brendan,' Doherty broke in, 'that Willard fellow did everybody a favor a couple of years back when he took Johnson apart in Havana, so let's move on…'

'There isn't a day I don't mourn the loss of John L. Sullivan,' Eugene Maloney intoned from the directors' end of the table, covering over the young man's gaffe. 'Now there was a bare-knuckler who knew how to win at all costs.' Maloney was still fuming that in April the U.S. Supreme Court had dismissed his Market Street Railway's suit against the City, clearing the way for a publicly owned transit system. 'Frankly,' he turned abruptly to the Police Chief, 'that's how you oughta treat those bums down on the docks. Striking for lighter loads, bigger work gangs, and a share of the ownership to boot! Who the hell do they think they are?'

'It's a mess, alright,' the Chief acknowledged wearily. 'Some are even supporting the stevedores strike up in Seattle – the ones proclaiming their solidarity with the Russian Revolution…'

Malcolm Doherty's jaw dropped. 'You mean the goddamn Bolsheviks?'

The Chief nodded. 'Refuse to load weapons Uncle Sam's sending over to help the White Guards, saying capitalists are out to crush the new workers' state.'

'Jesus Christ, everything's outta whack!' the ruddy-faced

Maloney boomed. 'They're saying twenty percent of the country's goddamn workforce will walk off the job this year in a push for higher wages, shorter days, workers' rights and all that bullshit…We've just come out of a war, for Chrissakes – now's not the time to be greedy!'

''Oughta be grateful to have jobs at all,' someone said, prompting nods around the table.

'Damn right,' the railway executive insisted. 'And I'll tell you something else, Doherty, now's not the time for more regulations in the workplace! Now's the time to gear up for peacetime production, retool the factories, invest in infrastructure…'

'To harness our manufacturing capacity for what people need now,' Malcolm Doherty continued alertly, 'like homes and schools, modern appliances, automobiles…and more streetcars, too, of course. Now's the time to grow, not retract!'

Mahoney pounded the table with his fist. 'We've got the strongest goddamn economy in the world and we don't need to go shooting ourselves in the foot!' Looking again to Doherty, he spoke emphatically. 'I'm all for fairness and the Queensberry Rules, Malcolm, but it doesn't mean you go soft. You take this new boxer, Dempsey, for instance – he plays by the rules, but he's as ferocious as any of the ol' bare-knucklers…'

'Made short work of Freddie Fulton last year,' Doherty agreed, nodding knowingly to young Ahern across from him.

'The son-of-a-bitch is constantly on the attack,' Maloney went on, licking his lips, before turning to the Chief of Police. 'That's how you need to take it to those bastards down on the docks!' he said, pounding the table again.

After returning from Sunday mass, Malcolm Doherty liked to

begin his week by perusing the *Call Bulletin* while enjoying the finest Brazilian coffee from the ornate silver service set out for him. Nothing thrilled him more than coming across his company's advertisement in the newspaper. His ritual was to stand and pour himself another cup of coffee, then look out the bay window to the steamships jamming the waterfront in the distance, evidence of the city's progress of which he felt an integral part. Only this morning as he looked out over the city, mulling over news stories about whether a waterfront strike could be averted and how many rounds Jack Dempsey would need to take the heavyweight title from Jess Willard later that summer, he suddenly he became cross. Morgan had been home four months now and had yet to engage in the family business – it was high time for a father-son talk.

Privately, he worried his son's exposure to life in the east might have corrupted him: when not sitting behind a desk at Army Headquarters in Washington, Morgan was always off to parties, or away to the big cities on the weekends. Though it was his wife who had persuaded him to reach out to some highly placed politicos to keep their son out of harm's way, Mr. Doherty felt the responsibility was ultimately his. He'd been keen to see just what kind of political pull he had – now he was chagrined to see what his son was becoming. When moments later Morgan sauntered into the drawing room in his pajamas, looking washed out and cradling some sort of tomato-juice concoction, Mr. Doherty peered over the top of his newspaper and said with exasperation, 'Good of you to make an appearance…'

'How's that?'

'I say it's about time you got up.'

'Oh, right. Good morning, Father,' Morgan said, seating himself gingerly on the couch. The light from the tall windows, the sound of his father's voice, even the smell of the lilies on the mantelpiece all seemed amplified to such an excruciating degree that he winced in pain.

'In another ten minutes you can wish me a good afternoon,' Mr. Doherty offered dryly as seated himself in his armchair. 'Any sign of your sister?'

Morgan shook his head and tentatively sipped his drink. 'Hair o' the dog, Dad,' he explained, ignoring his father's scowl, '—rather stressful evening, you know.'

'So your mother tells me,' Mr. Doherty said with a sigh. 'Let's hear your version.'

'Oh, God, it was simply awful,' Morgan began, eying the cigarette case on the coffee table, then thinking better of it. 'I'm afraid the poor dear was in for the shock of her life – carried away by all the pageantry one minute, in the trenches the next...'

'Brutal business,' Mr. Doherty muttered, before eying his son sharply. 'And where the devil were you, Morgan? You know how sensitive she is...'

Morgan looked down at his slippers. 'Well, Edward and I had left her chatting with another girl while we went to say 'Hi' to an old friend, see...Anyhow, I suppose we stood out, literally the only ones standing there among all the men in wheelchairs...' He pronounced it "litrally," one of many upper-class affectations he'd acquired at college that made his father cringe.

'Ridiculous!' Mr. Doherty said irritably, 'She should never have been left unattended. You've got to behave more responsibly, Morgan.'

He stood abruptly and began pacing the room, saying, 'And so as we've discussed, you'll be starting in at the office this week. You'll need to familiarize yourself with the accounting and scheduling departments first, is that clear?'

Morgan nursed his hangover remedy as his father spoke, sorry to hear this tiresome refrain again; he knew he'd done a poor job concealing his dread of a desk job. Smart and well-spoken, Morgan had acquitted himself well in the army; he'd met some interesting, important people, and got a sense of how far his wit and charm could take him. How ironic, he thought, to have "come of age" like so many of his peers – boys to men in two short years – but in altogether different ways.

'Yes, Father,' he replied obediently,' but I do hope we can abbreviate the orientation phase. I'd be of much more use traveling and drumming up business.'

'Yes, yes, I know,' Mr. Doherty said, turned to the window now, hands clasped behind his back, 'but we currently have a good man in that area – perhaps when Dobbs retires we can revisit the subject.'

Morgan regarded his father, always impeccably turned out, a man of quintessential managerial bearing. 'He'll die before he retires, Father…He looks nearly dead now.'

Not turning around, Mr. Doherty said, 'He's been loyal to us from the start and I hope you'll learn the value of this…For now, get to know the ins and outs of the business, and remember that sales is your Uncle Hector's domain, Morgan – you've got to prove yourself in the home office first.'

Morgan rolled his eyes at the thought of "Humorless Hector" who never trusted anyone, even the most obsequious. 'I hope

I can count on you to put in a good word for me...'

Mr. Doherty smacked his lips. He tolerated his son's cheekiness because the boy had the smarts to keep the business going after he retired, and he couldn't risk alienating him altogether.

'Oh, Morgan, dear, what a pleasant shock!' his mother said gaily as she came into the drawing room from the foyer. 'Are you well? I hope you haven't slept poorly.' She chortled under her breath, knowing just how to pluck her husband's aggravations.

'He's made himself a medicinal tonic, Clarice,' Mr. Doherty said sarcastically.

Morgan strained to look over his shoulder. 'How's our Little Darling, Mother?'

'Well, I've just looked in on her and she's beginning to stir, poor dear.'

Ten years younger than her husband, Clarice Doherty was the daughter of a prosperous fruit grower on the peninsula. She'd been raised in San Francisco and had first met Malcolm when she was attending the Convent of the Blessed Sacrament and he was doing business with the sisters and the prominent families of Pacific Heights. He'd been a dashing blond with piercing blue eyes, always smartly dressed, the very picture of success. He made a point of calling on her family down in Menlo Park while outfitting summer homes in the area, always arriving in a handsome carriage, bearing fresh cut flowers for her mother and imported cigars or liqueurs for her father. In time, impressed by the young man's vitality and solicitous nature, her father was duly convinced this up-and-comer could give his daughter a good life.

Now running her fingers over the satin upholstery of the

couch, she said to her husband, 'Why don't you check on Constance, dear? Edward will be calling on her soon and I think she'll rally for you.' She knew her husband saw a good deal of himself in Edward, such a bright and dutiful young man, not of high station, perhaps, but estimable nonetheless. Mr. Doherty nodded and looked at his pocket watch before leaving the room.

Mrs. Doherty sat down on the edge of the couch opposite her son, took a cigarette from the porcelain case and leaned forward so he could light it for her. 'Tell me,' she said, drawing forth the aromatic smoke, 'your father expects you down at the office this week, is it?'

'Yes,' Morgan said, defeated.

'And you've broached the subject of traveling for the company, I'm sure,' prompting another nod, '...only to be told your Uncle Hector will have the final say?'

Morgan could be bothered by his mother's inquisitiveness, but on this matter, he was grateful for her interest. 'Precisely,' he said.

Mrs. Doherty regarded her son a moment in silence. Though he was shrewd, it pleased her to know she still had something to teach him. 'You and Edward have known each other for how long, Morgan?'

'Ten years now – since starting Sacred Heart together.'

'And you know him to be intelligent...You trust him, I mean.'

'Of course. He's a stand-up fellow and should go far.'

'And since leaving school he's been working where? Something to do with textiles?'

'American Thread Company, why?' Morgan was hungry, and

the salutary effects of the tomato juice concoction had worn off. 'What's this have to do with me?'

'Why everything, dear,' his mother said coolly. She got up and made her way to the bay window where she savored another drag of her cigarette, leaving her son to languish in petulance a moment longer. 'He's so devoted to his parents, he'll need to stay local, though I daresay rising through the ranks in the textile trades would be difficult for someone of his ilk...'

Morgan watched his mother looking out to the horizon, arms crossed, the cigarette in her right hand pointed up just so. Where his father was quick with figures and had a gift for ingratiating himself with other successful men, his mother had always been more discerning. Growing up, Morgan knew his father to be forthright, even uncomfortably blunt at times, but in his mother's words he could detect layers of meaning. Now as she turned and looked at him with a pleasant smile, he immediately appreciated her line of thinking.

'Edward is ideally suited for Doherty Brothers,' Morgan said, holding out the ashtray for her. 'He could guide the operations at the main office while I go after new business.'

Mrs. Doherty stubbed out her cigarette and looked at her son as though this were the most sensible idea she'd heard in a long time. 'I'd better go see to Constance,' she said. 'We'll want her looking her best for Edward...'

Chapter 6

Edward stood before the great door of the Doherty's stately home in Dolores Heights and paused before ringing the bell. He turned around to look down the hill, passed the twin spires of St. James Church to the blunt bell tower of St. Peter's down in the flats. For many years this had been the Dooley's parish – until the earthquake and fire forced them to move – and Edward grimaced at the thought that his mother's dream of one day making it to the top of the hill might never come true.

He knew that Honora's disdain for the "two-toilet" Irish was really all about envy. She'd come to serve as governess for an upstanding family a generation earlier, and her success with those children confirmed her belief that gentility came from proper breeding. Alas, aspirations for a proper family of her own had come a cropper – something she laid at her husband's feet like a burnt offering. She also took a rather dismal view of her offspring: Colm for his belligerent streak, Katherine for her sour disposition, Walter for his diffidence, and Baby Deirdre for her foolishness. Edward, thank heavens, was the exception. Convinced he would go far with his intelligence and easy grace, Honora would say to him,

Watch your thoughts, Edward, for they become words
Watch your words for they become actions
Watch your actions because they become habits
Watch your habits because they become your character

*And watch your character, Edward, because it will deter-
mine your destiny.*

Now looking out from the landing of the Doherty's home,
Edward knew some part of him bore his mother's ambitions.
And yet for the second Sunday in a row, here he was with
another mess to clean up. Honora had gone on and on this
morning about his duty as a gentleman to protect Constance
from the kind of trauma she'd experienced at the ball the night
before; what she didn't know was that last Sunday he'd been
compelled to apologize for ungentlemanly behavior of another
sort.

Constance hadn't taken his calls the day after their seaside
outing – her parents explaining that she was under the weather
– so Edward decided to go to Sunday mass at St. Paul's, the
English Gothic church at the top of Dolores Heights that the
Dohertys attended. He lingered out front after the service, and
spotting Constance with her parents he approached tentatively,
doffing his hat. When Mr. and Mrs. Doherty happily assured
him that their daughter was now fit as a fiddle, he asked if he
might walk her home, and they encouraged her to go.

The two set off down Church Street pretending to be interested in the shop windows, until, out of sight of her parents,
he said miserably, 'I don't know where to begin…'

'An apology would be nice,' Constance said, staring off into
the middle distance.

He stopped to speak, but she kept walking. Hurrying to
catch up to her, he said, 'I do apologize, Con! Oh, I feel just
awful and hope you'll forgive me…' In truth, his recollection
of the disastrous evening was spotty, but outside a dress shop

where she'd stopped to take in the window display, he ventured, 'I know I behaved abominably. There are no excuses…'

'You were drunk and gloomy for some reason,' she said, studying the summer styles. 'I don't remember ever seeing you like that, Edward. You seemed like a different person.' With a glance, she added, 'I wasn't sure I knew you at all – or if you even cared about me…'

'But of course I care about you!' he exclaimed, taking her hands in his. 'I'm *so* sorry, Con – I know I've been distracted ever since I got back, but I shouldn't take it out on you.'

Averting her gaze, she said, 'I was…shocked, that's all.'

Edward hung his head, vaguely aware that he'd behaved boorishly in the backseat of the Maxwell but not recalling the details. 'I don't suppose it helps, but there were men I knew overseas who went around chasing the French and Belgian girls, and I just want you to know,' he said, releasing her hands, 'that I'm not that kind of person...'

Fingering her clutch, Constance said, 'I've always known you to be a gentleman, Edward…You've been through some terrible times, I'm sure – and you certainly weren't yourself Friday – so let's just put the whole episode behind us, shall we?'

Edward turned to her. 'I assure you I'll never behave like that again.'

Constance nodded, her eyes brimming with tears. Anxious to change the subject, she took off walking again and excitedly suggested they join her friends Gary and Ophelia for the new Douglas Fairbanks comedy that evening. Edward laughed, and taking her hand in his he swung their arms as they walked, just like in the early days of their courtship.

He was caught off guard when the Doherty's door opened behind him.

'You've been standing out here so long, Edward,' he heard Mrs. Doherty saying, 'that I wondered whether you'd forgotten how to ring the bell.' Turning around, he found her regarding him with an oddly patronizing glare. Always arrayed in understated elegance, she wore a coral crepe de chine this unseasonably warm Sunday, which accentuated her high cheekbones. He hastily removed his hat and stepped into the foyer, asking after Constance.

'Oh, she'll be fine, don't you worry,' Mrs. Doherty said as she directed him to an armchair in the drawing room. 'Just a case of nervous exhaustion – what with all the excitement last night...' No sooner had he seated himself than Mr. Doherty stepped into the room.

Edward bounded to his feet, and practically shouted, 'Good afternoon, sir!' Shaking the man's hand in earnest, he said, 'Mr. and Mrs. Doherty, I want to apologize to you both for what happened last night. Morgan and I certainly never intended for Constance to—'

'No harm done, my boy,' Mr. Doherty interjected, 'no harm done.' He beckoned the young man to reseat himself, then he and his wife sat down on the couch opposite. 'You'll find her completely recovered,' he said with a chuckle, while Mrs. Doherty smiled pleasantly.

'Tell us, Edward,' she said, 'have all the festivities just worn you out?'

Edward pursed his lips. 'Well, to tell the truth, I am glad it's over...'

'I'm glad for Constance, too. It's been hard on her, you

know,' Mrs. Doherty said, meeting Edward's eyes with a gaze that nearly made him shiver.

There came a bustle from the staircase, then Constance entered the drawing room, looking pale. Edward stood quickly, worried that not only must Mrs. Doherty resent his inattentiveness to her daughter the night before, but worse, she might now have an inkling of his boorish behavior the week before and think him a cad. As much as he wished he could summon a gallant greeting for Constance, he only managed to remark on the lovely dress she wore.

'Do you like it?' she said, smoothing the pleats. 'You don't think it's too plain?'

'Why, no, the color suits you splendidly,' Edward replied, pleased to see her smile.

'Très chic!' Mr. Doherty declared. 'I don't think I've seen that one before.'

'Why sure you have – at Easter,' Mrs. Doherty said as she escorted the young couple into the foyer. From the coat rack she pulled a shawl which she handed to her daughter. 'Now take this pashmina so that you don't catch cold, dear. And Edward,' she added in a cool admonishing tone, 'don't keep her out too late – she needs her rest, you know.'

Edward winced and promised to have her home by dinnertime, then with Constance on his arm, they descended the steps, and Mr. Doherty called out, 'Enjoy the afternoon, children!'

They were carefully making their way down the steep slope of Dolores Street when a Peerless Roadster roared passed, a dandy in a riding cap and goggles at the wheel, feigning brake trouble to elicit peals of terrified laughter from his female passengers.

'Some people ought to grow up, scaring women like that,' Edward said indignantly.

'Is that meant to be funny?' Constance asked, 'After last night, I mean.'

Edward bit his lip and they walked in silence until they reached Dolores Park, where he steered Constance to a bench. They looked out to the downtown skyline for a minute before he took her hand, and said abjectly, 'I'm so sorry about last night, Con. I hadn't intended for you to see any of that. Morgan and I just wanted to say hello to an old friend from Sacred Heart...'

'These Sunday apologies are wearing me out, Edward,' Constance said, looking down at their hands entwined. 'Can't we just put it all behind us?'

'I wish it were that simple...' he said at length. Watching a father push his child on a swing in the playground, Edward went on, 'I knew men who were killed over there, Constance, and yet it's men like Fitz who come home shattered that's even worse...Why I've returned unscathed I just can't understand...'

'Because God has a plan for you, Edward,' Constance said. 'A plan for us...'

'I don't know about God anymore, to be honest.'

'Oh, now, you don't mean that. There's a reason for everything, Edward – there has to be.' Opening her purse, she added, 'As Daddy says, we have a duty to ensure that those who have made the ultimate sacrifice did not die in vain.'

'Things are a lot less clear up close, I'm afraid,' Edward said with a sigh, '—lofty ideals lose their meaning in the face of death...'

Constance checked her face with her compact, then returned it to her purse and stood up. 'C'mon, there's something I want to show you…'

She took him down the street to Mission Dolores, the old adobe structure dating back to the city's founding by the Spanish in 1776, now dwarfed by the grand basilica going up beside it. Constance brought Edward into the old sanctuary, where it was cool and quiet, and by candlelight they could make a few elderly women in the pews bent over their Rosaries. She led him along the side to a vestibule that connected the sanctuary to a small garden cemetery. Edward had never seen this place, dank in the shade of palm and fig trees, hidden from the street by a high wall. Sauntering along a path lined with ferns, he recognized some of the names on the headstones – Arguello, Moraga, Guerrero, and Sanchez – as those of early alcaldes and commandants of the original settlement.

'Here we are,' Constance said as they approached a tiny clearing in a corner of the garden. Above three small headstones inscribed with the names Cora, Casey, and Sullivan, a wooden placard read, "Victims of the Committee of Vigilance – 1856."

'Daddy showed me this last fall,' Constance said, 'after Missy O'Connor and the Ferguson twins were taken by the influenza.'

'Who were these men?'

'They were Irish, Edward,' she said. When he didn't reply, she offered more of an explanation. 'I'm sure you've heard the stories of lawlessness all those years ago – the violence, trials without juries, the hangings? Well, these men were hanged, Edward. Daddy says they were victims of injustice and that it's important we remember them so that their sacrifice will not be in vain.'

While well aware of her father's pro-Irish sentiments, these men may well have been criminals for all he knew, and Edward shook his head. 'I'm sorry, but what's this got to do with the war?'

'Well, maybe not the *war* exactly,' she said, disappointed, '—but the point is they should not be forgotten. Their deaths were tragic, just like the people taken by the Spanish Flu.'

Constance wasn't one to engage in causes – it was her mother who found her a volunteer role in Del Monte's shipping office after America entered the war – and Edward had no illusions that she gave a lot of thought to philosophical questions. But where he didn't expect to confide his darkest moments of the war to her, it irked him nonetheless to think she was content to rely on platitudes and trite truisms to cope with grief.

'I wouldn't lump the flu in with the war,' he found himself saying defensively, '—the war was man-made, after all, and we have to come to terms with all the devastation it's caused...'

'We've had plenty to deal with here, believe me,' Constance rejoined irritably.

'Yeah, but what I'm talking about is different. What I'm talking about is war – men being killed, *butchered*, by other men. Friends, people I served with – it was horrifying.'

'Well, it's been horrible here, too,' Constance protested. 'It's horrible seeing people taken in the prime of life – women and children, too! Everyone wearing masks for protection, not knowing if it's safe to go out, not knowing who to trust...'

'There were plenty of women and children killed in the war,' Edward said, suddenly feeling ridiculous for the turn the conversation was taking, but unable to stop himself. 'I wish you could have seen the destruction, the villages blown to bits...

Last Christmas I was part of a detail where we gave money we'd raised to a widow and her five children and do you know—'

"I'm sorry, Edward," Constance cut in, strident now, "but I don't think you realize just how bad it's been for us here. The papers say over half a million Americans have died so far, and according to Morgan American casualties in the war were only about three hundred thousand…'

'Only!' Edward exclaimed, stepping back. 'Listen, Constance, I don't see why we're arguing here. I just want you to know what I've been through – Morgan doesn't know, he wasn't overseas. *I'm* the one who has to live with what happened!'

'Don't shout at me, Edward,' Constance said, greatly agitated now. 'How are you going to live with *what happened* at Rockaway Beach? That's what I'd like to know. Isn't there something you want to ask me? What are you waiting for?'

The taunt took Edward by surprise and he licked his lips to buy time. "Okay, Constance, now look – I'm sorry about that. I've apologized for that. I feel terrible about it…"

"What if I'm pregnant?"

'What?' he said, not meeting her eyes, stymied again by his spotty recollection of that evening, 'No, you can't be…'

Choking back tears, she said, 'You forced yourself on me, Edward! You can't abandon me…'

'No, dear, of course not,' he said, hastening to her side and putting his arm around her. Stunned to think that instead of trying to come to terms with what he'd seen overseas he now found himself knee-deep in a new predicament, he added vaguely, 'Everything's going to be fine, you'll see—we'll get through this.'

Everything was happening too fast; he needed time to sort things out – ironic, Edward thought, given the many months he'd languished in western France after the Armistice with nothing to do. At the moment, it was all he could do to salvage the afternoon and get Constance home without any more tears. He walked her over to Bergman's Pharmacy and sent her ahead to claim the one remaining booth while he waited at the counter to place their soda orders.

Though he was a bundle of nerves, when finally he sat down opposite her, he took her hands in his and smiled wearily. "I'm sorry if I've seemed a bit distant lately."

Looking wrung out, Constance said, 'There's so much to look forward to, Edward. You want us to be happy, don't you?'

How desperately he wished it could be that simple – that he could put aside his lingering torments and move on – but he wasn't the same man anymore. Nevertheless he managed to muster a smile. "Of course," he said, just as their ice cream sodas arrived.

For a few minutes they savored the refreshment and looked at the other couples around them, delighting in the colorful candy display case and the Gibson Girl pin-ups on the walls. Carried away in the excitement, Constance looked coyly at Edward. "You know what would make me happiest of all..."

Edward averted his eyes demurely. 'I know, but remember, Con, let's be prudent' he said in low voice. 'Let me get established first so that I can ask for your hand properly.'

'Oh, but Daddy already thinks the world of you.'

'I'll be returning to work tomorrow, and if things go well over the next few months, maybe I can ask Mr. Breslin about a promotion.'

'Actually, I believe Daddy would like to talk to you about something along those lines.' She flashed a curious smile.

'Pardon?'

'It's just that I overheard Morgan talking to him before you called for me today.'

'Talking about what?'

'Why, bringing you on at Doherty Brothers, of course.'

Before the war such a prospect would have elated Edward, but now he found himself even more surprised by his reaction than Constance was. 'Well, look, if there's one thing I've learned over the past couple of years, it's that I've gotta get by on my own.' When she regarded him strangely, he added, 'I just mean that I need to make my own way.'

'But don't you see what a wonderful opportunity this would be for you? For us?'

Edward's throat was dry and he probed the bottom of his parfait glass with his straw. Above all he needed time to think – but reminded of his short-term objective to stave off any more tears, he summoned his good manners, and said, 'Of course I do, dear.'

With a self-deprecating smile he reached over, and gently brushed her cheek with the back of his fingers. That sweet look in her eyes – oh, how foolish he was being, blurting out that bit about getting by on his own! To think he might impulsively break off this long-standing relationship, that he could just let this golden opportunity slip by brought to mind the reproachful image of his mother.

Chapter 7

'More pie, Sergeant?' Nurse Luchetti stood beside Jimmy Fitzsimmons in the hospital dining hall, holding a tray of desserts. She didn't know whether he was actually a sergeant, but she'd addressed him this way from the start because she felt it suited him, and because he never corrected her. 'I know how much you like the boysenberry.'

'No thanks, maybe De Silva there,' he said, indicating the heavyset man across from him who was scraping his plate with his fork, 'He's got a sweet tooth.'

'Geez, I already gave him mine,' Yost said, incredulous, 'Where the hell's he puttin' it?'

'Just tryin' to grow my leg back, fellas,' De Silva said, holding the nurse's gaze as she came around the table to serve him.

Yost turned to Kruger who could always be counted on for a biting remark. 'Bet you crap about a leg a day, Sal,' Kruger said on cue.

'Fuck you, Kruger, you one-armed ape.'

'Lemme plug that pie-hole of yours, De Silva…' Kruger said, pretending to get up.

The nurse smiled, familiar with their banter, and slid the plate in front of De Silva. 'What do you boys have on tap this afternoon?' she asked as she proceeded to clear the table. 'More bridge?'

'Yost cheats,' Kruger said bitterly, '—plays with a marked

deck…'

'Just wasn't your day yesterday,' Yost retorted, elbowing Fitz, who smirked.

Each of the men had lost at least one limb in the war, and but for sporadic rehab, they spent most of their days in wheelchairs. As the largest man in the group, and because of the bandages that covered his head wound, Fitz stood out. Yost had served with him in the same machine gun battalion when the 3rd Infantry pushed the Germans back at Chateau Thierry the previous July, and though he was from Bakersfield, he'd requested permission to accompany Fitz to Letterman Hospital to help with his buddy's recovery. There was something indomitable in Fitz's nature that caused the others to look passed his injuries; he'd become the point man of the group.

'No marathons, though,' the nurse cautioned, 'The Sergeant needs his rest.' Turning to Fitz before leaving the table, she said, 'I'll look in on you at the end of my shift.'

Angela Luchetti had come to San Francisco certain of her calling to be a nurse. She had progressed quickly through the training such that by the time of the Armistice, she'd garnered a reputation for dependability and could hold her own against the surliest of men. Adapting was difficult for many of the returning wounded – not only to prosthetic devices but also to how loved one's looked at them. A keen observer of family interaction, Angela admired how well most mothers hid their anguish, and how important fathers were to bolstering their sons' spirits and calming younger siblings. Most of all, she was impressed by the war brides and sweethearts who came often to help in their men's recovery and get them home. Though she'd never been in love herself and was not particularly senti-mental, she derived tremendous satisfaction seeing men regain their confidence and prove worthy of their women's devotion.

She'd come to San Francisco from Stockton out of a sense of duty, after boys she knew in school had been called up in the draft. From her father, a vegetable farmer who'd emigrated from Italy, she'd inherited a tireless work ethic and a headstrong nature. Her mother was a devout Catholic and would take Angela and her brother to St. Mary's, where the Latin mass bridged the language barrier among the Anglo, Italian, French, and Filipino parishioners. To Mr. Luchetti, St. Mary's as less a spiritual community than an arbiter of social standing – where events in the parish hall seemed little more than opportuni-ties for parishioners to show off their prosperity, and weaken ethnic ties.

By contrast, Angela's mother was eager to see her children succeed in ways that would have been impossible in Italy. She encouraged her children to make American friends, and by the time Angela was in fifth grade she was riding the trolleys downtown in the company of girls with names like Hansen, Wheeler, and McGrath. Together they'd watch paddleboats on the waterfront and buy candy at the Five-and-Ten; later, it was picture shows at the Avon Theater, strolling down Main Street to admire the new fashions in the windows of Kuechler's, and watching handsome couples alighting from gleaming motorcars at the Hotel Stockton.

Mr. Luchetti resented his daughter's assimilation into a culture that was foreign to him. Though he worked hard currying favor with the white landowners to expand his farm-ing operation, at the same time he was wary of the bustle of modern life and disapproved of the impudent manner of the young people he encountered in town. His wife tried to allay his concerns, saying that a certain level of independence was required to be successful in America, but privately she worried her husband and daughter were on a collision course. Little was said between father and daughter when Angela announced that she was leaving home.

Whenever Angela thought about those times now, she felt particularly ashamed about the heated exchange she'd had with her mother on the eve of her departure. They'd been making gnocchi together one Sunday. Angela had decided to leave the following week, and despite her mother's repeated pleas to stay, she would not be dissuaded.

'I'm going to San Francisco because that's where they need nurses the most, Mama. The army is there, and I want to do my part…just like Peter, and Dory's brother, George, and Mr. Cappaciola next door…'

Her mother shook her head as she peeled the boiled potatoes. 'The city is a dangerous place. You can be a nurse later – your father needs your help here now.'

'He can handle things,' Angela said, pushing the potatoes through a ricer.

Her mother drizzled a whisked egg and flour over the mixture, not looking up as she spoke. 'It's about that Clayton boy, no?' When Angela did not reply, she said, 'Your father, he means no harm, Angela. He loves you.'

Angela pursed her lips in disappointment, for while she resented her father's brushing the episode with the Clayton boy under the carpet, it irked her that her mother was content to simply regard it as a case of youthful infatuation ending in tears. That her mother's loyalty to her husband came at the expense of supporting her daughter's independence felt like a betrayal to Angela, and as she watched her mother deftly blend the potato mixture into a light crumble, Angela was overcome with bitterness.

'Papa's not capable of love, Mama,' she remembered saying. 'Those are empty words.'

Her mother had looked up a moment, then returned to the task at hand. With a feathery touch she proceeded to knead the dough into rows about an inch round as Angela waited for her to say something. But when she said nothing, Angela spoke the words she'd come to regret.

'I feel sorry for you,' she'd said with a rueful air, as she cut the dough into one-inch segments, '—having to pretend with Papa. He only thinks of getting ahead, as if that were all that mattered. His heart is frozen, Mama, but I guess he's all you have...'

Angela would never forget the image of her mother rolling the segments into little logs, her eyes moist with emotion as she managed to say, 'I will have Giancarlo when you leave...' Pressing the little logs lightly into the tines of a fork with her thumb, she went on, 'Your life, it is just beginning. Someday you will get over all of this and see we all must make sacrifices.'

'No, Mama, maybe someday *you'll* see...' Angela said, hastily arranging the gnocchi side-by-side on a tray. 'You'll see that you missed your chance to break with the past.'

Her mother was standing at the sink, about to fill the pot with water. Not turning around, Angela heard her say, 'Cara mia, you break my heart...'

Jimmy Fitzsimmons's father had fallen out with his well-to-do family from Baltimore when he was twenty-one. His life of adventure started with a stint on the B&O Railroad, followed by two years on a Mississippi riverboat, a turn with a New Orleans cotton exporter, and eventually Buenos Aires, where he found ranching work on the pampas. Later, Gerald became foreman of a railroad gang in Guatemala, until a brush with malaria sidelined him. Eventually, he boarded a banana steamer bound for San Francisco, where he enjoyed remarkable success as a gambler and came to own a Kearny Street saloon – convenient to the gambling houses, bordellos, and opium dens of Chinatown – that enabled him to amass a respectable fortune.

Jimmy's mother came to San Francisco in 1892, as part of a singing and dancing variety act backed by a New York vaudeville impresario. Adele Carew was a tall, striking redhead from Hartford who'd come from a long line of entertainers – her mother once opened for Sarah Bernhardt in Boston – and had dreams of becoming the next Lotta Crabtree, only to be swept off her feet by the dashing Gerald Fitzsimmons. After a whirlwind three-month courtship in Hawaii, Vancouver, and Alaska, Adele returned to San Francisco exhausted and pregnant. She and Gerald were married and moved into a fashionable Edwardian in Jordan Park.

Having ingratiated himself with political boss Abe Ruef, Gerald's future looked especially bright, until the great earthquake and fire destroyed his saloon. In the aftermath, when the shenanigans of the Schmitz mayoral administration came to light, a new breed of civic leaders cracking down on vice made sure that the days of the Barbary Coast were over. Gerald tried to restart his business in the booming Western Addition, but a newly emboldened temperance movement and disputes with his partners scuttled his plans. Eventually, he staked what was left of his fortune on an interest in a local semi-pro baseball team and a roadhouse tavern in the outer Richmond District.

Moving the family to a modest Second Avenue walk-up didn't sit well with Adele, however. Now in her late-thirties and mother to a new baby girl, she already had her hands full with Little Jimmy. She became increasingly irritable, and despite a ten-year hiatus from show biz, secretly began contemplating a comeback. She met up with some old friends when Will Rogers played the Orpheum, and ended up following the show to Portland.

This only became clear six months later, via postcard from Sioux City, where Adele reported that she was living her dream and would look the family up when the show came west in the spring. Instead of being on bills with the likes of Harry Houdini and Eubie Blake, however, Adele had to settle for the role of assistant to an ornery magician with halitosis, playing burlesque houses in places like Galesburg, Wichita, and Memphis; if she ever made it back to San Francisco over the years, neither Gerald nor Jimmy was aware of it.

By the time Jimmy started Sacred Heart, Gerald had moved his Guatemalan girlfriend into the house on Second Avenue to help raise Jimmy's sister. After graduating, Jimmy was on the road a lot playing ball, but in the off season he'd make a point of coming home to help his father at the roadhouse tavern. Resigned to this latest chapter in his life, Gerald took satisfaction in his son's success, and one night after they'd closed up and finished cleaning, he tried telling his son how proud he was of him.

'You're lucky, you know, Jimmy,' his old man had said, sliding a pint of Acme Beer across the bar. 'You found out you were good at something right from the start. 'Took me years – and some folks never do…'

'Like Mom?'

Gerald sighed. 'She was good at something once – maybe lost her way…'

Jimmy raised his pint. 'Well, thanks for pointing me in the right direction, Dad.'

'Hope you don't feel I forced you into it, son,' Gerald said, sipping his whiskey. 'I used to worry about that, but then I figured if you didn't like baseball you'd find something else."

'The game suits me fine,' Jimmy assured him, 'and anyhow, I don't overthink it – I find that holding on to things too tightly doesn't usually work out so well.'

'I'm glad you see it that way, son,' his father said. He lit a cigarette and cocked his head philosophically. 'Tell me something, Jimmy, I'm curious. What goes through your mind out there when the ball's put in play?'

Jimmy chuckled because sportswriters asked this all the time. For them he had a pat, humble answer they could use in their columns, but with his father he could be honest.

'Well, it goes something like this…when the ball's hit, see, out of all the possible scenarios I look for the best one to fall into place. Everything seems to slow down 'til I'm able to see what's gotta happen…' He took a swig of his beer, and continued, 'Now if I'm gonna be part of things, I start putting it together piece by piece. I'll pivot my foot and turn my head a certain way, depending on where the sun is. There's a charge in my gut that triggers my glove hand and the fingertips of my throwing hand start to tingle…' He glanced at his father, pleased to see how intently he was following this. 'Okay, so the ball's coming, see, and I have the glove down low so when I catch it I have time to pat it once in the mitt while my legs catch up with my arms. Then I'm set to throw.' He looked down with a faint smile, then said, 'That extra pat is like my throwing hand is applauding my catching hand…'

When Angela pulled the curtain aside at four o' clock that Sunday afternoon, she found Jimmy Fitzsimmons dozing in his wheelchair, a copy of the *Call Bulletin* folded carelessly across his lap. His bed was on the third floor, at the far end of D Ward, to afford him more privacy. Each ward was comprised of thirty-two beds, sixteen to a side, facing each other. Those along the north wall had a view of the Golden Gate, though generally patients just looked at one another across the aisle. From time to time, a nurse or an orderly would walk through the ward which smelled of hydrogen peroxide, but otherwise the atmosphere was somnolent.

Angela was particularly attentive to Fitz because while other nurses tried valiantly to disguise their dread at the sight of his wounds, Angela saw him as a man of evident character who'd simply suffered a tremendous misfortune. Over the many months of his stay, she learned that his setbacks were compounded by an inattentive family. His sister came sporadically – always with an acquaintance, and only to talk only about old times – and Angela felt sorry for how drained Fitz seemed afterward. His father, a sickly man with a sour disposition, had stopped coming altogether after only a few visits.

Lightly tapping Fitz on the shoulder, Angela said in a soft

voice, 'Glad to see you getting some rest, Sergeant, but a chair's the wrong place for it.'

'Huh?' he snorted, tilting his head to get his bearings.

'You have to lay in bed or else you'll end up curled like a pretzel.'

He dragged the back of his left hand across his mouth to catch the drool from his lips.

'Straighten up and lean forward,' Angela said, stepping behind him and pulling the throw off his shoulders, 'and I'll give you a back rub before transferring you to the bed.' He promptly complied, and she began to run her hands firmly across his neck and back.

'You boys have a good game?'

'Kruger lost his temper – we broke off early.'

They were silent for a minute while she massaged the muscles of his middle back with her thumbs and the heels of her palms. His body odor was ripe, but she pretended not to notice. The war had wrecked his body, and she could see he'd need all his courage if he was ever going to be able to care for himself. He let his head droop until his chin touched his sternum.

'No Molly this weekend?' she said, referring to his sister.

'Nope.'

'I thought she might make it to the ball last night...' Aside from the two young men who'd come over to Fitz, there'd been no other visitors.

He shook his head. 'Goes to the pictures on Saturdays...'

'Uh, huh,' Angela muttered, not bothering to mask her disdain for his sister's thoughtlessness – she'd once overhead his sister saying she was going to be a movie star herself one day. Angela worked on his shoulders, lost in thought about how alone in the world soldiers like Fitz must feel.

'Ever had a sweetheart, Jimmy?' she asked, running her palms down his back.

'Thought I did,' he said, chin on his chest. 'She came with Molly the first time…'

Angela thought back but didn't remember anyone in particular. 'I'm sorry,' she said.

She continued to work on his upper back and shoulders, and after a moment he lifted his head and twisted his neck from left to right, as if undoing a kink. He propped himself up with his left arm, immobilizing Angela's hands between his back and the chair. She laughed lightly.

'Touch it.'

His tone was neither helpless nor demanding. She pulled her hands free, and laying them on his shoulders, said, 'Excuse me?'

'Please…' he said, pushing away the newspaper to reveal that his gown was undone, and that his penis was engorged, though not yet erect.

Angela was startled a moment, then came around the right side of the wheelchair and stepped back to face him directly. He turned his head demurely to the side.

'No, I won't,' she said, leaning down to catch his eye, 'Sorry.'

Suddenly embarrassed, he shook his head from side to side and hastily gathered the newspaper across his lap. She waited for him to look at her, imagining that were it not for the bandages on the left side of his face, she might discern something in both eyes beyond shame or sadness. She gave no indication that she was about to leave.

'That's okay,' he said finally, looking up.

Angela placed a hand on his knee. She wasn't a religious

person, but she did believe in fate – there were no coincidences, there was a reason she'd come to know this man. Looking him squarely in the eye, she said, 'I know what it is to be cast aside, Jimmy, made to feel cheap and worthless. Well, you're not worthless – and you deserve better.'

Chapter 8

Edward Dooley was more aware of the economic forces at work in the world than most of his peers. The bitter disappointment he felt having to leave school had been somewhat assuaged by his coming aboard a great capitalist enterprise straightaway. The wife of the Dooley's landlord, Mrs. Greenberg, had relatives in the textile trade, and one day she pulled aside the usually haughty Honora to say that she'd heard about an opening down at the American Thread Company. She was aware that Edward had been making inquiries to general contractors and shipping companies, 'but *this*, this could be good for your Eddie,' Mrs. Greenberg said. 'He's a bright boy with good manners, and more important,' here she peered over the rims of her spectacles, 'they're lily white down there and he looks the part, if you get my drift.'

American Thread had been a major concern since 1898, when it was incorporated by the English Sewing Cotton Co., an amalgamation of British textile companies that had purchased thirteen mills in New England. Their aim was to go head-to-head with a Scottish consortium which had already established subsidiaries in the U.S., and by the time Edward joined ATC, the two conglomerates were producing two-thirds of the thread in North America.

His first visit to American Thread's west coast offices at 536 Mission Street could not have been more auspicious: a senior executive from the east coast mistook him for a department head, and in politely rectifying the man's error, Edward made a very favorable impression with management. Together with his smarts, it also didn't hurt that what was assumed to be his genteel Irish ancestry was already well-represented at the firm. The deference paid to senior management, particularly to the partners of British extraction at the company's New York head-quarters, was absolute. No one dared speak unless spoken to, let alone laugh aloud or venture an opinion on anything other than sports (and never boxing). To mention anything religious or political was unthinkable: employees refrained from ever uttering the words Catholic, Pope, Irish, or independence, for fear of drawing loathsome looks.

Edward's start happened to coincide with an anti-trust suit by the Justice Department which alleged price-fixing by American Thread and its chief rival. While this resulted in structural changes in management, the consensus among Edward's bosses was that the government's oversight was intrusive and even discriminatory against Great Britain, a war ally after all. Instead, they complained, Uncle Sam ought to be going after the socialist rabble-rousers within the International Workers of the World – a labor union derided as the "Wobblies".

Edward had been in the army only a few months when to his surprise the subject of the Wobblies came up. At a Christmas dinner with fellow recruits six months before they were to ship overseas, Joe Blanchard, a taciturn miner from Idaho, said that soldiers had a right to ask what they were fighting for. He dismissed newspaper stories about German atrocities against women and children as propaganda intended to draw

America into the war – and when his cynicism was challenged by Miller, a rancher from Laramie, Blanchard launched into a diatribe about how the capitalist oligarchy was repressing the working classes.

'The capitalist what?' the rancher drawled.

'The exploiters of labor – the rich, the corporations, and the bankers. We say, "A fair day's wage for a fair day's work!"'

'Aw, you're not one of them goddamn Bolsheviks, are you, Joe?'

Ignoring the provocation, Blanchard explained why the Western Federation of Miners had joined the IWW, and said the organization now represented dock workers, migrant pickers, lumberjacks, and garment workers, too.

Though Edward rarely spoke up in the group, at the mention of his line of work he felt it advantageous to plant himself firmly in Miller's camp. 'The Wobblies have always been a headache to the textile trades,' he ventured. 'Five years ago, they got twenty-thousand workers to walk off the job in Massachusetts, and the very next year they led a strike in New Jersey where a couple thousand silk workers were arrested.'

Undeterred, Blanchard opined that the workers' grievances had no doubt justified the strikes. When this elicited grumbling around the table, relishing the role of the underdog he went on to say that the Wobblies also accepted women, immigrants, even Negroes and Orientals, then pulled out his IWW membership card to show that, indeed, it was red.

'Shit,' the cattleman said, disgusted, 'the Wobblies are nothin' but a rag-tag bunch of anarchists like Debs, De Leon, and all them others, and I for one say it's a good thing they're finally bein' rounded up for opposin' the war effort.'

'Says a lot about the war effort, if you ask me,' the miner retorted. 'The warmongers are out to make money in this thing. Think about it...'

Edward had had plenty of time to think about it over the next eighteen months and still he was uncomfortable with the idea that instead of a clear moral imperative to repel German aggression, there might have been dark forces behind the war effort. As an American who'd never known real economic hardship, religious intolerance, or political repression, it was difficult to fathom how a dispute over commercial interests could have driven men to fight on such an enormous scale. Only cynics would conclude that economics and politics went hand in hand in – that the revolution in Russia had more to do with rejecting an economic order than with guaranteeing personal liberties.

It was easier to think that America was leading the world forward in a great march to modernity – the first constitutional democracy, the land of opportunity where hard work paid off and progress was a birthright. The wisdom of the American way of life was confirmed by unprecedented prosperity – where individual initiative, rather than a rigid caste system, determined success. Worrying about the rights of the working man belonged in the past: wages weren't so bad, and Congress had recently approved an eight-hour workday, after all. As for Blanchard, he was dead and buried in the Argonne.

For all his misgivings about returning to a desk job, Edward was glad to be working under Cecil Breslin, an ambitious, quarrelsome man whose modus operandi as long as Edward had known him was to exceed the expectations of the New York muckety-mucks. Breslin had seen something of himself in the teenage shipping and receiving clerk assigned to him in 1913. He put in long hours at the office, what with a high-strung wife and two children at home – and with not much of a home life himself, Edward happily stayed late to learn the ropes.

Edward thought of his short, stocky boss as a bulldog, always with a five o' clock shadow on his chin and a cigarette between his teeth. But he also considered him a mentor, some-one who could help set him up in the business world. Amid the boisterous homecoming at the Ferry Building two weeks ago – Edward's parents, his work mates, and his sweetheart were among the hundreds on hand to greet the returning Doughboys – Breslin hovered in the background until the American Thread entourage prepared to head back to work.

'Listen, Eddie,' Breslin said, taking the returning hero aside, 'I don't expect you back for a couple of weeks, alright? You'll need time to regroup…I'm sure you've got a lot on your mind.'

Now late on the Wednesday of his first week back to work, seated across from his boss in a wooden booth at The Loon, Edward listened as the bulldog of a man talked about coming home from the Spanish-American War a generation earlier. 'Sometimes it seems like only yesterday, slogging through the jungles of Samar, bored and scared to death at the same time,' he said, then, catching his Edward's eye, 'I'm sure you know the feeling.'

It was Edward who'd invited his boss out for a beer, but he was in no mood to trade war stories; he grimaced and nodded but made no reply.

Breslin was reminded of his young protégé's knack for diplo-macy, how he would employ a dignified silence to mollify a demanding client or a gruff supplier – as if by sidestepping a rancorous or tasteless turn, Edward was offering his counterpart an opportunity to step back and consider a more reasonable, respectful course. So Breslin chose not to put the young man on the spot, according him the one privilege due a veteran – to keep the grim details to himself.

Clearing his throat, he said, 'So, let's see, there's a lot to get you up to speed on. Daly's gone, but you know that – went over to Coats & Clark, the bastard…' Impatiently he pulled out a cigarette, lit it and took a long drag. 'Cummings quit on account of his heart,' he continued, rolling his eyes as he exhaled, 'and Dowling's in Los Angeles now trying to drum up business.'

'Darlene told me Cummings was pushed out,' Edward said, cradling his pint glass.

Breslin laughed sardonically. 'Darlene oughta mind her own business.'

Edward smiled. 'But with three million out of work now, I suppose businesses are cutting back everywhere, getting by with less for a while…'

'That kind of thinking's for suckers,' the stocky man said irritably. 'Unlike the other guys, we've always had more than military contracts to fall back on. 'Fact is, the boys back in New York are looking to grow. Take Willimantic, for instance,' he said, referring to the company's flagship thread mill in Connecticut, the largest in North America, 'they've decided to add spool cotton and hosiery yarn there now.'

Edward raised his eyebrows, impressed. 'But what about declining demand? Can we really keep the mills running full tilt?' Lighting a cigarette of his own, he went on, 'Given how bad things are overseas, maybe American Thread ought to get into the relief effort...'

'Leave the charity work to others, Eddie,' Breslin said dismissively. 'With the war over, we'll go after the competition hard, see? Wear 'em down 'till they have no choice but to close their doors. Let 'em go back to making twine,' he added with a sneer, '—this is *our* business.'

Draining his glass, he nodded to the barkeep. 'This prohibition thing is horseshit, by the way,' he groused. 'Better get your fill now, Eddie, 'cause come January, it's bottoms up.' Edward caught the barkeep's eye and raised his index finger for another.

Though he had a standing invitation to return to American Thread, for months now Edward had been nagged by the thought that going back to a desk job would be sadly anticlimactic. With his boss now going on about how the name of the game being expansion, however, Edward grew more hopeful about the pitch he had in mind. And yet for all the gumption it had taken to call the meeting in the first place, he suffered a moment of stage fright, and blurted, 'So, how're Edith and the kids?'

'Oh, fine,' Breslin said as two more beers arrived. He lit another cigarette with the end of the one he'd just been smoking. 'Annie got engaged, finally – to a boy from Livermore. 'Good fellow – family's in the hardware business.'

This news struck Edward as fortuitous, there having been a time when he feared his boss might have wanted him to take an interest in his daughter (who bore an unfortunate resemblance to her father). Learning there was a son-in-law on the horizon meant one less encumbrance to the proposition Edward had in mind – he felt positively giddy, sensing there was little risk of disappointing his mentor now.

The genesis of his proposal stemmed from an unusual visit he'd had with Morgan on Monday evening. His friend had stopped by the Dooley flat quite unexpectedly after dinner and invited him out for a drink to hail his return to the workforce. Edward appreciated Morgan's grandiosity, particularly his choice of the Redwood Room at the Clift Hotel, where they sat at the bar, facing a colorful assortment of liquor bottles. Edward described his first day back at work, and when he said little had changed at American Thread, Morgan seemed especially pleased.

'You've done well by the firm, Edward,' Morgan said with curious finality, 'but don't forget, they've done pretty well by you, too. They'd have lost that Seacrest account if it hadn't been for you – a fair exchange all around, I'd say.'

Edward sipped his Dewar's, not sure where his friend was heading.

Morgan leaned in and lightly touched Edward's forearm. 'I've been speaking with Father recently about how invaluable you'd be to Doherty Brothers...' He let the remark linger in the cigarette smoke a moment, hoping to conjure images of discussions between father and son going back several weeks, when actually he'd only approached his father the day before.

Looking down, Edward studied Morgan's delicate fingers and thought, not for the first time, that it was too bad his friend had never pursued his talent with the piano. Listening to him go on about the reputation his family's business had built up over the years, Edward nodded and smiled at the thought that perhaps his friend's most skilled instrument was his tongue.

While it was considerate of Morgan to advocate a high-level management job for him, just as Constance had intimated the day before, Edward was skeptical of his friend's off-hand response to his question about what role he would play in his family's business. 'Oh, business development, I suppose,' Morgan had replied with a weary sigh, '—you know, living out of a suitcase, traveling over hill and dale, glad handing all those cigar-chomping suppliers…'

But Edward knew Morgan, knew his friend considered San Francisco to be provincial, that it was more likely he was hoping to convince his father the time had come to branch out into other cosmopolitan areas – preferably east of the Mississippi. He knew Morgan preferred to be where the action was.

On his trips to and from the war, Edward had caught glimpses of bustling metropolises like Chicago, Cleveland, and Buffalo; on furlough in New York City, he'd taken an exhilarating stroll up Broadway to Times Square. Now given the fact that he'd gone overseas, and Morgan hadn't – that he'd faced hell and Morgan hadn't – it didn't seem fair that he should be the one stuck in a desk job.

With his whole life ahead of him, why shouldn't he take his shot? Why shouldn't he climb the ladder, get by on his wits and make something of himself? He'd like to see the country, stay in nice hotels, take clients to lunch in fine restaurants. Who's to say he shouldn't be where the action was, that he couldn't reach for the brass ring himself?

Now at The Loon, in the grip of a sort of reckless exuberance, Edward decided it was time. Sliding his pint to the side, he folded his hands in front of him and leaned forward. 'Mr. Breslin…*Boss*,' he said, underscoring his deference, 'I've been doing some thinking over the past few months – I've had a lot of time for thinking, you know – and I think I could be more useful to the company bringing in new business. I can represent ATC well and—'

'You mean sales?'

'Well, yes. You see, I've done a fair amount of traveling lately and I guess you could say I'm used to it. I like it, actually. And I understand the business – I'm bullish on American Thread, sir.' He smiled, pleased to sound so convincing.

Breslin eyed the young man carefully. 'Glad to hear it.'

The bulldog of a man had long worried that key executives in New York and London still considered California the distant frontier, and that therefore he might be overlooked in the new expansion. Here was a young buck he'd trained and knew he could trust. He leaned forward now, his elbows on the table, and spoke with conspiratorial urgency.

'The way I see it, American Thread's gotta pick up where we left off before the war. These are modern times – nobody's making their own clothes anymore. The money's in the ready-to-wear business and those're the customers we gotta go after.'

Edward cocked his head, curious.

Breslin glanced left and right, as though he were about to divulge something top secret, and said in a hushed tone, 'We undercut prices, see, sell for less, win out on volume – simple supply and demand.' He sat back and spread his hands on the table like a sultan.

When he was sure Edward had absorbed this wisdom, he lit another cigarette and continued, 'Look, the ladies' magazines take care of the demand side. Women today aren't satisfied with just two or three good dresses in the closet – not when they wanna look like Mary Pickford.' He blew a sharp stream of smoke to the ceiling and shook his head at how vain women could be. 'On the supply side we align ourselves with the manufacturers who command the cheapest wholesale. Like the guys from Rochester, for instance – they're looking for a shot out here in California. By undercutting prices, we crush the competition…'

Edward pursed his lips. 'It'll cost a lot of people their jobs, though, won't it?'

Breslin took a swig of beer as if he were dousing a fire. 'What are you, Eddie, a goddamn Bolshevik or something? It's survival of the fittest out there. Listen, we did our part retooling for the goddamn war – now American Thread's got a right to make up for it, and if something's gotta give it'll have to be wages.' Puffing irritably on his cigarette, he added, 'People oughta be grateful for what they can get nowadays…'

Edward thought of Blanchard and wondered whether a pay cut and a return to the twelve-hour workday was the way to go. But he was careful to hold his tongue. It was a new day now, and it was only natural that there'd be a period of economic adjustment as everything got sorted out. It was important to get on board because America would soon be on the move again.

Breslin squinted as he studied Edward, imagining how he could make the case with his superiors in New York. Edward could help raise Breslin's profile by covering a lot of territory in the west – and he could also trust that Edward wouldn't try to upstage him. But Breslin would only back a winner, and without sympathy, he asked, 'Are you sure you're ready for a salesman's life, Eddie? What about responsibilities to your family…to your girl?'

Edward would remember this moment as if the clouds had cleared and the future was right there within his grasp. 'Sure,

I've thought about that,' he replied, going with his gut, 'but my parents will be fine because I'll still be helping out financially.' He looked down at his beer, at the tiny bubbles rising to the surface, and was reminded of his mood after Sunday's visit with Constance – the last thing he needed was that kind of pressure.

'As for my girl,' he said with a strained smile on his face, 'I'm not ready to settle down just yet. I'd like to get out on the road while I've still got the chance…'

Chapter 9

'Good for you, boyo!' James Dooley said when Edward told him the news. Finding the kitchen empty when he got home, Edward had been resigned to call it a night until he discovered his father dozing in the sitting room, the stylus grinding along the inner ring of the gramophone. Rising too quickly from his easy chair, Mr. Dooley gripped his son's shoulders to steady himself. 'Your mother isn't back from her church guild meeting, is she?'

'No, I don't think so. Like I say, I just got in myself.'

'I was listening to my Adelina Patti record,' Mr. Dooley explained as he bent down precariously to tuck away the fifth of Scotch he kept hidden in the maple secretary.

'Don't trouble yourself, Father,' Edward said, beating him to it.

Mr. Dooley gathered up his newspaper instead, saying, 'I tell you, though, son, seeing how your mother regards salesmen as little more than itinerant hucksters, you better tell her it was Breslin who approached *you*, sayin' it's you he wants to bring in new business, you being a war veteran and all.'

'I suppose it is kind of a promotion,' Edward ventured, '—on account of the company expanding and all.' Grateful for the advice, he shook his father's hand, and Mr. Dooley gave his son a reassuring pat on the shoulder, bidding him goodnight.

After washing up, however, waiting to be carried off by slumber, Edward's thoughts became muddled and some part of his mind began to work at cross purposes, questioning his prospects for success as a salesman. He doubted how far his sincerity would get him, whether he could stomach the repeated rejection. What's more, he felt uneasy about trading on his record as a war veteran, and when it occurred to him that the next day would be the twenty-ninth, he broke into a cold sweat.

The war had left him pessimistic about fate and more attuned to superstitions. He couldn't help but read significance into numbers now – like adopting eleven as a lucky number after the Armistice – and the twenty-ninth had been the day of the division's reckless advance into enemy fire the previous September. In the days that followed, recuperating in a medical unit, Edward learned that the twenty-ninth of July been the day of the division's inauspicious arrival in France; precisely one month later, it happened to be the very day orders came to move up to the front. Prophetically, on October the twenty-ninth the battered division was ordered to the front once again, this time in Flanders.

Edward anxiously regarded the shadows on the ceiling, desperate to ward off another night of fitful sleep. Three months earlier an army doctor, addressing the regiment as part of the demobilization exercises, had explained that nightmares were perfectly natural and largely attributable to disrupted sleep patterns. Edward came to resent the man's blithe assertion that the nightmares would ebb over time – grim battlefield imagery would continue to dominate his dreams for years. But since his return he'd confided this anxiety to no one – not even his brothers, fearful that to describe the truly horrifying bits would trigger emotions that he wouldn't be able to control. He'd concluded that these nightmares were his unfortunate burden to bear, something he'd have to work to forget; other veterans he encountered seemed to say as much with their eyes.

The nightmares always began as though he were being held down against his will, thrust back into chaos with the deafening roar of exploding mortars echoing in his ears, where he could taste the mustard gas again and feel the oily rain on his hands. Frightful images would tumble by like in a zoetrope – explosions of dirt and bodies cart-wheeling through the air, men shouting but making no sound, lumps of flesh, the open eyes of dead men – images repeating, sometimes appearing in reverse and eventually running together, faster and faster, until he'd find himself sitting upright, jolted to consciousness, panting.

Only this night for some reason he was borne away to an earlier trauma, when as a boy of ten he'd been caught up in another kind of maelstrom. It began with violent shaking in the dead of night – probably one of Colm's pranks, he remembered thinking to himself – before the sounds of pots and pans cascading onto the kitchen floor upstairs and the crash of grandfather clock suggested something more ominous. In this rendition of the familiar dream he had the odd sensation of relaying the story to Private Miller late one cold, damp evening while on watch, speaking with matter-of-fact detachment, as if simply to pass the time.

My brothers and I slept in a make-shift room down in the basement, and when the shaking stopped I remember hearing my sisters shrieking upstairs, Father's heavy footsteps, and the pitiful wails of Seamus, our setter, who was pinned under the clock. Colm went racing up the back stairs and when Walter started fumbling with the kerosene lamp in the dark, I thought I smelled gas and told him not to light any matches…

We went outside where it was eerily quiet and the streetlamps were flickering. Morning was coming. I remember stepping across a gash in the street to join our friend, Jimmy Potts, and then the neighbors started to gather, the Rileys and the O'Rourkes, all in robes and dressing gowns, whispering so as not to waken anybody who might have slept through the trembler.

'Very considerate,' Miller deadpans, a vague shape in the murky night, the glow of a cigarette concealed behind his palm.

Then Walter shouted across to me. Our walk-up had a staircase that stuck out like a tongue, but when I looked over there was something peculiar about the angle of the roof against the pink sky. Maybe the roof was wracked, or the foundation had shifted, but before I could say anything Father came out onto the landing holding Baby Deirdre in his arms.

'Oh, Christ…'

All of a sudden there's a pop and the stairs started twisting, then he loses his grip on the baby and goes skidding down the risers on his back. Mother and my sister Katherine are screaming from the doorway and Colm bounds over the landing onto the sidewalk where Father's sprawled across the lower stairs, crying, 'Oh, Jesus! Bloody Jesus!'

Miller groans.

Dede was quiet and her eyes were closed, but somehow she was still with us. I remember clearing the hair away from her forehead and Walter putting his robe over her to keep her warm. Mother and Katherine rushed back inside and down the back stairs, while Colm managed to waylay a scared Italian milkman for his horse and wagon to get to the hospital. Father's hands were shaking when he took the reins, and Mother passed Dede to Katherine in the rear of the wagon before climbing up to the bench seat. She told Walter to pack up what he could from the house, told Colm and me to get downtown to check on the shop, then turned to Father, and said, 'Now drive like the wind, James Dooley!'

'Damn, Eddie, a hell of a story…What about the fires? I heard the whole town burned down…'

Oh, yeah, we never did see the sun that day, the skies were so full of smoke – but at this point it wasn't fully dawn yet. Colm and I and the Corcoran brothers took a horse and wagon from Kerrigan's stables, then picked our way through the rippled streets, passed vacant-looking people pushing carts and pulling trunks, making their way to the waterfront. There were crumpled wooden shacks everywhere and brick rooming houses reduced to rubble. At 3rd and Folsom the crowd was so thick – men shouting, women and children wailing – that we had to leave the horse with Joe and Matt and continue on foot. We wandered through the smoldering ruins, gagging at the stench from the tanneries and scorched smithies, and at the foot of Tehama Alley we climbed over a barricade of dead horses and found Father's shop. The tin walls were leaning badly, so Colm used an iron bar to prop up a header so I could shimmy inside.

'You surprise me, Eddie – didn't know you had it in you…'

I was able to find the ledger and the business license, a box of files, and Father's signed photograph of Gentleman Jim Corbett, before Colm told me to get the fuck out of there…

Edward hears Miller chuckle, then a canteen plows into his chest. 'Here, take a swig of this, it'll keep you warm…'

Well, by the time we make it back to York Street, soldiers are on patrol everywhere. Katherine tells us it's pandemonium down at the Southern Pacific Hospital, that Mother won't leave Dede with the nurses, that there's no telling where Father's gone. So, while Colm and Katherine cram the wagon with our family belongings, Walter and I go over to help the nuns at St. Peter's packing up statues and crucifixes…

'Good Catholic boy, Eddie, that's nice to hear…'

The nuns were headed over to their convent in Oakland and we moved to a camp set up at Precita Park. I can remember scampering to the top of Bernal Heights at twilight with a gang of boys to watch the fire devour downtown. There were stories about Tong gangs crawling out of Chinatown like cockroaches, about General Funston's drunken troops dynamiting Van Ness Avenue, and tycoons jumping to their deaths from the windows of the Palace Hotel. Colm showed off his prize, a handbill he'd torn from a downtown lamppost that said, 'Mayor orders: Shoot-to-kill!'

'Sure, when in doubt, start shootin'…' Miller says, his profile caught momentarily by the flare of a match as he lights another cigarette.

I woke up Thursday morning coughing for all the smoke and ash in the air, bits of books and ticket stubs falling all around like snowflakes. Katherine returned in a panic to tell us that the army is gonna blow up the S.P. Hospital for a firebreak and that Mother is taking Dede to a tent hospital the Sisters of Mercy are setting up out near Golden Gate Park. So Walter stayed at camp to keep an eye on our stuff while Colm and I went with Jimmy Potts and the Corcoran boys to pull people out of the Valencia Hotel that had collapsed into a sinkhole.

We were probably there less than an hour when some guy rushes up and grabs Joe Corcoran by the arm to tell him there's a mob at his uncle's jewelry store and that he better get over there. For a while Matt and Jimmy and I helped the nurses bring blankets and soup to the old-timers, then we headed over to Mission Street where across from Guilfoyle's Jewelers we find Joe. He's propped up in a doorway, bleeding from his stomach, and Colm is screaming, 'The fuckers shot your brother, Matt! He was trying to protect the place and they shot him!'

Through the crowd we could see a group of National Guardsmen holding off Mr. Guilfoyle with rifles and bayonets while other soldiers are coming out of his store with full knapsacks. When Colm confronted them, he got treated to the butt end of a rifle – the guy says that they don't tolerate looters, that they gave Joe fair warning…

'Amazing what they can get away with when all hell breaks loose,' Miller snorts, '—not all that different over here, really. So, your brother, how'd he take it?'

I think I've told you, Colm can be a hothead, but somehow he managed to bottle up his anger. He wiped his bloody nose on his sleeve, put Joe in a wheelbarrow, told Jimmy and me to get back to camp, then he and Matt pushed Joe all the way to St. Luke's Hospital.

When Colm showed up the next morning with a horse and wagon, he looked like he'd been up all night. He told us Joe was dead, and that he was moving us out to Golden Gate Park to be closer to Mother and Dede. We packed up the wagon without another word, and then he whipped that skittish mare through the wreckage of the Mission District and out the length of the panhandle where he dropped us with the hoi polloi and took off. There were people crying, some were cursing, but most were too tired to move. We waited all day only to be told it would be another day 'til army tents arrive. So off we go, lugging our stuff into the park, where we strung a tarp between some trees and munched old bread for supper.

In the morning Colm stumbled in, bent over in pain, his left eye swollen shut and his chin caked with dried blood. While Katherine bandaged his broken hand, he mumbled that the fire had been stopped, that 'some fucking soldiers' had stolen the horse and wagon. Then he passed out...

Miller emits a long sigh. 'You say he ran afoul of some noncoms at Camp Greene and is still stateside, right?'

He's the one you want over here, Miller – but you got me instead...

You got me instead...me instead. The words echoed in Edward's head as his consciousness returned to the present. An unlikely soldier, miscast for Colm and tossed into the cauldron, befriended by the likes of Miller with his hardened sensibility, then allowed to escape unscathed – and for what? To return to a comfortable life with all the trappings of success? Or to take up a harder, less assured journey, an obligation to make good on his reprieve, to accept life not as he wished it to be but for what was in store for him...

Chapter 10

Of his many impressions of the Panama-Pacific Exposition of 1915, none would have a more lasting impact on Edward than Mayor Rolph's audacious keynote address. On a sparkling February morning, Sunny Jim had stood before a crowd of a hundred and fifty thousand in the Court of the Universe – a McKim, Mead, and White confection with triumphal arches at either end symbolizing the rising and setting sun – to commemorate the new canal that joined east and west for the first time. Doffing his stovepipe hat, he intoned magnanimously, 'It is to the new San Francisco, the first city of the west, the commercial mistress of western waters, the city which has come out of flame fired with enthusiasm and throbbing with the spirit of conquest, that as Mayor I bid you a most hearty welcome!'

After a deafening ovation, Mayor Rolph spoke of the tireless efforts of civic leaders to realize Daniel Burnham's vision of San Francisco becoming the "Paris of the West." 'We've rebuilt a city that shall be great morally, industrially and commercially,' he declared, 'a city beautiful, wholesome, ambitious to be materially great, and inspired to be artistically delightful!' Moments later, President Wilson himself pressed a golden telegraph key in Washington, which sent a signal to an antenna on the Tower of Jewels that opened the great doors to the exhibition halls. With the crowd cheering and cannons booming,

San Francisco's triumphant return was thus proclaimed to the world.

Only, for Edward, something was lost in all the jubilation that day, in the lofty rhetoric that would prove as ephemeral as the fair's chicken-wire and plaster edifices. As unexceptional as a western breeze, it was something he'd seen in the eyes of Joe Corcoran, propped up against that storefront on Mission Street – that a great trauma was being swept under the rug, the truth obscured and history rewritten.

Chapter 11

Edward worked through the twenty-ninth in a funk, burying himself in his accounts, rarely looking up. Mr. Breslin knew to steer clear, having attributed such moodiness in the past to tensions at home. At four-thirty Edward pulled his jacket and hat from the coat rack and silently slipped out of the office. He crossed Market Street and boarded the "D" car on Montgomery, rode it through the financial district and up over Russian Hill, across Van Ness Avenue and through Cow Hollow, to the end of the line at Greenwich and Lyon. He entered the Presidio at the Lombard Gate, wincing as he passed the Enlisted Men's Club from which he'd been brusquely ejected two years earlier. It was nearly half passed five when he stepped into the lobby of Letterman Hospital – temporarily home to some twelve hundred sick and wounded soldiers returned from Europe – and made an inquiry at the front desk.

Convalescing veterans typically congregated in a recreation lounge in the afternoons, when the fog pushing through the Golden Gate made it too chilly to be out in the courtyard. But Edward was directed to a sunroom off the courtyard that was used occasionally for morning visits with family. Furnished with wood paneling, thick carpeting, and heavy silk drapes, the room was divided into two seating areas, each comprised of a high-back easy chair, a pair of couches on either side of a coffee table, and a space to accommodate a veteran in a wheelchair.

By late afternoon, the French doors admitted an anemic light which suffused the room with an unsettling gloom. As Edward entered he made out the silhouette of a lone figure, seated in a wheelchair, facing out to the courtyard. He approached tentatively and touched the man's shoulder.

'Fitz,' he said softly as he leaned down, 'it's Edward Dooley.' He was unable to immediately make eye contact when he came around, owing to the bandage that masked the right side of the veteran's face. Fitz looked up from the newspaper in his lap and Edward leaned against the edge of the couch across from him. 'Morgan Doherty introduced us the other night at the Victory Ball?'

'Dooley,' the big man repeated.

'You and my brother Colm were in the same class at Sacred Heart.'

'Colm Dooley.'

'Right…but I'm Edward.' His self-assurance wavered and for a moment he worried that the gravely wounded veteran might find this visit bothersome. 'Eddie,' he said now, '—at least that's how I was known in high school.'

'Fought with the Powder River boys…'

'That's right!' Edward exclaimed, 'Boy, what a memory.' Relieved, he reached over to shake the Fitz's left hand. 'They told me I'd find you back here.'

'Only quiet place this time a day.'

Edward was reminded that Fitz had difficulty pronouncing certain sounds. He tried to imagine him without the bandage on his head, the right side of his face symmetrical with the left, recalling how handsome he'd once looked in his Seals uniform covering third base.

'How's your sweetheart?' Fitz asked.

'Oh…she's fine, thanks,' Edward said, grimacing at the memory. 'Quite a scene that night…I really appreciated your help…'

'Ol' Jeb's not so bad – just angry is all.'

'Sure, 'guess it stands to reason.'

'Angrier now, I expect, after being shipped up to Sacramento.'

'Sacramento?'

Fitz turned his head in a curious way. 'Didn't give him much of a reason – some cock-n-bull stuff about logistics…'

Reminded of Morgan's specious offer of hospitality, Edward wondered whether his friend actually had the clout to arrange a transfer. Seeing Fitz was eyeing him, he became uneasy, not sure how to get to the point of his visit. He wasn't really clear why he'd come, only that he had to. Bad dreams were part of it, but even when he was awake he was having a hard time. So much on his mind, like a weight he couldn't carry by himself – not yet, anyway.

'I imagine it's gotta be hard,' he began awkwardly, looking down at his hands in his lap, 'being there at the dance…on the sidelines and all.'

Fitz nodded, but when he said nothing, Edward's thoughts began running together, as they often did when it came to transitioning from soldier to civilian. In his darkest moments, he'd think of Cousin Michael, who hadn't been called up on account of his age and was now thinking about a religious calling. How nice to dwell on spiritual matters, never having been forced to look evil in the face. When Edward learned that the fight in the Marne that took Michael's brother, Patrick, had cost a thousand men a day, he wondered how Michael's merciful God could countenance such slaughter.

The man across from him cleared his throat, startling Edward from his reverie. 'So, ahh, Fitz, how're you getting on then?' he stammered, 'You got back in, what, January?'

The big man nodded again.

Edward leaned forward and took a pitcher of water from the coffee table, nervously poured two cups and handed one to Fitz. 'Feel like you're getting your strength back?'

Fitz sipped from a straw then put the cup down. 'Bit by bit, 'best I can...'

'Any more surgeries?'

'Dental mostly...some skin grafts. Lots of rehab.' They heard a commotion from the elevator lobby down the hall. Something metallic, maybe a bedpan, crashed onto the tile floor, and Edward could make out a testy exchange between a caustic male, probably a patient, and an exasperated female, probably a nurse. 'Then I can get outta here,' Fitz said, as if on cue.

'I'm sure your folks'll be glad to have you home.'

'Uh huh,' Jimmy said, looking off to the side.

Sounds of the squabble faded in the background, and Edward continued, 'Morgan says your father and sister come by sometimes.'

'Never together, though,' Fitz said as he folded the sporting green with the long fingers of his left hand and laid it on the coffee table. When Edward looked puzzled, he added, 'Molly's going off to Hollywood...to be in pictures.'

Edward tried to look impressed, though it didn't sound like good news. 'So, when you're done here, you'll be moving in with your father?'

Fitz shook his head. 'Remember the Claremont Roadhouse robbery?' he asked, referring to the night four men in handkerchief masks had robbed the place at gunpoint. 'My Dad's joint. They pistol-whipped him – 'he hasn't been the same since.'

'Jesus…' Edward shook his head. 'A policeman was shot trying to catch 'em, right?'

Nodding, Fitz said, 'Nabbed the bastards in Los Angeles - doing life in San Quentin now…'

'Christ, Fitz,' Edward said with a sigh, 'I'm sorry about your dad.'

Fitz tilted his head philosophically. 'Led a pretty fast life.'

A steady buildup of noise in the hallway alerted Edward that everyone was on their way to dinner. 'You probably want to get going, huh, Fitz?' he said, deflated.

'Nope. 'Not 'till six.' He nodded to the clock on the coffee table.

'I'll be happy to take you whenever you say.'

'Sure thing.'

Edward was glad the visit wasn't over. He regarded Fitz a moment, impressed by the man's calm demeanor despite all that he'd suffered; he seemed to exude strength, not the stoical kind, something more centered and self-possessed. Edward had an idea that maybe the man opposite him understood why he'd come.

'Mind if I ask you a question, Fitz?'

'Shoot.'

Edward dug out a pack of cigarettes from his jacket and bent forward to offer one to Fitz. The disabled man brought the cigarette to his lips and Edward lit it for him, then, after lighting one for himself, he sat back and crossed his legs.

'I've been home a few weeks now, just went back to work this week, in fact – I'm in sales down at American Thread…' He exhaled and felt a knot loosen in his neck. 'Anyhow, I figure it's gonna take a while adjusting to being back. It's good to be home and all – everybody's happy to see me, of course – but it's not the same.' Looking distractedly at the clock, he took another drag of his cigarette. 'I guess nothing will ever be the same.'

'Nope.'

'I suppose everybody's been changed by the war in some way,' Edward ventured.

'Only there's some who don't know it yet.'

Edward regarded Fitz a moment. 'Well, that's right…that's what I'm driving at, I guess. I know I've got to get on with things,' he said, leaning over to the ashtray on the coffee table, 'but I just don't see how you're supposed to compartmentalize it all. You know what I mean?'

'Life isn't fair.'

Looking across, it was as if the wheelchair and the bandages didn't exist. 'I keep having these awful dreams,' Edward confessed without reservation.

'I know.'

'Yeah, but you must think you're living a nightmare,' Edward said, swallowing hard. 'I mean, with all that's happened, how do you hold yourself together?'

'Like I say, life isn't fair,' Fitz said simply, shaking his head in resignation.

'And with all your talent…'

Fitz stubbed out his cigarette in the ashtray. 'Sure, I'm mad about what happened. 'Figured I'd play ball a long time…' He straightened up and stretched his arm. 'Funny thing is – I just realized this a couple of months back – nothin' can take away what I got outta baseball.'

Edward leaned forward, elbows on his knees, listening intently.

"Prob'ly never heard of Charlie Sweeney,' Fitz said with a chuckle. 'Set the major league record with nineteen strikeouts back in '84? Anyhow, when he was washed up he came back here and bought a stake in the Haverlys, the old minor league team, then lost it in a card game to my dad. That's how we got involved with the Pacific Coast League...'

'All on account of a card game...' Edward said, shaking his head.

After a moment's reflection, Fitz said, 'Some folks say you shouldn't look for the meaning of life in baseball. It's just a game, they say...'

Edward looked at Fitz, afraid to speak, afraid he might break a spell of some kind, until he got the feeling the vet was waiting on him. 'So, what's the game taught you, Fitz?'

The big man didn't respond right away. He stared out to the courtyard, which was dark now, the sunroom shrouded in shadows, but for the lamplight that caught Fitz's profile like an aurora. 'Patience,' he said at length, '—control what you can, accept the rest.'

The words hung in the air a moment. Edward looked over to the newspaper on the coffee table, the box scores folded in on themselves, and remarked, 'I used to wonder how you guys could take those heartbreakers.'

'When it all slips from your hands...' Fitz said with a snort.

This reassured Edward enormously, and looking to the big

man, he said, 'Remember that series you had against the Oaks when everything seemed to unravel? What was it, nine runs you guys gave up in the eighth?'

'Couldn't *buy* a third out,' Fitz said with a sheepish grin. They burst out laughing and Fitz took another sip of water, but when the laughter caused him to choke and cough, Edward grew alarmed. Waving him off, Fitz wheezed, 'Remember McGee's bunt?'

The two of them convulsed in howls of laughter until Edward, his eyes full of tears, held up his hands in surrender. Fitz pinched his nose to choke off his chortling, and when he regained his composure, he said, 'Bet the whole fiasco was fun to watch…'

'Oh shit!' Edward sputtered, wiping his eyes with his handkerchief. The laughter was so cathartic, he looked over gratefully. 'You got some kind of courage, Fitz, let me tell you.'

Fitz smiled softly. 'Brought more outta the Marne than I took in with me, Eddie.'

They got to talking about major league ball, about how Fitz's former Seals teammate Ping Bodie was tearing it up for the Yankees now, about how the White Sox looked unstoppable this year. This prompted Fitz to mention that he'd met one of his heroes, Buck Weaver, when the Sox played the Senators the year before, just before the 3rd Infantry shipped overseas. 'Only third baseman in the league Cobb won't bunt against,' Fitz said admiringly. 'He's that quick.'

Caught up in a kind of euphoria, Edward tried to describe how he used to marvel at Fitz's defense, the way he could snag a grounder, letting the force spin him around while making the exchange to his throwing hand, then use his right leg like a catapult to uncork a flare to first. 'It was like a dance out there,' he said, staring into the middle distance, before realizing it might have been inappropriate describing something Fitz would never replicate. He was feeling self-conscious when he caught sight of a nurse coming into the sunroom, and Fitz, who'd been eyeing Edward appreciatively, now turned to see who was coming.

'Angela!' he said, waving her over.

'I just got off my shift, Jimmy,' she said, approaching, 'but I see you have a visitor...'

Fitz dismissed the apology, saying, 'This is a veteran friend of mine, Edward Dooley. Different regiment, same war.'

Edward stood up. 'How do you do?' he said, offering his hand. She looked familiar, green eyes and chestnut hair, shapely figure – but it was the wry smile on her lips that synched it. 'Oh, didn't I see you the other night at—'

'At the Victory Ball,' she interjected, recognizing him as the man who'd knocked over her coffee tray when the fireworks started. 'My name's Angela Luchetti,' she said, shaking his hand. 'I was so sorry about all the ruckus...tell me, how's your lady friend?'

'Oh, much better thanks,' Edward said, suddenly flustered, '—a bit of a shock is all.'

'Of course.' She was struck by his fine features and wisps of fair hair, unusual given the toll fighting had taken on heartier men. But recalling his dutiful demeanor, she said, 'It's good to get the men out of the hospital – but it can be dicey. I felt so badly for her...'

'Well, that's very kind,' Edward replied, anxious to bring

the big man into the conversation. 'Good thing Fitz was there to save the day!'

'Yes, it was.'

'We'd be a sorry bunch without Angela,' Fitz said, then eyeing Edward, he added, 'She keeps us in check.'

'Have you been at this long?' Edward asked. He was about to retake his seat, then thought better of it.

'Since we entered the war,' she replied, straightening Fitz's sweater. 'To do my bit…'

'Talk about courage, Eddie,' Fitz said, dusting cigarette ash from his knee.

'Don't be ridiculous, Jimmy,' she said as she gently pushed him forward to pull up his back cushion, 'I just believe in hard work, that's all.'

'Same difference,' Fitz said.

Looking at Edward, she said, 'Do you come from a big family, Mr. Dooley?'

'Two sisters, two brothers – right here in San Francisco.'

'Then I'm sure you know all about hard work…'

'Oh, sure.'

'The sergeant here has very little family to speak of,' she said, catching Edward's eye, 'so I'll keep him busy with his exercises if you'll promise to stop in from time to time.'

'I will,' said Edward without hesitation.

'Good. Well then, I look forward to seeing you again.' With a warm smile, she shook Edward's hand once more, then touched Fitz's shoulder before she turned and left the room.

'Heart of gold,' Fitz remarked, as Edward watched her disappear down the hallway. 'Wish I could say that about the others around here, but you know how it is…' Edward was lost in thought as Fitz prepared to back up, saying, 'I don't plan on staying at Letterman any longer than I have to – 'figure I'll find a residence hotel where I can be around regular folks...'

Edward snapped out of his trance, and taking the wheelchair by the handles, he turned the big man around, saying, 'When that day comes, Fitz, you can count on me.'

'Thanks, Eddie. 'Much obliged.'

'No, Fitz, it's me who's obliged to you,' Edward said as they emerged from the darkened room into the brightly lit hallway. Making conversation on the way to the dining room, Edward asked about what had happened to Charlie Sweeney after he'd lost his stake in the Haverlys.

'Didn't end well,' Fitz said after a moment. 'Killed a man in a barroom brawl and spent a few years in jail before TB got him.'

'Wow, what a sorry fate...'

'Fate?' Edward couldn't see his friend's face, only the top of his head. 'Fate's got nothing to do with it,' he heard Fitz say matter-of-factly. 'Just didn't play his cards right.'

PART TWO

Chapter 12

Edward was not naturally inclined to soldiering; he'd never been a contentious person.

He was a city boy – something he had in common with one in five Americans at the time – though San Francisco wasn't highly industrialized, nor was it roiling with ethnic tensions like the bigger cities back east. Far removed from the demands of farms or factories, Edward lived a relatively comfortable life: he worked in an office, frequented movie palaces, went for picnics in Golden Gate Park and kicked up the surf at Ocean Beach. Were it not for the great earthquake and fire, nothing in the first two decades of his life would have prepared him for war.

As a ten-year-old he was witness to ineptitude and outright anarchy; he'd learned there is a difference between what actually happened – that people's lives had come apart – and what is recorded for posterity. One photograph from the '06 disaster particularly irked him: a group of Victorian gentry is smiling, like spectators at a regatta, as they take in the catastrophe from the relative safety of Russian Hill. By contrast, Edward would never forget the sight of his father, reunited with the family at the make-shift refugee camp in Golden Gate Park after Katherine had found him at the tent hospital. He'd stood there like a miserable dog, smelling of whiskey, sweat, and bile, as she tearfully recounted the miracle of Baby Deirdre opening her eyes for the first time in three days when she heard him.

The Dooleys made the best of it for several weeks, huddled among the eucalyptus trees with hundreds of other families, the smoke from campfires indistinguishable from the fog wafting in from the ocean. One afternoon, after another dispiriting meeting with the equivocal insurance men downtown, James returned to camp and announced that he'd received a telegram from his sister, Hildie, offering to take the children for the summer.

Hildie and her husband, Aidan, lived with their four children on a farm up in Sonoma, and what began as a favor to help James and Honora get back on their feet became a tradition for the Dooley children, for a few years anyway. The annual stay in the country was billed as a chance to get out of the dreary city fog and to get to know their cousins, but as the family's economic circumstances worsened, it turned into an annual hiatus for Mr. and Mrs. Dooley. The entire clan would typically arrive the first week of July, and following the July 4th festivities, James and Honora would return to San Francisco for six weeks.

'Let us know how you get on with those new contracts,' Hildie would say to her brother as she and the children waved goodbye from the train platform. But she was under no illusions. As her brother usually looked worse for wear when he and Honora returned in mid-August, she surmised that his fatigue had less to do with business troubles than with his wife's harangues.

For the Dooley children, summers in Sonoma meant milking cows and feeding chickens, pumping water from a well and using an outhouse. There was never any shortage of work: the boys in their hand-me-down dungarees would mend fences, dig drainage ditches, repaint the barn, turn a fallow field; the girls in gingham dresses worked mostly indoors, Katherine and Cousin Cora bent over wash boards or mending clothes when not preparing meals, while young Maggie looked after Baby Deirdre, whom she adored.

Though two years younger than Cousin Patrick, Colm had no trouble matching his stamina. After morning chores, the two would spend the day in Mayacamas Mountains, returning with stories of rattle snakes they'd taunted and rabbit traps they'd set. Though the older boys would tease Walter and Edward for being scrawny, their younger cousin Michael never did. Three years Edward's junior, Michael was big, but reserved where his brother was boisterous. Both O'Shea boys were adept with their hands. Patrick liked repairing engines, and Michael built model ships and tinkered with clocks; his bird sketches were displayed in the town library, where he was a regular.

Edward became accustomed to hard work over the course of several summers – he filled out a bit and developed calluses on his hands, overcame his fear of heights, and no longer turned away when Uncle Aidan slaughtered a pig. He was seventeen in the summer of 1913, when he and the other boys managed to plant one hundred Gravenstein apple trees in a single day. In the flatbed of Uncle Aidan's Ford on the ride back to the farmhouse at twilight, Edward beamed with satisfaction when Cousin Patrick gave him a hearty slap on the back.

The boys having exceeded his expectations, Uncle Aidan drove them up to a favorite fishing hole the next morning (after promising the girls that he'd take them to a dance at Boyes Hot Springs on Saturday). He dropped the boys at a filling station in Eldridge, saying he'd be back at five, then, laden with daypacks, fishing poles, and a tackle box, Patrick and Michael led their cousins up through the dry grasses into the wooded creases of the rolling hills.

It was a day Edward would remember as full of promise, like a gift. He felt especially invigorated, taking long, easy strides, tracking the majestic arc of a red-tailed hawk, smelling the licorice in clumps of anise and pepper in the marigolds. The boys followed Patrick across a meadow covered with poppies and purple lupine, and down a deer path into a musty dell so thick with ferns and mossy boulders Edward half-expected to find a leprechaun. A series of granite outcroppings formed a crude amphitheater along the banks of a stream, where Patrick set about demonstrating proper casting technique.

Unfortunately, the Dooleys never met with much success fishing, and it wasn't long before Colm grew restless and handed his rod back to his cousin, saying, 'Fly fishing stinks! I'm gonna have a look around…' An hour later, he reappeared on the opposite side of the stream, shouting breathlessly that he'd found a hunting lodge under construction a few miles off. Seeing the excitement in the others, Patrick conceded that the fishing expedition had been a bust and packed up the tackle box.

Colm led the way through groves of scrub oak and manzanita before they came out on a dirt road, where they were immediately passed by a convoy of trucks racing down the hill. Through a whirl of dust they made out what appeared to be a fortress up around the bend – high stone walls canted inward, supporting a handsome timber-frame structure above. A lone truck parked under the portico and the tap-tap-tap of work within the walled compound drew the boys through an archway into a central courtyard, where two men were bent over redwood timbers set up on sawhorses. The second-floor veranda projected like the prow of a ship, pointing to a pergola at the opposite end of the courtyard which framed a commanding vista of the valley below. The timber framers had begun packing away their chisels when the burly one said, 'I suppose you boys want a tour.'

He brought them into the great room which featured new Stickly furniture, sumptuous Persian rugs, and a stone hearth big enough to stand in. The enormous posts and beams had been rubbed with tung oil to match the hutches in the dining room and the bookcases in the library. Upstairs there were rooms with four-post beds and armoires, bathrooms with ceramic tile floors and the latest porcelain fixtures, and a master suite with a balcony facing east to Mt. Veeder.

When their guide mentioned that the pool in the courtyard would be stocked with mountain bass, Patrick scoffed, saying even that wouldn't be enough to attract experienced outdoorsmen. 'Everybody knows the best quail and deer hunting is miles from here.'

'Well, he ain't much of a hunter, son,' the timber framer explained. Seeing quizzical looks from the boys, he said, 'Any of you ever read *The Call of the Wild*?'

Michael turn to the man. 'This is Jack London's place?'

Not to be outdone, Patrick said, 'Come to think of it, I heard he was buying land up here around Glen Ellen, only I thought it was just another one of his crackpot farming schemes.'

The timber framer chuckled at the teenage know-it-all. 'It's kinda hard keeping a place with twenty-six rooms and nine fireplaces a secret,' he said, turning to lead the boys back downstairs. 'Ol' Jack's callin' the place Wolf House…He and his wife move in next month.'

Rushing back to meet up with Uncle Aidan, the boys talked about novels like *The Call of the Wild* and *White Fang* that had made London rich enough to build his dream house, about the brutality of the wolf pack, the fine line between savage and civilized. 'It's about survival of the fittest,' Patrick said with finality, as they scrambled down an embankment.

'I don't buy it,' Michael offered from the rear, '—because that means the world is a hopeless, godless place. That everything's random and without meaning.'

'Not random,' his brother countered, '—just selective. The weak get weaned out.'

'Justice, pure and simple,' Colm put in.

Undaunted, Michael said, 'For animals, maybe, but we have free will. We can choose to not act like savages because we've been blessed with a soul.'

'Wish I could believe you, Mikey,' Patrick said after a minute, 'but when push comes to shove, I'm not sure we wouldn't just go back to being animals.'

That evening after supper, with Uncle Aidan and Aunt Hildie reading the paper on the porch, the older boys tinkering with a tractor motor in the barn, and Walter playing "Hearts" with the girls in the parlor, Edward and Michael brought a chessboard into the dining room. They were setting out the pieces when Edward returned to the afternoon's conversation, saying 'So, Michael, do you think Darwin was wrong? I mean about man being descended from apes?'

Michael smiled. 'Well, it might explain how we're similar as a species,' he said, 'but not how we're different…That's why I like *The Sea Wolf* better than the other books, because London is finally dealing with *human* nature.'

Edward was pleased to hear this. Though he'd been frustrated the first time he read the book as a boy, only when he read it again in high school, after studying Augustine and Aquinas on the nature of good and evil, was he able to fully appreciate it. As the chess match unfolded, he and Michael discussed the debate London sets up between the intellectual protagonist lost at sea, Humphrey van Weyden, and the merciless Captain Larsen who rescues him.

'Larsen calls him "Hump" as if idealism were a deformity!' Edward said with a laugh.

'Larsen's a worthy foe, though,' Michael countered. 'Life at sea is unforgiving and seal-hunting's a brutal business. He has good reason to believe our only motivation is survival.'

With that, he went out to the hall and pulled a dog-eared copy of the book from the shelves beneath the staircase. Returning to the dining room table, he found the page where Edward could quote Hump arguing how Larsen misunderstands Darwin when he concludes that the struggle for existence sanctions the wanton destruction of life.

'Because man is endowed with a *soul*,' Michael declared, 'and that's what makes him different from other beasts.'

'And by resisting the temptation to do evil, he can win eternal life!' Edward rejoined.

Michael smiled, but then flipped to another section, quoting Larsen again,

Ah, you have eternal life before you. You are a millionaire in immortality...and it is all very beautiful, this shaking off of the flesh and soaring of the imprisoned spirit...So why cling to life – what's there to be afraid of when you are sure of your resurrection?

Edward looked at his cousin expectantly, who ventured, 'We cling to life because it is God-given, and we honor Him by protecting it.'

'Resurrection comes to those who have earned it through faith,' Edward observed.

The two had laughed at the heady exchange, but after the war Edward would look back on this as the point where his path and Michael's crossed. At the time he had no idea that the quarrels consuming his parents that summer would result in his having to quit Sacred Heart to help the family make ends meet; or that Aunt Hildie had persuaded her husband that Patrick could take over the farm, enabling Michael to pursue his education (at the Christian Brothers School in Martinez, no less, an irony lost on everyone but Edward it seemed.) While never one to hold a grudge, Edward would forever equate the twist of fate that befell him that summer with the news of Jack London's dream house going up in flames days before he was to move in.

Chapter 13

Scanning the headlines while riding the streetcar to work the following June, Edward had no idea how profoundly a random shooting in someplace called Sarajevo would affect his life.

The United States had little at stake in the conflict that erupted among the imperial powers that summer. Two years later most Americans were still content to be bystanders: Woodrow Wilson won reelection in November 1916, by sticking to his promise of keeping America out of the war. But when his appeal for peace fell on deaf ears in December, an inexorable slide ensued. First, Germany resumed its U-boat warfare in February, prompting the U.S. to break off diplomatic relations; then a telegram intercepted in March suggested a German-Mexican military alliance should the U.S. enter the war. In early April, declaring that 'right is more precious than peace,' President Wilson made the case to Congress that America had a moral responsibility to stop the madness in Europe and to defend democracy around the world.

When Congress declared war on Germany, U.S. forces numbered just three-hundred thousand – consistent with the Founding Fathers' reluctance to maintain a standing army, lest the republic devolve into the kind of imperial power they'd rebelled against in the first place. When the Selective Service Act was passed in May, the country's top soldier, General

John J. Pershing, was charged with mobilizing an army of two million men in twelve months. It was a frenetic summer as young men across the country bid farewell to family and friends and reported for duty. Some were more eager than others.

'Lucky son of a bitch,' Colm said of Cousin Patrick at dinner one night, '—he'll probably be overseas by Christmas.' Patrick had joined the National Guard the year before and was among the first soldiers to be mobilized. Ignoring his mother's glare for using profanity, Colm continued, 'We shoulda gone in *last* summer after those radicals blew up the Preparedness Day parade,' referring to the blast on Market Street in San Francisco that had killed ten and injured dozens.

'That was the work of anarchists, though – not a foreign invasion,' Edward said, still hoping for cooler heads to prevail.

'Anarchists put up to it by the goddamn Kaiser, for all we know,' Colm retorted. 'Let's face it, everything's coming apart and it's about time we took charge over there...'

Edward wasn't the only one left reeling by the President Wilson's about-face. He couldn't get his head around the idea that America was being pulled into the quagmire, that something so remote and abstract would suddenly be bearing down on him personally. As soon as the draft passed, and with his twenty-first birthday coming in June, he began to lose his appetite and have trouble sleeping. Consternation within the Dooley household caused a rash to break out on his hands, what with Honora insisting her husband write the Selective Service to exempt Edward from serving.

Though cowed by their older brother's bellicose pronouncements, Walter tried to assuage Edward's anxiety by saying that Uncle Sam couldn't take all three of them, that Edward would be needed at home. The third week of May Colm dragged Walter with him to the Presidio where they signed up with the San Francisco regiment, the 30th Infantry. Edward anxiously awaited news from the draft board for a month, but in the end his parents' appeal made no impression – goaded by Colm, Edward registered the day after his birthday.

By that time, with the 30th Infantry already filled, Edward's orders were to report to Camp Lewis in Tacoma, Washington, after first going through an introductory boot camp at the Presidio. On a foggy afternoon in late August 1917, he stepped off the "D" car at the end of the line and was waved through at the Lombard Gate. Bracing himself for the ordeal, what little poise he had he attributed to his business suit, the Homburg he'd borrowed from Walter, and his father's leather suitcase, which had acquired the tawny color of a fine cigar. He strode onto the base, stirred by the marching platoons and the men on horseback wending their way through truck convoys. He followed a young soldier who swept passed him on his way to a three-story building identified as the "Enlisted Men's Club". Its broad veranda teeming with men in uniform, Edward mounted the steps and was passing a group of soldiers coming down when one of them offered him a jaunty salute.

The lobby smelled of hot dogs and coffee wafting in from a canteen at the rear of a social lounge, where soldiers were gathered around pool tables. Edward's attention was drawn to a flyer which read "Amateurs Report Upstairs". In the weeks since being drafted he'd tried to calm his nerves by thinking of the army as a kind of fraternity, and assumed the flyer hinted at some good-natured hazing to come. He followed the low murmur of male voices coming from the assembly hall upstairs, and as he approached the doors, several sharp claps summoned everyone to attention. But instead of finding recruits lined up at sign-in stations, about a hundred men in uniform were seated on folding chairs, facing a stage.

Edward quickly took a seat in the rear among a smattering of other men in suits, just as three soldiers in BVDs and wool breeches stepped onstage. With their fingers laced up under their chins, they batted their eyes coquettishly and sang in a ragged falsetto, '*Three little maids from school are we, pert as a school-girl well can be...*'

The audience erupted in raucous laughter, leaving Edward confused and vaguely embarrassed. A young man in a striped necktie and straw boater turned around and said, 'The one in the middle ought to shave his mustache, don't you think?' Edward watched as a large fellow wearing a baggy union suit and a dour countenance now lumbered onto the stage and addressed the curtsying trio in a rich baritone. This was enough to dislodge an older soldier, an officer standing at the foot of the stage, who slowly came up the aisle tapping a riding crop against his thigh. As soon as he passed, a man across from Edward gestured over his shoulder, and quipped, 'Every regiment has its Pooh-Bah!'

Edward laughed uneasily until the riding crop struck his shoulder.

'You college boys in Hardie or Keyes?' the sergeant hissed, drawing a blank stare from Edward. "The Bachelor Officers Quarters," which wing?' When Edward became flustered the older man bellowed, 'What's your name, boy?' causing many heads to turn. To his great mortification, Edward learned that he'd stumbled upon a rehearsal of *The Mikado* at officers' training school. He was gruffly directed to the induction center for plebes on the North Cantonment, and as he hastily made his way to the exit doors the sergeant called after him, 'They're gonna eat you alive, Dooley!' causing the hall to explode with laughter.

'Oh, you poor thing!' Constance said, alarmed at the sight of Edward's sunken cheeks and badly sunburned forehead.

'All part of the rite of passage,' he said, trying to sound nonchalant. With a day's furlough to say his goodbyes, an afternoon coffee at the Doherty's would be his only chance to see Constance. 'It'll make the adjustment to Camp Lewis that much easier.'

In fact, he would remember boot camp as one of the most grueling experiences of his life. After his humiliation at the Enlisted Men's Club, he'd been subjected to a degrading physical exam and a barrage of inoculations which resulted in nausea, headaches, and chills that lingered for days. From the flimsy barracks on the windswept North Cantonment where new recruits were assigned, Edward could make out the Parthenon-like Oregon Pavilion, which had been turned over to the army after the fair to serve as a dance hall for officers – off-limits to the likes of lowly draftees.

Two weeks under the thumbs of the grizzled veterans of the Spanish-American War and the Philippine Campaign had been miserable; but for summers in Sonoma, Edward was certain he could never have endured the long hikes with full packs, the bad food and poor sleep. Now sitting with Constance in her front parlor, he was determined not to indulge in self-pity, lest he break down altogether.

'We're so proud of you, Edward,' she said, massaging his badly blistered palms. One of the few girls with a beau old enough to be called up, her eyes now welled with tears. 'Oh, Edward, you will be careful, won't you?'

'Don't cry, Con,' he said, his throat tightening. 'General Pershing won't send us over until we're ready.'

'Oh, the Germans have behaved so abominably,' she said, dabbing her eyes with a handkerchief. 'I think I've mentioned Fr. Seifert, Mother's friend who teaches down at Santa Clara? He attended the Catholic university in Louvain, you know, where the Germans have burned all those medieval manuscripts...'

'Yes, I remember Morgan mentioning it when he started at Stanford. Speaking of which, how's his summer project working out?'

'Well, he hasn't been home in over a month. Father says the government may have an interest in the demographics work he's doing with some professor there...'

Edward smiled. 'Who'd have thought our man of letters had a head for statistics?'

'Father's written Senator Phelan,' Constance went on, refreshing their coffee, 'to see if there might be a place for Morgan in the War Department.'

Edward was silent a moment, then unable to resist a self-indulgent remark, he said, 'And I'm the one cut out for the infantry – a natural-born fighter, that's me.'

'Oh now,' Constance admonished, 'you'll make a fine soldier. And you know Morgan – he's never been very athletic.'

Chapter 14

Like most recruits, Edward had never ventured more than a hundred miles from home. He'd never crossed the Carquinez Strait by rail ferry, nor had he ever seen Sacramento, let alone the Klamath Mountains, the Willamette Valley, or the Columbia River. The magnificent string of volcanoes he saw from the train on the way north, from Lassen Peak to Mt. Rainier, were enough to remind him of his humble place in the grand scheme of things.

Camp Lewis was one of thirty-two cantonments around the country, a great swath of forest cleared away for barracks, latrines, and mess halls – a gold rush boomtown, where the crackle of rifle fire from the shooting ranges and the far-off thunder of artillery drills seemed incessant. Under the watchful eyes of overbearing sergeants, platoons were forged into fighting units, and pity the poor private who couldn't keep up.

Recruits were drawn primarily from the Pacific Northwest – miners and mountaineers from Idaho, cattlemen from Wyoming and Montana, sheepherders from Utah and Nevada. Edward met sailors from Seattle and stevedores from San Pedro, lumberjacks from Eureka, farm boys from Fresno and Provo. Outnumbered by the rough-and-ready types, he was circumspect: whenever anyone asked him a direct question – like how fast the cable cars were in 'Frisco or whether he'd ever frequented a Chinese bordello – he'd respond using as few words as possible. He also made a point of never mentioning books, fearful of raising the suspicions of those for whom schooling had been a perfunctory affair.

The army taught Edward that he could endure more than he thought possible: he wasn't the only one to get tangled up in a rope ladder or fall face-down in the mud, to be plagued by black flies or afflicted by foot fungus as a result of daily marches on mushy trails. In time his shoulders grew accustomed to the straps of his pack, and he found that he was a decent shot, something he credited to time spent at Bronco Billy's Shooting Gallery at the Pan-Pacific Fair.

The 91st Division, nicknamed the Wild West Division, was comprised of two infantry brigades, each brigade made up of two regiments, each regiment made up of four battalions, each battalion made up of four companies, each company made up of five platoons, and each platoon made up of four squads of ten men each – together with supporting artillery, medical, and supply units, forty thousand soldiers in all, the best of the west's young manhood.

While there was experience at the top – the Major General and Brigadier Generals were all West Point graduates – privates only interacted with corporals and sergeants, who, in turn, reported to captains and lieutenants. Commanding E Company of the 362nd Infantry Regiment, Edward's unit, was Captain Maynard Gates, West Point '05, who claimed to have served under General Pershing himself during the Pancho Villa expedition. Edward's platoon was headed by First Lieutenant Grainger, a soft-spoken railroad engineer from Billings who'd done a turn in the Philippines. Below him was Sergeant Asa Shaw, a tall banker from Boise so stooped and gray that some wag called him a dead ringer for the Civil War vet they trotted out on Decoration Day back home. By default, this made Corporal George Richter, a stout rancher from Corvallis with the disposition of a bantam rooster, the platoon's taskmaster.

Mitch Pitowski was a wheat farmer from Omaha whose size and stolid demeanor accorded him the unofficial leadership role in Edward's squad. In the first week he'd defused an altercation between Jacobs, a haberdasher from Sacramento, and Crowley, a Reno carpenter prone to using racial slurs. He also indulged the feints and jabs of Oscar Pereira, a diminutive artichoke farmer from Watsonville who fancied himself lightweight champion Benny Leonard – 'C'mon, let's go, you big palooka,' he'd say to Pitowski, 'I'm gonna put your lights out, see?'

Duncan Miller was a no-nonsense cattleman from Laramie who struck Edward as a character out of a Zane Grey story – of the endless drills the laconic cowboy would say, 'Just give me a goddamn rifle and send me over.' Miller took an immediate interest Edward because his brother had taken him see the San Francisco Seals play in Portland the year they won the Pacific Coast League pennant. He was still talking about the triple play they turned that day.

Karl Steinkoler, a quiet fisherman from Anacortes, overheard Miller breaking down the remarkable play and unexpectedly put in that he'd seen that same Seals squad dismantle his Seattle Indians team. 'Couldn't hold a candle to 'em,' the fisherman confessed. Miller took a drag of his cigarette and smiled. He liked Steinkoler because he only spoke when it mattered.

In early December E Company drew the short straw – no leave until the second week of January – but they were granted a liberty pass for Christmas Day. When Steinkoler mentioned that he was going up to Seattle to see his sister, a Red Cross nurse, Joe Blanchard, a taciturn miner from Idaho with 'no family to speak of,' asked if he could come along. Edward and three others quickly followed suit.

On Christmas morning the six privates were on the first truck convoy to Tacoma. In their wide-brimmed campaign hats and olive-drab tunics they strode shoulder to shoulder down Pacific Avenue, the lampposts festooned with ribbons and wreaths, trolley conductors ringing their bells as they passed the Doughboys. At the Northern Pacific Train Depot they listened as holiday revelers took up the new ditty making the rounds,

Tramp, tramp, tramp, the boys are marching
I spy Kaiser at the door
We'll get a lemon pie and squash him in his eye
And there won't be a Kaiser anymore!

Grateful soldiers waiting for the train to Seattle then launched into spirited renditions of yuletide favorites. Seated at the coffee counter with his buddies, Edward overheard a young boy ask his mother if the soldiers were heroes. He stole a glimpse of the young woman, with three children and an armload of packages, and caught his breath when he made out the words '...because their service will safeguard your future.'

Faced with the prospect of an overcrowded train, Steinkoler led his pals down to the docks where they boarded the Nisqually steamer. Pereira spent the next hour bent over the stern, but the others were thrilled to stand at the bow as the boat navigated the intricate waterways, making mail drops at tiny islands cloaked in cedar and fir. When from a distance they heard the sounds of industry coming from two cavernous sheds, Steinkoler announced that they would be stopping off to see his uncle, a steamfitter at the Puget Sound Navy Yard, on half-shift that day.

Bremerton was a colorless town, the streets awash in mud, makeshift storefronts strung together along well-worn board-walks. In a ramshackle diner Steinkoler found his uncle, a thick, middle-aged man with a bristly gray beard running along his jaw like an ancient mariner's. Over platters of runny eggs, boiled potatoes, geoduck clams and deep-fried cod, he entertained the six army recruits with stories of his days as a deep-sea fisherman in the Straits of Juan de Fuca, before various ailments sidelined him and he took to repairing ships.

'A few years ago, them Annaplis boys shut the yard down on account of all the bawdy houses and opium dens,' he said, pulling out papers and a pouch of tobacco, 'but soon as this war starts up, whaddya know, they need us again. First we helped the Brits, but now with us in it, we got three thousand sailors working seven days a week here...' Fumbling with the front of his overalls, he pulled out a flask and poured something dark into his mug of greasy coffee.

Miller raised his eyebrows. 'Christmas cordial?'

'Well now, where's my manners?' the weather-beaten man said with a sneaky smile, 'It's Christmas, fer Chrissakes!' and with a chuckle he poured a dollop into each of their mugs.

Hoisting his mug, he said, 'Damn shame the state goes dry just as you boys get here. Inhospitable and unpatriotic, too!' Then he lit a cigarette and took a long drag before bemoaning the teetotalers of Washington State. 'There's a fella in Seattle they call "the Good Bootlegger" 'cause supposibly he's on the police force, too. Who cares, I say? His whiskey's smooth, comes from Canada...' As they sipped their coffee, he added, 'I'll tell you something if you haven't figured it out already – there's good guys and bad guys, only it ain't always clear who's who...'

Edward knew the world wasn't black and white, but he hadn't lived long enough to see much gray yet. As the steamer pulled into Seattle that afternoon his eyes were drawn to the Smith Tower skyscraper and the spires of St. James Cathedral on the hill, monuments to capitalism and religion. Remembering the words of the old mariner, he wondered for the first time whether there might be less than honorable reasons for America getting into the war.

Montgomery McSweeney's prize possession was the silver steel Colt revolver he'd inherited from his granddad on his mother's side, a Battle of Vicksburg veteran cited for bravery. His father had also been in the military – an Irish recruit in General Terry's unit that discovered the remains of the 7th Cavalry at Little Big Horn – though eventually he lost his health, his livery business, and his mind to drink. Young Montgomery aspired to his granddad's legacy instead, and although he amassed a poor record at the Wentworth Military Academy, he considered impudence a badge of honor. Audacity couldn't be taught, it was inherited – at twenty-seven he was convinced that his time had come.

After a few drinks with fellow officers upstairs, McSweeney was smoking a cigarette in the entry court of the Hotel Sorrento, a fashionable Italianate hotel on First Hill that was home to senior military personnel, when something disturbing caught his eye. Beyond several well-dressed couples gathered in lobby, McSweeney spied what looked like buck privates gathered in front of the Ladies Parlor, the temporary Red Cross headquarters that this evening was being used for a Christmas reception. If there was one thing that especially galled the stocky Second Lieutenant, it was the presumption of new recruits drafted from the civilian ranks. Grinding his cigarette into the gravel, he marched into the hotel.

'What the hell do you think you're doing?' he demanded as he came up to the five privates. When Pitowski explained that their buddy had come by to visit his sister, McSweeney said curtly, 'This reception's for officers only – you shouldn't be here at all.'

Blanchard pointed out Steinkoler in the parlor, but the red-haired officer was having none of it. 'Beat it before I call the MPs,' he growled.

'Aw, now wait a minute, Lieutenant—' Miller began.

McSweeney looked up and squinted. 'Take a step closer and I'll have you in the brig for threatening an officer.'

'Threatening?' the rancher replied indignantly, 'The hell I was…'

McSweeney's his eyes twinkled. 'What's your name, soldier?'

'Miller, *sir*,' his emphasis on the last word ambiguous. 'E Company, 362nd Regiment.'

Hands on his hips now, McSweeney said sharply, 'I'll inform Captain Gates that you've been insolent, Miller – belligerent, probably been drinking.'

With a sneer he directed Edward to get Steinkoler and his gang off the premises, ASAP, then crossed his arms and stood implacably in front of the others. Miller rolled his eyes and pretended to study the ceiling molding while Pitowski and Blanchard stared straight ahead. But Pereira couldn't contain himself, and shifted his weight from one foot to the other until he blurted out, 'Jeesh, Lieutenant, it's Christmas – we don't want any trouble!' Pitowski tried nudging him, but it was too late.

McSweeney grinned. 'Looks like they let anybody into the army these days,' he said, pleased to be looking down at a shorter man.

Pereira stiffened, but Miller held him back. 'I reckon Oscar here has more fire in his belly than you'll ever have, Lieutenant,' the rancher jeered.

'Why you son of a bitch!' McSweeney hissed, stepping forward, fists clenched.

But the man from Laramie didn't budge, and in a low, disgusted drawl he uncorked some long-simmering resentments. 'They asked for fightin' men and here we are, goddammit. Now as for your kind, Lieutenant, you better stop bullying us, see, 'cause we'll be the ones carryin' the load over there while you're shittin' your pants, screamin' for reinforcements!'

McSweeney was livid and no one moved.

'Trouble here, Monty?' All eyes turned to a tall captain approaching the group whose insouciant tone suggested he liked getting the better of the Second Lieutenant.

'*My* men know better than to crash an officers' party,' McSweeney snarled, annoyed by the interruption, particularly by a ninety-day wonder from the officers' training pool.

Just then Edward and Steinkoler arrived, and the group was turning to leave when the Captain blocked their passage. 'You boys have lady friends in there?' he asked mildly.

'My sister's one of the nurses, sir,' Steinkoler explained.

'Oh? Well, I imagine that must be a big sacrifice for your family, both of you in the service,' the Captain remarked. 'What's your name, soldier?'

'Steinkoler, sir, from the 362nd, E Company.'

'Steinkoler…' the Captain repeated curiously. 'What's that, German, Jewish…both?'

The fisherman's eyes went round like saucers. 'Sir?'

There was an awkward silence before the Captain laughed. 'Just kidding!' he said, 'You never know about the Kaiser, what with the Black Tom sabotage and all…' Seeing a senior officer coming from the Ladies' Parlor, he added hastily, 'Unfortunate name, though – 'ought to think about changing it, like the King did,' before going ram-rod straight and bringing his arm up in salute.

'Merry Christmas, men,' the Colonel said, returning the salute in cursory fashion. Edward noted the expert tailoring of his worsted serge tunic, how neatly his Sam Browne belt was drawn across his chest. He held a teacup of eggnog in his left hand that smelled of brandy.

After being apprised of the situation, the Colonel said, 'I don't have to tell you how proud we should be of our women – they'll be holding down the home front in our absence, after all.' He looked down at the cup in his hands. 'Who knows how long that'll be?' he said absently, 'Some say we'll make quick work of the Boche, but with the Bolsheviks taking Petrograd last month, I'm afraid we can count on the Germans turning their attention west just in time to meet us in Le Havre…'

An uncomfortable silence filled the air until the Captain,

covering for the Colonel's lapse in discretion, said, 'We'll be ready for them, sir.'

'They haven't seen the likes of us yet,' McSweeney added for good measure.

'Indeed,' the Colonel said with a polite smile, before setting off for the lobby.

The Captain shot McSweeney a condescending glance before heading into the Ladies Parlor. Incensed, the Second Lieutenant briskly escorted the six privates out to entry court where he ordered them to stand at attention. With the strains of "Here We Come A-Wassailing" wafting from inside the hotel, he proceeded to exorcise his many frustrations in an expletive-laden diatribe that he concluded directly in front of Miller. He thumped the chest of the inscrutable rancher while assuring him of the fire in his belly until Miller decided to see for himself and suddenly drove his fist deep into McSweeney's stomach. Pitowski managed to catch the crumpled man and lay him gently in a flower bed where half an hour later the mayor and his wife were shocked to discover him, passed-out in a puddle of boozy vomit.

Such unbecoming conduct was enough for Major General Greene to declare Seattle off-limits to military personnel on New Year's Eve. Within a few months, with the help of Tacoma's Rotarians, a wholesome entertainment zone was built across the Pacific Highway from Camp Lewis, complete a bowling alley, an ice cream parlor, and a Chinese restaurant.

On a tip from Steinkoler's uncle the six privates enjoyed a Christmas dinner of steamed salmon and boiled ham, string beans, succotash, and mashed potatoes, in the back room of a hostel for retired seamen. Beer and whiskey flowed freely, and the air was thick with tobacco smoke and the boisterous laughter of three dozen servicemen, mostly sailors, but also a few soldiers and marines, engaged in card games and spirited conversation. Periodically a carol would start up at one table and spread throughout the room, building camaraderie, keeping homesickness at bay. Where Edward might be inclined to self-pity – picturing Constance enjoying eggnog with her family in their festively decorated drawing room, or his sisters unsuccessfully choking back tears at Christmas dinner over the absence of their brothers – he found himself oddly consoled in the company of his new buddies, however improbable that would have been were it not for the war.

After their table had been cleared, Miller was shuffling a deck of cards when Blanchard asked Steinkoler whether he'd ever been called a German sympathizer before.

The fisherman shook his head. 'I prefer pickin' the fights I'm in, not the other way around.'

'Corporal Richter says the Huns give his people a bad name!' Pereira said with a laugh.

Blanchard sneered, 'He's just the type who'd fall for stories about Boche barbarians spearing babies with bayonets and raping the Belgian girls, cutting off their breasts...'

'Jesus, Blanchard,' Miller muttered as he started dealing a hand of poker.

'The kind of stories that quashed the resistance to the draft in England,' the man from Coeur d'Alene continued, 'though I bet plenty of those blokes didn't give a damn about Belgian neutrality.'

'But the Germans *are* the enemy,' Miller said as everyone

studied their cards, '—they wanna take over everything.' He looked to his left. 'Mitch, you wanna kick things off?'

The farmer tossed a nickel to the middle of the table, followed by Edward, who said, 'We've got to stand up for our allies.' Pitowski echoed the sentiment, saying that the momentum had shifted since the victories at Vimy Ridge and Cambrai.

'Don't believe everything you read,' Blanchard said, dropping a nickel of his own, as did Pereira and Steinkoler. 'I've got relations in Canada who say the Tommies suffered a quarter million casualties at Passchendaele last year – to advance all of five fuckin' miles.'

Miller broke the silence that followed. 'How many cards you want, Mitch?'

When it got around to Blanchard, the miner said, 'It's a fair question to ask why we're going in now. What with the Russians quitting the fight, the bankers who loaned all that dough to the Brits and the French are probably worried about getting their money back…'

'Christ,' the rancher groaned as he dealt Blanchard two cards. 'Where do you get all that bullshit, the *International Workers* paper?'

'Jack Reed, actually: "Leave it to the poor guy to fight a rich man's war."'

'Another socialist nut like Debs and De Leon,' Miller said dismissively. 'You and your Wobbly friends can sit the war out for all I care.'

'Who?' Pereira asked.

'The International Workers of the World,' Edward explained, '—a rag-tag group of anarchists and socialists.'

'Sure, I've got no sympathy for industrialists who'd sell

weapons to both sides if it meant a good profit,' Blanchard said as he saw Edward's bet and raised it. 'But that doesn't make me a traitor. I'm willing to fight – I just wanna know what I'm fighting *for.*'

Before folding, Steinkoler said that only last year five Wobblies had been shot on a ferry in Puget Sound, their bodies thrown overboard. Edward recalled a story about vigilantes in San Diego taking it to a group of Wobblies for agitating free speech, but he said nothing.

The bet back to Miller, he tossed two more nickels into the pot. 'Okay, Blanchard, since you oughta be objecting on principle alone, tell us why you're fightin'…'

'On account of my father,' the man from Coeur d'Alene said, just as Edward and Pitowski dropped two nickels. 'He was a miner, too, but I barely knew him – killed in a strike eighteen years ago…I've always wanted to set the record straight.'

Miller tapped ash from his cigarette into a stamped tin ashtray, waiting.

'I'm a good American,' Blanchard declared as he let two nickels fall. 'My people have worked hard building this country up, and we're entitled to the same freedom as any of those mine owners or New York financiers.'

Pereira peaked at his cards, said he was out.

Blanchard brought up Bill Haywood of the IWW, recently arrested under the Espionage Act for supposedly using labor disputes to intimidate factory owners and hinder the war effort. He said that as head of the Western Federation of Miners ten years earlier, Hayward had been framed for the assassination of Idaho's governor – retribution, supposedly, for persuading McKinley to send in federal troops to crush a miners' strike back in '99.

'Where your father was killed?' Pitowski asked.

Blanchard nodded. 'Haywood's trial was about what America stands for – whether the mining companies, backed by Uncle Sam, could set a guy up like that.' After examining his cards, he said, 'Well, the bastards couldn't make the charges stick, so Haywood was acquitted.'

Miller rolled his eyes. 'And that makes him a great American.' He turned over his cards to reveal a straight. Pitowski offered up three Aces; Edward sheepishly showed two pair.

'So I'm fightin' for democracy, even if it ain't perfect,' Blanchard said, eyeing the rancher now. 'We've got a duty to protect freedom, and I'll be damned if anybody's gonna spit on my father's grave 'cause he was a union man.' Turning over a king-high flush, he said, 'Now gimme a cigarette, Miller…'

Everyone looked on in astonishment as Blanchard calmly gathered up the cards for another round. The rancher slid over his pack of cigarettes, and when the man from Coeur d'Alene pulled one out, Pitowski struck a match for him. After a long, satisfying drag, the miner began shuffling the cards, saying to no one in particular, 'He was no traitor to this country, and being killed by the U.S. Army doesn't make it so.'

Chapter 15

From the shadows of the boxcar Steinkoler murmured that it was a bad omen, but Corporal Richter tried to reassure everyone, saying it was just an unfortunate accident. Miller lit a cigarette, briefly illuminating the somber faces, and said that the injured ones were lucky, that their fight was over even before it started, "cause when your time's up, it's up.'

It was half past three in the morning, time marked by the click-clack, click-clack of the iron wheels on the rails, members of the platoon propped up against the side walls on tufts of hay, the middle of the car a mountain of knapsacks. While idling outside a tiny village at midnight, a speeding French locomotive had plowed into their troop train – killing thirty-two, maiming sixty-three, blood and severed limbs everywhere – a harrowing debut to their great campaign.

What had begun with an auspicious rendition of "We won't come back till it's over, over there!" while steaming out of Hoboken two weeks earlier; had soared amid cheers of "God Bless the Yanks!" from the women, children, and old men of Liverpool; took on dramatic purpose at the docks of Southampton where the Y-men offered tea and doughnuts and a hollow sendoff; had devolved finally into a hurried march through the crooked streets of Le Havre with its foul-smelling latrines and gruff girls whistling provocatively for cigarettes.

The gaps in the planking of the boxcar offered scant relief

from the stifling humidity and the stench of horse manure, and after a minute, Edward spoke up. "I don't know," he ventured, in response to Miller's caustic assessment, "I gotta think life's more than just a matter of chance."

'You gotta think that, do you, Eddie?' the rancher said, dragging on his cigarette. 'Keep your head down, you never know when there'll be a bullet or a bomb with your name on it.'

'I'm with Dooley,' Pitowski put in, 'God's gotta be watching over us – otherwise, what's the point?'

'I can see how a farmer might feel that way, Mitch – but maybe on account of my working with animals all the time, I see it different. There's not much that's up to us 'cept what we do in the moment. We're born, we live, we die – that's it.'

'Miller's right, men,' Richter said. 'Better to live in the present. Don't look back, don't over-think things...'

'Better yet,' Blanchard offered with obvious irony, 'don't think at all.'

The 91st Division was billeted on training grounds a hundred miles southeast of Reims. In the first few days of hiking over the rolling hills, Edward was struck by how much the herbaceous smells and the vivid colors of wildflowers reminded him of that glorious day in the Sonoma Valley when he and his cousins had given up their fishing expedition to see Jack London's dream house; by the second week, the drudgery of the drills had all but expunged such happy boyhood memories.

One evening in late August, after another backbreaking trek in full packs, the platoon was sprawled around a campfire when Pitowski cautioned Crowley against any more late-night excursions.

'They're not messing around,' the big man warned, 'A private over in Dammartin was court-martialed last week for tapping some farmer's wine barrel.'

'Stupid shit,' Crowley jeered. 'Nah, we got to talkin' to some a them Poyloos…'

Laying his wet socks on a rock, Miller said, 'Since when did you learn French, Frank?'

'Some things don't need translatin',' the Reno man replied with a salacious grin.

'A carton of cigs don't hurt neither!' Charlie McLeod, one of Crowley's posse, added with a laugh. 'There's a farm 'bout five miles passed that ravine we crossed yesterday where they keep these beauties up in a hayloft.'

'Beauties I bet,' the rancher scoffed.

There was ribald laughter around the campfire, but Pitowski wasn't amused. 'It's a risky business, Crowley, and I'm not covering for you. It'll come down on the whole platoon.'

'So what if I get the clap?' the Reno man said, 'I'll be shot up soon enough anyways…'

Miller was disgusted. '*You're* the stupid shit, Crowley.'

The first letter from Constance arrived a couple of days later:

July 13 – San Francisco

Dearest Edward,

We've heard from Morgan that the American forces number over a million now, so I'm heartened to think things might be winding down just as the 362ⁿᵈ arrives.

It gives me great satisfaction knowing that my volunteer work at Del Monte's shipping offices is contributing to the war effort. Chances are the salmon and sardines you get in your rations come from the canneries down in Monterey!

Unfortunately, those Wobblys you've mentioned have been pushing for unskilled cannery workers (mostly Italians) to join their union. Now they're picketing, demanding $2.50 per day, which has Father incensed. He says I should be canning peaches rather than sitting at a desk!

On a serious note, a Mrs. Fulton at work lost her nephew in April (he was in a Boston regiment) and I can only imagine how terrible that must be. Please take care of yourself, Edward, and write to tell me where you are and how you are doing.

Yours affectionately,
Con

In the spring of 1918, having amassed thirty-seven divisions and six thousand guns along a forty-mile stretch of its western front, the Germans launched a final offensive against the Allies. They'd advanced to within fifty miles of Paris, when, in the summer, French forces bolstered by American reinforcements managed to dig in at Chateau Thierry.

In August, General Foch decided that the American Expeditionary Forces would form the bulwark of a grand counter-offensive to break the German salient. In early September, packs bulging with blankets, tarpaulins, and extra boots, half a million American soldiers stealthily assembled along an eighteen-mile line running from the Argonne Forest in the west to the Meuse River in the east. Among the fifteen American divisions, the 91st was one of four comprising V Corps, which was charged with leading the assault up the middle.

For seven days they waited, as wildflowers closed up and heavy rains began.

The 362nd Infantry Regiment was assigned a billet that had been recently vacated by the 92nd Division, which had moved up the line. Learning this, Crowley quipped, 'I guess "Nigger Jack's" more bullheaded than I thought…' For the benefit of the squad, he explained that General Pershing had earned his nick name (softened in the press to "Black Jack") after leading the Buffalo Soldiers of the 10th Cavalry up Kettle Hill in Cuba years earlier, before adding with a chuckle, 'Thought for sure he'd leave the coon divisions for the French to command since they'll prob'ly just run off when the shootin' starts anyway!'

'Not if they're anything like those soldiers from Senegal we saw the other day,' Blanchard observed. Then, shaking his head, 'Beats me what they get out of all this…'

On the afternoon of the twenty-fifth of September orders arrived that the attack would commence early the next morning. Few slept that night as men cleaned their guns, wrote letters home, played cards to pass the time. At midnight, a relentless American bombardment intended to soften the German defenses started up from the rear, and at precisely 05:30 the 91st Division charged to the top of a ridge. Members of E Company came upon a basin of fog and proceeded to pick their way down into the murky valley below without firing a single shot. As they passed deserted trenches someone murmured that the nighttime bombardment had probably overwhelmed the enemy.

Edward's platoon had just entered the woods when from

his left he heard the pop of a sniper's bullet, then saw the head of someone in front of him detonate in a cloud of vapor. A broadside of machine gun fire erupted on the right and the men scattered pell-mell. Explosions, ripping sounds, and pitiful screams filled the air as Edward rushed forward, tripping on a tree root. He had just raised his hand to brace himself on Pitowski's shoulder when the big man suddenly went stiff, pivoted at the ankles, and fell face down in the muck. Edward scrambled to his feet and tried looking back, but was yanked forward – 'Move it, goddammit!' someone yelled, 'Move it!'

The mayhem unfolding around him was incomprehensible, ridiculous – men cut down like stalks of corn, great blasts of flesh and blood, smoke and shouting, soldiers groaning on the ground with stumps for arms or legs. Terrified, Edward managed to stagger out of the woods and dropped into a trench already crammed with other men from the platoon whose faces he didn't recognize. Lieutenant Grainger appeared above them and immediately ordered everyone out, telling them to proceed fifty yards ahead to a stream.

Over the next ten hours, the tedious, incremental advance continued – through muddy ravines and belts of barbed wire, passed concrete emplacements and routed machine gun nests where dead Germans looked oddly prim in their gray field uniforms. Some clearly had died agonizing deaths; others, but for a bullet hole in the temple or a bayonet wound to the chest, seemed to be sleeping. Twice the platoon passed a shambling line of prisoners being escorted to the rear, some sullen, others docile, every now and then a man so frightened he begged for his life to anyone who would catch his eye.

At dusk the exhausted platoon took refuge in the shelter of

a hill outside a small village. Men were sprawled against a low stone wall, absorbed in their own thoughts as they cleaned their rifles and glumly picked at their rations. Edward closed his eyes and tried to sleep but horrific details of the day wouldn't leave him in peace. He was aghast at what he'd witnessed and for a time was consumed by resentment that neither Colm – kept stateside for a disciplinary infraction – nor Walter – serving in a clerk capacity at the Presidio – would ever have to experience anything so traumatic. Once again, he'd have to carry the burden they could not.

By the dim light of a damp fire, Miller started complaining to Sergeant Shaw about the French Chauchat rifles they'd been issued jamming all the time, but Corporal Richter testily cut him off. Meanwhile, Edward overheard Blanchard asking Crowley how he could have been so cold-blooded that afternoon.

'What, you mean the prisoner?' the man from Reno said before coughing up a wad of phlegm and spitting into the fire. 'Don't kid yourself, Blanchard – they'd do it to you if they had the chance...'

'But that was a fuckin' execution,' the Idaho miner said. 'The guy had surrendered—'

'Goddam Krauts,' the carpenter sneered. '"Kinder, kinder," my ass – I doubt that bastard had any kids, and even if he did, they can rot in hell for all I care...' Leaning to his right, he borrowed McLeod's cigarette to light one for himself. 'What's the matter with Pereira, anyway?' he said of the artichoke farmer who was sitting apart from the group against a tree stump, looking morose.

'It's Mitch,' Steinkoler explained. 'He thinks we shoulda

gone back.'

'He's right,' said Jacobs, the Sacramento haberdasher, 'but a sergeant told us there'd be guys coming up behind us to take care of him – only now I don't believe it.'

Edward had never spoken much with Aaron Jacobs, but that evening, on patrol together in the shadow of a charred elm, he found Jacobs was uncharacteristically talkative. 'I can't get it out of my head why Crowley would shoot the poor guy point blank, like an animal,' the man said.

''Cause he's crazy,' Edward said, concealing the light of his cigarette in his palm. After a minute, he went on, 'I'll tell you something else, Jacobs, as a Christian I've always felt bad for the way he picks on you…'

'Thanks, but I'll be alright,' came the reply, 'We Jews have thick skin…'

Edward stubbed out his cigarette on a rock. 'You know, being in the garment trade like you, I don't see Jews and Catholics being all that different.'

After a moment, not looking over, Jacobs said, 'I know the Irish get picked on, too, Dooley – but sometimes I think we Jews were born to suffer…'

At first light the men of the 362nd had started advancing on the village of Epinonville when without warning shells began raining down on them from behind. Soldiers scattered in panic, diving for cover, not knowing how to proceed, while red flares sent up to raise the artillery went unheeded. The platoons suffered tremendous casualties until out of the chaos Colonel John "Gatling Gun" Parker emerged. Named for his exploits at San Juan Hill in the previous war, Parker swore a blue streak waving the men forward toward the German gun emplacements and beyond the reach of the friendly fire.

The dreadful incident sapped what confidence remained in the regiment, and it was all the men could do to make incremental progress that day. At night, dug in on a hillside, a high explosive German shell landed not fifty yards from Edward's squad, obliterating five officers of E Company – Captain Gates among them – who'd been studying a map by flashlight. Before dawn the 362nd regiment was ordered to shore up the 361st whose ranks had been cut in half trying to dislodge the enemy from their battlements.

The twenty-ninth of September was a Sunday, but Edward had lost track. After three days of battle and grimly determined advances amid a relentless bombardment, he wasn't thinking clearly. Existence had taken on a dream-like quality. His eyes stung with fatigue, his hands were dry and cracked, he'd soiled his underwear more than once. Like the rest of the regiment, in seventy-two hours he'd undergone a metamorphosis from untested Doughboy to haggard combat veteran. Inured to the violence, resigned to the drudgery, he was operating on adrenalin and fear. Before dawn, hundreds of mud-encrusted men rose stiffly and peered down into thick woods, beyond which lay a barren plain separating them from the town of Gesnes.

No sooner had the first rays of sunlight peaked over the town's lone steeple than the regiment was assailed by a withering artillery barrage. One by one platoons began making their way down through the woods until eventually they'd all assembled at the foot of the great plateau. Shortly before three o'clock that afternoon Lieutenant Grainger returned to announce that the regiment was to commence attack at precisely three-forty.

'They're outta their goddamn minds,' Blanchard said, drawing Corporal Richter's glare.

'Gesnes is of top strategic importance,' the Lieutenant continued, 'and the advance must be continued at all costs. Our artillery and machinegun battalions will start up at three-thirty to give cover.' He looked over the platoon. 'Now is the time, men – I know you'll do your duty.'

There was some grumbling as the soldiers readied their rifles, but when Richter saw Blanchard grousing to Miller, he came up and said sharply, 'I don't wanna hear any bitching!'

'It's suicide, Corporal, and you know it,' the man from Coeur d'Alene said.

Richter looked menacingly at the miner. 'This order's from Major General Cameron of V Corps. He's gotta know something we don't, so shut the fuck up.'

'But he's five miles from the front, for Chrissakes!' Blanchard said challengingly.

With the confrontation beginning to attract attention, the bantam rooster corporal stepped forward, and hissed, 'We got it on good authority that's the First Prussian Guards out there – the same sonsabitches who were on their way to Moscow a year ago. They've been brought in to hold the line, only our regiment's not gonna let 'em, see?'

'The Prussian Guards! Are you kidding?' Blanchard exclaimed. 'Our division doesn't even have a tank to its name… let alone any goddamn air support!'

Richter clenched his fists, seething now. 'The 362nd is gonna drive those bastards back, and either you get with the program, Blanchard, or I'll have your ass court-martialed, so help me God!' The miner was opening his mouth to speak when the corporal cut him off. '*Goddammit!* I've had enough of your second-guessing! What's your deal, anyway, huh? Are you really some kind of goddamn union agitator?'

'Fucking idiot!' Blanchard yelled as he lunged at Richter, driving him to the ground. 'You'd shoot your own kind if Uncle Sam told you to…'

Edward, Miller, and Steinkoler managed to pull him off the corporal, who got to his feet and growled, 'Don't think I won't, you yellow-bellied bastard!'

It wasn't long before the 347th Machine Gun Battalion opened up behind the regiment, a strangely comforting sound, like a reassuring clap on the shoulder from an older brother. With the various platoons of the Wild West Division readied for the charge, a spirited contingent from Montana and Wyoming started up a low chant – *Powder River! Powder River! Powder*

River! – which at three-forty became a full-throated roar as thousands of young men took off across the barren plain. With rifles and bayonets pointed straight ahead, they charged like mad bulls, heedless of the bullets whizzing by and mortars exploding around them – an all-out stampede, a profligate sacrifice, nothing less than a defiant declaration of their humanity…

The earth erupted beneath them, sending men cartwheeling through the air. Edward surged forward, driven on by the barbaric looks of Miller, McLeod, and Crowley, by Blanchard sprinting by without his rifle, cursing the faceless foe. Periodically Edward would drop to the ground to reload his rifle, then come up and fire vaguely into the distance – as though by hitting a target somewhere out there in the smoke he could repel all that was being hurled against him.

Despite the rain and a relentless enemy bombardment, the 362nd managed to advance steadily throughout the afternoon. By dusk platoons began breaching the barricades around Gesnes, engaging in vicious skirmishes amid the ruins until all the German forces had been dislodged, the last of them frantically lashing their horses as they fled east into the night. But the mood among the Americans was anything but celebratory. Exhausted and numb to all the violence and noise, they staggered among the ruined buildings, passed the smashed dugouts and machine gun nests where in the course of the day the enemy had resorted to stacking their dead to bolster their defenses.

Edward's squad came upon two Germans propped up against the wheels of caisson, arms limp at their sides, their mouths twisted in pain. Miller knelt down to get a better look at one of them, and satisfied that he was still alive, he stood up and brutally bashed in the side of the man's head with the butt of his rifle. When the other man flinched ever so slightly, the rancher raised his rifle threateningly, but seeing that the man's mid-section was blown open and his legs were badly mangled, he simply pushed him over onto his comrade. 'Pleasant dreams,' he quipped, before moving on.

Edward regarded the helpless man a moment, trying to bring to mind Pitowski, Captain Gates, and Blanchard's suicidal charge by way of girding himself to finish the man off. But standing there, he grimaced, knowing he was no murderer: having seen the man's eyes, he could no more kill him out of revenge than put him out of his misery as a kindness. Instead, he hung his head and followed the rest of the squad.

As night descended, the weary troops could make out the sound of ambulances and supply trucks crisscrossing the battlefield behind them. A harried medic came through the village and reported that hundreds had been killed or wounded, that some companies had been reduced to only a few dozen able-bodied men.

Eventually three-quarters of E Company, including Edward's platoon, was reassembled in a cemetery behind the church. While most were grateful to see familiar faces, the mood among the men grew grim as word was passed about who was still unaccounted for. It was understood that Blanchard had been shot dead, that Sergeant Shaw had been wounded, that Pereira had gone missing. Many men had been exposed to gas, and the worst off, those badly blistered and gasping for air, had been evacuated to aid stations.

It was around nine o'clock when Lieutenant Grainger and

Corporal Richter returned from a meeting with their superiors. The Lieutenant was ghostly pale as he announced that the regiment had been ordered to fall back to the original position at the other end of the great plateau. 'Seems we got too far ahead of the 361st and the 363rd,' he explained, '—and now we're vulnerable to counterattack.' In the flickering lantern light men looked at one another in stunned silence. Shaking his head wearily, Grainger felt compelled to add, 'A problem with the telephone wire apparently – orders calling off the advance didn't reach us in time…'

Emotions ran from disbelief to contempt as the soldiers synched up their packs for the march back. A few muttered acerbic asides in the frosty air, but most said nothing, the exhaustion, hunger, and cold having already sapped what little was left of their morale. The clouds cleared for a time, and by a sickly moonlight the ragged platoons made their way across the devastation where so many of their brethren had died in vain.

The disjointed route through the pockmarked landscape made for a haphazard return march, and soon Edward became distracted by the bobbing lanterns of the medical units patrolling the eerie battlefield, listening for signs of life. The daylong bombardment had left him with a ringing in his ears, and as rain clouds returned and blotted out the moon, he staggered along, increasingly disoriented. He fell behind his squad as he stumbled into craters and over mounds of dirt, coming upon the faces of dead men, mouths agape, eyes open to the heavens.

When an icy rain started up again, he burrowed into a small cover of upset earth, clutched his knees to his chin, and closed his eyes tight. He drifted in and out of consciousness as the storm came crashing down around him. When at last it had passed, he tried to get his bearings, but was frightened by the rivulets of rainwater and blood that meandered into his crude shelter like snakes. Shivering, overcome by fear and rage, he let out a wretched wail and frantically disgorged himself from the mud. He took off in a desperate sprint, until the rail of an upturned artillery wagon caught his head and swept his feet out from under him. Dazed, he brought his hand to his forehead, and tasting warm blood, he howled like a dog before setting off again in a mad dash.

Chapter 17

'And this one?'

'Banged up a bit – 'just bandaged his head.'

'Why's he strapped to the cot?'

'Convulsions. Unconscious since they brought him in.'

'Whose is he? What battalion?'

'Second Battalion, E Company – Dooley's his name. Luckily he still had his dog tags on – not much else, I'm afraid…'

'How's that?'

'Medics found him wandering around out there, practically naked. Gone nuts, I guess…'

'Poor bastard. Make sure Grainger knows he's with us – for a day or two, anyway.'

The sound of canvas flapping. By spectral lantern light he makes out two shapes moving away from him. A large tent, evidently an aid station; next to him immobile men, but for the intermittent rise and fall of their chests. Wool blankets irritate his skin, but when he tries twisting he finds that he's been restrained. He closes his eyes, tells himself not to panic. Had he been wounded? Where is the pain coming from? Does he have all his limbs?

Warily Edward began to survey his body, first making a fist with each hand, then wiggling the toes of each foot. He tightened his gut, flexed his glutes. When he engaged his quadriceps to bend his legs a piercing pain in his left knee nearly caused him to shout out. When he tried filling his lungs with air he felt an acute soreness on the right side of his ribcage. But aside from a dull ache at the crown of his skull, he surmised that his body was intact.

For several minutes he listened to the pitter-patter of rain on the sagging roof while trying to piece together his memory of the retreat. Found practically naked, unconscious. They spoke English – so he wasn't a prisoner, but where was he? Near the front? Was that shelling in the distance? What had become of his unit? Might his condition merit a discharge? At this thought, his sphincter relaxed, and he was enveloped in a rush of diarrhea.

Edward stayed a week and a half with the medical unit and during his convalescence he overheard two doctors talking about the 91st Division having suffered over four thousand casualties in the first six days of the Meuse-Argonne Campaign; he learned from a discharge officer that the 362nd Regiment had lost five hundred men on the twenty-ninth of September alone. The magnitude of the carnage shocked him. The senselessness of two massive armies hurling themselves at one another left him numb and speechless – even as he watched the men around him going about their business as though it were the natural order of things.

Edward was delivered back to E Company on the morning of October 12, when the 91st Division was eventually relieved. Approaching his squad on crutches as they stood in line at mail call, Miller was the first to catch his eye.

'Hey, look, it's Dooley,' the cattleman said. 'Thought we lost you, brother…'

Edward shook his hand and, in turn, greeted Crowley, McLeod, and Steinkoler. As the line moved up to the mail wagon, Edward remarked on how run down so many men in the regiment were and learned that dysentery had been running rampant. He was also told that Blanchard's body had been recovered, that there was still no sign of Pereira, that Jacobs had been removed to an evacuation hospital suffering from shell shock. Edward found all of this difficult to fathom – as if he'd just learned that Colm and Walter were gone forever from his life.

'We got shot up all to pieces,' Steinkoler was saying. His skin was blotchy and he'd developed an odd facial tic. 'Kept telling us reinforcements were coming, but they never showed...'

Edward asked about Jacobs and Miller told him that the haberdasher had panicked during an aerial bombardment. 'The Gerries were using phosgene or some shit we hadn't seen before,' the cattleman said. 'I had a hell of a time gettin' the kid's mask on—'

'Crowley had to clock him,' McLeod interjected with a grin.

Miller spit into the dirt. 'I was holdin' him down just fine...'

'The Jew-boy was givin' away our position!' Crowley exclaimed. 'Out of his gourd!'

A commotion started up at the mail wagon when the YMCA man called after a recruit for postage due. This prompted some profanity-laden grumbling from Crowley, and by the time the squad reached the wagon, the Reno carpenter was seething. Looking up at the middle-aged supervisor, he growled, 'You Y-men got some gall, you know that? First it's chargin' us for hot chocolate and donuts – and now for postage due, too! You cheap bunch of bastards!'

'Now wait a minute, soldier,' the man began, 'we're here to support the troops. We supply the—'

'Just give us our goddamn letters!'

'We give out stationery for free,' the man persisted, 'but how do you think your letters gets back to the States? We've got to defray expenses...'

'Defray expenses, my ass!' the Reno carpenter roared. 'I bet folks back home donated them cigarettes yer sellin' us.' The Y-man grew red-faced trying to restrain himself, but offered no response, and turning to go, Crowley added dismissively, 'And you call yourselves a Christian organization...Sh-e-e-it, more like a bunch a kikes, I'd say...'

Edward was fortunate to receive two letters that day, but he resisted the temptation to tear into them until he had bedded down for the night. The first was a dishearteningly thin missive from Constance.

August 14 – San Francisco

Dearest Edward,

'Sorry it's taken me so long to write. Morgan tells us that with all the British and French equipment already overseas, there's room on our ships to send more men over – and Daddy says General Ludendorff's recent surrender is a sign that the end is near.

We ran into your parents at the Cathedral Sunday and your Mother asked if we knew anybody who'd like to buy some nice brocade curtains. That didn't sound very good, so Daddy's putting in a good word down at the chancery for a bid your father submitted recently.

How are you? I imagine it must be awful. We miss you terribly and want you home soon!

Yours,
Constance

Edward was disappointed by how remote Constance seemed, as if she were writing from another planet altogether. In his letters he'd been careful not to convey any of the trauma he'd experienced so as not to upset her – still, given general assumptions about the horrors of war, how hard could it be to express more than passing empathy in a one-page letter?

Thankfully, the second envelope was a newsy chain letter from his siblings.

September 6

Dear Edward,

Thank you for your reports from France. You've probably been moved to the front by now and are seeing action which I am sure must be horrible. We pray for you every day.

All's fine here, more or less. The rationing isn't too hard – canned corned beef is palatable and we do okay on 'Wheatless Wednesdays.' Our victory garden in the backyard give us more tomatoes and squash than we know what to do with.

Mother's in high dudgeon over this influenza business. The other day Maeve Mulcahy and her Brigid paid her a visit – they still live downtown where the crowded conditions are especially worrisome. Mayor Roth has ordered 18,000 'Hope's Rose' inoculations from

Boston in an effort to stem the spread of the disease.
  Be safe Edward and don't take any chances!
  Yours devotedly,
  Katherine...

  Hello Eddie - we miss you so and all we do is hope for you return safe. Daddy and I lite a candel for you at church when we walk Mother to her meeting on Wedns Wened *Wendsdays after supper. The Cathedral is grand with all the candels but it makes me sad. Auntie Hildie came last weak to see Mr. McCormick becose they need help with the harvest since Cousin Michael is at colige and Maggie* volin*voluntears at the post office. Cousin Cora has a fellow now but he works at the bank. Okay, I have to say goodby! WE LOVE YOU EDDIE!!*

  Your adorig sister - D...

                                                    September 12

Dear Edward,
  Sorry, Dede left this for me to finish but I haven't been by for a couple of days now. I stay at the barracks most nights because of the long hours and because I can do with some peace and quiet (if you know what I mean). Mother's been riding him pretty hard since the Diocese job fell through – she says it brings shame on the family, but it wasn't a very big job and I don't think anybody really noticed. (Collin Duffy asked last night at the Liberty Bond drive whether I might be able to help him with his books. Now wouldn't that bring shame on the family?!)
  Yesterday the Red Sox won the series but nothing was said about

the sixteen people who dropped dead in Boston on account of the influenza – I heard that from Collin. It's bad in Philadelphia and New York, too, and so far there isn't a vaccine that works. Folks wear masks now and some tie mothball sacks around their necks to ward off infection!

The papers report that it's cropping up overseas, too, and Colm says there's a rumor in the ranks that it might have started at Ft Riley in Kansas. It sounds cynical, but wouldn't it be ironic if the boys we sent over to win the peace end up infecting the world instead!

Be careful over there, Edward. Your loving brother,

Walter

Edward shook his head and folded the chain letter back into its envelope. How like Walter to be droll – he could afford to be as he was well enough out of harm's way. As for all the talk about making the world safe for democracy, all Edward wanted to do at this point was make the world safe for the likes of Dede. And as for Katherine, tough love may be all that he could hope for, but at least he got that much – some of the men never received mail at all.

Chapter 18

In late October the Wild West Division was restored to full strength with greenhorns from the recently arrived 84th Division. Grainger and Richter had been transferred to the depleted 361st Regiment, and looking at all the new arrivals, Edward could only cynically conclude that he was no more than a pawn, easily replaced. E Company was now led by Second Lieutenant Henry Foster, an insurance man from Lexington, Kentucky, eager to get make a name for himself. 'I understand you boys saw some action up in the Argonne,' he drawled, addressing the platoon for first time, 'but that's nothing but a warm-up for what lies ahead…'

'What a jackass,' Crowley muttered. The new sergeant glowered at him.

'The 91st is moving up to the Yipps Salient in a week's time,' Foster continued, 'where we'll be joining forces with the Poyloos. It's gonna be close proximity fighting from now on, so consider your bayonet your best friend…'

'How's about givin' us guns that work?' the Reno carpenter sang out.

'What's that back there?' Foster said irritably.

'This French shit's useless, Lieutenant – how's about them Browning automatics we was promised?'

'What's your name, Private?'

'Crowley, Sir. And another thing, we ain't never had enough

rifle grenades and it's damn near impossible to take out a Boche machine gun nest without 'em…'

Sergeant Roy Bostick, a lumber mill operator from Dayton, said, 'Better cool it, Private.'

'And what's more,' the Reno man went on, 'we ain't seen a single Stokes mortar in all the time we been here. Our signal apparatus is for shit, too, and the horses are all skin-and-bone affairs – they can barely pull themselves, let alone artillery…' A few of the men snickered.

'That's enough, goddammit!' the lieutenant boomed. 'Look here, there's plenty of damn rifles and ammo to go around, we'll have a first-rate machine gun battalion alongside us, and there's enough one-pounders to blow their machine gun nests to smithereens. Now the next one of you who starts bitching and moaning about equipment will be first in line for a court-martial. You hear me, Crowley?!'

The carpenter nodded sullenly. "Sir.'

Flushed with anger, Lieutenant Foster looked over the platoon contemptuously. 'Lieutenant Grainger says you cowboys in E-Company think you're a pretty tough bunch. Well, as far as I'm concerned, you're nothing but a bunch of redneck cowpokes, and from now on you'll keep your mouths shut. Do I make myself clear?'

'Yes, sir!' came the rousing response, and Miller winked at Crowley.

Four new privates had joined Edward's platoon, and over the next several days the Lieutenant rode Private Wayne and Private Mickelson especially hard. One afternoon Edward and Miller were refilling their canteens at a trough when the cattleman tried to size up another new officer across from them, John Stagby.

'You and Sergeant Bostick been with the Lieutenant long, Corporal?' Miller asked.

Stagby was a shrewd-looking man from Elkhart, Indiana, with blue eyes and flaxen hair. 'Since Officers' Training at Camp Taylor, why?' he said, gauging the rancher carefully.

'Well, if you don't mind my sayin', the real thing's hard enough – it's no good messin' with the heads of the slow ones at this point.'

Corporal Stagby glanced at Edward, then with a sigh, said to Miller, 'The Lieutenant's anxious to get out there, is all.'

'Visions of glory…' Miller observed rhetorically as he concentrated on filling his canteen. 'Listen, there's no telling what a man's gonna do in the thick of things, but it's better not goin' into it all mixed up…'

Stagby gave a barely perceptible nod. 'We'll try getting the Lieutenant to back off…'

On a cold night during the train trip north a week later, Edward was standing between the railcars getting some air when the Corporal happened by. He offered Edward a cigarette, which he lit with a silver lighter, before lighting one for himself. Leaning on the iron railing, watching the silhouette of hills going by, Stagby said, 'So what do you do back home, Dooley?'

'I'm with the American Thread Company, sir – almost five years now.'

'Kinda young to have that much time in already, aren't you?'

'Had to leave high school early…'

'Hard luck,' Stagby said, '—I never got to finish, myself.' He took a long drag of his cigarette. 'A good education can set you up,' he ventured. 'College boys get to run the inside track – as for us, it's a longer race…'

'I never thought of it like that.'

'We'll get there, though,' the Corporal continued. 'The more our motivation is tested, the more pure it becomes.' Taking a last puff of his cigarette, he flicked it into the darkness. 'Too many run just for the sake of running – not knowing where they're headed – and after a while, they lose their way…'

At length, Edward said, 'And you, Corporal, what business are you in?'

'Haven't settled on anything yet,' Stagby replied, looking straight ahead. 'I've done lots of things so far – started out plying the Great Lakes on an iron ore barge, then worked in a steel mill, tried bookkeeping, even banking for a while…They say there's room for advancement in the army, but I've got my sights set on making some real money.'

'That's the American Dream,' Edward said.

Stagby turned and smiled. 'The pursuit of happiness,' he rejoined, a twinkle in his eye.

The division disembarked near Passchendaele. They marched east for three days, an icy wind at their backs, through a wasteland of shell holes and tangled barbed wire, where charred trees and burned-out tanks stretched across the horizon in every direction. On the twenty-seventh, allied aeroplanes slashed through the sky overhead, racing to the front. The sound of distant cannon fire reawakened Edward's anxieties of the month before.

The division's advance now amounted to seizing a farm, then a village, then another farm, in a tedious, enervating routine.

Because of his knee, Edward was not part of the scouting details that engaged in hand-to-hand skirmishes among the hedgerows and abandoned buildings. Assigned late night watch, he tried quelling his agitation during the relentless bombardments by smoking incessantly and taking a swig of wine, whiskey, or cognac whenever he could get it. One night the squad was gathered around a campfire in a drafty grange when Crowley opined that the Frenchmen they'd been advancing with were fighting like they had nothing to lose.

'That's 'cause they don't,' Miller said. 'The only thing they're fightin' for at this point is revenge. Whatever Gerries they get now they line up along a gully and mow down.'

'Goddamn!' someone said.

'We'd do the same if we was defendin' Boise or Cheyenne,' McLeod declared.

Edward got up awkwardly on account of his stiff knee. 'They've been fighting so long they don't even bother with gas masks when the wind shifts,' he said, before tossing the remnants of his bitter coffee into the campfire. 'Guess they figure they're bound to die sometime – whether in a week or ten years from now doesn't make much difference...'

Miller looked at Steinkoler. 'Eddie,' the cattleman said, 'why don't you get a little shut-eye tonight, huh? Karl and I'll take the watch...'

Two days later the platoon had come upon a village purported to be abandoned when suddenly they came under fire. It took over an hour, but members of Edward's squad managed to work their way to the village square where they holed up in an old dining hall. Edward and Steinkoler pushed upturned tables

175

against the broken windows as barricades, while Miller went to a side room to get a better look at the square.

Crowley came careening into the hall and asked if they'd seen the Lieutenant. As Edward was saying he thought Foster was back with McLeod, shots were fired from the second floor of a building across the street, splintering one of the dining tables.

Wild-eyed, the man from Reno said, 'Whaddya say we flush them bastards out?'

But Miller poked his head into the room to dissuade Crowley. 'We gotta get the church first,' he whispered urgently. 'I think there's a sniper in the steeple…'

A volley of return fire came from just outside the dining hall before Lieutenant Foster stumbled in with two of the new privates in tow. 'Anybody know where Sergeant Bostick is?' he asked, breathing hard as he approached the broken windows to size up the situation. When the response came back negative, he said, 'Now listen up, we've gotta take the building across the way or else they'll have us coming and going. Miller, you and Dooley bring Riggs with you and take cover in those market stalls on the other side of the square.'

Miller shook his head and gestured over his shoulder. 'Gotta hit the church first – there may be a shooter in the belfry…'

'We don't have time for that,' Foster insisted. 'Go around the *back* of the goddamn church and come into the market from behind, then wait for my signal. *Now get going!*'

Edward got up with Steinkoler's help and followed Miller and Riggs out the rear of the dining hall. A few minutes later, with Steinkoler set up in the side room with Private Wayne, and Crowley readying a recently requisitioned Lewis Gun, Corporal Stagby arrived with Mickelson and McLeod.

'Stagby, you're here!' Lieutenant Foster said from the windows. 'Look, we're going after the building across the way, see? Miller and the others are on their way to the market stalls over there, so now I need you three to get in position behind the fountain in the square. We'll give you cover.'

'Let's wait on Bostick,' Corporal Stagby said, '—he and his guys'll be along any minute.'

'No, we need to go now before the Gerries get wise to how many we are. We'll strike from three angles,' he said, surveying the square with binoculars. 'Good! Miller's in position. Okay, Corporal, you three move out to the fountain from that door there. Okay, Crowley.'

Before Stagby could speak, Crowley had pivoted the machine gun through a window and began unleashing a ferocious salvo on the building across the street. As soon as a firefight had erupted between the buildings, Foster waved Stagby's team out to the square. The diversion was working until Mickelson, a large, overweight young man, tripped short of the fountain – only there was something wrong in the way he fell.

'Aww, *fuck*!' Foster shouted. 'Mickelson, goddammit, you're supposed to keep your head down!' Furious, the Lieutenant twisted through a window opening and fired his rifle vaguely toward the church only to be rebuffed by a barrage of gunfire from across the street.

Seeing an opening, Miller and Riggs burst from the market stalls and charged across the square, lobbing grenades into the ground floor shops; Edward hobbled along in their wake, shooting vaguely at the windows upstairs. Meanwhile, covered by McLeod, Corporal Stagby managed to drag Mickelson into the shadow of the fountain. When the sniper in the church belfry signaled to his comrades in the building across the square, Crowley stepped out into the street with his rifle, drew a bead, and dropped the shooter like a prized buck.

When all the noise had subsided Miller and Riggs peered into the smoky shops to confirm the slaughter, but hearing the shuffle of feet upstairs, they quickly pulled back and clung to the outside wall on one side of the door. Miller signaled to Edward to hold up on the other side.

Lieutenant Foster appeared in the square now, his hand raised, yelling, 'Hold your fire! Hold your goddamn fire!' Approaching from the fountain, he said, 'Dammit, Miller, you were supposed to wait for my signal!'

'Are you crazy?' the cattleman said. 'We had a man down – all bets were off.'

The Lieutenant squared up. 'I'm the one in charge here, Private, is that clear?'

'You rushed it, Foster, you know damn well – the Corporal and his men were sitting ducks…'

'I'll have your ass for that remark, so help me God!' the Lieutenant hissed. 'Now what's the goddamn situation in there?'

Stagby came up from behind. 'Lieutenant, we're going to need a medic…'

'You work that out,' Foster said dismissively as he eyed the rancher. 'What's the situation, Miller?' he repeated.

'All clear, Lieutenant.'

Edward glanced at Miller, dumbstruck, as Foster barged passed him with Corporal Stagby a few steps behind. 'Jesus Fucking Christ!' the Lieutenant bellowed as through the smoke he got a sense of the carnage.

'Sir, I wouldn't go any fur—' Stagby was heard to say just as Lieutenant Foster caught sight of something coming over the stair banister, something that for a split second reminded him of the egg tosses he'd enjoyed as a boy at the Fayette County Fair…

Chapter 19

A week later the regiment was poised on the western banks of the Scheldt River. Edward's platoon had made camp in the ruins of a school, where in the garden lay the decomposing corpses of thirty-five German machine gunners.

'Seems only fair to leave 'em another day or two,' Sergeant Bostick said, as he, Crowley, and Edward sat smoking cigarettes at dusk. 'Rough justice, maybe, but blood's good fertilizer – nitrogen helps the roses grow faster.' Hopping off the low stone wall into the garden, he added, 'At least the folks around here'll get a nice garden out of it.'

'Jesus,' Edward muttered.

'What's wrong, Dooley?' Crowley said, whittling a stick, 'It'll be pretty.'

'I don't see anything ever being pretty again,' Edward said with a grimace. 'Imagine Mickelson's mother in her garden after finding out that her boy's dead…'

'Aw, you can't think like that – it all evens out in the end, don't ya see?' Crowley said. 'That poor bastard was bound to come up short sometime, either gettin' kicked in the head by a horse or run over by a tractor. Nah, there's rough justice at work, just like Sarge says.'

'It makes no sense. First Mitch, then Blanchard…Pereira…'

'Look, it's every man for himself out there. I don't know about Pitowski, but them other two was asking for it.'

Edward lit another cigarette. 'How 'bout Lieutenant Foster – how do you figure that?'

'That's easy,' Sergeant Bostick broke in, as he ambled about in the muck of the garden. 'He wanted to be a hero and he will be – he goes out with a Distinguished Service Cross for fearlessly leading a raid that took out six Boche. His sons'll grow up worshiping his picture and hoping someday they can measure up to their old man.'

'Too bad this is s'posed to be the last war,' Crowley said with a grin, nudging Edward.

'The one I can't figure is Stagby, to be honest,' the Sergeant went on, thrusting his hands into his pockets, '—too damn cruel a fate.' The carpenter grunted his assent. 'There was always something about him when we were coming up together – a light in his eyes, like he could see a long way off...' Shaking his head, Bostick said, 'He made corporal just when we were leaving Camp Taylor, but there were no hard feelings 'cause nobody doubted him.'

Edward took a long drag of his cigarette. 'He did seem to know what he wanted...'

Crowley closed his knife and stood up. 'Some men are natural born leaders,' he declared, before chucking the stick into the garden and heading back to the schoolhouse.

Edward and the sergeant lingered a few minutes longer in the fading light.

'The army wasn't Stagby's calling,' Bostick ventured while probing one of the corpses with his foot for medals or other souvenirs. 'Something else was driving him, something I'm not sure even he could put his finger on... not until he met *her*, that is.'

'Who's that?' Edward asked.

'Lily I think her name was,' Bostick said as he resumed his pacing. 'Pretty little thing – a debutante from one of Louisville's leading families. They'd throw these soirées for the officers, see, and, well, he fell for her and hard...'

Edward flicked his cigarette butt into the garden, recalling his conversation with Stagby between railcars, how impressed he'd been by the Corporal's ambitions.

Bostick stepped over the low wall, and he and Edward were halfway to the schoolhouse when he remarked, 'They made a handsome couple, but now, what with half his face blown off, I doubt she'll have the gumption to stick by him...'

To say the Armistice struck Edward as anticlimactic would be only half right. For over six weeks he'd been functioning on a very primitive level, sustained by caffeine, nicotine, and alcohol. He was so sleep-deprived, so driven by adrenaline, that he was almost heartsick when the end didn't come in a last gallant charge, some apocalyptic fireball. Instead, as of the eleventh hour of the eleventh day of the eleventh month, he was simply told it was over, that along with millions of other men it was time to turn around and go home.

When the guns went quiet, the men of the Wild West Division jubilantly embraced one another and howls of relief filled the air up and down the line. But after a raucous celebration that lasted the better part of two days, a familiar malaise settled over the division that had been dispersed across the wet and battered countryside. Nights became bitter cold and morale sagged with each passing week as rumors spread that there might be a long-term occupation of Belgium, or that they'd have to shore up the White Russians in Siberia or fight another war in Mexico. In early December the division finally was ordered west – a bleak journey through Flanders by way of Ypres, where wooden crosses marked the graves of more than half a million men.

Edward's spirits were especially low. He hadn't received mail in over a month, and with hopes of being home for Christmas dashed, he'd grown sullen and withdrawn. The long marches were especially galling, seeing trucks and trains used to transport artillery ahead of the Doughboys themselves. While the likes of Crowley and McLeod took full advantage of the grateful Belgian girls along the way, Edward kept to himself. He said little at mealtimes and would quietly cry himself to sleep at night; even Miller and Steinkoler steered clear of him.

Christmas 1918 was spent in and around the tiny village of Oostvleteren. Money was collected from the companies of the 362nd Regiment to buy presents in Dunkirk for the local children. On Christmas Day the Americans hosted a party in the dilapidated town hall, where eggnog and cocoa were served, and the army band played holiday music.

The regiment managed to raise additional money for the poorest families in the area, and late in the day Edward, Steinkoler, and a fellow named Gustafson from F Company, were dispatched to a farm about a mile from the village. A boy of perhaps fifteen ushered them into a dim, one-room farmhouse that smelled of boiled cabbage. An old wardrobe separated the private quarters, with a ladder leading to a sleeping loft, from a large kitchen with a fireplace, a cast iron stove, and a long wooden table around which sat five more children. Their widowed mother wore her black hair tied back in a bun, and wiping her hands on her apron she beckoned the soldiers to the table.

'Americains, oui? Parlez-vous Français?' she asked as the men stepped into the light.

'Pas beaucoup,' Gustafson said, 'désolé – I'm sorry.'

Dismissing his apology with a wave, she instructed the two young girls seated closest to the stove to make some coffee for their guests; the three youngest children looked up at the visitors before turning back to the game of jacks they'd received that morning. The woman gestured to the remaining space on the two benches, and Gustafson set down a box of oranges and chocolate bars on the table before the soldiers seated themselves. An awkward silence fell over them as the boy stood off to the side anxiously watching his twin sisters prepare the coffee. Their mother looked to her happily distracted younger children at the table, and cupping her hands over her nose, she appeared to mist over.

'We tank you for zees tings,' she said, gesturing to the game and the gifts.

She turned abruptly and muttered something to her daughters. One of them removed a pan of sweet bread from the oven, while the other disappeared into the shadows and emerged with a jar of fruit preserves. When the coffee and the holiday bread had been served, the mother held her cup aloft, saying, 'Merry Chreesmas to you – we tank Yankees for to come to us!'

She spoke in French to Gustafson, saying it must be hard for them to be away from their families at Christmas, and Gustafson relayed this to Edward and Steinkoler. In kindergarten English, and with Gustafson's occasional assistance in French, the three soldiers went on to describe where they were from and how many brothers and sisters each of them had. In the stilted conversation that followed, they were surprised to learn that their hosts were familiar with words like cowboy, movie star, and baseball. While Edward and Steinkoler tried to explain that their hometowns had rival baseball teams, Gustafson drew a map of the United States on the lid of the box to show how far from New York City each of them lived.

Fascinated by his talents with a pencil, the twins asked him to draw various animals, and their brother somehow engaged Steinkoler on the subject of fishing. Edward's gaze wandered until he spied a photograph on the mantel, a medal hanging from a ribbon draped over one corner of the frame. It was a picture of a man in uniform, his soft smile all but hidden beneath a mustache. Edward blushed when he discovered the woman of the house looking at him.

'Zair fattur,' she said, pursing her lips, 'A goot man.'

'I'm sorry,' Edward said, just as the twins laughed at something Gustafson had drawn.

Looking sympathetically at Edward, she said, 'You have cheeldrin also?'

Despite his height, Edward had always been self-conscious that his pale complexion made him seem younger than he was. Now to be thought of as a father, he wondered how much he'd aged over the past few months. He shook his head and looked down uncomfortably.

Later, as mother and son were escorting the soldiers to the door, Gustafson turned and said, 'Madame, nous voudrions vous donner quelque chose en plus pour vous aider...' He pulled a worn brown envelope from his tunic and handed it to her. 'We want you to have this.'

It was a large envelope, folded over once but not sealed, and as she pulled back the flap and saw what amounted to more than eighty American dollars, she was overcome with emotion. Edward and Steinkoler managed to grab hold of her the moment her knees gave way, and as her son reached over, Edward caught his eye. In a split-second, reminded of what he'd been called upon to do for his family at seventeen, and knowing how much greater a burden this young man would bear, Edward was ashamed for ever having felt sorry for himself. Where he'd sometimes likened the weight of family responsibility to his "cross to bear," in light of what he'd been able to endure in this war he now had a glimpse of his purpose in life.

That night, after a serviceable turkey dinner with all the trimmings, Edward made an effort to fraternize with his platoon for the first time in weeks and was grateful to be welcomed back into the fold. Much like the year before, the men made the best of the situation with their temporary family – reminiscing about Christmases back home and musing about Christmases to come. Edward made it to bed after midnight, and warmed by holiday brandy, he opened the letter he'd received from Constance two days before. He'd been saving it for a Christmas present, only it turned out to be a belated Thanksgiving greeting.

November 18 – San Francisco

Dearest Edward,

We are overjoyed that the terrible war has ended and that you will be coming home to us safe and sound. You are in Belgium now, which is closer to the sea and therefore closer to us – so we will raise a Thanksgiving Day toast to your speedy return!

Oh, but it's been such a terrible fall with this Spanish Flu, I hardly know where to begin. My dear friend Missy O'Connor passed ten days ago, and then just last night the Ferguson twins were taken to the hospital, and they're teenagers! People were wearing cotton masks at the Armistice parade and Father says a City Health Inspector shot a man for refusing to put one on.

I don't know if there is any way you'll be able to make it home for Christmas, but it would certainly raise our spirits. Morgan's not sure that he can, given how much work is involved in getting you all back.

I saw Walter at a Sacred Heart function the other day and he passed along the sad news about your cousin Patrick. You weren't anywhere near there, I hope. Anyway, my heart goes out to your family. God keep you, dearest – we need your brave presence here now!

Yours—
C

A week after Christmas, the 91st Division finally boarded trains heading west. On New Year's Day they passed through the outskirts of Paris and Versailles, but there was no time for sightseeing as rest and recuperation were the orders of the day. The division was billeted around Le Mans, and for many it was the beginning of a long road to recovery – if not delousing, then being treated for the flu or venereal disease, or coming to terms with losing a limb. For able-bodied men, the drills and marches meant to relieve the boredom of waiting never let up – a wait that would stretch on for ten more weeks.

In early March the division's four regiments were assembled for review on a makeshift parade ground in an empty field. With billowy clouds passing overhead and a row of poplars providing a backdrop for the temporary stage, the commanding officers addressed the twenty thousand strong. Unfortunately, heavy winds and a weak public-address system made most of the proceedings unintelligible to the men of Edward's platoon standing at the rear – and what they could make out provided little clarity on when they'd be going home.

Major General Johnston's farewell address was full of praise for the men of the 91st: for how well they'd born up under the strain of nine days and nights in the Argonne, for never having hesitated in the face of vicious enemy fire. He cited specific occasions where each of the four regiments had achieved a particular goal, and culminating with the 362nd, he declared, 'No exploit of the division can match when you took Gesnes and pushed on to the army objective beyond it.' When he likened it to carrying the ball up the middle for the American First Army, the cheer from the regiment didn't sit well with Miller.

'I hate that bullshit,' he groused, '—like it was nothin' more than a football game.'

'Makes for a good story in the papers, though,' Sergeant Bostick observed dryly. 'Gives the folks back home something to visualize, something to help 'em make sense of it all.'

'Let 'em visualize the friendly fire we took that day outside Epinville…'

'I heard about that,' Bostick said, shaking his head. 'But listen, Miller, somebody's gotta write it up and it might as well be us. So what if we take a few liberties here and there? It's one of the spoils of victory.'

'Don't believe everything you read in the papers,' Edward said, quoting Blanchard, which prompted knowing glances from Miller and Steinkoler.

The reference wasn't lost on Crowley, and when Johnston had wrapped up his speech, the man from Reno said, 'Look, Dooley, you gotta trust in the system. They're never gonna tell it like it was 'cause they don't want to go offendin' the women and children…' As the Major General saluted the division for the last time, Crowley added, 'That wouldn't be good manners.'

'I say fuck polite society,' Miller declared amidst the hearty applause that followed Johnston's exit from the stage, 'They're the ones who got us into this mess in the first place.'

Crowley laughed. 'Can't argue with you there, Dunc.'

'Let 'em get a taste of what it's really like,' Miller went on, 'and maybe they won't want to send their sons off to the next one…'

The balance of the afternoon was devoted to commending each regiment in separate ceremonies at the four corners of the parade ground. Even General Pershing himself came by to address the 362nd at one point, though his most memorable remark was an offhand comment about how the men who took Gesnes deserved better boots than what he saw them wearing.

As citations and promotions were being doled out, Sergeant Bostick observed that opportunities were to be had in times of transition. 'That could be you up there, Miller,' the Sergeant said of Riggs who was being promoted to corporal. 'Nothing against Danny, mind you,' he added, 'but he's just a kid.'

'Sorry, Sarge, but soldiering's not for me,' the cattleman said. 'All the ass-kissin' and anglin' for promotion, waitin' around for another war – you can have it.'

'But it's like that in any line of work.'

'Not in ranching. Promotions oughta be based on merit, not in how well you play yer cards.'

'If you say so…'

For the men of the 362nd the highlight of the day was seeing Colonel John "Gatling Gun" Parker again. Seriously wounded during the assault on Gesnes, he'd been recovering in a Paris hospital and had made a special effort to attend the gathering. He stood up near the end of the ceremony, and braced by a pair of crutches, he bid the men of the 362nd farewell, wishing them a safe trip home. 'I'm not one to get sentimental,' he said before leaving the podium, 'but I hope that someday, perhaps on some happy hunting ground in Montana or Wyoming, we can pitch tents together again.' A roaring ovation started up and he waved as he made his way off the stage.

'Liked that fella from the get-go,' Crowley said.

'He's the real deal, alright,' Miller agreed. 'Not a bad hunter, either, I'll bet.'

After a minute, Steinkoler said, 'That'd be a good way to stay in touch, don't you think? Maybe fly fishin' on that Powder River of yours sometime…'

The regiment had been dismissed, and turning to go Miller put his hand on the fisherman's shoulder. 'Sounds good to me, Karl. Like t'get you up to the Tetons, too.' Looking passed Steinkoler, he added, 'Whaddya say, Eddie?'

'We could hunt black bear up at Medicine Bow,' Crowley put in.

Edward smiled at Miller, grateful for the consideration.

'Or maybe duck hunting?' the rancher said, eyeing him,

determined to elicit a response.

Though he'd never quite understood it, Edward had always appreciated Miller's friendliness – and even though he knew he'd never hold a rifle again, he didn't want to disappoint the cattleman. 'Sure thing,' he said.

The regiment's disintegration began on the docks of St. Nazaire. Broken into three groups, they were loaded onto the Floridian, the Luckenback, and the Lancaster, and set sail for New York on April 2nd, escorted by a fleet of battleships and destroyers. When the Statue of Liberty came into view on the fourteenth, there was no hooting and hollering, only a profound silence among the men. Ten days of demobilization exercises followed at Camp Merritt, then they boarded trains in Hoboken for the trip west – to rejoin their families, resume their lives, and do their best to put the recent past behind them.

from *A Shropshire Lad*
A.E. Housman

The winds out of the west land blow,
  My friends have breathed them there;
Warm with the blood of lads I know
  Comes east the sighing air.

It fanned their temples, filled their lungs,
  Scattered their forelocks free;
My friends made words of it with tongues
  That talk no more to me.

Their voices, dying as they fly,
  Loose on the wind are sown;
The names of men blow soundless by,
  My fellows' and my own.

Oh lads, at home I heard you plain,
  But here your speech is still,
And down the sighing wind in vain
  You hollo from the hill.

The wind and I, we both were there,
  But neither long abode;
Now through the friendless world we fare
  And sigh upon the road.

Stanza XXXVIII

PART THREE

Chapter 20

Edward had barely been back six months when Colm was arrested. Edward and Walter were now sharing an apartment on the fringe of Pacific Heights, and they answered the knock on their door at three o' clock one morning to find their effete neighbor in his smoking jacket looking none too pleased. After announcing that their father was on the telephone, he led them down the hall to his apartment shaking his head – with the war over, all sorts of young people were coming to San Francisco, and though the Dooley brothers struck him as earnest, the fact that they shared a studio suggested they didn't come from much.

When they'd hung up the telephone, they informed their neighbor that their older brother had been in an accident, and that they were off to the hospital – when, in fact, they'd just learned that Colm was being held at Northern Police Station.

'Well, I hope it all works out,' the man said as he brusquely showed them out, then called after them, 'And let Western Electric know you want a telephone of your own...'

As Edward and Walter made their way over Nob Hill, revelers were still trickling out of the Fairmont Hotel, where hours earlier the Dooleys themselves had been toasting the one-year anniversary of the Armistice with friends. Music wafting from the penthouses overlooking Huntington Park suggested the festivities were still going strong. The predawn fog had begun to lift, and descending Taylor Street the brothers could make out the twinkling lights of Oakland across the bay. At the bottom of the hill, they followed in the wake of two inebriated couples being escorted from the back of a paddy wagon into the police precinct.

'Been like this all night,' the desk sergeant groused to Edward and Walter after the drunk-and-disorderlies had been booked and led away. 'With Prohibition not goin' into effect 'til January, New Year's oughta be a goddamn riot!'

The Dooleys smiled politely and inquired after their brother. After they waited nearly an hour in a small room down the hall, a thick-necked cop with a billy club shoved Colm through the doorway and down into a chair. Colm's wrists were cuffed in front of him and his right hand was swollen. There was a nasty cut above his left eye, and a trickle of reddish saliva seeped between his bloated lips; some of the wounds look fresh.

'World class bare-knuckler, this one,' remarked the police lieutenant who dismissed the cop after Colm had been seated. Timothy Egan wasn't a tall man, but he stood ramrod straight, with a granite chin and piercing blue eyes. 'Had himself quite a time beating the daylights outta some well-to-do at The Clift,' he said, not bothering to sit down. Periodically Colm mumbled the word "lies" as Lieutenant Egan gave an account of the alleged episode. He told Edward and Walter that he'd have the incident report written up by the end of the day.

When they returned with their father that evening, they were informed that Colm faced serious charges, especially if victim didn't make it.

'Victim, hell!' Colm said through a wire grate. The bastard was puttin' on airs, buttin' in on a girl we were talkin' to…'

'You and Morgan?' his father asked.

Edward had since learned from Morgan that after their own party had broken up, he and Colm had stopped in at The Clift for a nightcap. Though it troubled Edward that Morgan had left Colm after the fracas, his friend explained that without a telephone number for Edward he'd had no choice but to contact their father instead.

After a day of his wife's hysteria, Mr. Dooley looked haggard as he explained that evidently the young man was the son of a prominent businessman.

'I don't give a damn *who* he is. Nobody calls me a "Dumb Mick"!' Colm snarled.

Edward hung his head, and Mr. Dooley said dejectedly, 'You'll be charged in the morning, boyo. Could end up being manslaughter or murder – it all depends…'

Honora's shame was complete when her son was identified by name in the morning edition of the *Call Bulletin* under the headline "Ohio Steel Magnate's Son Fights for His Life at S.F. General." The story read that the scion of an esteemed industrialist had been senselessly attacked in one of the city's elite hotels, the alleged perpetrator listed as "Colm Aloysius Dooley, a thirty-year-old war veteran and tinsmith from San Francisco, being held without bail by the authorities."

Several anxious days followed before the young man managed to turn the corner. Then to the dismay of his father who'd just arrived from Cleveland, the Chief of Police announced that an eyewitness had come forward with a statement contradicting the claim that the assault had been unprovoked. Colm's wounds were held up as serious enough to cast doubt on whether he'd brazenly attacked an innocent man or had simply been defending a young woman's honor, and in the end, the embittered steel executive was unable to press charges.

'Well that's just typical!' Honora jeered after Colm's release, 'The papers are in no hurry to retract their spurious allegations – I suppose "exoneration" is too much to expect for a lowly "tinsmith"!'

It was Cousin Michael's reaction to the whole episode, however, that bothered Edward more. The two were smoking in the garden after Thanksgiving dinner at Old Man McCormick's, a tradition made bittersweet this year for the absence of Cousin Patrick. When Edward relayed the story of Colm's recent misfortune, Michael remarked that Colm had acted rashly.

'But Colm didn't provoke the fight,' Edward said, 'He acted in self-defense.'

Michael tapped ash from his cigarette into an urn. 'Aquinas said fighting and war were justified if the central purpose was a desire for peace, not for power or self-gain.'

'Something gleaned from books, maybe, Michael, but not from life experience. In *real* life, self-defense is part of survival, and I have no doubt your brother would have done the same in Colm's circumstances. Patrick wasn't one to be pushed around – he saw the world as it is.'

'Given what he saw of human nature in the war,' Michael said, looking off to the side, 'I can only hope that when he died he wasn't blind to seeing the world as it should be.' He stood to go back inside, and added, 'I'd like to think that in the end he could have refrained from a fistfight simply to show how tough he was…'

Edward sat at a café table in the Rose Room of St. Francis Hotel on New Year's Eve, with Art Hickman and his Jazz Orchestra banging away in the background, waiting for the girls to return from powdering their noses, and for Morgan to return from the bar with more drinks. Savoring a cigarette, he considered that whereas exactly a year ago he'd been in a leaky tent watching Miller poke at a dead gopher with his bayonet, here he was in a fine hotel drinking champagne cocktails. As recently as June, he'd been in poor health, wallowing in self-doubt, apprehensive about the future – but now, with a new year starting, he could finally smile with relief.

On the work front, he was settling nicely into his new role. He'd familiarized himself with key accounts up and down the West Coast and had accompanied Mr. Breslin on calls to several California apparel makers. In August, he'd gone to the Pendleton Woolen Mills in Portland to ink a contract for a new line of woolen sports shirts; twice in the fall he'd been to Los Angeles to help American Thread's man there, Fred Dowling, make inroads with manufacturers converting from military uniforms to working men's clothing.

Getting an apartment with Walter, who'd found work as a municipal bond trader, had been less traumatic than they'd feared. Honora and Katherine had their hands full with Aunt Mildred, as Deirdre had relocated to Sonoma to help her aunt and uncle with the farm; the departure of Edward and Walter meant that much less cooking and cleaning. Even after devoting a good portion of their incomes to supporting the family, the brothers were able to afford a new elevator building a stone's throw from Lafayette Park.

With his newfound independence, Edward was better able to

appreciate Constance and forgive some of her frivolity. If being a salesman meant adjusting the loneliness of life on the road, time apart from Constance actually helped to ease tensions, making their time together more enjoyable. She became more relaxed when her cycle continued uninterrupted; for his part, Edward was more chaste than ever. Their dates were light-hearted once again, and when they went out dancing with friends, his stiff knee didn't bother him as much.

Through all the changes, Edward remained faithfully devoted to Fitz, visiting twice a week and supporting him through various reconstructive surgeries. That very afternoon, in fact, he'd talk to his friend about helping him find a place of his own in the coming year.

Now seeing Constance approaching so happy and full of life, Edward felt a surge of euphoria, and reaching into the pocket of his rented tux he fingered the small velvet box that contained the engagement ring he planned to give her at the end of the evening.

'Why the Cheshire Cat grin, Edward?' she said as he stood to pull out her chair.

Alas, euphoria is but a temporary affliction. In the early spring, at a baptism for one of Mrs. Doherty's grand-nieces, Edward overheard something that brought him back down to earth.

It was a heady time for St. Paul's Parish – since January, the interior of the English Gothic church had been festooned with garlands and shamrocks, commemorating the one-year anniversary of the Irish Republic's Declaration of Independence. Now in late March, surrounded by stalwart families like the McDonoughs, the Healys, the Dohertys, and O'Neills,

Monsignor Malloy was presiding over the baptismal font. Having arrived late, Edward looked on from the edge of the gathering and spotted Constance across the way, standing behind the parents of the newborn and engaged in furtive conversation with her second cousin, Jack Healy. Morgan had once remarked that Edward bore a striking resemblance to Healy, who worked for a brokerage house and was a member of the Olympic Club, and as Edward regarded his courtly double, a conversation in front of him caught his ear.

'That Miss Doherty is a looker, alright, but I've heard she's rather high strung.'

'Not the sharpest knife in the drawer, either...'

'Knowing her mother, I'm sure it comes as a great relief to be marrying her off.'

'I should say...but then her beau there didn't have much choice after what her father did for his family.'

Edward didn't know the speaker, a large woman in a broad-billed hat, but recognized the other middle-aged matron as a Mrs. Flaherty, who now said, 'How do you mean?'

Edward had difficulty making out the women's whispers, what with Monsignor Malloy bringing his rich brogue to bear on the Latin incantations, but he did manage to catch the words "brouhaha" and "call to the chief." The infant's squeals as the water was dribbled onto its head prompted some good-natured snickering in the crowd, and then Edward heard Mrs. Flaherty say, 'I didn't think Malcolm Doherty had that kind of clout.'

'Mind you,' the large woman sniffed, 'if the young man had died there'd have been no getting that Colm Dooley off.' The Monsignor was leading the infant's godparents through recitations when the woman added, 'It's simply preposterous seeing Honora Dooley putting on airs down at the cathedral when she's got that hooligan for a son...'

Looking at Constance and her supposed fiancé across the baptismal font, Mrs. Flaherty remarked, "Tis hard to believe that boy's from the same family, isn't it?'

Over a month went by before Edward got up the nerve to mention the conversation to Constance. They were seated among the crowd awaiting the start of a Sunday afternoon concert in Golden Gate Park when he described what he'd overheard at the baptism.

'I don't know what you're getting so worked up about, Edward,' Constance said, fussing with her handbag, looking for her lipstick, 'Your brother's not in jail and the whole matter is behind us...'

'But I know Colm's got a temper – and I don't feel good about circumventing justice...'

'You astound me, Edward,' Constance said amidst the applause of the crowd as the musicians took their seats in the band shell. 'I've always admired your loyalty to your family and now here's an instance when you ought to be standing by your brother...'

Edward sighed. 'I'm just uncomfortable with favors, is all...'

With the overture to Bizet's "Carmen" starting, Constance said in a low voice, 'I don't know whether Daddy had any influence, and you'd only make him uncomfortable by asking him about it.' After a moment, she added, 'Gossiping old biddies – pay them no mind...'

As they listened to the music, Edward didn't know which

was worse: that her father may well have interceded on Colm's behalf or that Constance was content to know nothing about it.

Chapter 21

Fitz left Letterman Hospital in May after a fifteen-month convalescence. With most of his right jaw and cheekbone gone, his face was badly misshapen – nevertheless, he'd regained sight in his right eye, extensive dental work had enabled an adequate bite, and a series of skin grafts had masked much of the burn damage. Despite lingering inner ear problems and a numb right hip – disabilities his doctors believed would prevent him from getting by on his own – he had three advantages in his corner.

The first was Nurse Luchetti, whose ability to motivate him through a grueling physical therapy regimen spelled the difference between giving in to life as an invalid and taking a chance on starting over. The second was his friend, Edward Dooley, who came Wednesdays after work and every Saturday (with chewing gum, cigarettes, and the latest baseball periodical) when he would insist on pushing Fitz around the Presidio grounds in his wheelchair. The third advantage was that, together, Edward and Nurse Luchetti were able reach out to some of Fitz's former Seals teammates and capitalize on their faithfulness: led by Harry Heilmann and Sam Bohne, money was raised so that Fitz could afford a place of his own.

The Hotel Senate was in the heart of the Tenderloin, the downtown residential district that had been rebuilt after the '06 disaster. Comprised of hotels and apartments catering mostly to singles, the Tenderloin was a haven for nightlife, with musical theaters, burlesque houses, card rooms, billiard halls and boxing gyms – and though prohibition had been in effect five months by the time Fitz arrived, "blind pigs" were springing up everywhere. The Hotel Senate itself was considered a respectable establishment, a favorite among sports enthusiasts, its ornate lobby featuring portraits of the leading sports figures of the day, like pitcher Earl Averill, welterweight Packey McFarland, tennis star Clare Cassell, and golfing great Walter Hagen. When the manager heard Jimmy Fitzsimmons needed a place, he offered him a special monthly rate.

Moving day was a Friday. In the morning, Colm and Edward used the Dooley job truck to bring over some furnishings courtesy of Catholic Charities, and Angela set about fixing up the room when they headed off to the Presidio to pick up Fitz. His mid-afternoon arrival at The Senate was deliberately low-key – Edward accompanied the unsteady veteran through the empty lobby to the elevator while Colm and the manager brought a trunk and a folded wheelchair up to the sixth floor. Angela was setting out a card and fruit basket when Fitz first entered his room, big enough for a bed, a dresser, a table and two chairs. A pair of double-hung windows looked out onto an alley separating The Senate from another apartment building on the next street.

Several maxillofacial surgeries had left Fitz with a face vaguely reminiscent of what had been recorded in photographs before the war, though his upper lip was now rather bulbous, and a reconstructed brow kept his right eye deep in shadow. With no cheek muscles beneath the skin grafts on the right side of his face, it was difficult for Fitz to make recognizable expressions, but Edward and Angela had grown accustomed to looking passed his flat affect and finding him through his eyes.

'How're you getting on today, Fitz?' Angela asked, stretching up to peck his left cheek.

'Exciting ride over…'

'Oh, yes, isn't Auto Row magnificent?'

'I meant Colm's driving.'

Edward laughed. 'Always in a hurry,' he said as he unlatched Fitz's trunk at the end of the bed, 'He'd make a good cabbie!'

Angela directed Fitz to the table where he took a seat and looked over the half dozen signatures from his teammates on the card. While she unpacked, Edward took the opportunity to read off hotel logistics such as mealtimes, laundry service, and social hours in the lobby. It was hard to tell whether Fitz was listening, until he turned to Edward.

'Remember when you first came to see me at Letterman, Eddie?'

'Sure do. You were in the sunroom – looking over the box scores, if I'm not mistaken.'

''Member what I said about life not being fair?' Angela looked up from filling the dresser drawers and caught Edward's eye.

'Well, it's not,' the wounded vet said, closing the card and resting his left hand on it. 'And that's too bad, but it's just like baseball: you learn to control what you can and accept the rest.' He looked up. 'Anyway, I wanna thank you both for helping me get back on my feet.'

Angela smiled warmly at Fitz, and pointing to the basket, said, 'Edward, pull out that apple cider there and let's toast the wisdom of baseball.'

A few weeks later, Walter met Edward at the Hotel Senate after work as planned so they could walk to Market Street together to join Constance and Morgan for the evening. After Edward and Angela had said their goodbyes to Fitz in the dining room, however, Edward felt a pang of regret realizing that Angela would have to make her way home alone. He invited her to come along.

Morgan and Constance were waiting in front of The Strand, the newest movie palace in town, and when they recognized Nurse Luchetti from their occasional visits to Letterman – and always in Edward's company – they commended her on her tireless devotion to Fitz's recovery. Seeing her out of uniform, Constance found Angela rather plain, but she was glad for Walter because he was so painfully shy and seldom had an opportunity to meet girls.

Way Down East was currently the biggest picture out – the story of a New England girl tricked into a phony marriage and later abandoned when she becomes pregnant. Over the course of the film the guileless Anna Moore, played by Lillian Gish, matures from innocent country girl to giddy bride, betrayed lover, and, ultimately, noble heroine.

D.W. Griffith's provocative film was sure to spark debate among moviegoers, and Morgan was up to the challenge. With characteristic panache, he persuaded the maître d' at the Duquesne Club, a popular late-night eatery on McAllister Street, to give the group a table in the corner. The acoustics in the tasteful dining room (featuring embossed ceiling panels, brass wall sconces, white octagonal floor tile) made it impossible to carry on intelligible conversation, but holding court in the corner Morgan was able to kick things off without shouting.

'Would someone please tell me how I'm supposed to settle my nerves with a soft drink after a movie like that?' he asked in an aggrieved tone.

Edward smiled. 'Looking for something stiffer after all the high drama?'

'They're just going to have to legislate milder pictures,' Morgan said, shaking his head. 'Someone should have foreseen this. I mean, it's one thing to deprive the working man his beer to keep him from beating his wife, but how're the rest of us supposed to unwind?'

'Sacramental wine's exempt,' Constance offered. 'Maybe go to church more often?'

'A nice brandy would do the trick, sis,' Morgan said with a wink.

Walter began to explain that their Cousin Michael was in the seminary with the Christian Brothers when Angela cut him off. 'What's got you so jittery, Morgan? Was it poor Anna wandering out onto the ice flow and nearly going over the falls?'

'Oh, God no – that was pure melodrama. No, it's before she bolts out into the blizzard, when the truth comes out that she'd had a child out of wedlock. She points a finger at Lennox Sanderson…' Here Morgan clutched his chest with one hand while pointing to Walter with the other, then he cried out in a distraught falsetto, 'I was an ignorant girl betrayed by *him*, your honorable guest!'

Walter was flummoxed, but the snickering around the table came to an abrupt halt when Angela said, 'A conveniently dead baby at that…'

'Excuse me?' Morgan said, taken aback.

'Listen, if the baby had lived Anna would have had no choice but to slink off in shame,' Angela explained. 'But with the baby dying she's not entirely ruined because there's David, the saintly farmer who knows nothing about her past, and he's quite happy to redeem her.'

'Good bible-thumping American stock,' Morgan said with a righteous nod, 'and not some upper crust scoundrel like Lennox.' Looking to Angela ironically, she granted him a wry smile.

Dinner arrived – Salisbury steak sandwiches for the men (aka "hamburgers" before the war), a tuna melt for Constance, and a chicken pot pie for Angela.

'Pictures like that just pander to the masses,' Morgan asserted between bites. 'Show us a man in a tux and we're supposed to think he's hollow – that the breeding and the high moral standards are all a fraud. And do you know why? Because pictures today have to appeal to the unwashed masses who flock to the theaters to get their minds off their troubles.'

With mock indignity, Edward said, '*I* bathed today, thank you very much!'

'Being from the lower classes doesn't makes someone low-class,' Angela observed, undaunted, 'any more than being blessed with advantages necessarily ensures virtue.'

'Are we sparring here, dear?' Morgan said, feigning offense.

Hoping to prevent a scene, Edward ventured anxiously, 'Isn't the movie about character? That anyone can improve his station in America by living an upstanding life.'

'And undo the humiliation of being ostracized?' Angela asked.

Edward was regarding her curiously when Constance declared, 'Anna was a fool because she went against what's decent in society. She deserves what she got.'

'I was thinking of Lennox, actually,' Angela retorted. 'He should have been shamed for having set up the sham marriage in the first place.'

'Now look here,' Morgan said testily, 'any girl who thinks there's a rich prince charming out there ready to sweep her off her feet has got what's coming to her...'

'The moral being, stick to your own kind...' Angela said mildly.

Morgan patted the pockets of his jacket, pretending distress. 'Where the devil is my flask!'

Aggravated now, Constance said, 'Really, Angela, you needn't be cynical about it. Women need to be careful about who they associate with nowadays. They have their honor to protect, after all.'

'Not get into jambs and all that,' Angela said, nodding agreement. 'But then everyone knows there's a double standard for men. They can behave boorishly and get away with it, whereas one slip-up on the part of a lady and she's done for...'

'Oh, please!' Morgan scoffed.

'You *do* have to be smart about reading people,' Edward put in.

'No disagreement here,' Angela said, 'It's no good judging a book by its cover...'

There was general, if grumbled, assent around the table and thankfully coffee and dessert arrived just in time to relieve the tension. But before the conversation could be steered in a new direction, Angela spoke up again, which caused Morgan to wince.

'It *is* about character, Edward,' she began, 'just as you

were saying. In America, we have a responsibility to improve ourselves no matter what class we're from.' With her coffee cup raised to her lips, looking vaguely toward the middle of the table, she went on, 'They say it's a new era, that women ought to finally be accorded equal status with men – well then, we all have a moral duty to society to be our best selves, no matter where we come from…'

A silence fell over the group until Morgan looked across the table, and said beseechingly, 'Oh, dear, Walter, now I've heard everything. As if the eighteenth amendment weren't bad enough, it's the nineteenth that spells the beginning of the end…'

Chapter 22

After the Republican landslide in November 1920, those opposed to women's suffrage would crow that female voters had turned out for Harding because he was photogenic. In fact, newsreel coverage of Senator Harding's folksy front porch pronouncements resonated with voters across the country just as the publicists thought it would – because most Americans longed for a return to simpler times. Democrats had been in disarray ever since Wilson's return from Paris the year before when he declared, 'At last the world knows America as the savior of the world!' He would soon discover that his arrogance dissuaded congress from approving the Treaty of Versailles; his insistence that the 1920 election be a referendum on the treaty made for a contentious convention in San Francisco that summer.

The subject of the election had come up in the course of a train ride Edward and Angela shared in mid-October. (Edward had teased her about being more mindful of her family after learning from Fitz that she hadn't been home in over a year; when Mr. Breslin asked Edward to do some scouting in Stockton, Edward insisted that Angela show him her hometown.) This would be the first presidential election for Edward, and, with the 19th Amendment ratified as of August, for Angela as well. While they suspected their politics weren't completely aligned – Edward supported the vote for women, but he and Angela had crossed swords over a walkout by railcar operators in Oakland – it wasn't until they were traversing the San Joaquin Valley that the two discovered just how far apart they stood on the upcoming election.

'Really?' Angela said after listening to Edward's ringing endorsement of Harding. She looked out at the delta, then back to Edward, seated across from her, riding backwards. 'I'm surprised, that's all…'

'Surprised how?'

'Well, it's just I thought you'd support the president's push for peace. I would think that as someone who fought, you'd want to see the treaty signed.'

Edward put down his newspaper. 'At the end of the day, I'd have to say that the treaty's not in our best interest.'

'But maintaining the peace *is* in America's interest.'

'Yes, but this League of Nations business, see…deep down it's flawed – they say it may even be unconstitutional.' He shook his head as he looked to Angela, saying, 'I wouldn't want foreigners dragging us back into another war…'

'That's just what Republicans want you to believe,' Angela quipped as she looked out at the scenery again. 'The president says there's a way for America to be in the League and still maintain our sovereignty.' Turning to look at him, she continued, 'Too bad you weren't able to hear him speak at the Civic Auditorium rally last September, Edward. I know you were away on business, but he was very persuasive about it being in everyone's interest that America sign on. Otherwise, without a sensible world body we could end up making the same mistakes that led to the Great War in the first place.'

'Believe me, I don't want us ever getting into another war,' he said, watching telephone poles disappear into the distance, 'But we can't be the world's policeman, either. With Europe in ruins now, we ought to expand trade and help them rebuild their industries…'

'But that's not what Republicans are saying, Edward. They want us sticking to our own affairs, basically saying to Europe, "You started the mess, you dig yourselves out of it."

Edward found her feisty nature appealing – her green eyes flashed, her auburn hair seemed more red. Egging her on, he said, 'Well, that makes a certain amount of sense, right?'

'No, not anymore,' she replied as she bent down and began searching for a tin of mints in her bag, 'not when things are as interconnected as they are. There's no use pretending the rest of the world doesn't exist – we have a role to play in world affairs or else we'll live to regret it.'

'I don't know…' he said before turning away abruptly, ashamed that his eyes had lingered on her breasts as she dug into her bag. He wasn't sure if it was a new frock or a different brassiere, but then he hadn't really looked at her that way before. Clearing his throat, he said solemnly, 'The agreement's flawed – we shouldn't ratify it if we can't fully support it.'

At last she came up with the tiny tin. 'The treaty might not be perfect, Edward,' she said, offering him a mint before helping herself, 'but it's all we've got.'

Stockton was the epicenter of the San Joaquin Valley, an inland seaport seventy-five miles east of San Francisco that was gaining distinction as the "breadbasket to the world." Angela's father, Gaetano, had built up a five-hundred-acre farming operation on the east side of town, growing asparagus and red onions with other immigrants from the Italian Piedmont (while the Tuscans and Neapolitans grew peaches, plums, and apricots in the delta wetlands to the west). She looked forward to showing Edward that it wasn't a hick farm town but a major business center with a burgeoning downtown to prove it. For his part, Edward was too much of a gentleman to tell her that in his days as a schoolboy in San Francisco it was common to say Stockton was full of crazies because it housed the state's insane asylum.

The two arranged to meet late the next morning in the sumptuous lobby of the Hotel Stockton, Edward's expense account being sufficient to afford the best the town had to offer. Main Street was humming with streetcar and automobile traffic as Angela took him on a stroll down the sidewalk which was crowded with well-dressed women perusing the shop windows and businessmen on their way to lunch. She paused at Hunter Plaza to show off the splendid San Joaquin County Courthouse and later called his attention to the city's newest skyscraper, the ten-story Farmers and Merchants Bank, as well as the new J.C. Penney's department store.

She'd arranged for them to have lunch at The Clark Hotel, which boasted an elegant dining room framed by Corinthian columns with gold leaf accents. They were escorted to their table by a punctilious maître d' who presented each of them with a bound menu the size of an atlas. Predictably for a Friday, they each ordered fish.

Angela asked about the tour he'd made that morning of the Holt factory. Edward pursed his lips and shook his head, and looking very polished in his Brooks Brothers suit he told her that the building was too old, that the company was too deep in debt. He explained that during the war Holt had expanded too fast supplying military tractors and now found themselves at a disadvantage to rivals who were able to fill orders for conventional tractors more quickly.

'Adjusting to a peacetime economy can be tricky,' Edward said authoritatively.

Angela buttered a roll, saying, 'And how's your company making out?'

'Oh, American Thread is no small concern. We've always been well diversified across the garment industry.' He looked every bit the budding executive as he folded his arms and explained that the company was headquartered in New York City, and that there were five manufacturing plants back east, including the largest thread mill in North America. 'There's been talk of opening a plant on the west coast, you see, but Holt's factory just isn't big enough…We make over four thousand kinds of thread, after all!'

'My,' Angela said.

'Our thread is found in the apparel you find in the best department stores – Macy's and Lord & Taylor in New York, Marshall Field in Chicago… Bullock's in Los Angeles, Meier & Frank up in Portland…' Splitting a roll in two with his thumbs, he said, 'Now the labels you find at Penney's – Nation Wide, Ramona, Waverly – they're cheaper, of course, but there's a reason…' He speared a pad of butter with his fork. 'For one thing, they don't use our thread!'

Angela smiled. 'I assume there are unions at your plants? I ask because I remember the terrible steel and coal strikes last year and wonder if that's affected your business…'

'No, not really,' Edward said, munching his roll. 'Our industry went through its own growing pains about ten years ago.

Strikes in New York built up the ranks of the Ladies' Garment Workers' Union, and then before the war a walk-out in Chicago led to the Amalgamated Clothing Workers. Things are good now, though…'

Angela nodded, impressed, but Edward seemed distracted as he apprised the caliber of the businessmen at other tables. Suddenly impatient for their food to arrive, Angela said, 'I guess the difficulty for steelworkers and coal miners last year was that management wanted them stick to the same contracts they had during the war.'

Edward looked at her, bemused. 'Oh? Well, I wouldn't know the particulars. The economy's in a period of adjustment right now. People have to be patient while things are worked out…'

'But as I understand it,' Angela pressed on, 'the steel and mining companies were saying that the war wasn't over until the peace treaty was signed. Only the war *is* over.' She looked at Edward as if for confirmation. 'Anyway, it just didn't sound fair to the workers, that's all.'

'Well, there's more to it…' Edward said, vaguely irritated when their lunch was finally served. 'The AFL has started a lot of these strikes hoping to swell its ranks by bringing unskilled workers into their tent.' Taking a bite of his sea bass, he added, 'They're itching to take on big business.'

'But what about fair labor agreements?'

Edward reached for his iced tea. 'Listen, Angela, there are two sides to this thing, see? What I mean is, there's lots of outside influences these days and they don't always have America's best interests in mind…'

'You mean union agitators,' Angela said, picking at her fillet of sole, '—the socialists.'

217

'You bet. You've heard of the "Wobblies"? Bent on stomping out capitalism, uniting workers in a social class and abolishing wage labor outright?'

'Oh, I don't know, Edward,' Angela demurred as she concentrated on her food, 'I think this Red Scare has just been trumped up to sell newspapers.'

Edward put down his knife and fork. 'Now look, this Bolshevism business is no put-on. There *are* enemies in America who resort to violence...Palmer was right about those raids last year,' he said, referring to the attorney general's efforts to round up alien agitators.

'They want you to believe it's all the result of outside trouble-makers,' Angela said mildly, 'but that general strike in Seattle last year, and the Boston Police Strike – those seemed pretty homegrown to me. That's not a revolution – it's just people demanding fair pay.'

Edward was incredulous. 'What about those race riots in Chicago and Omaha...and Cleveland? They found communist leaflets—'

'I don't buy it,' Angela cut in. 'Racial unrest is a homegrown problem, not some foreign plot. I mean, do you really think those black men in Chicago – Doughboys like you – were put up by the Bolsheviks to defend their neighborhoods?'

'There're foreigners everywhere now,' Edward retorted as he returned to his meal in earnest. 'I went through a pretty dicey part of town this morning, in fact – all kinds of Orientals. Who knows what they're thinking?'

'Oh, that's just Japantown and Little Manila,' Angela scoffed. 'They come to Stockton to work the fields.' She took a sip of water, then looked at Edward as she spoke. 'That's why people come to America, Edward – for opportunity. So what if they don't speak English yet – they're hard workers trying to make it just like everybody else…'

Later that day Edward was smoking a cigarette in front of the Hotel Stockton waiting for Angela, when the doorman brushed passed him to wave off a battered Ford pickup that was pulling into the taxi zone. To Edward's surprise, it was Angela in the passenger seat, and a dark young man beside her gripping the steering wheel as though it had a mind of its own. Flicking his cigarette to the pavement, Edward stepped nimbly around the doorman and squeezed into the pickup next to Angela.

'I would have hopped in the back,' he said dryly as the truck lurched forward, 'but I don't think the doorman would approve.'

Angela laughed and introduced her sixteen-year-old brother, Giancarlo. Edward looked over and smiled, but the young man was too caught up making a turn to acknowledge him. Darker than Angela, he had a strong nose and brow, and a shock of black hair slicked back with pomade. The man Edward would come to refer to as "the matinee idol" because of his resemblance to Rudolf Valentino was intent on his driving.

Edward wondered whether he spoke any English, and looking passed Angela, at length he said, 'So, what do you like studying in high school?'

'Oh, biology mostly,' the young man said with a shrug.

'Giancarlo volunteered at the state hospital during the flu epidemic,' Angela explained.

'Getting the patients used to wearing masks – no easy task,' Giancarlo said, then, with a glance to Edward, 'It's the mental

219

hospital, you know...'

Edward raised his eyebrows and nodded. 'I understand not everybody in San Francisco was keen on the masks either.'

'Did you see many cases of the flu in the army?' Giancarlo asked after a few moments.

'Among other things...' Edward said cryptically. 'I don't know how the doctors managed to cope with it all.'

'The same as you, I expect,' Angela offered, staring straight ahead.

'And you were being shot at,' her brother said, hands clasped comfortably atop the steering wheel now as they sailed along.

The Luchettis lived on the east side of town off Copperopolis Road in a residential neighborhood of one-story bungalows, most with garages, utility sheds, or chicken coops in back. Angela's mother met them at the screen door. She was a short woman with black hair, a broad brow, and the full lips that she'd passed onto her son. Holding Edward's hands in both of hers, she said in a heavy accent, 'You are Angela's friend, the soldier.'

She beckoned him into the house that smelled of garlic and basil, the well-worn plaid upholstery of the oak furniture warmed by the afternoon sun. For an instant Edward felt as if the dour-looking ancestors in photographs on the mantel were following him as he was led to the dining room. The table was draped in white lace and a crucifix hung over the door to the kitchen. Through this door came Angela's father, a short, serious man with a bushy mustache, his green-grey eyes difficult to read behind spectacles. He offered Edward a perfunctory handshake with rock-hard hands.

For supper Mrs. Luchetti served cioppino, a seafood stew,

and Edward complimented her on the dish more than once. He also had a second helping of the bow-tie pasta and several slices of thick Italian bread which Angela taught him to dip in olive oil. Giancarlo found Edward's messy attempts to master this very amusing. Mrs. Luchetti shuttled back and forth to the kitchen and her husband ate in silence until Angela happened to bring up the coming election.

'I agree Republican,' Mr. Luchetti suddenly blurted out to Edward, 'America first – no foreign tangle up!'

Caught by surprise but feeling obliged to respond, Edward said, 'Why, yes, sir. We can't solve the world's problems – there's plenty to do right here at home.'

'Like tolerating dissent,' Angela remarked, which drew a hard look from her father. Turning to Edward, she said, 'We're a democracy after all – it's no time for isolationism, for deporting people simply because we don't like their views…'

'Be still, Angela,' her mother put in, 'we have a nice time.'

There was a split-second of silence before Giancarlo declared with a screwball laugh, 'All Wops are Galleanists!'

Edward was immediately on guard. A series of mail bombs the previous spring had resulted in the deportation of Luigi Galleani, a self-professed Italian anarchist; just a month ago, a deadly bomb blast on Wall Street was said to be the work of Galleani's followers. Edward worried that the matinee idol's facetious remark might trigger an angry outburst from his father, and indeed, no sooner did Edward look over than Mr. Luchetti began spewing recriminations.

'Galleani, no! Crazy man!' he asserted, pretending to spit to the side. 'Dangerous to America, Land of Opportunity.' Then, with a dismissive wave of his hand, 'Gone him!'

Mrs. Luchetti sighed and began clearing the table. She admonished her son under her breath as she passed, then beckoned her daughter to help her in the kitchen. Angela gathered up the plates, but at the kitchen door she turned around. Looking passed her brother with the sheepish grin on his face, she said, 'You never know who you can trust, isn't that right, Papa?'

A couple of weeks later, Edward was gratified to find his political views affirmed in more familiar surroundings. The occasion was Mr. Doherty's birthday and the family was gathered in their handsomely appointed dining room for supper. Morgan was going on about the new Harold Lloyd comedy when Constance opined that the movies were a frivolous escape from more serious matters, such as which direction the country was headed. Morgan countered that, in fact, the newsreels were keeping him up to date. Citing the coverage of Senator Harding speaking to admirers from his front porch, he observed, 'Anybody who loves people and dogs as much as he does deserves to be president.'

As the laughter died down, Uncle Hector's wife, Jillian, always a bit wary around her nephew, remarked innocently, 'He does seem very agreeable.'

Malcolm Doherty shot his son a cautionary look, then proclaimed, 'Harding will be a breath of fresh air after all this country's been through. We ought to stick to our knitting right here at home…'

'Enough with idealism,' Morgan exclaimed, 'We want capitalism!'

Though it was his birthday and he would have loved nothing

better than to trade witticisms with his son, in consideration of his guests Mr. Doherty turned to his future son-in-law, always the model of decorum. 'Tell me, Edward, how do you see things adding up?'

'Me? Oh, well, I'm bullish on the Republican ticket, of course,' Edward replied. 'As much as Teddy Roosevelt wanted America to be engaged in the world, now is the time to make sure America is secure and strong at home. We can't be the world's policeman, after all...'

'Put that big stick away!' Morgan chimed in.

'I don't want to see America drawn into another war,' Edward continued, 'and I think joining the League would put us on a very slippery slope...'

'Indeed! Wilson and his League can go hang for all I care,' Mr. Doherty declared. 'He sold Ireland out last year and he deserves his comeuppance!'

Patting her fiancé's forearm, Constance said, 'Edward also thinks the Republican platform is good for business, don't you, dear?'

'I do,' Edward said. 'It's time we got back to work and turn our attention to the future.'

'Hear, hear!' Malcolm Doherty assented, and indeed, a week later the Republican Party's "Return to Normalcy" platform carried the day.

Chapter 23

In the summer of 1914, while in Paris collecting art and furnishings for her home in San Francisco, Alma de Bretteville Spreckels also managed to persuade the French government to contribute a pavilion for the international exposition being held there the following year. So please was she with the small-scale replica of the Palais de la Legion D'Honneur that after the war she decided to have a full-scale reproduction built to show off her collection of Rodin sculpture and other European art. But the choice of a promontory overlooking the Golden Gate rekindled a controversy that had surrounded the creation of Lincoln Park a decade earlier. To diffuse the uproar over digging up an additional fifteen-hundred graves from the original potter's field cemetery, Alma arranged a Memorial Day ceremony in 1921 to dedicate her new museum, then under construction, in honor of the San Franciscans who'd fought in the Great War.

Seated with various dignitaries under a tent adjacent to the worksite that fine May morning, Mr. and Mrs. Spreckels looked out over an audience of several hundred patriotic citizens. Among the veterans in the first row at the foot of the stage sat Fitz, dressed in a new gabardine uniform (courtesy of Morgan's Presidio connections), his right sleeve pinned at the shoulder. Morgan, outfitted in crisp serge, was seated further back among fellow officers, while Edward and Walter wore business suits and sat among the civilians. (Colm had begged off, saying, 'What I want is the war bonus they promised us, not a fucking ceremony for swells.') The proceedings got under way with Mayor Rolph declaring the Spreckels' gift a fitting tribute to the thirty-six hundred San Franciscans who'd given their lives in the war and concluded ninety minutes later with a ceremonial tree-planting presided over by none other than French General Ferdinand Foch.

Relieved to no longer have to hold their programs at odd angles to block the mid-day sun, the audience quickly retreated to a neighboring tent pavilion where a buffet luncheon had been set up. Edward, Walter, and Angela assisted Fitz to a round table in the corner, and Angela stayed behind while the Dooley brothers went to stand in line for food. Fitz confided to Angela that he found the prosthetic mask Morgan had commissioned very uncomfortable. Though she objected to the mask, Angela nodded and patted his shoulder reassuringly just as Morgan and Constance arrived with two attractive women in tow.

Molly Fitzsimmons pretended to kiss her brother on the cheek, then introduced her friend, Alice Terry, who'd come up with her from Los Angeles the night before on the *Lark*. Morgan, their chaperone for the day, sat next to Miss Terry, while Molly dutifully took the seat on her brother's left. Constance chose the middle of the three remaining seats so that she would be flanked by Edward and Walter.

Alice was the embodiment of Hollywood success – she'd had a bit part in *The Devil's Pass-Key* the year before – a striking green-eyed brunette in a cranberry-colored Crepe de Chine dress and a broad-brim bonnet. When she thanked Angela for buying them red poppy boutonnières, Angela explained they were to benefit the war orphans in France and Belgium.

'Well, it's a wonderful tribute, and I'm so glad I could be here today,' Alice said brightly. Without missing a beat, she then turned to Fitz who was sipping lemonade through a straw. 'Molly says you've got a place of your own now, Jim.'

Fitz nodded. 'Suits me fine.'

'I do hope you can come by sometime, Molly,' Angela said.

Even if she'd yet to score her big break in show business, Fitz's sister was also stunning to behold – her fair skin and blond hair perfectly complemented by a sea-foam green chiffon drape and matching silk taffeta turban. She offered Angela a tight smile just as Edward and Walter returned with sandwiches and crudités.

Morgan introduced the Dooley brothers to his guests, and Constance was surprised when, instead of Walter, Edward took the seat between Angela and her.

'Well-known ballplayers stay at the Hotel Senate when they're in town, right, Fitz?' Angela asked, in hopes of encouraging Molly to pay a visit.

'Tom Seaton had stories to tell about his time with the White Sox,' the big man replied.

It was difficult to understand him through the mask, and to dispel the awkwardness, Morgan said jauntily, 'You mean the Black Sox, don't you, Fitz?'

Though everyone knew about the ongoing trial to determine whether the team had thrown the World Series two years earlier, Morgan's attempt at humor fell flat, and to break the uncomfortable silence, Alice said, 'Speaking of Chicago, did you know the Cubs were in Catalina for spring training this year?'

'Really?' Morgan said, grateful for the rescue. 'Come to think of it, I did hear Wrigley was building a hotel and gambling casino there. Perhaps you and I can have a look the next time I'm in Los Angeles,' he said with a wink. Alice laughed. They'd only met that morning but she liked Morgan – it wasn't often she met a man who quoted poetry without sounding rehearsed.

'My, it seems everybody's going to Los Angeles these days,' Constance remarked, amused by her brother's presumption. She liked to think she belonged to the smart set, too, that Convent of the Blessed Sacrament had been her finishing school. She was feeling confident in the company of the Hollywood girls – she wore a robin's egg blue linen frock with a side-rolling hat – and yet something wasn't right. A new dress always elicited a compliment from Edward, but today he'd merely pecked her cheek and squeezed her about the shoulders.

Molly was going on about how important Los Angeles was becoming thanks to the movie business, when Morgan said, 'If not for Hollywood, that town would be nothing but a backwater of buttermilk and meatloaf, what with all the Midwesterners retiring to the orange groves there...'

A ripple of laughter around the table stopped dead at Molly, and Alice winked at Morgan.

'It's true,' Angela said. 'Did you know that Los Angeles boasts the largest membership of the Women's Christian Temperance Union in the country?'

Constance was confounded by how self-assured Angela seemed, despite the gingham dress that was several years out of date and the tam-o'-shanter that looked positively dotty.

'My company's thinking of opening an office there because it's so business-friendly,' Edward ventured, 'but with just soda pop to drink, I'm not sure I'd have the zip and zowie it takes to succeed…'

'Zip and zowie!' Angela exclaimed, prompting another round of laughter, except for Constance who was startled to see Angela squeeze Edward's forearm.

The truth was that while Edward's job did keep him extremely busy, he was reluctant to admit that his interest in Constance was on the wane. When he wanted to unwind, he found it was in the company of Angela Luchetti, something that began one Saturday when she'd come by The Senate and found him reading the newspaper in the lobby.

'I forgot Fitz was going to a ballgame today,' Edward explained, 'but then I thought maybe you and I could have a visit ourselves for a change.'

Over cherry pie at a nearby coffee shop Angela was surprised when he asked about the tension between her and her father. She explained that her father believed one must work hard and play by the rules to get ahead, before concluding, 'Well, he's worked hard, alright – but he's taken advantage of a few angles, too.'

'Oh, like what?' Edward said mildly.

'Let's just say he's made himself a favorite among the big growers…'

When Edward cocked his head, she looked down at her coffee cup, saying, 'I guess he and I differ on the "how" of it. To him, everything's black and white – either you support capitalism because it's what America is all about or you're against it and you can't be trusted.'

Edward smiled. 'Speaking of which, I suppose you saw where that Wobbly big-wig, Bill Haywood, skipped bail and fled to

Russia a few days ago?'

'Sure, but nothing's ever as simple as it seems,' Angela said, nodding to the waitress for a coffee refill. 'Take Tom Mooney, for instance,' Angela continued, referring to the man serving life for the 1916 Preparedness Day bombing in San Francisco, '—labor leader or militant socialist? Now they're saying his conviction was based on perjured testimony and everybody's calling for his release…'

'Ten people were blown up and forty injured,' Edward said skeptically, '—somebody had to be responsible.'

'But that doesn't justify putting away an innocent man, Edward…Just because the government's behind something doesn't mean it's morally correct. As for Haywood, who knows if he's a traitor or a patriot – some people are impossible to understand.'

Edward frowned and his thoughts became muddled as he recalled the way he'd looked at her on the train trip to Stockton. She certainly had an attractive figure, but it wasn't just that. As she went on about the foibles of labor leaders, he saw that there was something in her eyes, the way they seemed so clear – the way she seemed to look right into him.

And he had to look away.

Morgan and Walter went to fetch coffee and cookies while Angela and the Hollywood girls visited the ladies' comfort station. Edward tried to include Constance in his conversation with Fitz about the baseball season, but she soon excused herself saying she needed to powder her nose after all. Instead, she waited by the empty tent that had accommodated the dignitaries earlier, and when she saw Angela she beckoned with a friendly wave. No sooner had Angela stepped into the shade than Constance said in a low whisper, 'I know a flirt when I see one...'

'Excuse me?' Angela said.

'You stay away from Edward, do you hear me? I don't like how you act around him.'

Angela knew such a confrontation was inevitable, but she had hoped Edward might have broached the subject already. She wasn't sure how much Constance knew.

The Sheik was a wildly popular movie that spring, the story of a charming Arab chief, played by Rudolph Valentino, infatuated with an adventurous Englishwoman who is traveling in North Africa. Some regarded the salacious innuendo as unfit for polite society. Despite all Morgan's teasing, Constance refused to see it on principle, while Edward looked anguished by his friend's devilish wink for he'd secretly taken in the film – with Angela Luchetti, no less! She'd proposed it almost as a taunt one Saturday after they'd visited Fitz, and with Constance going to a friend's bridal shower that evening, Edward took her up on the offer.

Over dinner afterwards, he asked in a nonchalant tone, 'Are modern-thinking women always so foolish?' referring to the escapade where the lady is abducted by the sheik.

'Men would like to think so!' Angela replied with a demonic laugh. 'Isn't that what you men dream of? Commanding women to obey you?'

Picturing Angela as a sultry temptress, he retorted, 'Only if it's what she deserves...'

Angela smiled and rolled her eyes.

Now seeing Constance tremble in anger, Angela said, 'And

I've seen how you act around him – I'm afraid you don't know much about love. Why not let him make up his own mind?'

A string quartet came to life in the lunch pavilion just as Constance hissed, 'I do know Edward. We've known each other since childhood and if you think—'

'A romantic notion, maybe,' Angela interrupted, 'but war does something to a man.'

Greatly agitated, Constance said, 'Edward's a good man and I'm not going to let him be bamboozled by somebody who just happens along when the worst is over…'

'He's not the man for you, Constance. It's hard, but you need to face it.'

'How dare you!' Constance exclaimed, shaking now, 'I've devoted myself to him while all you've done is feed him clap-trap and make him feel guilty about that Fitz character. Well, you're not taking him away from me because he's mine, do you understand?'

'What you want he can't give you,' Angela said in a soft voice one would expect of a confidant, 'and clinging to him won't get you what you want – because he doesn't love you.'

'He *does* love me!' Constance insisted. She started to move around Angela, then pulled up. 'Who do you think you are, anyway, insinuating yourself into our circle? Find yourself some invalid at Letterman and go back to where you came from…' She was walking away when Angela's words stopped her.

'I may be a country girl but I bet I know more about human nature than you ever will. What you're looking for is comfort and security – a pass on the messiness of life – and as a girl who's never wanted for anything, you'll probably get it.' Constance turned around, and Angela went on, 'But you'll never have real security – true love – because that you can't buy. And you're no gambler because you'd never risk your heart.'

Constance had never been spoken to this way before and was surprised in that moment to find something fierce had awakened in her. 'You're nothing but a two-bit meddler, the conniving daughter of some greedy immigrant,' she sneered. 'My father can find out the kind of people you come from – out there in Modesto or Manteca or wherever it is…'

Angela sighed. 'It's a free country,' she said as she brushed passed Constance. 'Give everyone my regrets, won't you? I'm leaving.'

Chapter 24

'Edward's got a soft spot for foreigners, don't you, dear?'

Though Constance said it in jest, Edward didn't like being put on the spot and his retort – 'Speak for yourself' – caused all eyes to turn to him. The Doherty clan had gathered for the 4th of July in Ben Lomond, the Santa Cruz Mountain retreat of the Callan's, Clarice Doherty's people. Supper on the great flagstone patio was over, the smell of barbecued pork still lingered in the air, and from the woods came the sounds of the children resuming their games.

'You're not opposed to the new immigration law, are you, Edward?' Mrs. Doherty prodded her would-be son-in-law.

'Well, even though more workers are good for industry,' he began, noting the serious looks directed at him, 'I agree it's time we slowed down the flow…to keep America strong.'

'And pure, of course,' Morgan said, winking at Edward.

Malcolm Doherty cleared his throat, summoning the attention of all the men and their dour-looking wives around the table. 'American culture is descended from the Anglo-Saxon, Nordic, and Germanic peoples, and it would be sacrilegious if this great country were sullied by too many Southern and Eastern Europeans…'

'—to say nothing of the Asiatics,' one of the Callan men put in.

'It can only help your industry, Edward,' Mrs. Doherty said

with a provocative smile.

'The Jews have taken over the garment trade, that's for sure,' her husband agreed, prompting Mr. Callan to wince for Clarice's father hoped that by now Malcolm would have learned to be more discreet.

Noting Mr. Callan's uneasiness, Edward was reminded of his conversation with Jacobs during the war when they'd commiserated over how both Jews and Catholics were persecuted – how ironic, Edward thought, that the Irish in America could afford to look down on the Jews. And yet, as much as he resented insinuations that the garment business was shady, he knew better than to challenge that assumption here.

'So much of the business is in New York, of course, but it's different here in the west,' he said, though he knew this to be false – he'd been making trips to Los Angeles twice a month, calling on manufacturers with names like Zukin, Rosenblum, and Klein. Looking at the Callan men, all flushed jowls and silver hair, he added, 'Pretty soon, American made will mean made by Americans again!'

'Bully for us!' Morgan exclaimed, but bothered to see his friend on the hot seat, he went on the offensive. 'While we're at it, let's root out all the criminals and degenerates – and not just foreigners, but the insane and feeble-minded, too,' he said, daring a glance to his Aunt Jillian.

'That's enough, Morgan,' his father admonished, 'No one's suggesting we go that far.'

'I'm only citing science, Father,' Morgan said. 'Eugenicists have confirmed the genetic superiority of the white race – our last, best hopes are sterilization and euthanasia…'

Morgan squeezed out the back of his Peerless roadster into the glare of headlights and dust stirred up by all the cars pulling into the clearing. Everyone was returning from the fireworks show at Quail Hollow Ranch, and Morgan was eager for rum toddies and backgammon. Edward had driven the roadster and Constance called after her brother that they'd be along in a minute.

'Well?' she said, when the last of the revelers were headed up to the main house.

Edward was still agitated after all the firecrackers, the hissing sparklers, and the explosive crescendo of the show's finale – his nightmares about the friendly fire incident outside Epinonville had not entirely subsided, and he realized belatedly that he should have begged off as he had the year before. Now desperate for a dark, quiet room, he wiped his brow with the back of his hand. 'Well, what?'

'Don't you think you owe me an apology, Edward? For your behavior at the barbecue?'

'How's that?'

'Why, your snapping at me, of course. Humiliating me in front of my family...'

'I don't know what you're talking about, Constance.' He licked his lips, anxious for a drink. 'It seems to me you were the one putting me in an awkward spot with your relatives...'

'Hah!' she scoffed.

'Listen, I'm pretty jittery after all the fireworks, so go easy on me,' he said, shaking his head to get his bearings. 'What's this all about, anyhow?'

'I'm sorry to have to spell it out, Edward,' she said, fiddling with her handbag, 'but these past several months you've been distant and careless toward me. I'm your fiancée, after all…'

'Oh, I see.'

'And don't try passing it off as a work thing because I don't believe that anymore,' she said defiantly. 'I know you're tired, everybody's tired, but this is different – you don't talk to me like you used to.' Her voice cracking, she added, 'It's as if you don't want to be with me…'

'Oh, now…' he began, reaching over to touch her hand, but she pulled it away.

'It's that Angela – the *Eye-talian* girl – isn't it?' she sneered. Edward looked into the dark woods, inscrutable. 'We had words, you know, Edward, at that Memorial Day affair. I don't trust that girl and I never have…Who does she think she is, anyway?'

'How do you mean?' Edward said, trying to buy time.

'You and I are engaged, you know – she has no right to be so familiar with you!' Edward rubbed his face with his hands, and, exasperated now, Constance said, 'Do you expect me to believe that she just happens to bump into you whenever you go to see that Fitz fellow? Do you take me for a fool?

'No, of course not,' he said, blinking hard, 'that's not it.'

'That's not it?' she repeated with a little laugh. 'What a curious thing to say, Edward. Then what *is* it? Are you in love with her?'

'Listen, I'm a wreck – can't we talk about this—'

'Well? Are you?!'

'No, of course not! Jeez, Con, I haven't done anything wrong…'

She turned away with a pout. 'Maybe not, but I bet you've thought about it – a woman knows when a man's being unfaithful...'

He pinched his brow, fighting back images of Gesnes, of Blanchard rushing by without his rifle.

'To think we've been engaged eighteen months...' she continued, but when he said nothing, she smacked her lips. 'What a fool I've been to trust you! After all my family and I have done ...'

His head pounding, Edward mumbled, 'Don't, Con, please...'

'What was I thinking? A thug for a brother, your dad a drunk, your mother...a shrew!' With a mad cackle, she exclaimed, 'God knows, I can do better than Shanty Irish for in-laws!'

Edward opened his eyes blearily. 'Don't be a brat, Constance – listen to yourself...'

She fumbled crazily with the door handle before stumbling out of the car. 'You're a selfish, indecisive, middling little man, Edward Dooley!' she yelled. Pulling off her engagement ring, she threw it into the woods, saying, 'And you can go to hell for all I care!'

Edward stretched out on his cot and stared at the knotty pine ceiling. His insides churned with anxiety, yet he felt empty and morose, just like in the last weeks of the war, sustained by adrenaline alone. It had all come crashing down, certainties about the future had fallen away, revealing a vast and barren terrain. This wasn't what he'd planned at all – this wasn't what was supposed to happen – and feeling sorry for himself, he feigned sleep when Morgan returned to the cabin they shared.

On the one hand, he chastised himself for having led Constance along, for having maintained false hope in a relationship that was doomed. At the same time, the finality of the break left him feeling oddly reassured, and, unable to sleep, in the middle of the night he scribbled an apology to Morgan on the back of a business card and slipped out of the cabin. He walked for well over an hour before managing to thumb a ride with a dairyman heading down to Santa Clara. He took the SP commuter train to San Francisco, shaved and showered at his apartment, and went straight to the Presidio to see Angela.

She was surprised to see him, but asked that he come back at the end of her shift; so, tired and hungry, he got a sandwich at the commissary and spent the afternoon idly watching the flyboys in their biplanes doing tricks over the new Presidio airstrip. At supper he explained to Angela that he and Constance had broken up. Alternately giddy and gloomy, he gushed about how long he'd known the Dohertys, about his friendship with Morgan and his misgivings about Constance. Angela did her best to follow along and consoled him where necessary. She walked him back to his apartment, but when he asked her up for a nightcap, she kissed his cheek. 'Get some sleep, Edward. I'll see myself home.'

A couple of days later Edward telephoned Morgan and proposed that they meet for a drink; Morgan said he knew just the place. They met at the Flood Building after work and made their way up Market Street to the edge of the Tenderloin. At the Taylor Street corner Morgan stopped at a service door with the number 65 above it, and after issuing a staccato rap – six knocks followed by five – the door opened and an old man gnawing on a cigar ushered them in. Edward followed

Morgan down to the basement, a lively room full of merchant seamen, with throw rugs that smelled of mildew and snappy ragtime music coming from a player piano in the corner. The bar consisted of a mahogany plank laid across wine barrels.

'The usual, Clem,' Morgan said to the barkeep, 'and a high-ball for my friend.'

Where the sailors would spike Acme near-beer with grain alcohol, Morgan preferred spiking grain alcohol with "Lime Rickey" soda pop. 'A poor man's Tom-Collins,' he called it, before assuring Edward that the whiskey he'd ordered was the same being poured at the upscale speakeasies.

After clinking glasses, Edward said above the noise, 'I'm sorry for leaving abruptly the other night, Morgan – I hope it didn't cause a fuss.'

'No, not at all,' Morgan lied, recalling his mother in high dudgeon the morning after. 'I thought it was a rather daring escape, myself…'

'I feel so bad for Constance – I suppose she's told you?'

'Didn't come as a complete surprise, if that's any consolation,' Morgan replied, lighting a cigarette and offering one to Edward, who accepted. 'From what I can tell, you two have been going in different directions for a while now…With you on the road so much, who knows where or when you'll settle down.' Smiling to someone in the crowd, he added, 'I'm sure she'd rather stay put here in San Francisco, anyhow.'

Edward nodded, surprised how pragmatic it sounded, then pursed his lips. 'But I do feel bad, breaking off the engagement after all this time. I feel I've let your whole family down.'

Morgan patted Edward's arm. 'Don't you worry about that – Mother always rides to the rescue where Constance is concerned. And maybe in time my sister will see that it's better this way. In any event, I'm glad you called,' he said, his hand on Edward's forearm as he hailed the barkeep for another round, then looking to Edward intently, 'and that we can still be friends…'

It was late August before Edward informed his parents that he'd broken off his engagement to Constance. When his abrupt announcement at the end of Sunday dinner was met with stunned silence, by way of explanation he added, 'Truth be told, we've been going in different directions for a while now…'

'What the devil is that supposed to mean, Edward?' Honora said, incredulous. 'You're to be married and then you'll settle down. That's always been the plan.'

Katherine lingered at the sink, hanging on every word, but Edward only shook his head. 'I'm afraid not, Mother.'

Mr. Dooley looked up with a sad smile. 'I'm sorry, son.'

'Sorry?!' Honora boomed, causing Katherine to fumble some cutlery. 'This is a disaster and all you've got to say is "sorry"?' With a contemptuous shudder, she said, 'Now, Edward, you've got to rectify this immediately…What is it she wants, anyway?'

'It's not what she *wants*, Mother – we're just not suited to each other, that's all.'

'Ridiculous! Listen, she'll do very well by you, Edward – you'll be a credit to the Dohertys, a hard-working, upstanding young man…a war hero.' She cast her eyes about, muttering to herself, 'I don't care how respectable they think they are…'

Disgusted, Edward said, 'Have you ever thought that maybe it's not what *I* want, Mother?'

'Hah!' Honora laughed at the idiocy of this statement. 'Mark my words, you're making a serious mistake. Now go home and get some rest and tomorrow you tell Mr. Breslin that all this travel has worn you down. You're not thinking straight, Edward. Don't be a fool!'

By early September, eight weeks since the calamitous July 4th episode, Edward was worn down by his own vacillating. The longer he went without speaking to Constance, the easier it became; on the other hand, he regretted hurting her – they'd been friends for so long and had shared so many good times together that it seemed callous of him to suddenly go silent. He liked to consider himself a gentleman and agonized over how he might have handled the situation better. Though he knew in his heart that it would have been disingenuous to lead her on any longer, he could understand how from her perspective the breakup had come as a shock.

So with her birthday fast approaching – September 4th would be a Sunday, normally their day together – he spent several anguished evenings composing a letter which he carefully transcribed onto a card and posted at the end of the week,

September 1st

My Dear Constance,

I can only imagine how difficult these passed two months have been for you. I want you to know that I care for you deeply and hope that I have not squandered our friendship which means the world to me.

I am at your disposal if you care to talk. In the meantime, please know that I am thinking of you on your special day.

Yours affectionately,
Edward

Chapter 25

Edward did eventually speak with Mr. Breslin as Honora had insisted, though the conversation wasn't what she'd had in mind. The bulldog of a man pulled Edward into his office one afternoon in mid-September to say that Dowling in Los Angeles had just blown up a deal with an important broker. He lit a cigarette and explained how the salesman had disappointed him twice before – once when Dowling's drinking had spoiled relations with a top customer, another time when a prominent ladies' undergarments manufacturer detected a whiff of anti-Semitism.

'The garment trade's incestuous, Eddie,' Breslin explained. 'Family connections between manufacturers and distributors mean people have a pretty good idea what to expect before a particular salesman even steps through the door. And now the dumb bastard's gone and made a stupid remark about the broker's daughter!'

When Edward asked how he could help, Breslin eyed him gravely and stepped in close. His breath sour, he gripped Edward's forearm, and said, 'I need you down there full time, Eddie – whatever it takes, I'll make it worth your while...' He brought his hands to his hips and began pacing the room, speaking to the floor. 'Now from what you've told me, I get the impression you and your sweetheart are through...but I'm just not sure how you'd feel being so far away from your family...'

When Breslin looked over he was surprised to find a conspiratorial smile on Edward's lips. 'On the other hand, maybe that wouldn't be so bad after all, eh?' His hunch confirmed, he came over and shook his protégé's hand gratefully and slapped him on the back. Then with a lecherous grin, he added, 'You'd better watch yourself down there, Eddie – I hear the City of Angels is pretty wild these days…'

Unbeknownst to Breslin, Edward had already developed a taste for furtive adventure following his breakup with Constance. Saturday evenings had become a standing occasion for dates with Angela – after visiting Fitz, they'd walk up Polk Street and go to the picture show at the Royal Theater, then he'd take her to dinner and walk her home to her rooming house.

Angela preferred dramas and romance pictures, and they especially enjoyed two Alice Terry films where she played opposite Valentino. Their love for each other proves invincible in *The Conquering Power*, despite having been thwarted initially by her mad stepfather. In *The Four Horsemen of the Apocalypse*, the Great War itself forms the backdrop a poignant love triangle where Terry, unhappily married to an older man, falls in love with a dancer in Paris. When the affair is discovered, her husband gallantly agrees to a divorce, but, alas, true love is foiled by the outbreak of war: the dancer is killed in combat and returns as a spirit when the war is over, urging his lover to remain loyal to her gravely wounded husband.

Edward and Angela saw *The Four Horsemen* a second time on the Saturday after Edward's startling encounter with Mr. Breslin. At dinner afterward, mulling over the implications of his relocating to Los Angeles, Edward asked Angela whether it had been difficult for her to move away from her family.

'It was time for me to go,' she said simply.

'You and your father didn't see eye-to-eye.'

She slipped his gaze and looked to the side. 'I wanted to be a nurse and do my part.'

'That's to your credit,' he said, returning to his meal. Lost in thought a minute, he mused, 'How I managed to survive the war I'll never know, but, whatever happens, I wouldn't want to lose touch with Fitz…'

'You won't,' Angela assured him. 'Trust yourself, Edward. It may not be as often, but you'll see him whenever you're back in San Francisco. I know you.'

Edward offered a faint smile, then to avoid becoming maudlin, he said, 'So, Nurse Luchetti, how do you think I'd do as a tango dancer?' referring to Valentino's sultry performance in the picture they'd just seen.

Angela laughed. 'I can't quite see you in gaucho pants, if that's what you mean…'

His mouth went wide in mock surprise. 'I'll have you know that even with my bum knee, I'm pretty light on my feet…In fact, I intend to prove it to you sometime.'

'Oh, really?' she said with a naughty grin, 'How about tonight?'

After dinner they walked up the street to the Fairmont Hotel where Paul Whiteman's Band happened to be playing the Cirque Lounge that evening. With the days of the waltz and the two-step fading fast, Edward and Angela happily joined the crowd dancing the fox-trot – everything from Whiteman's "Wang Wang Blues" to Eubie Blake's "I'm Just Wild About Harry." They proved a capable match on the dance floor, notwithstanding Edward's comical attempt at the tango when the "The Sheik of Araby" started up.

At two in the morning, with "Kitten on the Keys" echoing in their ears, they returned to Edward's apartment – Walter was away at a bond brokers' convention – where after a highball Edward impetuously kissed Angela on the lips and she promptly kissed him back.

It was breathtakingly unfamiliar territory for them both. Pulling off their clothes, they fell into each other's arms, Angela trembling at the feel of his hands cupping her breasts, at the heat of his breath on her neck as she opened up to this uncommonly sensitive man. For his part, Edward felt as though he'd found solid ground at last, free of the pretense he'd associated with romantic love for so long. He could finally be himself and not what someone else wanted him to be, and he nearly wept as she guided him into her.

He awoke first, a foggy Sunday morning, Angela beside him, her auburn hair twirled like a nest over her eyes. For the first time, the studio apartment's sole decoration, an etching of the Brooklyn Bridge that Edward had found at a rummage sale, seemed like a metaphor of his life so far – he'd never noticed the real thing the two times he'd traversed New York Harbor, and yet there it was now, right before his eyes.

When Angela awoke a few minutes later, she saw a far-off look in Edward's eyes. 'Penny for your thoughts,' she said.

He looked over after a moment. 'I was thinking we ought to get married…'

She laughed. 'It was a wonderful evening, Mr. Dooley, but let's not get ahead of ourselves!'

'But we're meant for each other, don't you see?' Edward

246

said excitedly, propping himself up on an elbow. 'We're such a good fit, we balance each other out – God knows I can be a bit wishful at times, and you, you're always so level-headed...'

'It's true I don't go in for rose-colored glasses, if that's what you mean,' Angela said, sitting up and pulling a throw over her shoulders. 'I've seen some bad behavior...'

Edward laid back down and stared at the ceiling. 'I've seen some ugly things myself, but I think it's better to look at life straight on, like you do...'

'What I can't stand is cowardice,' she observed rhetorically.

'Believe me, it's no good pretending bad things don't happen,' he assured her. 'At the same time, I've gotta believe there's hope in the world or else I couldn't go on!'

Angela looked down at him and smiled, for despite her lack of sentimentality she sensed that he would be true to her. 'What's always appealed to me about you, Edward, is that despite all the hypocrisy and injustice out there, you still look for the good in people.' Imagining herself steadfast by his side, she added, 'That's what I love the most about you.'

Certain of her strength, Edward reached up and kissed her. 'I love you, too, Angela.'

Edward and Angela were married at City Hall on October the twenty-first. Witnessing the proceedings were Walter and Colm, Angela's roommates Caroline Sprag and Gracie Taub, and Fitz, who, at the insistence of bride and groom, wore no prosthetic mask. Of all the pictures taken at the Polk Street portrait studio that day, the newlyweds' favorite would be the one where everyone is caught in a laugh, Gracie and Caroline on the left, Walter and Colm on the right, Angela and Edward in the middle, each with a hand on Fitz's shoulder, who is seated in the center. He'd been in the doldrums recently, ever since Buck Weaver and his White Sox teammates had been banned from baseball for life, but if his war wounds made it difficult to muster a smile, the humor in his eyes is unmistakable as he's caught pulling up the cuff of his trousers to reveal black-and-white checkered socks.

The group spent the afternoon in the back booth of a nearby chop house in a swirl of cigarette smoke and raucous laughter. Over seafood and steaks (and soft drinks fortified by Colm's flask), the newlyweds put up with good-natured ribbing about how an earnest, balding stick of a man had managed to win the heart of a Latin goddess. The maids of honor had brought a cake from Blum's for dessert, and by the time coffee was served, Gracie was in a feisty mood. Short and wiry, she liked shaking things up.

'So, what gets your mother more, fellas?' she asked Colm and Walter, bold as brass, 'Edward marrying an Eye-talian or not having a church wedding?'

'To her, the whole thing's an abomination,' Colm snorted.

Walter added, 'She thinks Edward hasn't been the same since his time overseas…'

'Knocked some sense into you, Eddie,' Colm said, 'and we're proud of you for it.'

Edward nodded and turned to Fitz. 'Nobody's the same as before.'

'Nah, but we get by…' the big man said.

Angela reached over and squeezed his forearm. 'No offense to the rest of you people, but when we move to Los Angeles, we're going to miss you most of all, Fitz.'

'True enough,' Edward said.

Gracie lit a cigarette. 'You go back down Monday, eh, Edward?'

He pursed his lips and nodded. 'My predecessor's dumped everything in my lap.'

'Well, listen,' Gracie said, 'I know you think your job is your top priority, but you'd better find a nice place for Angela. She's had enough of rooming house life...'

Edward smiled. 'Don't worry, I'm looking into it...'

'We've had enough of it ourselves, as a matter of fact,' Caroline put in brightly, taking Gracie's hand in hers. Caroline had soft eyes and a lovely complexion, which took on a hint of pink as she explained, 'We're going to rent a cottage of our own out in the Western Addition.'

Congratulations bubbled up around the table and Walter said, 'You know, you'll be able to walk to Letterman like I used to during the war – just up Presidio Ave to the gate and—'

'—and straight down "Lover's Lane,"' Colm said with a knowing grin.

'I like the sound of that,' Gracie said to Colm with a mixture of defiance and satisfaction. Colm nodded, as if to a worthy adversary.

'Guess it's as good a time as any,' Fitz said, pulling a fifth of Scotch from Gracie's bag and handing it to Colm to open. When everyone had been served, Fitz held up his glass. 'I was gonna say to Eddie and Angela that I can't think of two people who deserve each other more, but then,' tilting his head to Gracie and Caroline, 'maybe I oughta rethink that...'

Chapter 26

The next two months were a whirlwind with Edward spending weekends with Angela, then taking the overnight train to Los Angeles on Sundays. During the week, when he wasn't mending fences with customers in the downtown office blocks and garment factories, he was frequenting the various newsstands, cafeterias, and cigar shops; familiarizing himself the vaudeville theaters and movie palaces; learning where the high- and low-class speakeasies were and where one could discreetly buy a bottle of whiskey. He got in the habit of sitting in Pershing Square to read the newspaper and watch the Biltmore Hotel going up; sometimes after work he'd ride the streetcars out to see Boyle Heights or Echo Park, Montecito, the Crenshaw district.

Angela came down on Friday, the twenty-third of December, and the two spent a delightful weekend at the handsome Hotel Lankershim at 7th and Broadway. Christmas Eve was balmy as they took in the winter scenes in Bullock's display windows. At J.J. Newberry's he bought her a hand-embroidered voile frock for a Christmas present, then over patty melts and milkshakes at Van De Kamp's Cafeteria he playfully lamented the flapper fashions that required women to flatten their breasts and hide their hips. After lunch they took the streetcar out to a splendid park with a freshwater lake, complete with white swans and couples in canoes. A brass band played ragtime music in a gazebo, and Edward pointed out the facades of Westlake's fashionable apartment buildings peaking over the jacaranda trees and Canary Island Palms.

He led Angela through the park and up a side street to a small apartment building with Moorish accents where he buzzed the manager. 'I thought you might like to see our new apartment,' he said to Angela, 'though I'm afraid it won't be ready for another week…'

Mr. Olson was a pudgy man who reeked of Vitalis hair tonic. They followed him upstairs to a one-bedroom unit, currently being repainted, where he pointed out various modern amenities like a tub-shower in the bathroom and an icebox in the kitchen. After explaining that the ice box was restocked twice a week, he said to Angela, 'So, Mr. Dooley tells me you're Roman Catholics…'

She smiled and nodded, and Edward hastened to say, 'I've been over to see Fr. O'Halloran at Church of the Precious Blood, in fact.' Turning to Angela, he added, 'That's the new parish in the neighborhood.' She raised her eyebrows, amused by his alacrity.

'Mrs. Olson and I, we were raised Lutheran,' the manager explained, 'but coming to California has given us a new perspective on things. You two might like to attend one of Sister Aimee's faith-healing revivals with us sometime at the Foursquare Gospel Church.'

'Oh, well, we're creatures of habit…' Angela demurred.

'Not that we go in for quackery, you understand,' Mr. Olson said. 'You do get all kinds here in Los Angeles…Take the movie people, fr'instance. Now don't get me wrong, Mrs. Olson and I enjoy a light-hearted Chaplin picture just like everybody else, but there's some in that business who'll do anything for money and, frankly, it's breaking down the moral fiber...'

Angela put on a benign smile and squeezed Edward's hand.

'Take that Arbuckle fellow, fr'instance,' Mr. Olson went on, 'What he supposedly did to that girl up in 'Frisco,' he said, referring to newspaper stories of a lurid scandal at the St. Francis Hotel, "—well, it's deplorable is what it is, thinkin' he's above the law!'

As dubious as the stories seemed to Edward and Angela, Edward shook his head and Angela nodded gravely as if to confirm just how sound the manager's judgment was. With a resigned sigh they said their goodbyes, but Mr. Olson trailed after them, adding, 'If there's one problem with this town, it's the Hebrew element behind the pictures nowadays. Nothing's off-limits with those people, whether it's glorifying the movie stars or promoting "free love" in the magazines. I'm telling you, folks, you can't be too careful …'

Edward and Angela spent Christmas at the Santa Monica Pier, where cut-outs of reindeer and wise men with candy canes for staffs flanked the entrance to the Hippodrome Building. The pine scent of the Christmas tree was overwhelmed by the smells of sea air and hot buttered popcorn, and children squealed with glee on the merry-go-round while an old man in a Santa cap played carols on the Wurlitzer. The newlyweds laughed at themselves in the funhouse mirrors, rode the Whip three times, ate hot dogs and Cracker Jack, and walked barefoot in the sand.

In a seaside restaurant at the end of the day, Angela reached across the table and took Edward's hand. 'It's been quite a Christmas, Mr. Dooley – you sure know how to sweep a girl off her feet.'

'Oh, call me Edward, please,' he said with a grin, raising his glass of ginger ale. 'Here's to all the fun ahead in our life together!' They leaned in and kissed.

A few minutes later Edward was squeezing lemon juice over his shrimp salad when he said, 'Why don't you skip the trip to Stockton tomorrow, Angela – we can go up together next month so I can talk to your father man to man.'

Angela smiled. 'No, Edward, now don't worry. It has nothing to do with whether I married an Italian boy or not – he didn't like it when I moved away in the first place…'

'Well, how about your mother? I'm worried she might think she's losing you…'

'You're sweet,' she said, stroking his cheek. 'I'll let Mama know how you feel, and Giancarlo, too. And, who knows, maybe my father will come around…'

A week later Angela returned from Stockton with a trunk full of clothes and a watercolor landscape she'd done as a girl – asparagus fields in the foreground, the Sierra foothills in the distance – which Edward insisted on putting above their kitchen table. For New Year's Eve, after a candlelit dinner at home of overcooked game hen and undercooked turnips, they danced in 1922 to the sounds of the Abe Lyman Orchestra at The Piccadilly Hotel.

Over the next few weeks Angela acquainted herself with the burgeoning Mid-Wilshire district, getting to know the butchers and produce vendors, the cobbler and the Five-and-Ten. Twice a week she'd take the streetcar downtown to meet Edward for dinner and a show at one of the opulent movie palaces on

Broadway. Alice Terry's latest picture, *The Prisoner of Zenda*, had generated lots of buzz in the Hollywood press when it was discovered that while making the film she and her recently divorced director Rex Ingram had run off to Pasadena to get married.

The impetuous betrothal struck a sympathetic chord in Edward and Angela – and prompted an acerbic letter from Morgan which left Edward thoroughly baffled:

My dear Edward,

I must admit I was confounded by your clandestine departure in October. Only now it dawns on me – what with news of Miss Terry's scandalous affair and Mr. Arbuckle banned from pictures for life – that fickle morality drove you to make such a precipitous choice, then escape to the "City of Angels" of all places. Bravo, Old Chum, I didn't know you had it in you!

Not calling me was quite thoughtless of you, however – to say nothing of your callous disregard for the feelings of my poor, inno-cent sister. In fact, you left me no choice but to console her with another verse of the very Housman ode I quoted you two at the Victory Ball all those years ago:

> *Some lads there are, 'tis shame to say,*
> *That only court to thieve,*
> *And once they bear the bloom away*
> *'Tis little enough they leave.*

In case you're wondering, I prevailed upon Walter for your address in hopes that once the sting of shame has subsided you will reconnect with your oldest, dearest friend.

    Yours in depravity,

    Morgan

Chapter 27

Edward was meticulous about his clothing, as proper attire was considered a businessman's calling card, particularly in the garment trade. He maintained an assortment of suits and hats appropriate to every season – nothing ostentatious, just practical and of the highest quality. He had chosen the Park View Apartments for the ample closet space, and over time saw to it that Angela, too, had a variety of frocks to choose from, with hats to match – light bonnets for outdoor leisure, crocheted cloche hats for going to town, even a silk headdress for formal affairs. Though never one to put on airs, Edward took pride in the knowledge that his clothing was reflective of his good comportment; for her part, Angela appreciated the quality of her growing wardrobe, something she could only dream about as a girl growing up in Stockton.

Since the turn of the century, New York City had been the epicenter of the country's apparel industry with a labor pool comprised predominantly of Jewish immigrants from Eastern Europe. By the 1920s, Los Angeles saw a significant influx of secular, Yiddish-speaking Jews transplanted from New York – first in the film industry, but increasingly in the textile trades as well. So when Harry Breitstein telephoned one day to invite Edward to lunch, Edward couldn't believe his luck: Breitstein was a key broker between major clothing manufacturers, wholesalers, and retailers in the city.

But as Edward approached the storefront restaurant on South Spring Street (in a modest, three-story building that looked like a throw-back to the horse-and-buggy days) he grew doubtful that this would be the high-end meeting he'd imagined. He entered the dingy restaurant and a heavyset man with unruly gray hair beckoned to him from a corner table.

'Dooley!' the man exclaimed, not getting up. He wiped his mouth with a napkin in his right hand, precluding a hand-shake, and with his left gestured to the seat across from him.

'You did say noon, didn't you, Mr. Breitstein?'

'Sure, sure,' the big man said, buttering a roll. Edward sat down and pulled a menu from the stack propped up between jars of condiments. 'Ach! Don't bother with that,' Breitstein grunted as he slurped his chicken soup, 'I've taken the liberty...'

An old waiter in an apron appeared with a plate that featured two slabs of a white gelatinous substance, with carrot slices and a piece of iceberg lettuce for garnish. Edward gulped, but with the big man looking on, he was compelled to try it. The slimy texture was unlike anything he'd ever tasted, and it was all he could do to suppress his gag reflex.

'Here,' Breitstein said, opening a condiment jar and spreading a forkful of its contents onto Edward's plate, 'Gefilte fish can be kinda bland– try it with horseradish.' Choking down another bite, Edward's sinuses caught fire, his eyes began to water, and he gasped for breath. The big man roared with laughter, then, pouring Edward a glass of water, he said to the waiter, 'Sol, bring the kid a creme soda and some soup, will ya?'

Edward blew his nose while Breitstein explained that he'd worked in San Francisco for years and had always considered Cecil Breslin a straight shooter. 'He asked me to keep an eye on you while you made the rounds here,' the big man said. 'You're a hard worker, Dooley—earnest as all get out, but that's not so bad. Sure beats the guy over at Coats & Clark...'

'Well, thank you, Mr. Breitstein.'

The big man smiled, seeing his instincts were right. 'I cover everything west of Denver, Dooley, and I can tell you that with all the new department stores coming on line here there'll be lots merchandise to move.' The waiter reappeared with a platter of what Edward recognized with relief as corned beef, along with a bowl of steamed spinach and a plate of dumplings.

'Suppose you heard about the exclusive I got for Hickey-Freeman over at Bullock's,' Breitstein continued as he ladled a massive serving onto Edward's plate. 'Now, Hickey can afford to pass along the shipping cost of their suits, but they're the exception. What we need out here in Los Angeles is more manufacturing, for Chrissakes!'

In the course of lunch, Breitstein rattled off the names of a number of several local up-and-coming manufacturers and wholesalers and encouraged Edward to introduce himself. 'Tell 'em you and I have talked' he said, and Edward nodded gratefully.

They were sipping coffee when a young man walked in and ordered a sandwich to go. 'Nathan!' Breitstein shouted, 'I wanna introduce you to somebody.'

Nathan Leopold was as tall as Edward, with black hair, full eyebrows, and a square jaw. As the two shook hands, Breitstein said, 'Eddie here's with American Thread – supplies both Joe Zukin and Max Marks,' high praise, given that the two women's wear manufacturers were fierce competitors. 'Nathan came out from Cleveland a year ago – from Joseph & Feiss.' The name of the high-end men's clothier wasn't lost on Edward, and the two exchanged business cards before Nathan gave the big man a meaningful nod and returned to the counter for his sandwich.

'He's got fire in his belly,' Breitstein said as they watched Leopold leave the restaurant. 'Nothing motivates a man like revenge.'

With manufacturing in residential buildings outlawed in New York City in the first decade of the century, and big department stores relocating uptown in the second, a "garment district" sprung up in the 1920s on the blocks north of 35th Street and west of Fifth Avenue. During the same period, dozens of high-rise commercial lofts also went up in Los Angeles, making it the largest garment district west of Chicago. One morning a couple of weeks after having lunch with Breitstein, Edward called on Nathan Leopold at one of these factories.

Located on the eighth floor, the factory employed a hundred people: rows of men and women seated across from each other at sewing machines, with piles of partially finished garments between them. The room was stifling hot and Edward found Leopold in a glassed-in office at the far end where he and two other managers sat at desks overflowing with orders. Edward had started to unpack his spool kit and color card binder when Leopold suggested they go downstairs where it was quieter.

Over coffee and crullers at a Boos Brothers Cafeteria, Leopold preempted Edward's pitch with a wave of his hand. 'Harry tells me you've been in the trade since before the war…'

Edward nodded. 'And he said you were with Joseph & Feiss, only your card says Brownstein & Louis.'

'Brownstein's the son-in-law of Moritz Joseph,' Leopold said, sipping his coffee. 'We sell Joseph & Feiss merchandise under the B & L label – but you're not supposed to know that.'

'Oh.'

'I grew up in Rochester, see, and in '08 my father's firm, Beckel, Baum & Leopold, merged with Hickey-Freeman. It was going swell until Jacob Baum decided to ice my father out. I was at Camp Dix when my father died of a heart attack, and Baum assured my mother he'd pull some strings to get me stationed stateside – but the bastard never did a goddamn thing.'

Leopold produced a pack of cigarettes, lit one and pushed the pack across to Edward. 'So, on the introduction of a cousin, I went to Cleveland after the war where Joseph & Feiss was building a big factory to go head-to-head with Hickey. Hickey doesn't advertise nationally – they offer their wares to only one retailer per region. It's their Achilles' heel…'

He exhaled a stream of smoke. 'I'm glad for Harry but his deal won't last. We're gonna clean up out here before Hickey-Freeman figures out what they've missed…'

'Sounds like dog-eat-dog, alright,' Edward said, 'but why tell *me*?'

Leopold cracked a thin smile. 'You want to know why, Dooley?' he said, taking a drag of his cigarette, 'Because I think I can trust you…'

'Well, look,' Edward began, 'Coats has had a lock on Joseph & Feiss for years now…'

'That's true, there's no chance they'll change suppliers. And it's ironic that American Thread supplies Hickey-Freeman when they're the ones I want to beat.' Edward looked bemused until Leopold said with a grin, 'Don't worry, Dooley – you pitch me a fair price and I'll see that Brownstein goes with American – along with Smith-Reddick, Cohn-Goldwater, Rosenblum, and all the others who plan on giving the Rochester boys a run for their money…'

'Okay,' Edward said with apprehension, 'but what's the angle? What's in it for you?'

Leopold glanced left and right, then said, 'You're an honest man, I suppose.'

Edward had heard about kickbacks, but knew the downside outweighed any remuneration he might expect. He also resented the implication – coming from a fellow veteran of the Great War, no less – that honesty was nothing more than pretense. Stubbing out his cigarette, he said, 'You can count on it.'

Leopold laughed and held up both hands. 'Listen, Dooley, I'm not interested in anything untoward, believe me. I need someone I can trust, someone who sells a quality product and whose integrity is unquestioned. But if I'm gonna make inroads with the top retailers out here, I'm gonna need a good partner – an upstanding "goy" – or I'll never get passed second base.'

Indeed, Leopold and Dooley made a formidable team, successfully pitching production houses and buyers at the leading department stores. The two men got to be friends. Edward envied Nathan's education – he'd put in two years of college before being drafted – and Nathan, who'd served in the 78th Infantry during the final phase of the Meuse-Argonne offensive, was impressed to learn that Edward had been in the vanguard of the assault a month earlier. "V Corps – Tip of the Spear, Edge of the Knife!" he'd say from time to time by way of a compliment.

Nathan's blunt assessments had a big effect on Edward. One day after they'd had an unpleasant encounter with a purveyor of misses' sweaters, Nathan said, 'The old guard's Protestant, Ed, and don't you forget it. What do the Annandale, the Brentwood, and L.A. Country Clubs all have in common? No Jews, that's what.' Another time when Edward remarked on the meager presence of the Ladies' Garment Workers Union in Los Angeles, Leopold explained, 'The *Times* speaks for business interests here, Ed. Harrison Gray Otis himself made sure this would be an open shop town ten years ago when he orchestrated the bombing of his own goddamn building and then delivered up the McNamara brothers as rabid anarchists...'

The first time Edward invited Leopold over to dinner – he was a bachelor living in the West Pico-Wilshire district – it didn't take him long to launch into a diatribe, just as Edward had predicted to Angela. According to Leopold, the pioneering German Jewish aristocracy that dated back to the Gold Rush in San Francisco and Los Angeles regarded the newcomers as uncouth hicks from Eastern Europe. 'It's not the new money they mind, they just don't like you flaunting it 'cause it rankles the WASPs they rub shoulders with. That's why they can't stand the guys in the movie business,' he said, then with a wink to Edward, 'which is why we in the textile trade like keeping a low profile.'

'Always best to be discreet,' Angela observed.

Leopold smiled. 'The irony is that the two industries go hand and hand – Sam Goldwyn was a gloves salesman, Louis Mayer dealt in used clothing, Adolph Zukor sold furs. They just had bigger ambitions is all!'

Edward sent a portion of his paycheck home every two weeks in posts addressed to his father, with nary a mention of Honora. It was Edward's sisters who orchestrated the peace. They arranged a dinner party at a restaurant for their father's sixtieth birthday, including a fiddler and an Irish tenor, and got their mother to believe that Old Man McCormick wouldn't miss it for the world, even though he was in his eighties and in no condition to go. When Edward arrived and took the empty seat beside her, Honora was overcome with emotion and a grand evening was had by all. Thereafter, whenever Edward came to town for a monthly staff meeting, he would have dinner at the family flat. On one such occasion, Katherine answered the telephone and after some excitable chatter she returned to the kitchen to say it was Angela on the line.

'Angela, what a surprise!' Edward said from the telephone alcove in the hallway.

'I gather from your sister that you've spilled the beans already, Edward?'

'I know, I'm sorry. It just sort of slipped out!'

'We agreed to hold off until after the first trimester,' Angela said, adding with a sigh, 'but we can talk about it when you get back. The reason I'm calling is that I just got a telephone call myself – from Morgan, of all people, saying that Fitz has been arrested.'

'Arrested?! For what?'

'Morgan wasn't sure exactly. Somebody at The Senate got in touch with him.'

'Leave it to Fitz to find a way to get us back together, eh?' Morgan said brightly as he greeted Edward later that evening in the empty lobby of the Hall of Justice.

Edward was wary of his friend's cheeriness: he hadn't contacted him after the baffling letter he'd received, and now wondered whether Morgan took perverse satisfaction in Fitz's misfortune. 'How're things with you, Morgan?' Edward said, cautiously shaking hands.

'Oh, I can't complain. Business is booming – about to close a deal with a fellow named Smith, a hotelier who's building a lot of new hotels up and down the state.'

'Good for you. And Constance?'

'As you might expect – still a bit petulant.' They sat down on a bench across from the reception counter. 'Mother's got her busy in the Junior League these days, to keep up her social contacts…'

Edward offered a resigned smile. 'I'm sure I was persona non-grata with you all after eloping and that your mother's done her best to purge me from the family memory.'

Morgan raised his eyebrows. 'You don't come up in dinner table conversation, if that's what you mean. Anyhow, in time they'll see it's all for the best…' Patting Edward's arm, he said with a chuckle, 'Try as you might, you haven't burned your bridge with me! It's good to see you, although I don't know whether it's marriage or work, but you *are* looking a bit tired…' When Edward regarded him curiously, he continued, 'We ought to get together whenever you're up here for your staff meetings – take the edge off, you know…'

'Yeah, well, for now,' Edward said seriously, 'tell me about Fitz's situation.'

Morgan explained that the previous afternoon Fitz supposedly had groped a debutante coming out of the St. Francis and was facing charges of assault and public intoxication.

Edward grimaced. 'Sounds hard to believe.'

'Exactly,' Morgan said, 'so my father put a call in to the Public Defender today – a good man, born and raised here, his brother's a priest…'

'But you haven't talked to Fitz yet?'

'No, but we can see him together now.'

They waited in a basement office, where eventually Fitz was ushered in. He looked disheveled, his left wrist was cuffed to his belt and a scrape on his left cheek indicating that he'd been roughed up at the time of his arrest. Tired and sullen, he slumped into the chair across from Edward and Morgan.

'How're you getting on then, Fitz?' Edward asked. 'They looking after you okay?'

With a curt nod, he said, 'Ever since Egan showed up.'

'Egan?' Edward recalled the name from the time of Colm's arrest, and turning to Morgan, he said, 'Timothy Egan's the Public Defender now?'

'Since last year,' Morgan said, 'My father supported his campaign.'

'I don't need any favors,' Fitz growled.

'It'll help, believe me,' Morgan assured him. 'The girl's from a high-powered family.'

'Tell us what happened, Fitz,' Edward said.

'Nothing happened,' the big man snapped, '—that's the short of it. Minding my own business, sitting on a bench in Union Square at the end of a long day.'

Fitz worked for a cobbler on Mason Street, took his meals at diners, and went for a stroll in the evenings for some air. Edward had accompanied him once and was impressed by how deferential the shopkeepers in the neighborhood were to his friend. 'But you had an exchange with a young woman?' Edward asked now.

'Yeah, I helped her up.'

'What do you mean?'

'She takes a spill, see, so I go to help her and when she looks up she gets hysterical.'

'Were there a lot of people around?'

'Not at first. But then a crowd gathers when she starts pointing at me.'

'What happened then?'

'A cop rushes over and the next thing you know I'm in here…'

'Sounds straightforward enough,' Edward said, turning to Morgan. 'She got embarrassed, that's all. Egan can tell the judge and they'll drop the charges.'

'I can tell the judge myself,' Fitz said irritably.

'Egan knows the judge, though,' Morgan said. 'He can vouch for your character.'

'I don't know Egan – what's he know about my character?'

'Trust me, Fitz. It's the way the system works.'

Morgan was caught off guard when Constance telephoned him at the office the next morning. Having learned from their father that Morgan had seen Edward at the Hall of Justice the night before, she quipped, 'Was he turning himself in for being a cad?'

'Yeah, Sis, he's aged thirty years and wears a hangdog expression now...'

'It's all a game with you, isn't it, Morgan? I bet you just wanted to see Edward again.' Hearing nothing, she said derisively, 'Having Daddy call in a favor for someone you only mention once in a blue moon...Do you have any idea who Abigail Merriweather MacKay is?'

'An American princess, I'm sure.'

'Don't be funny – I've nearly been accosted by the beggars in Union Square myself!'

'You're a princess, too, I suppose...'

'You can go to hell, Morgan!' she hissed. 'I'm going to talk to Father about this. We don't know anything about that Fitz character these days and I'll bet—'

But Morgan slammed the receiver down on its hook.

Edward extended his trip by a day in order to join Fitz in a meeting with the Public Defender that afternoon (Morgan called to beg off, citing an emergency at work.) Edward and Fitz hadn't managed to say three words to each other when Timothy Egan strode into the basement office. Making no eye contact, he dropped a folder and a large book on the table.

'I'll be honest with you, Mr. Fitzsimmons,' he said, taking a seat, 'the circumstances of the encounter are dubious.'

Two nights in a dank jail cell hadn't improved Fitz's mood. 'I can't sit on a park bench?'

'Trouble is, you touched a lady.'

'She tripped.'

'So you say. The family's attorney claims witnesses will testify that you pulled her down.'

'Bullshit.'

Edward introduced himself, trying to cover for the profanity, then said to Fitz, 'He's just playing devil's advocate – hear him out.'

'In front of a judge,' Egan went on, 'her word will count for more than yours.'

Fitz grumbled.

'I'll make a case for your character,' Egan said, flipping through the folder, '30th Infantry – "San Francisco's Own"... quite the ballplayer once, if memory serves...gainfully employed now. I can explain your speech is slurred on account of the injuries you sustained overseas...'

Sensing doom, Fitz said, 'But?'

'Yes, I'm afraid there is a "but." The fact is, we have to give their attorney something – in the spirit of compromise...'

'Compromise?!' Edward blurted out.

'Can't help the timing,' Egan said, sizing up Edward. 'They're pushing to clean up the shopping district, see, and the Chief's been told to demonstrate aggressive enforcement.'

'So this is what you get for serving your country...' Edward said sarcastically.

'Dooley you said your name was? Any relation to Colm Dooley?'

'My brother, why?'

'I recall the Chief taking me aside up a couple of years ago to say we needed to go easy on him, even though he was nothing but a hothead.' Egan raised his head challengingly.

Edward swallowed. 'Now listen, Mr. Egan, Fitz here is no bum – you said as much yourself.'

'What compromise?' Fitz asked flatly.

'A plea, Mr. Fitzsimmons – to a lesser charge.'

'A plea,' Edward repeated.

'Here's the civil code.' Egan push the book over to Edward. 'Look up Order 783.'

Quickly skimming the entry, Edward said, 'But this is all about beggars displaying deformities to elicit sympathy...You'd have my friend cop to begging, Mr. Egan?'

'Watch your tone, Dooley,' Egan said. 'Their attorney's got us here. It's been on the books since Gold Rush times. Read Section 3 for us.'

Edward found the section and read aloud:

Any person who is diseased, maimed, mutilated, or in any way deformed so as to be an unsightly or disgusting object, or an improper person to be allowed in or on the streets, highways, thoroughfares or public places in the City and County of San Francisco, shall not therein or thereon expose himself or herself to public view.

Fitz broke the ominous silence that followed. 'Guilty as charged...for being ugly.'

'Six months jail time and a fifty-dollar fine,' Egan said.

Incredulous, Edward said, 'But don't you have an obligation to fight injustice like this?'

'My hands are tied,' Egan said succinctly. 'It's our bad luck that Miss MacKay tripped in front of you, Mr. Fitzsimmons, but there's the law. I'm only able to stick my neck out so far. You do the time and I'll see that the fine is paid.'

Edward was stunned.

'From the looks of the scoreboard, Eddie,' Fitz said, struggling to his feet, 'the game's over…'

Chapter 29

Angela suffered a miscarriage in November. She'd been able to conceal the bad cramping in the early months of her pregnancy, until one Wednesday morning. Edward's secretary managed to reach him at a coat factory where he and Nathan Leopold were making a presentation, but when Edward's telephone calls went unanswered, he hailed a cab and hurried home. He found Angela sitting ashen faced at the kitchen table, a tiny bundle in her lap, muttering the words, 'I thought I could be stronger, I thought I could be stronger...'

They brought the fetus to Los Angeles General, where Angela was admitted and cared for by the Daughters of Charity for several days. Before she was discharged, her doctor pulled Edward aside to say that uterine scarring might have contributed to the miscarriage. Edward wasn't knowledgeable about gynecological matters and suspected that perhaps a childhood illness was to blame. When he asked whether future pregnancies would be similarly compromised, the doctor told him it was hard to say. (It was several weeks before Edward broached the subject of a childless marriage with Angela – which she dismissed as needless worry, so committed was she to a new diet and exercise regimen to build her strength.)

Thanksgiving in Stockton was a bleak affair. Angela spent most of the time with her mother crying in the kitchen, and little was said at meals. Edward ran errands with Giancarlo, and felt especially bad for his father-in-law, to whom Angela barely said a word.

In mid-December Angela insisted that she and Edward spend Christmas in San Francisco as planned. Katherine immediately set to work refurbishing the rear bedroom upstairs in the Dooley flat that had been Aunt Mildred's before she passed a couple of years earlier. Because Honora had only met Angela in passing when she'd stopped by with Edward one Saturday after visiting Fitz, the family was on pins and needles when the couple arrived Christmas Eve. At supper, when the turkey had been carved and the platters and serving bowls were making the rounds, Honora addressed the guest of honor across from her.

'Edward says you've been thinking of volunteering at the Old Soldiers Home?'

'Yes, that's true,' Angela said. She'd seen the grounds the first time Edward had taken her to the seaside – hundreds of acres of manicured lawns and palm trees just east of Santa Monica. 'There are about a thousand veterans in residence there,' she explained, '—those with no family to speak of, and those who require special attention. I imagine it's hard for many of them to accept their new life for what it is…'

This struck Honora as eminently sensible. 'That, indeed, is the crux of it right there,' she said, passing a basket of biscuits to Colm.

Hoping this signaled the harmony everyone hoped for, James Dooley raised his glass to toast the Irish Free State, which had officially come into existence three weeks earlier. After a clinking of glasses, Honora spoke again to Angela as if they were dining alone.

'I've been doing some volunteer work of my own at the St.

Joseph's Orphan Asylum here, you know. So difficult finding homes for all the children...'

Edward looked alarmed, and Walter glanced uneasily at his father and sisters.

'Is that so?' Angela said.

Taking a bite of turkey, Honora went on, 'As you say, the hardest thing is for them to accept their life for what it is—'

'To be hopeful,' Angela said, serving herself green beans, 'and not succumb to doubt.'

'Precisely,' Honora agreed, catching Angela's eye. Then, turning to Edward, she said, 'See that Angela gets some of that relish there – your Aunt Hildie made it.'

The next morning the family was returning from Christmas mass at the cathedral when Honora took hold of Angela's arm as they walked. 'I don't suppose Edward's ever spoken to you about our Baby Mary?' she said, and seeing Angela was puzzled, she continued, 'No, he wouldn't have...' After explaining that the baby had been born between Walter and Edward, and had lasted but three months, she concluded, 'It nearly did my James in, you know – he was so fearful that he'd brought a cold into the house...'

Angela looked up at her mother-in-law. 'I didn't know – I'm sorry.'

'It happens,' Honora said, gazing down Van Ness Avenue. 'I was devastated, of course, particularly with three little ones to look after, but we got through it somehow. The point is,' here she patted Angela's hand, 'we've got to be strong for our men because there's a lot of ground to cover. I can see you're made of strong stuff, so don't despair – you'll be fine.'

Unbeknownst to Constance, the rapprochement between Edward and Morgan that had been occasioned by Fitz's arrest was fully realized over Christmas. Morgan joined Edward and Angela in paying Fitz a visit at the county jail, and after learning of Angela's miscarriage, Morgan was uncharacteristically subdued. Saying their goodbyes later, Morgan choked up and managed to whisper, 'You're a remarkable woman...' Though she'd always regarded Edward's friend as an odd duck, Angela was genuinely touched by his sympathy.

She'd heard about his affinity for Housman from Edward, but Angela nevertheless was surprised to receive a letter from Morgan a week later where he conveyed his condolences for their loss by quoting from *A Shropshire Lad*:

> *With rue my heart is laden*
> *For golden friends I had,*
> *For many a rose-lipt maiden*
> *And many a lightfoot lad.*
>
> *By brooks too broad for leaping*
> *The lightfoot boys are laid;*
> *The rose-lipt girls are sleeping*
> *In fields where roses fade.*

Edward's own grief was compounded when Uncle Aidan died of a broken heart that spring – carried off with the last of the apple blossoms, as Aunt Hildie put it.

Uncle Aidan's death came as a relief for his family because he'd never been the same after the telegram arrived in October 1918, informing them that their son Patrick had been killed in France. Since then, Aidan had hired and fired a succession of farmhands to help tend his beloved orchards, but none of them ever measured up. To the Dooleys, the irony was that Cousin Michael had been so well-suited to the job – before he went off to get an education with the Christian Brothers and ended up joining the order.

The funeral was a particularly bittersweet affair for Edward. Having recently buried a child of his own, he would forever have a heavy heart at the memory of walking with Michael afterward, down the very Gravenstein apple orchard they'd planted as boys.

Chapter 30

On a hot afternoon in August, Angela answered the buzzer to the apartment and was astonished to hear Morgan's voice on the intercom saying that he happened to be in the neighborhood. She buzzed him up, and moments later there he was at her door bearing a bouquet of yellow roses.

'Why, look at you!' he exclaimed, pausing at the threshold to unabashedly admire her swelling belly. 'Edward hadn't mentioned *this*.'

'He's keeping his promise this time,' she said, beckoning him in, 'and so should you.'

He kissed her on both cheeks. 'Cross my heart.'

She asked him to make himself comfortable on the couch while she took care of the flowers, but he followed her into the kitchen, which smelled of chicken, tarragon and rosemary.

'Edward doesn't know I've come to Los Angeles,' he said, sitting down at the kitchen table. 'I'm staying over at The Ambassador for a few days and wanted to surprise you both – though it's you I want to speak to first.'

Angela turned from the sink with a quizzical look.

Morgan crossed his legs. 'You're how far along now?'

'Four and a half months.'

'My heartfelt congratulations – I'm so happy for you both.'

Angela put the flowers in a vase, then made up a pitcher of iced tea and a plate of anisette cookies while Morgan explained that he'd promised Fitz he'd look in on his sister.

'She's living in Echo Park now and making a go of things,' Morgan reported. 'In fact, a couple of days ago we went up to Laurel Canyon to see Alice Terry filming a costume drama. It's set during the French Revolution – loads of fun. Alice plays the heroine opposite a dashing young fellow named Ramón Novarro – the next Valentino, they say.'

'My, don't you move in high circles,' Angela said as she came to the table.

'Oh, film people are terribly exciting. What parties they throw!'

'Yes, we read all about it in the tabloids. We even spot a celebrity ourselves once in a while – Wallace Beery lives at The Bryson, just across the way.' Taking a cookie from the plate, she said, 'So tell me, Morgan, why did you want to see me first?'

He sighed. 'I wanted to ask you something – thought it better in person.'

'Oh?'

'It's about my sister, you see. She's rushing into a rather bad marriage, I'm afraid, and I've had an idea that I can't shake.'

'What's that?' Angela said, taking a sip of her iced tea.

Morgan leaned forward and brought his clasped his hands to his lips. 'Edward's been the most genuine friend I've ever had, Angela. We go back a ways, you know.' She nodded. 'At first I didn't like that you took him away from my sister, but then, well…anyhow, it's taken me a while to concede that it was he who found you and not the other way around.'

Angela put down her glass.

'You and I can be frank with one another,' Morgan said. 'I'd never want to interfere, you understand – Edward's friendship means too much to me to lose it again – only my sister's always been a bit foolish, and now she's become headstrong to boot. I don't know whether she's doing it to spite our mother or what, but she seems determined to make a disastrous marriage.'

Fingering the condensation on his glass of tea, he continued, 'Now, Edward's known Constance since she was a girl. He understands her and can talk to her in a way that I can't. He can remind her of who she is, of the sort of life that'll make her happy.' With an awkward glance at Angela's belly, he added, 'Love and family, security in simple things…'

Angela's mouth twisted at the irony. 'And how is the man she intends to marry disqualified?'

Morgan now irritably drummed his fingers on the kitchen table. 'He's thirty-two, divorced, and comes from a lot of money – his father's with a big hydroelectric concern. The fellow looks to me to be a bit of a cad – and Constance, well, she's all of twenty-three and convinced she'll be an old maid soon. I'd like Edward to talk some sense into her – as a friend.' He took up his iced tea to quench his thirst.

Folding her arms across her belly, at length Angela said, 'You're not the marrying type, Morgan – otherwise you'd understand what your sister's going through. But I see that you're honestly concerned for her happiness, and I appreciate your calling on me like this. It shows the respect you have for your friendship with Edward.'

As she refilled their glasses, she cast her memory back to the confrontation she had had with Constance a couple of years earlier at the Memorial Day event. Bits of what she'd said came to mind – *What you want he can't give you…You aren't a gambler, you'd never risk your heart.* Looking at Morgan now,

Angela had little sympathy for the predicament his sister had gotten herself into.

'Edward's got a heart of gold,' she said as she set down the pitcher, 'but he can't save everybody, Morgan. God knows he'll always have his hands full with his family, but meddling in other people's love lives is a messy business. Please don't ask him to get involved.' She reached across and lightly touched Morgan's arm. 'Trust me. In her heart of hearts your sister's not the kind of woman to take the most important decision of her life lightly...'

When Edward came home from work Angela told him that Morgan had telephoned to say he was in Los Angeles, and that she'd invited him over for dinner. He arrived at half passed six with a bouquet of yellow roses and feigned delighted astonishment at Angela's pregnancy. Over cocktails he explained that he'd checked on Fitz's sister as requested, but unfortunately had to return home the next day and couldn't take Edward up on his offer to show him around.

Over dinner Morgan proceeded to monopolize the conversation by ticking off various conspiracy theories surrounding the death of President Harding in San Francisco two weeks earlier. 'To say that he wore himself down in the course of his cross-country adventures is too preposterous to be believed,' Morgan asserted. 'Presidents travel all the time and they certainly don't lack for comfort.'

'He did go all the way up to Alaska, though,' Edward said.

'Oh, please!' Morgan scoffed. 'It was all a diversion – he was glad to get out of Washington, what with Teapot Dome and all the scandals swirling around his administration.'

Edward remarked that the president had some surprising things to say on his trip, like coming out in favor of the U.S. joining the World Court, and even endorsing labor's right to organize.

'He did seem to go off script there at the end,' Morgan admitted, '—away from the party bosses. Maybe he found religion out here in the west, in the land of clean living...'

Edward and Angela laughed, he at his friend's sarcasm, she at his contempt for earnestness.

'Could be that he was shocked by all the shenanigans going on around him,' Edward offered, 'and thought he'd better start setting the record straight.'

'He seemed the genial sort, that's for sure,' Morgan said. 'Probably choked on his own guilelessness.'

The president's passing struck Gaetano Luchetti as fortuitous. When Edward and Angela came to Stockton in September, he noted over supper that the last president to die in office was succeeded by an energetic Republican not afraid to stand up to monopolists. 'Republicans for small business,' he declared, 'for self-made men in America!'

Edward felt Angela bristle beside him. She was five months pregnant now, and Edward had suggested the visit so that she could be with her mother. Anxious to curry favor with his father-in-law, Edward said, 'In just two years the Republicans have cut unemployment and federal spending,' and seeing Mr. Luchetti was pleased, he went on, 'and even managed to create worthy programs like the Bureau of Veteran Affairs.'

'Ach, the war!' Mr. Luchetti exclaimed, angrily cutting into his meat. 'Harding was right to say no to this League of Nations

– it does no pay to be allies with the British and French. Italy must stand up to the imperialists.' Holding up his knife for emphasis, he said, 'The Italian Prime Minister speaks of vindication for what Wilson and the others failed to deliver!'

'Mussolini's an opportunist,' Angela said flatly, 'Before the war he was a socialist, quoting Garibaldi and Mazzini, but now he and the Fascisti talk about a new Roman Empire!'

Mr. Luchetti put down his utensils noisily. 'Why should Britain get Persia and Palestine and the French get Algeria? Three hundred thousand killed at Caporetto and Italy gets nothing?'

'Italy can barely manage itself,' his daughter said dismissively. 'How can they expect to control Dalmatia and North Africa, too?'

Mrs. Luchetti stood up and turned to Giancarlo, hoping to change the subject. 'Tell your sister how you and your father are so busy – another five hundred acres at the Clayton farm.'

'Spinach and asparagus,' Giancarlo clarified for Edward.

'But what about your interest in becoming a doctor?' Angela asked irritably.

'Ach! Doctors make no good money,' Mr. Luchetti said as his wife cleared the table.

Mr. Luchetti liked to spend Sunday afternoons in peace, repairing mechanical things in his toolshed, which was no more than a lean-to off the back porch, a half level below grade. When Angela stepped through the doorway, the smells of grease and turpentine immediately brought her back to the times as a girl when she would keep him company while he cleaned a clock or tinkered with a carburetor. Now caught in silhouette by the naked light bulb overhead, her father looked up.

'Come sit,' he said in Italian, moving a stack of *Popular Mechanics* magazines off a stool.

Angela approached tentatively, careful to avoid snagging her sweater on one of the many hooks on the wall. Seeing that her father had the components of a small electric generator spread out on his workbench, she said in Italian, 'Still working on magnetos, Papa?'

He smiled. 'It's the smallest things that make the biggest difference.'

Hearing one of his favorite expressions again, she caught her breath as she sat down. It seemed like only yesterday he was letting her inspect the wear and tear on contact points of a magneto. After opening the cam lobe, he would say, 'Well, Angela? Should we replace them?' More often than not she'd say the sparkplug and points could go another week, and he would tousle her short auburn hair before resetting the point gap.

Angela mourned the distance that had developed between them in the years since, and hoping for something of a reconciliation, if only for the sake of her mother and her brother, she summoned her courage and gently leaned against him. 'Papa, you have always taught us that ambition is good…so why not let Giancarlo follow his dream of becoming a doctor?'

'Ach! Don't meddle, Angela – he does what he likes…'

'What *you* like, you mean.' She felt her magnanimity wavering.

'I need him here. He is devoted to his family.'

'And I am not?'

'You are not here – I don't know,' he said as he began fiddling with his tools.

'I had to go my own way. I had no choice…' Upset that this wasn't going the way she wanted, she couldn't help but challenge him. 'You did the same as a young man, Papa – does that make you disloyal to your family?'

'I am not disloyal! I came to America to help my family.'

'You're the American success story, alright,' Angela said in English now, '—you're rich!' When he scoffed, something in their shared stubbornness got the better of Angela and she added derisively, 'Leasing more acres from the Claytons year after year…'

Gaetano looked at the work in front of him and continued to speak in Italian. 'I do lease-to-purchase now, because he owes me…'

'He owes you? No, Papa, you owe *me* – for betraying me!'

'That's not true,' he said, shaking his head, 'you encouraged the boy…'

'We were schoolmates – I thought I could trust him!'

Edward happened to catch these last words as he approached the tool shed; alert to the argumentative tone he'd become sensitized to as a boy, he stopped short of the door.

'I lost a baby last year, Papa,' he heard Angela say bitterly, 'and for that I will always think of you, you and your black dreams…'

Suddenly anxious, reminded of eavesdropping on his parents' rows from the cellar, Edward stepped into the toolshed. 'Oh, there you are, Angela,' he said, feigning nonchalance. 'Your brother wants to take us out to the county fair…Say, what're you two working on?'

Angela stood up and took Edward by the arm, attempting a smile. 'Papa's always been fascinated by magneto engine starters,' she said as they turned to go. From the doorway, she glanced back. 'He's always said it's the smallest things that make the biggest difference...'

But Mr. Luchetti had returned to his work and pretended not to hear.

The next day, with Gaetano and Giancarlo gone to the fields and Angela down for a nap, Edward joined Mrs. Luchetti in the kitchen where she was making a peach pie. He offered to peal the fruit while she rolled the dough, and as they worked she asked about his job, confessing that it was getting harder to distinguish handmade from ready-to-wear garments these days. He assured her there would always be patterns for skilled seamstresses like her and offered to have a wholesaler he knew send a bolt of high-quality muslin up from Los Angeles.

When his mother-in-law commended his skills in the kitchen, Edward told her that he'd enjoyed baking with his sisters as a boy. Gemma asked about his siblings, and he explained that the baby would be his family's first grandchild. When she hung her head, Edward sensed an opening and confided that somehow Angela felt responsible for losing the baby the year before.

Gemma sprinkled ice water onto her dough, and at length said, 'Angela is always very serious since a long time...'

'I overheard her say something to her father yesterday about the Clayton boy,' he ventured, catching her eye. 'She's mentioned him before – I understand he upset her once. So why does your husband still do work for the family?'

'Oh, that's in the past,' Gemma said, wiping her hands on her apron.

'What happened – if you don't mind my asking?'

'Young love and broken hearts,' she said, pursing her lips. 'He's married now, anyway, with two children, I think. He runs his father's cannery on Waterloo Road…'

'Did he serve in the war?'

'Oh, I don't know,' Gemma said, dusting the dough with a pinch of flour. 'His family, they supply canned fruit and vegetables to the army then.'

'Whose family?' Angela said as she came into the kitchen, causing Edward to flinch. She looked to her mother. 'What are you two going on about?'

'Oh,' Edward broke in, 'I was asking about the cannery out on Waterloo Road…'

Gemma looked to her daughter. 'They pack string beans and beets there now, no?'

But Angela wasn't buying it, and suspecting her mother had said more to Edward than she should have, she jeered, 'All I know is they exploit the Filipinos there…'

'Oh, really?' Gemma said as she laid the rolled dough into the pie plate.

Just how irked Angela had been at the thought of her mother discussing past love interests with Edward became apparent several weeks later when he came home from work one evening and showed off a sample of the muslin that he'd just arranged to be sent up to Stockton.

'That's sweet of you,' Angela said, brushing passed him on her way to the kitchen. 'Perhaps you should send a bolt of fabric to another of your female admirers.'

From the stack of mail on the kitchen table she held up an

envelope. 'From Morgan,' she said as she pulled the letter out, '—chock full of news and witticisms, of course, but what he really wanted us – I mean you – to see is this.'

It was a clipping from the *San Francisco Chronicle* which read:

> *Mr. and Mrs. Malcolm Doherty are proud to announce that their daughter, Constance Healy Doherty, is to be wed at Three o' Clock on the afternoon of Saturday, October the Twenty-Seventh, at St. Paul's Church, to Mr. Chester Percival Bingham, late of Redding, an executive with the Great Western Power Company.*

Chapter 31

Baby Clara arrived three days after Christmas, underweight but otherwise healthy. Angela was greatly relieved; Edward was ecstatic.

Angela's mother, Gemma, had come to Los Angeles to help, and in January her husband joined her, though he insisted they stay in a modest hotel nearby so as not to be an imposition. He declined Edward's invitations to show him the city, preferring instead to spend the mornings reading on the couch while his wife looked after Angela and the baby; in the afternoons, he'd take long walks by himself and report at dinner on how ostentatious people seemed, how risqué the movie posters were. He returned to Stockton after ten days. A week later Gemma received a letter from him informing her that one of his brothers had sent him a telegram stating that that their eighty-five-year-old mother was gravely ill. No sooner had Gemma returned home in early March than he abruptly left for Italy.

When Edward and Angela announced that they would bring the baby to San Francisco for Easter, Honora insisted on arranging a baptism at St. Mary's Cathedral – evidence for Edward that his mother had fully accepted Angela into the family fold. On Holy Saturday, everyone was gathered around the baptismal font at the rear of the cathedral. Gemma wore a dress she'd made herself of the yellow muslin Edward had sent her, while Baby Clara was adorned in the same satin gown that Honora had made for Deirdre two decades earlier.

Afterward, Angela's friends Caroline and Gracie hosted a party at their Lyon Street bungalow. Despite a high fog, it was pleasant enough to set up a buffet table in the backyard, and people sat wherever they could find a spot. Aunt Hildie was seated on a low brick wall, along with her daughter Cora and Cora's new husband, a quiet, unassuming bank manager. When Hildie spotted Angela's mother coming away uncertainly from the buffet table with a plate of food, she beckoned her to join them.

Hildie made Gemma feel right at home. After introducing her daughter and son-in-law, she explained that her other daughter, Maggie, had been best friends with Edward's sister Deirdre since they were girls, and that her son, Michael, had been the one assisting the Monsignor with the baptism that morning.

'Such a nice family,' Gemma remarked, 'It is good for Angela…with no cousins.'

Cora nodded politely. 'Tell us, Mrs. Luchetti, we haven't heard how Edward and Angela came up with the name Clara. Is there a Clara in your family?'

Gemma finished chewing a bite of food, then said, 'Edward's mother wished for the name Claire, I think, but Edward wanted the Italian spelling. He's a sweet boy that way.'

'Yes, he's a sweet boy,' Hildie agreed. The four of them looked over at Edward who was mimicking a baseball stance in front of Fitz to demonstrate something to Giancarlo. 'He seems to have taken your son under his wing.'

'My boy is shy with people, like his father.'

After a moment, Hildie ventured, 'It must be difficult, with your husband being away...'

'He keeps the vigil,' Gemma said, '—His mother has eighty-five years.'

'We shall add her to our prayers,' Cora promised, squeezing her husband's hand.

Aunt Hildie was watching her brother, James, coming down the back stairs unsteadily when she noticed Edward's friend on the porch. Morgan hadn't been at the baptism (Angela had prevailed on Edward to keep the ceremony intimate) and was surveying the yard with an expectant grin when his eyes met Hildie's. With a wave he headed down the stairs, gave a clearly astonished Edward a pat on the shoulder as he passed, then made his way over to Hildie and her little entourage.

'Why, Mrs. O'Shea, it's been ages!' he exclaimed as he approached. 'I was so sorry to hear about your husband's passing last year...'

Hildie accepted a peck on the cheek, and after introductions, Morgan said, 'I knew Edward and Angela were coming for Easter, but I didn't realize the baby was being christened *today*. I wonder who the godparents might be?'

'Why, Angela's friend Caroline, and Walter, of course,' Cora said.

'Walter?' Morgan repeated, 'You don't say?' The news irked Morgan, particularly since Walter had recently announced that he was moving to New York to take a position in one of the big bond houses. Masking his surprise, Morgan chuckled and said, 'And I didn't think he even liked children!'

Aunt Hildie smiled, and asked mildly, 'Do you know

Caroline and Gracie?'

'Oh, we've got mutual friends,' Morgan said, before taking Gemma's hand in his. 'I can't tell you how glad I am to finally meet you, Mrs. Luchetti. This is your first grandchild, I believe – would you mind if I call you "Nonna"?'

Gemma blushed and Hildie winked at Morgan.

'I'm very fond of your daughter, you know,' he went on solicitously. 'She'll be a wonderful mother. She's so sure of herself – I suppose she gets those qualities from you.'

'She *is* strong, Mr. Morgan,' Gemma said, 'and very loyal, too.'

Edward was having lunch with Nathan Leopold when he mentioned that he'd received a telegram from an old army buddy saying that he was coming through town the following week. 'Well, not a buddy exactly,' Edward corrected himself, 'just a crazy S.O.B. by the name of Crowley who took to the trenches like a duck to water.'

'I know the type…Bullets, bombs, and bayonets, hurrah!'

Edward smirked. 'Tell me again about that reunion you had with your old Rochester crew a couple of years back.'

Picking tomato slices out of his sandwich, Leopold said, 'See, for some guys the war's the greatest thing they'll ever be a part of – they talk about it like it was a football game. Then there are others who're never gonna get over it, who've been drinking themselves to death ever since we got back, who can't keep a job or hold onto a girl…'

For Edward, fortunate to have served with men from places far from San Francisco, it had been easier to fall out of touch. In the five years since getting back, he managed to exchange

Christmas cards with Steinkoler, but never looked him up when he went to Seattle. 'Guess we oughta consider ourselves lucky to be somewhere in the middle…' he observed now.

The following Wednesday he met Crowley after work in the lobby of a hotel near Central Station. 'Well, I'll be damned,' the Reno carpenter said, fuller in the face now, 'Dooley's all grown up in a suit and tie!'

'How you doing, Frank?' Edward said warily as they shook hands. 'Good to see you.'

Edward said he knew a place where they could get a drink, and they caught up as they walked. Crowley explained that he was in town to take delivery of some Australian hardwood for his booming homebuilding business. He told Edward that he, Miller, McLeod, and Steinkoler made a hunting trip to Yellowstone every year, and that he was missed.

The speakeasy Edward led him to was a musty storeroom in the back of a cigar shop. No sooner had the whiskey and beer been served than Crowley began, 'Say, it sounds like yer doin' pretty well for yourself, Eddie – good job, a wife and kid. Bet yer in the stock market…'

'No, not really,' Edward said, not about to mention Walter, working in real estate securities back in New York.

'But you'd like to get outta that apartment and buy a house, though, am I right?'

'Oh, sure,' Edward said, sipping his beer, bracing for a pitch.

Sure enough, Crowley had an oil drilling scheme for some land in Fallon, Nevada, that he'd optioned under the reclamation act. After explaining that some of the same men who'd been in on the gusher near Elko two years earlier were on board, he leaned forward. 'Listen, Eddie, the stock market's for gamblers, but mineral rights are tangible and worth a fortune. Why get in bed with a broker you don't know from Adam when you and me go back aways!'

Edward ran his finger down his pint glass, and after a moment said, 'I appreciate you're thinking of me, Frank, but I'm afraid I'll have to pass.'

Crowley pushed back from the table. 'Woah! Bailin' on me right off?' When Edward didn't reply, the Reno man scowled and muttered under his breath, 'Miller said I couldn't count on you – 'matter fact, he's never liked how you've passed up his hospitality…'

Sensing he was off the hook, Edward said, 'Well, I'm not much of a hunter…'

'Shit! Come shoot quail with us then, fer Chrissakes!'

'Once a city boy, always a city boy…'

The Reno man shook his head, disgusted, and after a minute, said, 'You can't put the war behind you, you know, pretend it never happened. You can't forget your buddies…'

'Didn't you used to say it was every man for himself out there, Frank?'

'Yer a chickenshit, Dooley,' Crowley sneered before knocking back a shot of whiskey. 'Steinkoler says you married a nurse. She know yer a nut case? She ever seen the report?'

'What report?'

'After Gesnes. You know – after you cracked up. "Combat fatigue," my ass! I'm surprised you didn't shoot yerself in the hand or the leg.'

Edward pursed his lips and stood up. 'I'm working with a Jewish fellow these days, Crowley, and you know what he says about guys like you? He says, "There's no shortage of coal in hell.'" With that, Edward put two silver dollars on the table and walked out.

Edward invariably found Fitz in good humor when he would visit him at the San Francisco County Jail, which was located in the fogbound hinterlands of the Ingleside District. The two of them would sit in the recreation yard, the big man wrapped up like an Eskimo, and watch a softball game between an assortment of small-time crooks and chronic drunks who'd welcomed Fitz as a war hero.

He was less sanguine after his release, however. With the Hotel Senate under new management and disinclined to accept men who'd done time, Fitz had to settle for a nondescript rooming house at the corner of Mason and Ellis, also in the Tenderloin. The only sign of life in the narrow, three-story brick building was a French laundry on the ground floor. The first time Edward came by he almost missed the door to the dingy residences upstairs. A heavyset woman in a frilly housecoat sitting at a table just inside regarded Edward doubtfully a moment, before sending him up to Room 204.

Fitz was sitting on his bed fully clothed and reading the sporting green, the remnants of a ham sandwich and a soda on the nightstand beside him. The room was half the size of what he'd had at The Senate and smelled of cigarettes and aftershave. Fitz grinned as he got up from the bed and motioned Edward back out into the hallway.

'There's no place to sit up here, Eddie,' he said, 'Let's go downstairs and I'll buy you a drink.' Taking his Carnes' artificial arm from a hook behind the door, he strapped it on with difficulty before leading Edward back down the stairs.

'Buzz me next time, doll,' he said to the heavyset woman, 'Eddie's an old friend.'

'Looked like another traveling salesman to me – was gonna send him up to three.'

'Nah, my buddy's happily married,' Fitz said as he squeezed by her table to a door under the stairs. Edward followed his friend down a tight, dark staircase to the basement where Fitz drew back a heavy red velvet curtain to reveal an empty barroom decked out like the captain's quarters of a Spanish galleon. The low ceiling was expertly trimmed with box beams and a luxurious bar reclaimed from a Nob Hill gentleman's club dominated the long room, facing a wall finished with pressed metal panels and portholes repurposed as light sconces.

'All the charms of the sea, without the view,' Fitz deadpanned as he pulled up a barstool.

The proprietor emerged from the back – a squat, bald man Fitz introduced as Jerome – and drew a couple of beers. He explained that he used to run the Haymarket Dance Hall next door, until the dancers could no longer quench their thirst on account of Prohibition. 'Still, being so close to the St. Francis Hotel has its advantages,' he told Edward, 'cause the swells who get tired of being gypped at the high-tone speakeasies up the hill can get a good deal here.'

Fitz described the protocol, where the laundry served as the checkpoint. Old Mrs. Sarthou greeted customers at the counter and if she got the right password – known only to certain hotel doormen and maître d's – she'd wave them on to her son, a former middleweight contender, who would escort them down the back stairs.

Anxious to not appear too innocent, Edward said, 'You

know, a friend of mine took me to a joint down on Taylor a couple of years ago – The 65 Club, I think it was called.'

'Watch it,' Jerome said, lighting a cigarette for Fitz, '—that's where the queers go…'

Edward grimaced, and eager to change the subject, he asked Fitz about his sister. When he learned that she'd been in town recently shooting a DeMille picture, he quipped, 'Who knows, maybe she'll be a star after all…'

Fitz cocked his head. 'Maybe.'

'You'll be famous by association,' Edward said, then with a friendly nudge, 'and maybe Angela and I can finally lure you to Los Angeles for one of those glitzy movie premieres.'

'Thanks just the same, Eddie,' Fitz replied, then with a knowing glance to Jerome, 'but from now on I'm better off keeping a low profile…'

PART FOUR

Chapter 32

Mr. Breslin was so pleased with Edward's performance that he decided to send his protégé to American Thread Company's biennial sales meeting in New York City. It would be Edward's second visit to Manhattan. The first, before shipping overseas in July 1918, involved a ferry ride from Jersey City and a stroll up the Great White Way. With a tear in his eye he'd looked west from Times Square, the start of the Lincoln Highway that terminated in San Francisco, full of vague hopes about returning safely. Looking out from the ferry seven years later, the twin towers of the Hudson Terminal looked like a drawbridge to some magical metropolis, with the stately Municipal Building beckoning like open arms, and the Singer and Woolworth Buildings unabashedly declaring the sky was the limit.

Edward confidently strode up Broadway, exhilarated by the hum of commerce, buildings bristling with billboards as far as the eye could see. Flags on display in the stores and on every public building made him proud to be a veteran of the Great War, and he was eager to see the Victory Arch that he'd only seen in photographs. He hastened to the crossing of Broadway and Fifth Avenue, but found no marble edifice; instead, a passing businessman informed him that the wood-and-plaster tribute at Madison Square had been torn down a few years earlier, after a fundraising drive to make the arch permanent had fizzled.

American Thread was headquartered in an eleven-story masonry building, designed in the Renaissance revival style and rounded like a citadel where West Broadway met Beach Street. Along with other elder statesmen in the wholesale/industrial/warehouse district of the Lower West Side like the Textile Building and the Mercantile Exchange, it would soon be cast in shadow by the thirty-two story Mayan-inspired ziggurat then under construction, the offices of the New York Telephone Company.

At half passed eight on a Tuesday morning, ATC's sales managers from around the country were gathered in a conference room, all eyes on Chief of Sales, Ian Kirkpatrick, an abstemious bachelor whose Aberdeen ancestors supposedly had begun running woolen mills in the Middle Ages. After the sparest of welcomes, he had the salesmen introduce themselves: in addition to Edward, there were Charlie Gillespie and Sam Asher from the New York office; Declan Morrissey from Boston; Pete Ragali from Philadelphia; Herb Greene, who ran Cleveland and Rochester; Percy Schuster, St. Louis and Kansas City; and Ben Katzenburg from Chicago.

The Chief Operating Officer, Mr. E.G. Cross, entered the room at precisely 9 o' clock, and delivered a dry recitation on market share statistics. He concluded by warning of increased competition from Europe, citing mill expansions in Liverpool and Manchester, a munitions factory conversion in Amiens, and rumors of a manufacturing plant coming on line in Bavaria, which elicited groans from several veterans in the room. (Edward would learn that Morrissey, Katzenberg and Ragali had all seen combat, that Greene and Asher had served stateside in the National Guard, and that Schuster's 4F claim had been bogus.)

No sooner had Cross departed than Katzenburg held up a copy of the "Textile World Journal" saying, 'He must think we're a pretty dim group, Kirkpatrick, because it says here American Thread's going to slash factory pay another ten-percent,' then glancing around the table, he added, 'and that's on top of the thirty percent cut made over the past five years.'

'We're well aware of the competitive environment, thank you,' Kirkpatrick said irritably.

'Workers accustomed to what they made during the war now have to work twice as hard,' the Chicago man continued, unfazed, 'and overproduction leads to falling prices, which leads to more wage cuts…'

'That will do, Mr. Katzenburg!' Kirkpatrick boomed.

But there was something disingenuous in Katzenberg's nod, and later Edward learned that he'd come over from Coats & Clark before the war, bringing the Hart, Schaffner and Marx account with him – a coup that secured bragging rights for American Thread executives and earned him impunity from the Chief of Sales.

As usual, the salesmen were put up at the Broadway Central Hotel, a 400-room leviathan long since bypassed by tonier establishments uptown. Over lunch in the hotel's sparsely occupied dining room, Morrissey groused between mouthfuls of a mediocre beef bourguignon, 'You can bet senior management doesn't stay in dumps like this.'

'This "American Plan" is for the birds,' Katzenberg agreed. 'Give me a lousy room but let me use my expense account for a stiff drink and meals at a decent restaurant.'

'Alas, Prohibition did Delmonico's in,' Gillespie said with a sigh.

The Chicago man shook his head. 'Thank God there's no shortage of speakeasies here, Charlie, and what's more, the government's got no right interfering with my personal liberties. Hell, I fought for the government!'

'Yeah, I fought, too,' Morrissey sneered. 'And for what? *Freedom?* As far as I'm concerned, the government oughta stop coddling foreigners. So their wages get cut, Katzenberg – Who invited them here in the first place, huh? All this talk about labor commissions...Jesus!'

'Couldn't agree more,' Schuster from St. Louis said. 'You're on your own here in the good ol' U.S. of A. In fact, the company's no more loyal to us than the government is – you're only as valuable as your last sale...'

'Dozens of guys just itching to take your place,' Ragali from Philadelphia put in.

Edward thought of himself as a "company man" and was uncomfortable with this kind of talk. Though he hadn't said much at the morning meeting, his numbers spoke for themselves, and now he felt emboldened to say, 'I don't know if it's as bad as all that – there are plenty of deals to go around.' When this met with silence, he went on, 'Listen, the Hollywood studios are starting to market film fashion to consumers now – department stores like Bullock's and The May Company are going to start carrying the styles you see in the movies...'

'That's all well and good for you out in sunny California, Dooley,' Morrissey said, 'but here it's dog-eat-dog, see? Folks who've been here for years are fighting to keep their jobs on account of all these foreigners.'

'Send 'em all back to Warsaw or Calabria...' Ragali said with a wry grin.

'Damn right,' the Boston man agreed, returning to his meal, at which point Ragali winked at Edward.

Like the Broadway Central, the once-fashionable shopping district along 6th Avenue known as the Ladies' Mile had begun to fade after Macy's moved to midtown in 1902, followed by Lord & Taylor, B. Altman, W. & J. Sloan, and Bergdorf Goodman. The garment district that eventually comprised twenty-four blocks between 33rd and 42nd Streets was already the largest concentration of clothing manufacturers in the world in 1925, when Asher and Gillespie arranged visits for their colleagues.

Together with Pete Ragali, Edward went to tour a women's wear factory in a loft building on 7th Avenue. Fleury Couture was owned by Stan Herman, a short, handsome fellow, who'd also seen action in the Argonne (he named his company after the hospital at Fleury-sur-Aire where he was sent after sustaining shrapnel wounds). The factory consisted of double-wide tables oriented perpendicular to high windows that provided light and air. Electrical cords hanging down from overhead conduits powered the sewing machines at each work station. A great stack of cut fabric lay at the end of each table – currently a line of percale dresses. The staccato rhythm of the machines sounded almost musical to Edward, though the mood among the women working the machines was gravely serious.

'Must be exciting having your own business,' Ragali shouted to their host as he made his rounds.

'Always been a cut-throat industry,' Herman yelled back, 'One out of every four producers goes belly-up in the first few years, the margins are that tight.'

'Jesus,' Edward remarked, 'it's not quite that bad in California.'

'Jesus has nothing to do with it, Mr. Dooley,' the short man yelled, 'We're strictly Old Testament here...' Ragali laughed and Herman turned to be sure Edward took the joke in stride. 'West Coast's different,' he explained, '—unlimited demand and only so much production capacity. Out here there's always somebody happy to undercut you...'

When they returned to Herman's glassed-in office, a tall, stork-like man was waiting for them: Sid Finkelstein, ladies' apparel buyer for Parcher & Stein Department Store in Newark. He wore a bowler hat and spats and looked as old as the hills. 'Sid's my mensch,' Herman said as he poured stale coffee into a paper cup. 'He got his start about the same time Grant was holed up at the Broadway Central writing his memoirs...'

'We did good business 'til Appomattox,' Finkelstein deadpanned.

Leaning on a walking stick, he talked about the old apparel industry, explained how German Jews started the big department stores, leaving the middling work to the Yiddish-speaking peasants who came after them – 'My people, from the shtetls of Eastern Europe, the "Moths of Division Street,"' he said proudly. He explained how they'd get the fabric wholesale and then farm out the work to basters and sewers, pocket makers, buttonholers, and finishers.

'And now this,' he said with a stiff wave, 'so much efficiency and still so little profit!'

He had a raspy, infectious laugh, and seeing that Edward and Pete liked what he had to say, he declared, 'Your generation's got it made, boys. You've got the production problem solved and demand's going through the roof because you can appeal to people's vanity like never before.' Their interest piqued, he continued, 'See, nowadays the national advertisers make up some malarkey about American women being noted for their pretty ankles, and whaddya know, hemlines rise fourteen inches. Tell men that a snappy suit exudes confidence and they start lining up around the block. And you wanna know why?'

Here he leaned on his walking stick with both hands and grinned. 'Because it's not clothes you're selling, boys, it's hope – everybody's hoping to look better off than they really are. That's America for you!'

Later that day Ragali took Edward to the slums of the Lower East Side where children in rags hocked newspapers and street vendors haggled with headstrong matriarchs in strange-sounding dialects. 'We're no more entitled to the American Dream than any of these poor bastards,' Ragali said, returning to Morrissey's remarks at lunch. 'I bet Civil War vets were shaking their heads fifty years ago when they saw the likes of you and me coming over…'

To reinforce just how fortunate they were, Ragali concluded his tour in the financial district. They came through the breathtaking canyon of office blocks on Broad Street to the New York Cotton Exchange, a magnificent, twelve-story Renaissance revival building with a base of Roman arches on the street and a loggia with Corinthian columns at the top. Light streamed through the great arches as they entered the trading hall. From a catwalk above the row of teller windows, clerks scribbled on a chalkboard as prices were relayed from the exchanges in New Orleans, Memphis, Savannah, and Liverpool. The two young salesmen watched the frenzy in the trading pit at the center of the great hall for a while, then Ragali remarked, 'Cotton's been the country's leading domestic and export commodity for over a century now, Ed – and as long as people are wearing clothes, you and I'll be sitting pretty…'

Against the advice of both Pete Ragali and Sam Asher, before returning to California Edward went to Willimantic, Connecticut, to see American Thread's flagship factory, one of the largest thread mills in the world. Unfortunately, his visit coincided with a period of unrest between management and the thirty-five hundred workers employed there. When Edward showed up unannounced, the plant superintendent grudgingly agreed to give him a tour.

Edward was astounded by the magnitude of the operation in Mill No. 4. The newest of the nine factory buildings, it was five hundred feet in length, with rows of spooling machines on each of its four floors powered by belt-driven camshafts suspended from the ceilings. Above the waist-high spooling machines hundreds of bobbins were arranged in three tiers, each bobbin revolving at high speed on a vertical axel. Workers stood back to back in narrow aisles, manually attending to twelve bobbins at a time, leaving little time for chatter – unlikely, anyway, among the assortment of poor Connecticut Yankees, Poles, Irish, Italians, and Ukrainians.

The only sign of union activity Edward encountered was a group of men handing out leaflets near the entry gates to the plant when he was leaving. It happened to be between shifts, and after passing through the gate, he was approaching the men for a leaflet when over his shoulder he heard someone say, 'Who the hell's this guy think he is?' Before he had a chance to turn around her heard another man say, 'I seen him wit da super – probly mangem'nt…'

Belatedly aware how conspicuous he must have looked in his overcoat and fedora, Edward turned, and said, 'No, no, I'm just a salesman, actually…I'm out from California, Los Angeles, in fact, and I've just always wanted to see your plant…'

'Figure on starting a plant out there, do ya?' someone said. 'An open shop town?' Edward blanched as two large men approached him from the side.

'No, that's not it at all,' he said, trying to back up. 'I'm a salesman, see, and—'

The next thing he knew one of the big men was lifting him to his feet while the other one pressed his hat back into his hands. The afternoon sun was in his eyes as he tried making out the various voices: *You okay there, Mister?…Hey, back off!… Aw, shit, the bastard's bleedin'…Prop him up, Hal, and walk him back inside…*

Edward felt nauseous and had a strange sensation of walking while suspended by his arm pits, floating through crowds of men coming and going. When the world stopped spinning he opened his eyes and found himself in the factory infirmary, with the night nurse applying a poultice and a bandage to a bad bruise on his temple. When she asked him who he was, he deliberately garbled his words; when she excused herself a moment, he slipped out.

Fortunately, the wound caused by a lunch pail was confined

to his left brow and eye socket such that he could hide it behind dark glasses during his cross-country trip home. He was chagrined to report the incident to Angela, but otherwise felt that with no one the wiser he could put it behind him.

He'd been back to work only a few days when Mr. Breslin reached him by telephone, irate as he reported that he'd just been subjected to a humiliating dressing down by Mr. Kirkpatrick for Edward's foolishness. It turned out that the night nurse had contacted the plant security officer, who, in turn, had combed through the visitors' log and conferred with the plant superintendent. After coercing a disclosure from a spooler he knew to be ambivalent about a strike, the security officer was able to identify the missing man as Edward Dooley and place him at the union leaflet table at the time of the shift change.

In the days that followed, the United Textile Workers of America convinced the workers at the Willimantic plant to walk off the job, which led to violent confrontations between strikers and state police, and plenty of bad press for American Thread. In the end, the Company prevailed (replacing the strikers with French Canadians and recently laid-off textile workers in Rhode Island and Massachusetts). But however innocent his intentions, Edward had earned a black mark for having associated with union sympathizers.

Chapter 33

Angela suffered a trauma of her own later the same year – an experience that would force her to come to terms with her own limitations.

The first time she stepped into Barry Hospital she found the familiar smells of hydrogen peroxide and carbolic cleaning solution oddly reassuring. Everything about the Old Soldiers Home exuded a sense of order – from the tidy clusters of three-story veranda buildings on the well-tended grounds to the meticulous uniforms of the medical personnel and attendant staff – as if to refute the chaos that had resulted in grievous injuries to men who had served in Europe, the Philippines, China, and Alaska. Angela's volunteer work began with cataloguing supplies and pushing men in wheelchairs outside for fresh air. But when the Chief Superintendent of Nursing learned that she'd been a highly regarded nurse at the Presidio in San Francisco, she prevailed upon Angela to take on a supervisory role in the physical therapy ward.

With the country enjoying a wave of unprecedented prosperity, the badge of courage once accorded amputees had become a stigma, an uncomfortable reminder of times most people preferred to forget. Keenly aware of this, Angela endeared herself to vets who were eager to walk again, to shave and feed themselves, to get on in the world without becoming objects of pity. Small victories were immense sources of satisfaction for her – men who found work in the mailroom, men sure enough of their gait to leave the grounds and ride a streetcar, men so confident with their prosthetic arms that they could eat at a lunch counter without shame.

After Clara was born, Angela would return to the Old Soldiers Home from time to time to keep up with her patients. She would leave the baby to play on the mat next to the nurses' station while supervising the nurses and the male orderlies who guided men through their exercises; mother and daughter would eat lunch with the nurses in the cafeteria, and Clara would fall asleep on the streetcar ride home. One day when Clara was about eighteen months old, Angela got so caught up in reconfiguring the exercise room that she decided to stay after lunch, and put the baby down for a nap in the little room behind the nurses' station. When Baby Clara went missing a short time later, Angela was seized by fear and foreboding, and a frantic search ensued.

The Barry Hospital was a long, peaked-roof building with dormers windows at the third-floor residences, which were reserved for senior medical staff. Two MPs were assisting in the search when from the veranda a child's giggles could be heard directly overhead. Angela and the others raced up the back stairs to an empty apartment where they discovered Clara on a small balcony, clutched in the arms of a distraught veteran with split-hooks for hands. Though he'd jammed a chair against the doorknob to block access, Clara seemed strangely calm, and happily waved her stuffed bear when she saw her mother.

When Angela and the others rushed forward, the man turned and held the baby threateningly over the railing. Ward Supervisor Watkins quickly tried to defuse the situation by directing the MPs to leave the room. Seeing the man shoot a hateful look at Angela, she said, 'He knows who you are, Nurse Dooley. You can't be here – trust me. Go listen from the bedroom window if you want, but keep the shades drawn.'

From the adjoining room, Angela peered out anxiously from a crack between the shade and the windowsill. Nurse Watkins knew the veteran, Lieutenant Henderson, and spoke in a conciliatory tone to the him through the window that opened onto the deck. She listened patiently, drawing the man out on his various grievances – that no one liked him, that his father rarely came to visit anymore. (Angela later learned Henderson was from a prosperous Pasadena family, had sold luxury automobiles with his father before the war, and had lost his hands in an accident while delivering artillery to the front.)

For fifteen excruciating minutes Angela watched him grow increasingly agitated. Baby Clara was preoccupied with her bear as Henderson swayed from side to side, then Angela caught the words, 'I hate these arms, I hate my life! Who does she think she is, bringing a baby here?!'

'She means no harm, Dale,' Angela heard Watkins saying. 'Nurse Dooley is a great help to us here…She's married to a veteran, you know.'

'Able-bodied, I bet…'

'I wouldn't know – he may be…' then, after a moment, 'It's hard to understand the reasons why things happen the way they do…'

'You wouldn't know the first thing about bad luck,' he said gloomily.

'I had a beau once, Dale,' Angela heard the ward supervisor say. Despite her honey-colored hair and dimpled smile, there was a sadness about Emma Watkins that made her difficult to know. Now Angela heard her describe how she'd grown close to a soldier she'd nursed back to health at Camp Bowie in Texas, only to have a fiancée turn up in the end to reclaim him.

'The bitch!' Henderson yelled.

A sudden clanging from below caused him to look over his right shoulder, and in that instant a soldier clamored up from the veranda on his blind side and bounded over the balcony railing. Grabbing the veteran viciously by the collar with one hand, he snatched the baby away with the other. Meanwhile, three MPs had stormed the apartment and forced their way onto the balcony where they quickly apprehended the man. Angela ran out from the bedroom to take Baby Clara, who was screaming hysterically for all the commotion.

'Don't be so hard on yourself,' Edward said that evening, using the very words she'd used to console him when he'd returned from his fateful trip to the east coast. 'There's no telling where a lunatic might spring up – the point is that Clara's okay.'

'But this has thrown me for a loop,' Angela said, sobbing at the hopelessness of it all. 'I'm in over my head, Edward – I should have known better. Physical injuries are one thing, but nobody really understands how the brain can be damaged, the psychological scars…'

'At least "shellshock" isn't considered a hoax anymore,' Edward offered, reminded of Aaron Jacobs, evacuated after breaking down at the front. Putting his hands on her shoulders, he looked her in the eye. 'You'll always be a hero to me, Angela. Think of all the men you've helped retake control of their lives over the past seven years…'

Shaking her head, she said, 'There are so many others, though, and so much we don't know about the link between our minds and our emotions.' Overwhelmed with grief, she embraced Edward, and over his shoulder, said, 'I can't go back, I just can't...'

Edward eased up on business travel and insisted that twice a week Angela and Baby Clara take the streetcar downtown to meet him for lunch. He purchased a Ford Model T on credit and periodically the young family would drive the length of Sunset Boulevard in the evenings to enjoy fish-and-chips at a roadside diner on the Pacific Coast Highway. On weekends they might drive out to Glendale and stroll the grounds of El Miradero, take in a ballgame between the Seals and the Angels at Washington Park, or visit the aquarium in Venice Beach. Invariably these outings would include a drive through one of the new residential subdivisions that were popping up everywhere. Edward was especially interested in the houses going up in Hancock Park. He set his sights on making more money and sought investment advice from Walter in New York.

His motivation was now entirely personal as he worked hard to parlay even the most tangential connection into a new business account; his company man zeal was never the same after Mr. Breslin's tongue-lashing. The more he thought about how unfair it was – he'd been the one who suffered the black eye, after all – the more he questioned the prevailing wisdom at American Thread that union motivations were always sinister.

When he confided as much to Harry Breitstein over drinks one afternoon, the big man was amused. Regarding the whiskey glass in his hand like a crystal ball, Breitstein said, 'If it hadn't been for that blowhard Haywood the Wobblies coulda been a real force, Eddie. But then it was all won and lost in Lawrence back in '12 – the so-called "Bread and Roses" strike…'

Edward remembered hearing about the episode in school but didn't quite understand the significance. Breitstein went on to explain how two Italians working for the IWW had managed to unite a workforce of erstwhile enemies – English and Irish, French and Germans, Greeks and Turks – to sustain a ten-week walk out by twenty thousand workers in the depths of winter.

'If it weren't for Ettor and Giovannitti,' Breitstein concluded, 'those immigrants working sixty-hour weeks in the New England mills wouldn't have even earned a measly dollar a day. Those two got the public to pay attention and shook up the whole industry.'

'Score one for labor,' Edward said.

'Yeah, but then Haywood and his cronies got too political and squandered the whole thing. The very next year they pushed for silk workers to strike in Paterson, only this time police fired into the crowd and five thousand were arrested – the Wobblies were done for…'

'Score one for management?'

'Listen, Eddie, Willimantic is yesterday's news,' Breitstein said in a fatherly tone. 'No matter how hard the unions keep at it, the mill owners have all the leverage because it's the stockholders who call the tune. Why do you think American Thread's opening plants in the south now? Labor's dirt cheap and folks down there don't go for any of that socialist crap…'

Chapter 34

Gaetano Luchetti had been in Italy for nearly two years, but as the months went by and the family matriarch hung on, he and his brother Vincenzo decided to go into business together. Angela's mother learned this in letters, but also heard rumors that he was looking to sell his prized artichoke acreage out on Farmington Road. In September, after another of her husband's brothers came to take Giancarlo to Italy to see his father, Gemma's worst fears seemed to be confirmed, so Angela invited her to Los Angeles.

Intent on being unobtrusive, Gemma slept on the couch in the living room and was up before sunrise every morning to have breakfast ready for Edward. Her heart swelled when Angela and the baby would emerge from the bedroom, then Edward would take a last sip of his coffee before kissing each of them on the forehead, Gemma included, before leaving for work.

On Tuesdays and Thursdays Gemma would join Angela and Baby Clara on their trips downtown, where they would shop for produce at City Market. Gemma liked chatting with the farmers about their harvests as she picked out various fruits and vegetables. She was especially talkative one morning, and after saying goodbye to a kindly Japanese vendor from whom she'd bought peppers and zucchini, Gemma got on the subject of Italian nationalism.

'Pride is a silly thing, you know,' she said in Italian while Angela pushed Clara in her stroller. 'This "Risorgimento" is nothing but vanity – Mussolini thinking he's Caesar… The crazy ideas of disgruntled soldiers and impotent old men!' Somehow her sarcasm tickled Clara, who giggled.

Coming up to their streetcar stop, Angela said, 'Are you worried Papa might not come home, Mama?'

'He could be a Blackshirt now for all I know,' Gemma replied as she handed the shopping bag to her daughter so that she could hold Clara. 'Maybe he lost his way – coming to America with hope, then leaving angry and blind to the good future we have here.' She closed her eyes and sighed, then playfully nuzzled Clara, eliciting more giggles.

Gemma was still with the family in October when Edward arranged a birthday bash for Angela at the Cocoanut Grove. Morgan promised to come to town and bring Fitz's sister as his date, and Angela suggested they fix Nathan Leopold up with Emma Watkins – she owed a debt of gratitude to Emma, and having heard enough about Nathan's fleeting romances with salesgirls and manicurists, she thought he might appreciate someone of substance.

The Ambassador Hotel was considered the epicenter of the tony Mid-Wilshire District; its nightclub, the Cocoanut Grove, was popular with the Hollywood glitterati and featured an exotic Moorish décor inspired by Valentino's film *The Sheik*. The Dooley party was seated cheek-by-jowl with other tables beneath a canopy of palm fronds, steps from the dance floor, where couples spun to hits like "Sweet Georgia Brown" and "Yes Sir! That's My Baby." The cacophony of music and laughter, and the profusion of floral perfumes, musky colognes, and pungent cigar smoke, made for an intoxicating atmosphere, and during one of the slow numbers, Angela remarked to Edward that Emma and Nathan made a handsome couple.

Meanwhile, when he wasn't dancing with Fitz's sister, Morgan was having a grand time squiring her around the room. Molly was a brunette now and went by the name Marjorie Blake, hoping to resuscitate her career which had stalled after a bit part in a Mabel Normand comedy. When the Dooley party finally sat down to dinner, Morgan mentioned that Marjorie had a shot at being in one of Mack Sennett's "Bathing Beauties" features.

'Oh, that would be great fun!' Angela said brightly.

Marjorie smiled without enthusiasm as she picked at her food. Her skin was still fair, but a downturn at the corner of her crimson lips suggested a hardening of character.

'I imagine it's tiring work,' Emma offered. 'I was just reading in *Variety* where—'

'It's all about who you know in this town,' Marjorie interjected.

Covering for her brusqueness, Morgan said, 'We were just saying "Hello" to Ramón Novarro over there!'

'Oh, we just love Alice Terry's pictures, don't we, Edward?' Angela said. 'She and Novarro always look so good together.' When Marjorie pretended not to hear, Angela asked with a kind smile, 'Are you and Alice still friends?'

'Of course,' Marjorie said tersely, then, looking passed Nathan Leopold to an impish fellow with wild hair arriving at a nearby table, she said to Morgan, 'That's Sid Grauman.'

When this made no impression on Edward and Angela,

Morgan smiled benignly and looked across to Emma and Nathan. 'I bet these two never get up to the Egyptian Theater...'

'Hollywood's for single people,' Nathan said bluntly. That he didn't look at Emma as he said this disappointed Angela, but Emma caught her eye and smiled.

While the others focused on their dinners, Morgan was content to watch the goings on at Grauman's table. Brandishing a flask, he poured another dollop of gin into his tonic water, saying, 'I love that everything is so simple in America – if you've got dough, you're in!' When the others looked up, he continued, 'I mean, forget about breeding and centuries of tradition. Here with hard work and a little luck you can put the Warsaw ghetto behind you and hobnob with the likes of Douglas Fairbanks and Norma Talmadge!'

Nathan Leopold looked at Morgan. 'Money's always bought respectability in this country,' he said evenly, '—look how far the Irish have come...'

Morgan grinned. 'Oh, I don't know – we Irish are a pretty humble lot. From lowly laborers to peddlers of porcelain fixtures in, what Edward, three generations?! A few success stories maybe, like the Silver Kings or Doheny, the oil tycoon, but the rest of us just manage to eke out a living. As a people, though, I'd say the Jews are doing pretty well for themselves. Look, they've made it overnight – film's the fourth largest industry in the world now!'

'That's enough, Morgan,' Angela cautioned, 'It's my birthday, remember?'

But Nathan chuckled to allay any concern. 'My people have learned that you've gotta make it while you can,' then turning to Emma, 'You see, we don't blend in like everybody else. These here are the lucky ones,' he said, looking around the ballroom. 'They saw the writing on the wall and got out in time – not so for the poor devils who stayed behind, the ones loyal to the Kaiser or the Czar. Turns out, they're not even considered European anymore!'

Emma felt self-conscious and looked him squarely in the eye. 'If you knew me better, you wouldn't lecture me. People are treated unfairly on account of all sorts of preconceptions.'

'Hear, hear!' Morgan said. 'Listen, I'm afraid I got Mr. Leopold off on a tangent...'

'—and he ran with it,' Marjorie muttered under her breath.

This didn't sit well with Nathan. Putting down his utensils, he said, 'Whenever things go sour, like they have in Germany, it's the Jews who are the most convenient targets...'

'Thank heavens that doesn't fly here in America,' Edward put in nervously, hoping to change the subject, but before he could, Leopold touched his arm.

'But it's different with us, Eddie. We can't pass for Western European like you can.'

'That's absurd, Nathan!' Angela said testily. 'There are many well-respected Jewish peop—'

'No, he may be right,' Morgan interrupted. 'I had Jewish friends at college who used to call it "the curse of the chosen people" – outsiders since the days of the Pharaohs...' Angela glowered at him, but Morgan went on blithely, 'I used to say to them, "We were with you up until Jesus!"'

Edward groaned and lit a cigarette.

'Christians are so smug in their certainty,' Nathan countered, lighting one of his own.

'You have to admit it's a compelling story, though,' Morgan

said with a laugh, 'even if we do force it down people's throats. Let's face it, salvation sells!'

'Amen, brother,' Marjorie quipped.

Nathan stubbed out his cigarette and abruptly got to his feet. 'I've heard enough,' he said, holding out his hand to Emma. 'Would you like to dance?'

She returned a few minutes later without him, and explained that he'd been irritable and distracted on the dance floor, before offering a brisk apology and storming out.

'Oh, I'm terribly sorry to hear it,' Morgan said, looking genuinely glum. 'I liked your friend, Edward – thin-skinned, perhaps, but clever, nonetheless.'

Angela suffered a second miscarriage on the train trip to San Francisco at Christmas. She was several weeks along and the experience left her wan and without hope, for despite her best efforts to ensure robust health she evidently could not preclude a recurrence of that first traumatic episode. She was subdued throughout the holidays, spending most of her time alone in the rear bedroom upstairs that had once been Aunt Mildred's. Edward attended to Clara with the help of his sister and mother, and by the end of the stay Angela was able to join the family in the front parlor after dinner, where Clara delighted in Grandpa James's reading of "The Tale of Peter Rabbit," a favorite of Auntie Dede's a generation earlier. Angela came away from the visit grateful for the Dooley's support, and for Katherine especially, who saw to it that Honora respected her privacy.

Edward and Angela had been back in Los Angeles only a few days when one afternoon, after Angela had put Clara down for a nap, the telephone rang. It was Emma Watkins, calling to inform her that Dale Henderson had been struck and killed by a motorist early New Year's Day just outside the grounds of the Old Soldiers Home.

'Oh, how awful,' Angela said.

'And the worst part is that it could have been avoided. If only the administration had listened to our concerns about the south gate crossing – it's on a blind curve, remember?'

'That's right.'

'He was such a troubled man, Angela,' Emma continued, clearly still upset, 'but lately he seemed to be turning things around. He wasn't missing appointments like he used to and before Christmas he told me that he wanted to give the Carnes arm another try...'

'It's just terrible...' Angela said, sorry for this lost soul but also wishing that the memory of the incident with Clara could be expunged as well. She asked how his family had taken the sad news and Emma explained that his father had arranged for the body to be brought back to Pasadena to be buried in the family's plot.

Angela thanked her for the call but wasn't interested in staying on the line – though she liked Emma, she was well enough done with the Old Soldier's Home. 'Be well, Emma, and say "Hi" to everyone, won't you?' she said before hanging up.

A nagging suspicion prompted Angela to go to the library the next day and dig up the January 2nd edition of the *Times*. There she found an account of the incident in the back pages – the tragic story of a paraplegic veteran caught in a most unfortunate circumstance in the early morning hours of New Year's Day. Noting that Henderson had been struck and killed by a Pierce-Arrow, however, Angela wondered whether it had been an accident at all. The distraught driver, a widow on her way home from a party at the Los Angeles Country Club, reported that the young man had appeared out of nowhere.

Edward and Angela returned to San Francisco for Easter, where an odd encounter cast a pall over that holiday as well. Just as the Dooleys were preparing to leave for church Sunday morning, a small, unsavory-looking character in a rumpled suit appeared on the front stoop demanding to see Honora. Edward had answered the door, and when he asked what it was regarding, the man with a pockmarked face sneered, 'Tell her it's Danny Bogue – from another life.'

Katherine came up behind Edward just then, and the man blurted, 'Oi, remember me? Brigid Mulcahy's boy? You and your mam used to visit – you played checkers with me…'

With a wary look, Katherine went for their mother while Edward escorted their disconcerting visitor into the front parlor. Edward kept an eye on him as he looked about with a scowl on his lips – as though the lace curtains, the clock on the mantle, the air sweet with the smells of fresh carnations and lemon furniture polish summed up all the middle-class gentility he'd come to loathe. A commotion arose in the kitchen and suddenly Honora was marching up the hallway unpinning her hat, with Katherine on her heels.

'What is it you want, Danny Bogue?' she said curtly as she came into the parlor.

'Bet you thought I disappeared like me dear old Da,' the man said with a smirk, revealing crooked, yellow teeth. He sat down on the couch now and stretched an arm luxuriously across the top. Looking to Edward and Katherine, he said, 'S'posedly he was Shanghaied, or maybe murdered over a gamblin' debt, but who's to say? Me Mam, she held to the former – was sure he'd be back…'

'Your poor mother, Danny,' Honora said, shaking her head as she took a seat on the edge of the armchair. Brigid Mulcahy had come out from Boston with her and had made her way among the shanty Irish South of Market Street before marrying a roustabout named Dan Bogue. The man disappeared when Danny Jr. was no more than a toddler, and Brigid was pregnant again.

'Me poor mother, indeed,' Bogue repeated. From his jacket pocket he pulled a yellowed letter and handed it to Edward.

Edward and Katherine immediately recognized their mother's handwriting on the envelope; addressed to the Maudsley Sanitarium on Sutter Street, the letter they unfolded was dated October 1918, and read that she didn't know any Brigid or Maeve Bogue. The sullen man now explained that he'd come down from Vancouver earlier in the week at the urging of the matron of the sanitarium who was clearing out her files before retiring. Eyeing Honora coldly, he scoffed, 'Besides a few photographs and the death certificates she had that ta give me…".

'So you found an old letter, so what!' Honora said irritably, 'Holy Jesus, I was the one who referred her to the Maudsley in the first place. What with three sons off to war, my husband barely makin' a livin', and my sister-in-law dyin' upstairs, we had no room for sick people!' She shook her head again, disgusted. 'After all I did for your mother – the money, the meals, the cryin' on my shoulder…you and your sister always with snotty noses, wearin' nothin' but rags. Where in God's name were you, boy? Dodgin' the draft, I suppose. Hidin' out in Canada!'

His eyes dark beneath his brow, Bogue turned his attention back to Edward and Katherine and said menacingly, 'The kicker is the matron showed me some old logs where it's recorded that a James A. Dooley was adm—'

'Why you shiftless, no-good coward,' Honora hissed, getting to her feet and pointing to the door, 'You get out of this house this instant!'

The young man stood up and yelled, 'Cause yer feckin' husband's a mental case…' as Honora came at him, her hair like a white-hot flame.

Tearing at his clothes, she snarled, 'You're a bad seed, Danny Bogue! A bad seed from a pitiful, depraved woman who lost all self-respect!' Edward got hold of the young man's arms just as his mother toppled over the coffee table. Sprawled on the floor, her dental bridge askew, she garbled the words, 'Get out, Satan! Get out!!'

With the man flailing and sputtering obscenities and barbs about their being Christian hypocrites, Edward managed to drag him out the front door and down the steps to the sidewalk. The household was still composing itself thirty minutes later when a final indignity arrived in the form of a brick, hurled through the bay window of the parlor, Honora's letter wrapped around it with twine.

Chapter 36

In August, Valentino's death from appendicitis prompted Edward to say that he and Angela had been remiss, not keeping in touch with Giancarlo. Her brother had been in Italy for a year now and she'd not written him once, relying instead on periodic reports from her mother.

'He's got to be homesick,' Edward said. They were parked in the shade of a housing tract under construction one Sunday afternoon, with Clara napping in the back seat.

'Probably having the time of his life,' Angela groused, 'Mama hasn't said he's lonely...'

'Believe me, it's the last thing a boy wants to tell his mother...'

'Oh, maybe you're right,' she said with a sigh, only to quickly reverse course, 'But he hasn't written us either, Edward. Not for Christmas or Easter, or just for Clara...'

Taking her hand, Edward said, 'I don't want him to think we've given up on him, that's all. That he's got no life to come back to here.'

'Okay, dear heart,' Angela said, squeezing his hand, 'I'll write to him...'

In late December, Gemma received a telegram from her husband informing her that his mother had passed away. It was three months before Gaetano Luchetti and his son returned to Stockton, however, and in telephone calls home Angela got

326

the sense that all was not well, that there was an uneasy truce in the household. She and Edward arranged to visit for Easter.

Her brother had grown darker in the sixteen months he'd been away – he'd been doing farm work – and he seemed preoccupied as he and his father spent the days inspecting crops, and meeting with various suppliers and pickers. After Easter mass, everyone was seated in the shade of the rear porch, watching Clara search for the Easter eggs her Uncle Giancarlo had hidden in the garden, when Angela asked her father about his brother Vincenzo's farming operation.

'Is good,' Mr. Luchetti said with a crisp nod as he rocked in his chair, 'Five hundred hectares for corn, alfalfa, and wheat – government gives best prices...'

'The Prime Minister is a forceful leader,' Angela said with a sidelong glance to her mother.

'Italy is stronger now, yes – the "irredenta" is coming,' Mr. Luchetti declared, referring to Mussolini's territorial ambitions. 'Prosperity has returned and we are a proud people once again.' Looking out at the Easter egg hunt, he added dismissively, 'But in America they say Italians are anarchisti!'

'You mean Sacco and Vanzetti, Papa,' Angela said. Demonstrations around the world had prompted calls for a new trial for the two men accused of robbery and murder in Massachusetts. 'There'll be a clemency hearing this summer,' she assured her father.

'Ach, American justice! It goes on too long...'

'It will work out,' Gemma offered. 'They say the judge is not fair and will be changed.'

But alone later that evening, Edward questioned why Angela was trying to appease her father when they'd been following the case closely for years and had concluded that the men were guilty. 'They're avowed Galleanists, Angela – the evidence is more than circumstantial.'

'I know, I know,' she said wearily, 'but can't you see that his mind's made up? I don't want to argue with him – I'm worried he's looking for any excuse to leave for good…'

Her suspicions increased when she returned in July – Edward was on a business trip to the Pacific Northwest – and was able to have a heart-to-heart with her brother. They were having malts at a soda fountain one afternoon, and she had just confided that she might be pregnant again, when Giancarlo confessed that he'd gotten a girl pregnant in Italy.

'I can't tell Mamma,' he said, 'I'm too ashamed.'

'No, Giancarlo, don't be ashamed, never be ashamed,' Angela said, touching his arm as she studied him imploringly. 'Tell me what happened.'

He sighed, grateful to be able to talk with her about the tremendous burden he was under. The girl was a cousin, he explained, one of his uncle's daughters, and she was due sometime in the fall. 'It was stupid,' he said, looking down, 'I should have known better.'

'Well, but you can marry her and bring her to America, right?'

He shook his head. 'She'd never leave her family – she wants nothing to do with America…just like Papa.' When he looked at Angela, tears came into his eyes. In fits and starts he explained that their father was trying to sell his land in order to buy a Holt tractor and a thresher and ship them to Italy.

'For Vincenzo?" Angela asked. But when he wouldn't return

her gaze, she sensed the worse. 'But what about Mama?'

'He's planning on talking to her,' Giancarlo said simply, pushing his malt away.

The next day, on the pretext of needing darning thread, Angela asked her father if she could come along with him to the hardware store. They rode in silence and only after parking in the dirt lot behind the store did she turn to him.

'You're going back to Italy,' she said evenly. 'I know, Papa. For reasons I'll never understand, you've lost faith in America…'

He pursed his lips in resignation.

'And now Giancarlo has an obligation to go back – to honor his responsibilities,' she continued, lifting a hand to head off any demonstration. 'Brothers and sisters talk – don't be mad at him,' she said, then with defeat in her voice, 'He's doing the right thing.'

She turned and looked her father in the eye. 'You have to tell Mama everything because if she doesn't know, Giancarlo's leaving will break her heart.' Despite something inside her that resisted the urge, she squeezed his hand and said, 'Take her with you, Papa.'

Whatever he might have said he held back. Instead, he jutted out his jaw to fight back tears, and looking out the windshield, he nodded slowly.

But he never did talk to his wife. Instead, citing the whole Sacco and Vanzetti affair – the two were executed by electric chair in August – he abruptly returned to Italy with Giancarlo at the beginning of September. Angela learned this through her mother's sobs on the telephone. It came as a great disappointment for she had hoped her mother could have accompanied them for Giancarlo's wedding and the arrival of his child.

It was only later that Angela came to know just how callous her father had been. Gemma had come to stay with Edward and Angela a few weeks later, when the telegram arrived announcing the birth of Giancarlo's son. When Gemma burst into tears, Angela realized that her mother had been completely unaware of Giancarlo's predicament.

Chapter 37

With the economy running so strong, signs of strain were inevitable. Nathan Leopold snapped when heard that Hickey-Freeman, bowing to stockholder pressure, was starting to market ready-to-wear suits to multiple retailers – calling the new label "Walter-Morton" after the eldest sons of Jerry Hickey and Emmet Baum, Leopold's nemesis from Rochester.

'What really galls me,' Leopold sneered, 'is claiming that the label is for the discerning customer when it's the same goddamn suit Hickey's been peddling for years!'

Edward chuckled. 'Like passing Joseph & Feiss off under the B & L label?'

'The difference, Eddie,' Leopold said testily, 'is that we were here first…'

American Thread was also adjusting to the increasingly competitive climate. Its chief rival, Coats & Clark, had been gaining ground in Los Angeles after several big garment manufacturers opened West Coast plants. Cecil Breslin summoned Edward to San Francisco for an emergency meeting to strategize about how American Thread should respond.

'This fight's on our turf now, Eddie,' the man said over a lunch of sandwiches in the conference room, 'and rather than praying for the New York muckety-mucks to make new alliances, we've gotta see to it that producers out here stay ahead of the competition.'

'The one's touting the "Fun in the Sun" California look,' Edward said, as if on cue.

The bulldog of a man nodded. 'Linens, silks, and rayon especially.' Wiping mustard from his chin with the back of his hand, he said, 'Our big advantage out here is labor costs,' then with a wink, '—and I know how that sticks in the craw of your colleagues back east…'

It was a reference to the biennial managers' meeting the year before, where Edward had been reminded of how he stuck out like a sore thumb. The salesmen were gathered for dinner at Gallagher's, a West 46th Street steakhouse popular with businessmen, chorus girls, and gangsters – emblematic, like Mayor Jimmy Walker himself, of New York's brazen disregard of Prohibition. They dined like kings on oysters and filet mignon while trading bold predictions about various business deals in the offing, when eventually conversation took a more jocular turn. Percy Schuster, the St. Louis-Kansas City man, taunted their New York hosts about the Cardinals' World Series victory over the Yankees a few months before. 'Foolish of the Babe trying to steal second in the bottom of the ninth, wasn't it?' he said with satisfaction.

'Like Houdini taking one to the gut,' Charlie Gillespie replied, referring to the blow that had felled the magician recently. 'But don't worry, Percy, the Yanks'll be back!'

Still gloating, Schuster began prodding Declan Morrissey about the Red Sox, who had finished last in the league. But it was Pete Ragali from Philadelphia who spoke up first, saying he liked the new kid Boston was bringing on at third, prompting Edward to remark that the kid, Fred Haney, had actually started out with the Hollywood Stars in the Pacific Coast League.

'Yeah, and Cincinnati after that,' Morrissey muttered grumpily before suddenly coming alive and turning to Edward. 'Speaking of Hollywood and Reds, Dooley, any truth to the rumor that you're a communist sympathizer?' A few snickers bubbled up around the table, and Edward was reminded that his East Coast colleagues saw each other more frequently and probably enjoyed gossiping at his expense. 'I mean, given your affection for the factory workers and all, I wonder whether you might be going out to Passaic this time around,' referring to the strike of wool and silk workers, the first to have involved the "Workers' Party".

Edward glowered at the man, but Charlie Gillespie held his hand up to stifle any comeback. 'Look, Declan, Botany Worsted had no choice but to rescind those wage cuts, but that doesn't mean Red militants will ever be allowed back into the plants…'

'They did get a collective bargaining agreement out of it,' Ragali said, winking at Edward.

'Thanks, Pete,' Edward said, before turning irritably to the Boston man. 'Listen, I'm no communist sympathizer, Morrissey. I went to Willimantic the last time I came out because I wanted to see the factory, that's all – not to foment revolution. I'm a loyal company man.'

'Glad to hear it,' the Boston man said with a wicked grin.

But Edward didn't know when to quit, adding foolishly, 'I can't help it if mills keep closing all over New England…' which only served to rekindle Morrissey's ire.

Edward was leaving the office one afternoon to pay a visit to manufacturer of seersucker suits when he received a frantic call from his sister, Katherine, informing him that their father had suffered a stroke. Angela was now seven months along, and assured him that she could count on help from the Mother's Club of the parish, so he took the overnight express to San Francisco.

He spent the next day at St. Francis Hospital, where his father lay unconscious, calming his mother and sisters, and placating Colm who had been vocalizing his doubts as to whether the doctors and nurses were doing all they could. Edward reached Walter in New York by telephone and reported that their father had opened his eyes and appeared to recognize family members; unfortunately, he was apparently paralyzed on the left side of his body and unable to speak.

With Thanksgiving only a week away, Honora was intent on getting him home. The following Wednesday, Edward and Colm carried their father upstairs to the rear bedroom which had served as his sister Mildred's sickroom for years. Despite all Katherine and Deirdre had done to spruce up the room to his satisfaction, however, the fright in their father's eyes was evident, and his mumbling incomprehensible.

Aunt Hildie moved into Colm's old room down the hall for the next six weeks to help nurse her brother. Katherine went to Los Angeles to accompany Angela and the Clara on the train trip north for Christmas – though the holiday was joyless and Clara's fourth birthday party an afterthought.

One afternoon as Edward sat at his father's bedside across from Aunt Hildie, she reminded him of how as a baby his contentment had been a great consolation to his father.

'I only wish I could talk to him now,' Edward said gloomily

as his father slept.

'Oh, he knows you're here. Say what you need to, dear boy – it will bring him peace.'

Edward welled up, and after a few deep breaths he took his father's hand in his. It was cool to the touch, the once-familiar calluses gone. 'We love you, Pops, and…and we're coming along just fine…' he managed to say, before he was overcome with emotion.

James Aloysius Dooley, sixty-two years of age, passed on the 17th day of January 1928, a first-generation American, father of six (predeceased by his daughter, Mary), tenor, tinsmith, sentimental dreamer, a loving man.

Honora grudgingly honored his wish that the funeral mass be held at St. Peter's – the decidedly modest church in the flats of the Mission District where their children had been baptized. Edward, Colm, and Walter served as pallbearers, assisted by John Potts and Denny Collins, long-time employees of James's, and one of the sons of the McAvoy-O'Hara funeral director. The six men were solemnly bearing the casket out of the church at the end of the service when Edward caught sight of a woman shrouded in a mourning veil, seated in one of the rear pews between Morgan and a nattily dressed gentleman.

After the hearse had been loaded, the Dooley family formed a receiving line in the tiny narthex of the church to thank the forty or so attendees. The unfamiliar couple at the end of the line turned out to be Constance and her husband, who introduced himself as C.P. Bingham of the Great Western Power Company. Morgan, who hadn't mentioned that his sister would be in town for the funeral, now made a point of engaging

Honora to give Constance and his brother-in-law a chance to visit with Edward and Angela. The encounter lasted no more than five minutes and amounted to the barest exchange of condolences and pleasantries, before the Dooley family had to depart for Holy Cross Cemetery.

With John Potts muttering curses as he maneuvered his enormous Pontiac Six through city traffic, and with his wife hard of hearing, Edward and Angela were able to talk privately in the back seat on the way out to Colma. When Angela asked whether Constance had been fond of his father, Edward replied absently, 'Oh, I suppose – I don't recall really...'

'Maybe she just wanted to see what's become of *us*,' Angela said.

'—and maybe show off her prosperity,' Edward added with a sidelong glance.

Angela dug into her handbag and pulled out a tin of breath mints. 'Fortunately for her, the occasion called for a veil...'

Edward took a mint that she offered him. 'How do you mean?'

'It would've been hard to miss without the veil...'

'Miss what? Is she ill?'

'The heavy makeup over the bruises, Edward – her left cheekbone and temple?' Looking out the window, she added, 'Who wears a broad-brim hat and gauntlet gloves to a funeral?'

'My God, do you think she's hiding bruises on her arms, too?'

'He did seem pretty tightly wound...' Angela ventured.

'All business, that's for sure,' Edward agreed, shaking his head incredulously. 'When I mentioned that we lived in Los Angeles, he was quick to belittled the Owens Valley Aqueduct before trumpeting his great Feather River project...Jesus!'

'Well,' Angela said, patting Edward's hand by way of putting the episode behind them, 'living in Chico can't be the cosmopolitan life Constance had in mind – they'll be building dams up there for years...'

Angela went nearly full term, and in early February gave birth to a baby boy who had Angela's dark coloring. Once again at Honora's insistence, the baby – named James in honor of his dearly departed grandfather – he was christened at St. Mary's Cathedral in San Francisco on Holy Saturday. The Dooley women hosted a celebration at Old Man McCormick's, which unfortunately would be remembered for Colm's absence.

The previous fall he'd announced his intention to marry the daughter of Salvadoran immigrants whom he'd met through one of his employees. Fifteen years his junior, Rosa was diminutive but feisty, the youngest of five, whose imperfect command of English greatly amused Colm. Nevertheless, she kept him in check and he seemed to thrive in her unfamiliar culture. He got on with her father, a bricklayer, and liked the family's cooking so much that he put on a few pounds; he even drank less.

But where Honora had adjusted to the idea of Edward marrying an Italian girl, she was less accepting of Rosa, whom she derisively referred to as "the Mexican jumping bean." Colm had postponed the wedding planned for January due to his father's passing, then a heated exchanged between mother and son caused him to put it off indefinitely.

When in March Edward reached his older brother by telephone to ask that he be the baby's godfather – Angela's friend, Gracie Taub, was to be godmother – Colm had one condition.

'I'm not talking to Mother and I'm not coming to any damn party she's throwing…'

'Listen, Angela and I don't want to make things any worse between you two,' Edward hedged, 'Maybe I ought to ask Morgan instead…'

'No!' Colm said sharply. 'I want to be your son's godfather, Eddie – I'm honored you and Angela would ask me. As for Honora, she can go to hell…'

'Aw, she may be cool to your girl right now, but she'll get over it in time.'

'That's just it, brother, she won't get over it,' Colm said bitterly. 'Rosa knows it, so she broke off the engagement last month.'

'What? No, no, you've got to get her to reconsider – if you love her.'

'It's no use, Eddie – if you thought Mother was hard-headed…' There was silence on the line until Colm spoke up again. 'What gets me is why I didn't just go off and marry her like you did with Angela – instead, I give into Mother and end up losing the girl for good…'

Edward felt awful, and at length said, 'There'll be other girls, Colm…'

'Yeah,' came the unconvincing reply.

Chapter 38

The Yankees won the World Series in the second week of October behind three Babe Ruth shots over the right field fence in St. Louis. Meanwhile, the San Francisco Seals, behind a "Murderer's Row" of their own, were engaged in an epic battle with the Sacramento Senators in the PCL, which culminated in a championship showdown at Big Rec on October 16th.

With the ten-year anniversary of the Armistice drawing near, the Presidio Color Guard was on hand, the stadium was decked out with red, white, and blue bunting, and the franchise's six pennants fluttered above the "Booze Cage" in the bleachers (where the ticket price included a sandwich and a shot of whiskey). Twelve members of the pennant-winning Seals teams of 1915 and 1917, Fitz among them, formed a semi-circle behind Mayor Rolph as he addressed the crowd from the pitcher's mound before the start of the game. "Sunny Jim" led the crowd in the Pledge of Allegiance before ceding the microphone to opera contralto Louise Homer who gave a stirring rendition of the "Star-Spangled Banner". A row of San Francisco police officers then issued a three-volley rifle salute from the left field line, signaling it was time to play ball.

All the pre-game pomp was a distant memory by the end of the first inning, however: pitcher Elmer Jacobs was roughed up for two runs on four hits and the Seals' much ballyhooed batters failed to get on base at all. Edward, Morgan, and Fitz were sitting above the home team dugout just as the second inning was getting started, when Harry Heilmann appeared and offered to trade his seat behind home plate to a star-struck fan so that he could sit next to Fitz. Heilmann had played ball at Sacred Heart, too, and when Fitz introduced Edward and Morgan, the tall, lanky first baseman exclaimed, 'Any friend of Jimmy's is a friend of mine!' (Fitz explained that it was Edward who'd written on his behalf years before, asking teammates for help when he was looking to leave Letterman.)

Heilmann had been playing for the Detroit Tigers for ten years; he matched up well with his indomitable teammate, Ty Cobb, and won the American League batting title four times. Still, he was philosophical about his notoriety, and taking his seat, he said, 'Never been more than a spectator in October, fellas.' Between commenting on the impressive play of the Seals' Babe Pinelli at third and Frankie Crosetti at short, he caught up with Fitz – having heard about the arrest and jail time, he was glad his old teammate had a job and a place of his own again.

By the bottom of the seventh, with the Senators up 5-1, the air was thick with cigar smoke and frustration. With Pinelli on first and Ping Bodie on deck, there was a hush of anticipation as Roy Johnson came to the plate. He was a heavy hitter, but also something of a strikeout goat, and the count sagged to 1-2 before he launched a comet deep into the right field stands, unleashing delirium in the stadium. Bodie followed with a double, Dutch Ruether singled, and the Seals were off to the races – a five run inning. When in the top of the eighth south-paw Duster Mails discharged three Sacramento batters with what Heilmann called Ford assembly line efficiency, Morgan quipped, '—just the kind of productivity Hoover has in mind!'

'Jesus, you've gotta be kidding,' Heilmann said. 'The Republicans' hands-off business philosophy just makes the fat cats richer – ask any factory worker in Dearborn…'

'Aw, c'mon…' Morgan started to protest before he was cut off.

'Millionaires don't give a damn about the little guy,' Heilmann asserted above all the excitement that had gripped the hometown fans. 'I for one like Al Smith because he's for abolishing labor injunctions and for regulating the power companies…'

'Yeah, but his being against Prohibition is political suicide,' Morgan said.

'Calls it like he sees it,' the lanky man replied as he turned his attention back to the game.

The Seals' bats had come alive, and the relief pitchers the Senators sent in couldn't stop the bleeding. When they came up to bat in the top of the ninth down four runs, the San Francisco fans were on their feet cheering wildly.

Bodie recorded out number one, catching a high fly to left, and Morgan said, 'Look, Harry, nobody outside Boston, New York, and maybe Chicago is gonna to trust a Catholic in the White House. Sure, we can cheer on Skip Madigan's Galloping Gaels and the Fightin' Irish of Notre Dame, but as for the presidency, we've got as much chance as the Bolsheviks!'

After the second baseman quickly dispatched a grounder, Heilmann looked over to Morgan. 'You're a strange breed of Republican out here, Doherty, that's all I can say.'

The next batter went down looking; the Seals had won their seventh pennant.

Chapter 39

Angela was disappointed, though not surprised, that for the third time around Edward was backing the sensible business candidate. After eight years of economic growth, confidence had become the watchword around the country. The consumer revolution meant that the more one bought, the more America grew – from air conditioners to radios, electrical appliances to underarm deodorant, the promise of permanent prosperity made possible thanks to "buy now, pay later" consumer credit. *What will they think of next?!*

Edward was intoxicated by the boundless optimism in the air. Garment factories were humming sixteen hours a day, dozens of new skyscrapers were under construction in Los Angeles, and the San Pedro docks were second only to New York City in exporting American goods. Bullock's opened a new store on Wilshire Boulevard – now dubbed the Miracle Mile – that catered specifically to motorists.

The epicenter of all the consumer confidence was Wall Street, and the bull market seemed unstoppable. Popular periodicals touted the ease of investing and watching the tickertape had become a kind of national sport. For four years Edward had been making modest investments based on recommendations from Walter, and now, back in New York for the biennial managers' meeting, he was anxious to talk to his brother about accelerating his rate of growth.

Over dinner at a steak house in the financial district, Edward grew impatient as Walter waxed on about married life – he'd married his boss's niece and moved into a charming flat near Gramercy Park. Over coffee, Edward tried to sound casual when he finally broached the subject of stock tips.

Walter lit a cigarette, a new affectation that Edward found vaguely irritating. 'Well, I expect you've done pretty well by RCA, no?'

'Sure, but with the new baby and all,' Edward began, anxiously twiddling his coffee spoon between his fingers. 'You see, we've got our hearts set on a Spanish Mediterranean bunga-low in an up-and-coming neighborhood…'

Walter nodded judiciously. 'And you're still sending Mother money?'

'Every month, Walter, just like you – only with more respon-sibilities, I've got less to play with.' Ashamed to sound petty, he said, 'Listen, I just need another RCA…'

Walter was very deliberate in dispensing advice, talking up established companies like General Motors and General Electric, and cautioning against riskier, less well-capitalized concerns; he was circumspect about real estate securities, given the swindles down in Florida and knowing first-hand how commercial development was well ahead of demand. In the end, he suggested that Edward visit the branch office of the National City Bank in Los Angeles.

'Buy on margin?' Edward said. 'But that's pretty risky, isn't it?

'Of course, if you're not careful,' Walter agreed, glancing at the tab. 'Split it?' he asked, and as the two brothers dug out their wallets, he went on, 'Naturally, you've gotta do your homework on companies you're investing in. Even the best investors get stung every once in a while…Like the song says, Edward, "If you want the rainbow, you gotta have the rain!"'

After the sales managers' meeting the next day, mindful of Breslin's advice to keep his enemies close, Edward made a point of drawing out Declan Morrissey. He suggested the Boston man join him and Pete Ragali to see a trade show in the garment district, and on the subway ride uptown he skipped the chitchat and plunged into a sensitive subject right off the bat.

'Say, I imagine the strikes hit Massachusetts pretty hard,' he said to Morrissey as soon as they took their seats, referring to the walkout by fifty-thousand textile workers in New Bedford and Fall River the year before. 'What's the mood these days?'

'Pretty raw, as you'd expect,' Morrissey said with a scowl, 'what with the National Guard called in and people going to jail. But mostly because it just petered out…'

'Once you get blackballed as a striker, well…' Ragali put in.

'Unions don't have much clout anymore,' Edward opined, '—not with all the cheap labor in the south…'

Morrissey leaned forward, elbows on his knees. 'And you're all busted up about it, I bet…'

'No, not really,' Edward said sincerely.

Ragali chuckled. 'Ed's beginning to get how free enterprise works…'

'Look, I sell thread, I don't make it,' Edward said. 'If making it cheaper five hundred miles away means American Thread is more competitive, that's fine with me…'

The Boston man nodded. 'To make it in America you've gotta go where the work is – that's how it's always been. My granddad came over on account of the famine and worked as a laborer digging canals on Merrimack River. My dad moved to Boston and learned carpentry, then saw to it we got a decent education so we wouldn't have to use a pickax ourselves…'

With the subway car nearly empty, Edward stretched out his legs. 'My father's father came over during the famine, too, first to Kentucky, where I think he worked in livery. Then an Irishman sponsored my dad out to San Francisco where eventually he started his own sheet metal business – that my brother runs to this day…'

Pete Ragali explaining how his grandfather had come from Naples to Pittsburgh, only to backtrack to Philadelphia after an uncle was maimed in a foundry accident. 'We got into dry goods instead, which is how I ended up in the apparel trade… It takes a few generations.'

Morrissey looked over to Edward after a moment. 'The trouble with newcomers nowadays is they don't wanna blend in. They isolate themselves, then they put down roots. But capitalism's all about risk, top to bottom – you can't expect things to be handed to you.'

Edward nodded. 'You're always at the mercy of larger forces…'

'Factory work's a devil's bargain, that's for sure' Ragali agreed, 'Just when you think you've got it made, along comes somebody willing to do it cheaper…'

'It's survival of the fittest, alright,' Edward declared. 'You either adapt or you die!'

Upon returning from a business trip to the Pacific Northwest later that summer, Edward was eager to tell Angela about having looked up Karl Steinkoler in Seattle. Seated at the kitchen table holding Baby James while Angela worked on dinner with Clara, he reported that his old army buddy had a wife and four kids and ran his own commercial fishing business. Angela followed distractedly, but not until Edward asked about the odd little painting next to her Stockton watercolor on the wall did she look over.

'It's a camellia,' Clara said of the crude red flower with jagged green leaves. 'One of the old soldiers at the hospital gave it to me.'

'The hospital?' Edward said.

Angela reminded him that while he was away she and the children had accompanied Gemma to the Napa Valley to get out of the Stockton heat. She explained, again, that the Cappaciola family had moved there to be close to Joe, who'd been gassed in the war and now lived at the Yountville Veterans Home.

'You remember Rose, his sister – she still lives next door to Mama,' Angela said, bringing over a dish of pureed squash as Edward fastened Baby James into his highchair. 'Joe volunteered to serve in 1917, after getting his citizenship. Anyhow, Rose arranged for us to stay with Louise and the children while we were there, and so we paid Joe a visit together.'

'I'm not sure that was such good idea,' Edward said, looking cross. 'I thought we agreed it's better that you steer clear of those places...'

'It was only for about an hour,' Angela said, putting a bib on the baby.

As unfortunate as it was that some vets were consigned to living outside mainstream society, it irked Edward that a veterans' hospital still exercised a pull on his wife. He said as much later, after they'd put the children to bed and were washing the dishes together.

'Don't worry,' Angela assured him, 'I'm not going back to the Old Soldier's Home. It's just that our generation got caught up in the war, and like it or not, the ripples continue...'

'Yeah, well, I don't like you getting all worked up over it.'

She gave him a hard look. 'Listen, Edward, I can take care of myself, thank you very much.' She commenced to vigorously scouring a pot, saying, 'But it's not right thinking we can ignore the men who weren't so lucky, put them out of our minds...'

'I'm not ignoring them,' Edward said testily, 'but we've got to move on with our own lives – it's the best way we can honor the ones who didn't make it. That's what you said once.'

'Not to the point of distraction, it isn't.'

Edward stopped drying a plate. 'What's that supposed to mean?'

'It's just that you've seemed awfully pre-occupied lately, that's all,' she said, not looking up. 'It's work, work, work, all the time – then you come home exhausted and irritable...I don't want you getting caught up in the rat race and missing what's truly important.'

'Well, I'm sorry, but there's been a lot of pressure lately,' Edward said defensively, then demurred, 'It's just that I hate thinking of you crammed in here with the children all day...'

'I know, dear, but we're really okay. Don't put so much pressure on yourself – we don't need to have it all overnight, you know.'

'Right,' he said with a self-deprecating sigh.

They worked in silence a minute before Angela said, 'I thought a lot about Fitz while we were up in Yountville – it's

347

so lovely and serene there. I know he's a city boy like you, but maybe some time in the country would do him good. What do you think?'

Picturing Fitz in the basement speakeasy, Edward pursed his lips and shook his head. 'No, he's better off where he is – away from all the reminders of the war...'

A record-breaking heat wave swept across the country in August, mirroring the trading frenzy on Wall Street. The hit song on the radio was "I'm in the Market for You," the Babe hit his 500th homer, and the people of Los Angeles thrilled at the sight of the Graf Zeppelin as it soared overhead on its round-the-world tour. By the first week of September the stock market had reached an all-time high, and caught up in the euphoria, Edward was making regular visits to the NCB branch offices to up his investments (RCA shares that he'd purchased for $100 were now trading at over $300). Though not aware just how much he was borrowing on margin, Angela was noncommittal when Mr. Olson, the building manager, mentioned that a two-bedroom unit was coming available – several friends with children had moved to new neighborhoods like Larchmont and Windsor Square, and she wanted a new home as much as anyone.

Edward and Angela explicitly refrained from talking about their financial future for fear of jinxing it. Edward was smoking more and having a second whiskey after dinner, but Angela didn't call him on it; nor did he disclose his recent nightmares, which brought up war-time superstitions that he thought he'd put behind him. When the twenty-ninth of September passed without incident – the eleventh anniversary of the reckless advance on Gesnes – Edward took Nathan Leopold for an expensive lunch the next day, with no explanation other to say he appreciated their friendship.

On Monday, October 21st – Edward and Angela's wedding anniversary – the front page of the *LA Times* was upbeat with the news that President Hoover was joining Henry Ford and Thomas Edison in Dearborn, Michigan, to celebrate America's prowess as a beacon of prosperity by commemorating the 50th anniversary of the invention of the light bulb.

Two days later, Edward was standing with dozens of other businessmen at the corner of 6th and Olive to watch the stock market read-out on the wrap-around sign above NCB's corner entrance. But instead of the usual chatter about the imminent groundbreaking of the Los Angeles Stock Exchange, there was worried conversation about tremors in the market. The next morning, Edward was in a meeting with buyers at J.J. Newberry's when a commotion on 5th Street caused him to look outside. When he saw businessmen running on the sidewalk, his first thought was that they were giving chase to a pickpocket – that is, until Mr. Griggs, the dour manager of men's furnishings, stepped into the room to announce that there was a run on the market.

At that very hour a handful of financiers had gathered in the offices of J.P. Morgan in New York to craft a statement assuring the public that, just as in 1907, the banks could be counted on to inject more capital into the system. Indeed, the market began to stabilize on Friday. But Thursday's free fall had been bracing enough for Edward that he wired Walter, pleading that he make himself available to take his telephone call Saturday morning.

'How's the weather out there?' Walter asked nonchalantly, when the two were finally connected.

Edward was seated in a telephone booth in the lobby of the Ambassador Hotel. Anxiously whisking cigarette ash from his trousers, he replied, 'More importantly, how's the weather where you are, Walter? Blue skies, I hope…'

'Oh, a few clouds maybe, but they're breaking up – no need to panic!'

'What about all the market volatility? What the devil's going on?'

'Listen, I read everything I can get my hands on, Edward, and this is just a tempest in a teapot brought on by the debate in congress over that Smoot-Hawley bill. The Republican majority wants to go against the president's wishes and increase industrial tariffs. The market always gets jittery whenever there's a policy squabble in Washington…'

'Well, are *you* selling any stocks?' Edward asked, rubbing his chin.

'I've made a few trades – nothing too substantial, though. People get burned when they act impulsively. Steady and true wins the race, remember…'

'And you're down at the exchange every day, right? You know first-hand when the wind shifts?' Suddenly feeling claustrophobic in the stuffy booth, Edward blurted out, 'I've got everything in stocks, Walter – I can't afford to be careless.'

'Relax, Edward, what we saw yesterday shows that the market's strong – it's simply too big to fail. There's too much riding on it…'

When the sell-off resumed Monday, however, Edward began

to panic. He sent two desperate telegrams to Walter, but as the day progressed and the market continued its precipitous slide, he received no reply. He was short with Angela when he got home, prompting a crying jag from Baby James that rankled everyone's nerves that evening, and by the time he got to work Tuesday, the anxiety on the street was palpable. He spent the morning standing in line at NCB's jammed-packed offices trying to stem his losses (RCA was trading for $26 a share now). When the stock exchange closed mid-afternoon, Edward was among hundreds of stunned men wandering the streets of downtown Los Angeles trying to fathom a financial collapse of unprecedented proportions – $30 billion lost in two days, with more money out on loan to speculators than all the U.S. currency in circulation.

He came home that evening a defeated man. 'I'm…I'm sorry to say,' he stammered, his eyes welling up as he stepped through the doorway of their apartment, 'it's just that we're wiped out, dear, completely done in…' He shook his head woefully and drew a ragged breath.

'Oh, Edward!' Angela exclaimed, pained to see the anguish in his eyes. Gently cupping his head in her hands, she pressed her forehead to his, saying, 'It'll be alright, we'll be alright – it's only money…' He shut his eyes tight as he embraced her, and Clara came over to console her parents. As she fiercely hugged their legs, Baby James looked on from his playpen, wondering what game this was.

'Look,' Angela said after a moment, pointing to a Western Union envelope on the kitchen table, 'Walter sent you a telegram!' She wasn't sure if Edward was laughing or crying, but he squeezed her shoulders and said, 'Not now,' and went to the sink for a glass of water.

He said little at dinner while Clara babbled on about an episode of "Amos 'n' Andy" they'd all listened to on the radio Sunday evening; from time to time Angela caught his eye, and he tried valiantly to muster a smile. After they'd put the children to bed and done the dishes, he assured Angela that he would be alright and just needed some air. With a whiskey and a cigarette, he went up to the roof of the apartment building, his routine when he wanted to unwind and think about the future.

But even as he lit his cigarette he knew the glow on the western horizon would offer no consolation this evening. Holding the unopened telegram in his hand, he resented his brother, though in truth he was more disgusted with himself. Utterly exhausted, he sat down on a crate and smoked his cigarette, watching the fog roll in from Santa Monica. At length, after draining his glass, he tore open the telegram, which read,

```
NEW YORK, NY - OCT 29, 1929
SORRY LINES JAMMED MONDAY HOPE YOU
CLEARED CREVICE OKAY HARD LUCK LET'S
TALK WHEN DUST SETTLES YOURS TRULY =
WALTER
```

He let the paper fall from his hands. Then, glancing at it a second time, he noted the date – again that ominous date, in this case the very day eleven years earlier when the battered 91st had been called upon to advance one more time at all costs. He hung his head and proceeded to cry, soft whimpers at first, eventually giving way to deep, doleful sobs as he found himself filled with resentment that the war should continue to cast such a long shadow in his life, and that once again he'd trusted in a system that had ultimately let him down.

PART FIVE

Chapter 40

While many dreams were wrecked by the crash, still other dreams were born, some most unexpectedly: in April, members of the Dooley clan received invitations to Deirdre's wedding, to be held in Sonoma two months hence. Edward telephoned Katherine, who said that she and Honora were as baffled by the news as he was. She explained that Tommy Hoagland was the younger brother of Pete Hoagland, husband to Cousin Maggie for six years now.

This news immediately took Edward back to the summer day the Dooley and O'Shea boys had stumbled upon Jack London's dream house. Katherine had gotten all out of joint the morning Uncle Aidan announced at breakfast that he was taking the boys fishing, so he also promised to take the girls to the Boyes Hot Springs dance the following Saturday. Cousin Cora remarked excitedly that she hoped the Hoagland boys would be there – she was keen on Pete and suggested that recently Tommy had been giving Katherine the eye at church as well. When this elicited giggles from Maggie and Deirdre, Katherine lost her temper, which prompted Deirdre to burst into tears. In addition to her lisp and a lazy eye – stemming from her childhood injury – Dede had a sensitive nature, which her brothers and cousins hastened to mollify after Katherine's outburst.

Now, years later, Edward noted the same irritability in

Katherine's voice when she said it was preposterous that Deirdre would be getting married to Tommy Hoagland. 'It makes me wonder about his character – taking advantage of an innocent girl like that...'

'Well, Dede *is* nearly thirty...' Edward said, as though to himself. 'So how long's she been seeing this young man?'

'Young man!' Katherine scoffed. 'Why, he's got to be over forty – Maggie and Pete already have three children, you know. Deirdre's over there all the time...'

'I suppose that explains it, then.'

'Oh, for goodness sake – they may be friendly toward one another, but husband and wife? Really, Edward, I wonder if this Tommy is playing with a full deck himself...'

In fact, throughout the weekend-long wedding party in June, Edward was struck by the big man's intelligence and his gentle disposition. Where it was all Maggie and Pete could do to corral their hellion children during the wedding ceremony, the groom was gallantly attentive to his elderly mother and her lady friends. Before the ceremony got started, he even came over to Edward and Honora and offered his pocket watch to keep Baby James amused.

Angela, Katherine, and one of Tom's unmarried sisters were bridesmaids, while Clara, now six, served as the flower girl. As Deirdre came up the aisle of St. Francis Church escorted by Colm, Honora whispered to Edward, 'I only consented to this because of your father, you know. He always said he wanted a full life for Dede – I only pray that she's ready for it...'

'Mother, you astonish me!' Edward said as Colm delivered his sister to the foot of the altar and shook hands with the groom. Perhaps Honora's diabetes, a reminder of her own mortality, was softening her once-brittle demeanor.

Cousin Michael was now an ordained "Brother" at St. Mary's College where he taught philosophy, and at the wedding reception Edward was pleased to have an opportunity to engage him again. The two had sparred at Christmas over St. Augustine's contention that materialism led to a corrupting of one's soul; now Edward was better able to acknowledge how recklessly he'd been swept up in the stock market frenzy. Seated in the shade of a willow tree with plates of food on their laps, he confided that the crash had hit him pretty hard. 'I suppose I put more faith in the economy than was warranted...' he ventured.

'It goes to show that man's material reality is no more than an illusion,' Michael said, with more resignation than judgment. 'Plato draws the distinction between a reality that is perceptible, but not intelligible – like the stock market, say – and a higher reality that is intelligible but imperceptible.'

Taking a bite of potato salad, Edward said with a sidelong glance, 'I knew there was something I didn't like about Plato...'

Michael laughed. 'Listen, with a family to support I'm sure you were only hoping to see your money go a little further – I wouldn't call that greed, exactly. The thing is, by conditioning ourselves to always want more, we become softer for it – turning our attention away from God in order to satisfy our worldly desires...'

Edward was grateful that his cousin hadn't taken a righteous tone, because he didn't need a lecture on the consequences of hubris – he felt guilty enough for thinking he could live beyond his means, then rationalizing that it had been his due. These days, whenever he'd see a man in rumpled business suit washing windshields at a stoplight, or read about some poor devil leaping to his death from the Arroyo Seco Bridge, he'd remind himself that he didn't have it so bad.

Such were his thoughts that October as he stared at Malcolm Doherty's casket in the aisle of St. Paul's Church. Stunned by Morgan's telegram the week before, he'd rearranged his schedule to attend the funeral of a man whose energy and enthusiasm he'd always admired, the man who might have been his father-in-law.

Sitting well behind the Dohertys in a mixed crowd of San Francisco's Irish American gentry and some of Morgan's college chums, Edward reflected on the conversation he'd had with his friend over drinks the night before at a downtown speakeasy. While generally aware that Mr. Doherty had been hurt by the crash, he hadn't realized how bad it was until Morgan quipped that the "coronary arrest" had been a blessing, lest his father put a pistol to his head.

'Jesus Christ!' Edward exclaimed, 'Tell me you're joking…'

Morgan removed two cigarettes from his sterling silver case, and offered one to Edward, saying, 'We really had no idea how overleveraged he'd become until Uncle Hector issued a springtime ultimatum…' He flicked open his lighter and lit their cigarettes.

'Turns out, Dear Old Dad's faith in electricity got the better of him,' he said, taking a long, satisfying drag. 'Seeing GE's stock triple in five years, he decided to go in big and put up his ownership interest in Doherty Brothers as collateral.'

Edward winced at the news, knowing General Electric had lost nearly half its value in a matter of days. 'How could Hector let him do it?'

Morgan shook his head in disgust. 'The bastard had no problem watching his partner dig his own grave – in May he offered to buy him out for pennies on the dollar…'

'My God!' Edward said. 'So where do things stand now?'

Morgan pursed his lips. 'To keep up appearances, Hector's giving Mother a monthly stipend and letting her keep the house. As for yours truly, you know my uncle and I have never exactly seen eye to eye,' he said, tapping his cigarette ash into an ashtray, 'so I've decided to go into shipping!'

'Shipping? You mean the export business?'

'I'll get to see the world after all,' Morgan said with a coy smile.

At length, Edward mused, 'Well, at least Constance is taken care of…'

His friend sighed and shook his head. 'Oh, she'll have to get by on her wits, too, I'm afraid. You'll see her tomorrow, but without the water and power magnate…' When Edward looked over, Morgan said, 'I'm proud of her – 'turns out, Con's got gumption after all. She took a holiday to Reno recently with a lady friend. Six weeks to be precise…'

'Six weeks?'

'Hmm,' Morgan nodded, sipping his drink, 'Used to be the residency requirement for a Nevada divorce was six *months*! Can you imagine sis in that cowpoke town for six months?!'

Edward paused on the landing of the Doherty's stately Dolores Street Victorian and turned to look east once more, down passed the twin spires of St. James Church to the blunt bell tower of St. Peter's at the bottom of the hill. He'd once stood here with the world at his feet and his head in the stars – now it seemed too incredible to believe that the house no longer belonged to the Dohertys, that his friend had been turned out of the family business, and that his former fiancée was newly divorced. The sound of door opening behind him caught him off guard.

'You've been standing out there so long, Edward,' he heard Constance say as he turned around, 'I wondered whether you'd forgotten how to ring the bell.'

She asked him in and he pecked her on the cheek and squeezed her shoulders while offering his condolences. He'd chosen not to bother her in the reception line after the funeral; now seeing just how drawn out she was, he was glad that their first encounter could be more informal. In due course he would pay his respects to Mrs. Doherty – who would ask without irony how he and "the Italian girl" were getting on – and mingle awkwardly with members of the extended Callan and Doherty clans, including Uncle Hector playing the role of family patriarch in the front parlor. But for now he let Constance guide him through the throng back to the kitchen, where they sat in the breakfast nook and talked while various maids came and went.

Her hair was a stronger hue of red than he remembered, and he ascribed the puffiness around her eyes to so many recent tears. 'Poor Daddy meant well,' she began, 'but I can't help but feel sorry for him – what with losing his brother's loyalty and then mother making things so hard on him in the end…'

'How do you mean?' Edward said. 'I thought your father had a heart attack.'

'Oh, I thought Morgan would have told you,' Constance said, surprised. 'She might well have brought Father home for his last days, but instead she insisted that he be kept in a double room at St. Luke's – payback for his recklessness, I imagine...'

A maid brought them tea, and Constance stirred two lumps of sugar into her cup. Despite the wrinkles that hinted at the strain she'd been under, Edward noted her familiar vivacity, even if it were a bit more willful now. As if reading his mind, Constance said summarily, 'So much water under the bridge, Edward – but life goes on...'

Edward pursed his lips. 'It's for the best, Con – I'm glad you can make a fresh start.'

'Only this time it'll be on my terms...' she said, looking to the side.

'Well, I wish you every success. You certainly deserve it...'

She offered a light laugh. 'I suppose we get what's coming to us...' she remarked enigmatically, and when Edward didn't respond, she caught his eye. 'And you, Edward, have you everything you always wanted?'

'Oh, the crash was difficult, of course, and business isn't what it used to be...' he trailed off, feeling foolish to begin this way. Knowing how lucky he was to have a loving family and a job, he said, 'Why, yes, everyone's fine...adjusting, to be sure, but we'll manage.'

'Yes, and with Honora in poor health on top of it, what an awful lot of responsibility for you...' Constance said, not looking especially sympathetic. 'Well, I'm sure you want to pay your respects to Mother,' she said brusquely after a moment, and seeing that Edward had nothing to add, she slid out of the breakfast nook.

He followed her into the dining room where they found Morgan standing unsteadily before a cluster of uncomfortable-looking society matrons. 'Ah, my dears!' he said, clearly tipsy as he beckoned Edward and Constance to join him, 'I was just saying to these virtuous women that the new Hays Code for motion pictures is a complete hypocrisy, don't you agree?' Turning to the women, he slurred, 'What's a little suggestive nudity now and then? God knows the museums are full of it – it's just that their nudes don't wriggle about as much!'

Appalled, the women turned and scattered. Constance took her brother aside and urge him to behave himself, but he cackled shamelessly while refilling his wine glass from a decanter on the sideboard. Draping his arm across Edward's shoulder, he declared, '"Wake: the silver dusk returning; up the beach of darkness brims!"' When Edward smiled and bowed his head, Morgan took his sister by the hand and looked up at Edward. 'Remember what a trio we once made?' he said wistfully.

His eyes were rheumy and tinged with regret, but there was a fierceness, too, which Edward found admirable. Looking over to his defiant friend and embittered former fiancée, he replied, 'Seems like only yesterday...'

Chapter 41

'Things are going from bad to worse,' Nathan Leopold said bluntly over lunch one day the following spring. Edward had returned from the bi-annual sales managers' meeting in New York armed with data suggesting that the economy was on the road to recovery, but Leopold was in a sour mood and not interested in wishful thinking. He tore into his pastrami sandwich with a knife and fork, saying, 'Remember when Hoover promised "a chicken in every pot, two cars in every garage?" Now he wants us to trust that big business will turn things around – God, the American people are a bunch of suckers…'

'But consumers *are* starting to regain their confi—' Edward started to say.

'Oh Christ, Eddie!' Leopold snarled. 'The dumb bastard caved in to his conservative cronies and now our trading partners are gonna raise their own tariffs in retaliation!'

'We'll buy American-made goods,' Edward countered, 'to help our industries.'

Leopold rolled his eyes. 'Don't be a sap – nobody's buying anything. Investment capital has dried up, factories are closing, retailers are going bankrupt…'

Edward nervously picked at his lunch. He didn't like Nathan when he was irritable and was afraid that suggesting lunch had been a bad idea – and yet he didn't know how else to do it.

'And you know what really gets me?' Leopold continued,

flashing his knife for emphasis, 'It's all the goddamn sanctimony. Hoover used to boast of the high sense of moral responsibility in the business world – what a lot of horseshit! Now to make up for the blunders of the financiers, he calls for new taxes and public works projects. "Time to tighten your belts and pitch in, folks!" The fucking audacity!'

Edward grimaced, afraid Leopold's outburst was attracting attention. 'It's tough to swallow,' he admitted, 'but we'll just have to weather the storm…and adapt.'

Leopold bristled at the word "adapt." Edward had begged off a few pitches with him recently and instead was reaching out to lower-tier manufacturers supplying Sears & Roebuck and Montgomery Ward, whose new retail stores were targeted to the middle-class. Sensing a juncture in their relationship, Leopold put down his cutlery and wiped his mouth.

'So you're going over to chains now, Eddie, is that it? Mother Hubbard housedresses and overalls?'

'Look, Nathan, I can't afford to be choosy these days – I've got a family to support.' When Leopold scoffed at this, it was Edward's turn to be irritable. 'Sure, I'd like be flipping through menswear quarterlies, touting lightweight worsteds and gabardines, but for the foreseeable future I've got no choice but to promote brands like Fashionbilt and Dee Dee Deb…'

Leopold returned to his meal. 'Chain stores are nothing but windowless boxes for peddling merchandise to the masses – no clerks, just plenty of parking,' he sneered. Edward tried to laugh good-naturedly, but Leopold wasn't done. 'You'll be hawking sewing kits at Woolworth's before you know it…'

Edward scheduled his April meeting in San Francisco so that

he and Morgan could take Fitz to Opening Day at the new Seals Stadium. Morning fog gave way to blue skies by noon, and Edward prayed the day would pull Fitz out of his recent funk. None other than Ty Cobb threw out the ceremonial first pitch and the game itself didn't disappoint, an 8-0 rout of the Portland Beavers behind solid performances from veterans of the '28 squad as well as new talent like first-baseman Chicken Hawks and outfielder Henry "Prince" Oana.

It was an auspicious start to another pennant-winning season (the Seals would sweep the Hollywood Stars in October), but Fitz seemed distracted throughout. None of his former teammates stopped by to visit – Harry Heilmann was home in Detroit nursing arthritis that would cause him to miss much of his last season – and he left his seat three times to wander the windy corridors beneath the grandstands.

Morgan hadn't seen Fitz in over six months and was disturbed to learn that their buddy was spending all his free time at the main library researching the history of armaments. Edward called it a morbid obsession. He described his visits where Fitz would recite the particulars of various weapons – incendiary devices, projectiles, mortars, and heavy ordnance – all in use at the time of the Great War.

'I'm worried he's going off the deep end, Morgan,' Edward said when Fitz left his seat a second time. 'In February, it was all about how Vickers had settled a patent claim against Krupp over artillery shells the Gerries used during the war, and last month it was a lecture on the destructive capacity of shrapnel balls…'

'Jesus,' Morgan said, grimacing, 'some things are better left alone.'

'The worst of it,' Edward went on, 'is that apparently he's written the army demanding to know the order of combat on July 18th – the day he was wounded. He's convinced the French commander's orders to the 7th Machine Gun Battalion were misconstrued…'

'Oh, that's no good,' Morgan said, rubbing his forehead.

When visiting in March, seeing Fitz's room strewn with dog-eared munitions manuals, Edward had suggested that they retire to the basement for a drink. The speakeasy was crowded, and they sat at a small table in the corner. Edward recounted a recent trip to the park where Baby James had gotten a kick out of throwing bits of bread at the ducks – all by way of suggesting that perhaps the toddler had a future as a pitcher. Fitz pulled a cigarette from his shirt pocket using his left hand (for the better part of a year his artificial right arm had been buried beneath the sweaters hanging on the back of his door), and said distractedly, 'Have the scouts take a look…'

Edward sighed. Lighting his friend's cigarette and one for himself, he said, 'So, did you hear back from the army yet?'

Fitz shook his head, then after a moment, 'Did you know a 76mm field gun was designed to hit a target at seven thousand yards?' Edward wasn't sure whether to look impressed or dismayed. 'They designed 'em so that at that distance a half-inch spherical bullet released from a shrapnel shell would pack enough punch to disable an enemy soldier…'

'Okay…' Edward said uneasily.

'Only the typical combat range was about half that, Eddie. The trajectory was flat and the velocity was a thousand feet per second. That gave each bullet in a 3-inch shrapnel shell seven times the energy necessary to disable a soldier.' He took a sip of beer. 'That explains the artillery casualties on both sides – it was shear butchery…'

Edward hung his head, and at length, said, 'Your sacrifice wasn't in vain, Fitz, believe me. The country's in your debt – Congress just overrode Hoover's veto of the Bonus Bill, you know…' When the big man gave him a doubtful look, Edward leaned in. 'Listen, Fitz, I remember when you moved out of Letterman your telling Angela and me how much baseball had taught you. How you can only control so much, that you have to accept the rest…'

'That's the beauty of the game,' Fitz said as he watched a girl leading a salesman upstairs, 'but the game we were in over there, Eddie – that game was rigged.'

Chapter 42

Having put in sixty-hour workweeks in boom times, Edward was lucky to clock half that now – business travel out of state had been curtailed and invariably new contracts were on a quarter-by-quarter basis. He lunched with Nathan Leopold occasionally, but their relationship grew more strained after Edward closed a deal with a Mexican sweatshop in Torrance. When Edward asked Mr. Olson when a two-bedroom unit might come available – and proposed only a nominal step-up in rent – the building manager was cool to the idea. After Edward unloaded his Tin Lizzie to a dealer in Van Nuys, weekend outings amounted to streetcar rides up to Glendale or out to the beach. Angela organized the Mothers Club clothes drive for the parish, and Edward volunteered for cleanup duty at Sunday afternoon suppers for the indigent, held in the church basement.

When during Clara's First Holy Communion at Church of the Precious Blood in May Gemma suggested the family come to Stockton for an extended stay that summer, they jumped at the chance.

With the agricultural economy still going strong, the docks of Stockton were bustling with boats and barges; unemployment was virtually unheard of, and people were friendly, even if they wore hand-me-downs and drove ten-year old automobiles. Edward and Angela got in the habit of taking the children downtown to wile away the afternoons under the elms in Hunter Plaza. Strolling down Main Street with Gemma one afternoon, Angela suggested they stop in at Penney's to find an affordably priced gingham smock for Clara.

Where once he'd turned his nose up at the chain store, Edward now was keen to examine the garments made under the Fashionbilt, Waverly, and Lady Lyke labels; he proudly showed Clara the insignia in the collar of a junior frock coat that cited American Thread by name. With Baby James in his arms, he went off to inspect the merchandise in the men's department, while Clara went with her mother and grandmother to pick out a cotton dress.

While Clara changed in the dressing room, Gemma remarked, 'Last month I sent some fabric to Giancarlo and Gina for their little Sandro because there's no money for new clothes...'

'That's because Mussolini's "Battle for Wheat" is a failure,' Angela said bitterly of the state-run farming initiative. After a moment, she added, 'Does Papa admit that?'

Gemma pursed her lips. 'I only hear from your brother, but he says your father likes what Mussolini did, settling things with the Pope: "A united Italy keeps communism away."'

Angela rolled her eyes. 'He'll drag the country into a foolish war, Mama, and that makes me worried for Giancarlo.'

Gemma pretended to ignore the remark. 'Your father thinks America is finished,' she said at length, '—that greedy bankers have ruined everything and criminals are taking over...'

'Hah!' Angela scoffed, 'He's only sorry Al Capone got arrested!'

Edward received an odd telephone call from Katherine in September. Months earlier she and Honora had cancelled plans to come down for Clara's First Holy Communion, leaving Edward to assume that his mother was peeved that the sacrament wasn't being celebrated in San Francisco. Only afterward did he learn from his sister that Honora's poor health had prevented the trip – her diabetes was getting worse, she was gaining weight and complaining of numbness in her feet and hands. Now Katherine was calling to say she was fed up.

'The doctor prescribes insulin and says I'm to keep the patient comfortable. Well, I don't need to tell you what kind of patient Mother is, do I, Edward?'

'No…' he said wearily.

'No, I don't,' Katherine continued with vehemence. 'Day and night, up and down the stairs, nothing ever hot enough, or cold enough – oh, Edward, how she torments me!'

'And you can't afford help?'

'Not with what you and Walter are able to send. Some days she goes on about how we're never going to make rent, about how I should be making more clothes for the children – what with Walter and Emily's little girl, and Dede pregnant now…'

'No, Katherine,' he said, recalling the ghastly afghans she'd knitted for Clara and James, '—you've got your hands full with Mother…'

'I can't take it any longer,' his normally stoic sister said between sobs, 'I just can't…'

'It'll be alright,' he assured her, 'we'll think of something…'

'She's mean, Edward, really nasty. It may be the discomfort, but I wonder if it's what she really thinks.'

'Why? What's she saying?'

'Snide little comments, like "You're the clumsiest person on the face of the earth," or "You've got a mind like a sieve!" or "A trained monkey could do better."'

'Oh, Katherine…'

'Just the other day, I'm helping her with her bath and she says, "You'd never understand because you never had children!"' Edward was speechless. 'I hate her, Edward! I positively hate her! I've stood by dutifully all these years, first with Baby Mary, then Walter and you, Dede, Aunt Mildred, Father. The best years of my life and she says these things to me?!'

'Listen, Katherine, we all know how devoted you've been. Give me a few days – I'll call Colm and see how we can get you some help.'

But when Edward finally reached him after three days, his older brother was unmoved. 'You know what they say about rescuing a drowning person, Eddie – they'll pull you under. Katherine oughta just get the hell out of there…'

For weeks Edward agonized over what to do. He pleaded with Walter to contribute a bit more; he kindly declined Deirdre's offer to care for their mother in Sonoma, knowing how Honora abhorred the heat and wouldn't want to switch doctors; hopeful inquiries to old family friends were greeted with politely disguised evasions. Finally, in late October, Edward telephoned to ask Mr. Breslin whether he might be able to return to work in San Francisco.

'It would be a demotion, I'm afraid,' Edward explained to Angela later that evening. 'I'd have to give up what I manage down here and share whatever I can get in San Francisco.' She stared at her hands, folded on the kitchen table. 'I know it's not easy, dear,' he said, trying to make eye contact, 'but the family needs us…and, besides, we'll be that much closer to Stockton.'

Angela looked up. 'Your mother will be a handful, Edward, especially with the children. Katherine will be there to help, right?'

'Of course,' he said, immediately doubtful.

'And I won't live in that musty flat,' Angela declared. 'It's not a good neighborhood. There's no park and the nearest parochial school is in the Tenderloin – and we're not sending Clara there…'

'No, of course not,' Edward assured her. 'I'll find us a nice house, I promise!'

'With a back yard,' she said irritably.

'Look, I'm sorry, Angela, I really am,' Edward pleaded. 'I'm not happy about this but I don't know what else to do. I promise I'll find us a good place to live and a good school for Clara. Trust me, everything's going to be fine…'

'I expect to be in on the financial decisions from now on, Edward,' Angela insisted. 'You're asking a lot from me, and I won't be kept in the dark any longer.'

He disliked the position he found himself in – caught up once again in the nagging sense of obligation to his family – and it didn't help being chastised by Angela. He'd been well-intentioned, after all – it wasn't as if he'd lost it all at the track, though his wife would never accept the distinction. He nodded abjectly.

'I'll be sorry to leave our life here,' Angela said, shaking her head as she got up from the table, 'the friends we've made, the future we'd planned…'

'I know, dear,' Edward said, trying in vain to catch her hand as she passed.

She stood at the kitchen counter, her back to him as she resumed making Clara's lunch for the next day. Gently touching her shoulders, he said, 'Listen, we'll get through this and then we can pick up right where we left off…' but she wouldn't turn around.

Chapter 43

Though they never would speak of it explicitly, Angela and Edward's third child was conceived in an air of desperation. It was a miserable time for Angela, what with organizing the household for the move: Clara became moody and resentful at the thought of losing her school friends as her ninth birthday approached, and, in turn, Baby James grew more difficult to manage, as well. Caught up in the stress of packing up and saying their goodbyes, Angela spent much of December fighting the flu, and the family passed a bittersweet Christmas at Pleasure Pier in Santa Monica – where tears were shed as they watched the sun vanish over the horizon, apprehensive over what the future held.

The Dooleys returned to San Francisco the second week of January 1932, with just two weeks to settle in before Honora was to join them. Edward came home from work early the first Friday to find Angela in the kitchen overwhelmed with unpacking boxes, Clara home from school in bed with an ear infection, and James banging an empty coffee can in the dining room.

'Listen, let me finish this, dear,' Edward said, taking his wife into his arms. 'Katherine will be over first thing in the morning to help with the children, and it would suit me fine if you and I could just take a nice walk in the park tomorrow…'

'No, Edward, it's not that,' Angela said, pulling away and taking a handkerchief from her apron to wipe her eyes. 'I went to the doctor this morning, remember?'

'Is everything okay?' he said, alarmed. 'Did he give you something for your headaches?'

She placed a hand on an unopened box. 'Believe it or not, I'm pregnant...'

Edward stood there amazed, considering how seldom they made love anymore. 'How far along, do you know?'

'Two and a half months, maybe.'

He hugged her again, then stepped back and placed his hands on her shoulders. 'Well, that's wonderful!' he said gallantly, 'What a way to signal a new start!'

But Angela shook her head. 'It's the last thing I need right now, Edward. As it is, I don't know how I'll ever manage with your mother...'

'Well, maybe James can start kindergarten early, and with both kids in school—'

'—I'll have your mother to myself.'

'James, *James!*' Edward called out to his son in the dining room, 'c'mon, boyo, stop that banging, will you?' With a sidelong glance to Angela, he left the kitchen, saying, 'Why don't you and I find the box with the trains and give Mama some peace and quiet, okay?'

Edward had been operating from guilt for a while now. Every week in the fall he'd commuted to San Francisco, both to manage the transition with the man who was moving to Los Angeles to take his place, and to look for a suitable house. He'd spent hours poring over rental listings and squeezing in time to meet with various oddball landlords, including a flirtatious divorcée with a charming bungalow in the Inner

Richmond District who hinted it could be his in exchange for sexual services; he was so tired and overextended he had half a mind to take her up on it, but his conscience caught up to him.

In the end the best he could do was a three-bedroom flat on 41st and Cabrillo. The new arrangement met many of Angela's criteria – a quiet neighborhood next to Golden Gate Park, a Catholic church and grammar school just up the street, and a shopping thoroughfare on a streetcar line to downtown. On the other hand, the Outer Richmond District was the hinterlands: vast blocks of three-story apartment buildings joined side-by-side to subdue the shifting sands, wide streets which served to funnel the interminable fog from the ocean to the bay, and rear yards that were little more than rabbit warrens draped with clotheslines.

The flat itself featured hardwood floors and a fireplace, a gas stove and an ice box in the kitchen, and three bedrooms looking out over the rear yard. The one in the middle, reserved for Honora and accessed through what would be the children's room, jutted out like the prow of a ship, making it particularly cold when the ocean breezes picked up, and too hot on the rare occasions when the gray skies cleared. A family of four lived upstairs – the father a wiry auto mechanic and incessant smoker, his plump and bashful wife, a skittish twelve-year-old daughter, and a teenage son forever practicing the trombone.

Edward had hoped to entice Katherine to live with them in a room "off the garden," but when she took one look at the make-shift space at the back of the garage that smelled of mothballs and motor oil, she decided to get a place of her own instead. She agreed to come over Tuesdays, Thursdays, and Saturdays to help care for Honora and give Angela a hand with the housework. (In time, the children grew fond of their auntie, and, heartened by their company, Katherine was better able to take her mother in stride.)

Aside from budget constraints, Edward's ulterior motive in locating far out in the avenues was the proximity to the natural environment that he remembered as a boy. He imagined the family picnicking in the park, taking walks at Ocean Beach, and swimming in the heated saltwater plunge at Sutro Baths. Above all, with fond memories of the 1915 exposition in mind, he looked forward to taking the children to Playland-at-the-Beach, a ten-acre amusement park that featured a carousel and a Ferris wheel, a roller coaster, and a variety of game arcades.

On Saturdays, to give Angela a chance to rest while Katherine accompanied her mother on visits to family friends, Edward would spend the day with the children. When he wasn't taking them to Playland, it was up to the Balboa Theater to see cartoons and a new "Our Gang" feature, or riding the streetcar downtown to go sightseeing, visit the main library, or watch a parade on Market Street. Typically Edward would visit Fitz after work on Thursdays, but occasionally he'd stop by with Clara and James on a Saturday if they were in the vicinity. (They called him Uncle Fitz, and despite his odd appearance and the tawdry circumstances of the Tenderloin, they liked listening to him talk with their father about the old days.)

One Saturday morning they stopped in at Fitz's rooming house only to be told that he was up at Newman's, a venerable boxing gym located in the basement of the Cadillac Hotel. Edward led the children up Leavenworth, through a nondescript door, and down a flight of stairs where the trio came upon a somnolent scene. In the dimly lit ring a muscle-bound man was shadowboxing as his trainer hung laces out to dry on the ropes, while from the dark recesses of the hall came desultory sound of another boxer going at a speed bag half-heartedly. The hall was cold and smelled of stale cigar smoke, liniments, and Pine-Sol. A handful of boxing enthusiasts and gamblers sat in the first few rows of wooden seats at ringside. In the murky light Edward made out Fitz, and, to his surprise, Morgan sitting next to him.

'Why, Edward, here to place a bet?' Morgan said with a wry smile as Edward and the children came over. 'And with your backers, I see!'

Edward shook hands with the two men and had the children follow suit – they'd grown accustomed to shaking Uncle Fitz's left hand, and enjoyed Uncle Morgan's whimsical sense of humor. 'We were on our way to Union Square to do some window shopping,' Edward explained, 'but when they told me you were here, Fitz, I figured I'd show the kids a boxing ring – when there's not a bout in progress, of course…'

'Missed a doozy last night, Eddie,' the big man said, 'Tony Canzoneri made mincemeat out of some bum from Carson City.'

Edward winced, and ignoring Clara's remark about not liking mincemeat, said, 'And you, Morgan? What brings you here?'

'Oh, just seeing a man about a horse…'

Edward looked curiously at his friend, then took a seat in the row below the two men, with the children on either side of him. Clara thumbed through a discarded boxing program and James ran his toy car across the rail of the seat in front of him while the three men chatted.

When another boxer stepped into the ring and the trainer began to supervise a sparring session, Fitz said, 'Plan on teaching your Jimmy about self-defense, Eddie?'

'Oh, a bit early for that, I'd say…'

'Nah, they got classes for the little ones Saturday afternoons.'

Edward demurred with a grimace. Turning to his son, he said, 'We like playing "Knock-Out Fighters," though, don't we, Jimmy?' referring to the arcade game at Playland where mechanical boxers face off, their flailing arms controlled by pistol grips.

'"Pitch 'Em & Bat 'Em Baseball," too, Dad!' the boy said, eager to please Uncle Fitz.

Not to be outdone, Clara remarked, 'I'm really good at "Skee-Ball".'

Because Fitz didn't venture beyond the Tenderloin these days, Morgan felt obliged to describe the gauntlet one had to run at Playland's Fun House – the Mirror Maze, the Joy Wheel, the Barrel of Laughs, and the Rickety Bridges – just to get into the arcade hall itself. Fitz held up his hand, 'I'd never make it out alive…'

'The indoor slide's the best!' James exclaimed.

'Two hundred feet on a burlap sack,' Edward said, '—not a good idea after lunch…'

'But the *worst* part, Uncle Fitz,' Clara put in, 'is getting passed Laffing Sal – she's *sooo* creepy!'

Uncle Morgan laughed at her look of horror. 'Now, dearie, she's no one to be afraid of!' he teased, before explaining to Fitz that Sal was a buxom, gap-toothed animatron who loomed over the entrance to the Fun House with her frizzy red hair and a cackling laugh.

'Jesus, Eddie,' Fitz said in a tame rebuke, 'and you think it's too soon for boxing?'

'Oh, it's all just fun and games!'

'Yeah, that's what they said about the war,' Fitz deadpanned, before leaning forward. 'Say, Jimmy, you wanna hear about the sport of boxing?' When James nodded eagerly, Edward acquiesced with a smile, and Fitz went on, 'Well, first of all, there are three types of boxers – what they call the outside fighter, the inside fighter, and the brawler.'

'Shorter boxers tend to be "in-fighters,"' Morgan interrupted, 'because they like to swarm around their opponents like bees, punching fast and close to wear the bigger man down.' Edward grinned at the thought that some of Mr. Doherty's passion had rubbed off on his bantamweight son.

'Now the brawlers, see, they're "sluggers" who can stand there and take punches over and over,' Fitz started to explain before Morgan cut in again.

'Yeah, they're slow and they move around the ring like elephants but, boy, when they uncork a hook or an uppercut, it's lights out. *Pow!*'

James laughed as Morgan punched the air and jutted out his chin.

Worried that his friend might cite Max Baer as a brawler who'd killed an opponent right here in San Francisco a couple of years earlier, Edward hastened to say, 'But it's the "outside fighter" who's the ideal boxer, James. He stays outside or away from the other man, keeps his distance, deflecting punches, ducking and bobbing, biding his time – and then just like that,' he snapped his fingers, 'he strikes with a long-range jab when the other guy isn't expecting it. Remember my telling you about Gene Tunney?'

'—or Benny Leonard,' Fitz added.

The name immediately reminded Edward of Oscar Pereira, weaving and jabbing around Mitch Pitowski in boot camp, and he grew quiet and reflective while Fitz likened the three types of boxers to Rock-Paper-Scissors, something James was learning in kindergarten.

'Boxing experts figure it this way, Jimmy,' Fitz said, 'That the "outside fighter" will always beat a "brawler," a "brawler" will always beat a "inside fighter," and—'

'—and an "inside fighter" will always beat an "outside fighter,"' Morgan interjected. 'That's the way things turn out most of the time…'

'But not all the time, Uncle Morgan?' Clara asked.

'Well, dearie,' he said with a chuckle, 'I suppose there are exceptions!'

Chapter 44

In June, Angela gave birth to Baby Audrey after just thirty-five weeks – most likely owing to the anxieties associated with Honora having joined the family.

Initially the arrangement had seemed manageable, as she was pleased to have a bright room to herself and delighted to be in the company of her grandchildren. She proved incapable of keeping her opinions to herself, however, and the situation steadily began to deteriorate. Angela found it difficult to hold her temper when her mother-in-law insisted on offering advice on everything – not that she ever lifted a finger to help. A few tart exchanges could keep everyone on edge for days at a time, and no matter the flower bouquets or candy treats Edward might bring home, the best the two strong-willed women could manage was a frosty civility.

The baby's arrival was not at all routine – the obstetrician found Angela's blood pressure elevated during a routine check-up and immediately had her admitted to the hospital. After three alternately dull and agonizing days, labor was induced, and Edward had no choice but to leave an anxious Katherine to care for the household. Angela endured ten hours of painful labor, and when the doctor entered the waiting room at three a.m. to announce the birth of a baby girl, a haggard Edward was more relieved to think that his wife was finally sleeping soundly.

For some it was a joyful time – Deirdre had given birth to twins in the spring and Morgan informed Edward that Constance, now married to a Navy man from Norfolk, was with child herself – but for the Dooleys the difficulties kept mounting. Baby Audrey suffered from bronchial distress, and with the cradle in Angela and Edward's bedroom, her chronic coughing made for poor sleep. More than once Edward slinked out to sleep on the couch in the living room, leaving Angela to comfort the baby with a regimen that involved long sessions in the steamy bathroom followed by trips to the front door landing to rock the baby in the brisk fog.

Concerned for Baby Audrey's health, the family decided to accelerate her christening. As easy as it would have been to go to St. Thomas the Apostle's up the street, Angela was too exhausted to put up a fight when Honora insisted that the baptism take place at St. Mary's Cathedral. In turn, the family matriarch agreed to let Angela's friends, Gracie and Caroline, once again host a reception at their Lyon Street bungalow afterward.

The appointed Saturday was overcast. With three excitable children crammed into an old Buick that their upstairs neighbor had loaned them, Edward and Angela were worn out by the time they reached Fitz's rooming house. James was sitting in his father's lap playing with the steering wheel of the idling car while Edward tried soothing the baby in the seat beside him, when Angela and Clara returned to the sidewalk without Fitz.

'He's not coming,' Angela snapped as she and Clara got into the back of the Buick.

With Clara blubbering uncontrollably, Edward said, 'What's going on?'

'He got the days mixed up, I guess,' Angela said gruffly, reaching over to take the baby.

Edward tried unsuccessfully to make eye contact through the rear-view mirror. 'But I telephoned Fitz on Thursday to remin—'

'Never mind,' Angela cut in. 'He probably forgot about it – it doesn't matter, let's get going before we're late.' She gave her handkerchief to Clara, then turned fiercely to James. 'Now you sit on your bum and be quiet!' she scolded, which caused him to burst into tears.

Gathered around the baptismal font before the start of the ceremony, Morgan leaned into Edward. 'Trouble in paradise?'

Edward chafed at the satisfaction in his friend's voice – he and Angela suspected Morgan was hurt to have been passed over as godfather. 'Everything's fine,' he answered tersely, 'I just wish you'd been the one to get Fitz, that's all. He wasn't ready for some reason and it's got Angela all hot and bothered...'

'Gee, sorry, Old Chum,' Morgan said a bit defensively, 'but like I told you, the car's in the shop – he should've taken a cab like I did...'

Frustrated, Edward mused, 'I telephone him just the other day – Angela insisted that we come by for him.' Regarding her across the way as she handed Baby Audrey off to Deirdre, the godmother, with her husband Tom standing in for Fitz, he added, 'He didn't sound very good on the phone – do you have any idea what's going on?'

Morgan paused to greet Aunt Hildie, and when she'd settled in among the rest of the Sonoma contingent, he said to Edward, 'I'm afraid he's all wound up about the Bonus March fiasco,' referring to the army having forcibly removed forty thousand unemployed veterans and their families from encampments in Washington the week before.

'In June it looked like things were going their way…' Edward said rhetorically, feeling remiss for not having visited Fitz in a few weeks.

'I guess Hoover felt he had no choice, what with Congress divided and all,' Morgan said. 'I'm sure he never bargained for a hothead like MacArthur, though. Tanks and tear gas – the lunatic thought he was putting down a communist insurrection!'

'Jesus, what a mess,' Edward muttered under his breath. 'Fitz must feel betrayed…'

Quoting a bluesy tune popular in the early twenties when not everyone's fortunes were rising, Morgan sang softly,

> *Remember my forgotten man,*
> *you put a rifle in his hand;*
> *You sent him far away,*
> *you shouted hip hooray;*
> *But look at him today…*

Only that night, after putting the children to bed, did Edward learn from Angela just how bleak Fitz was really feeling. When they'd stopped by his place earlier that day, finding the entry door unlocked Clara had raced upstairs to surprise Uncle Fitz, with her mother slow to follow. Angela came upon her daughter shaking in the second floor hallway, the door to Room 204 ajar – inside, Fitz was seated on the edge of his bed, trousers down around his ankles, eyes closed, and groaning as he tugged at the hair of a women kneeling before him, bringing her head back and forth into his groin.

Chapter 45

A month later, his own spirits sagging, Edward prevailed upon Angela to let him accompany Morgan on an overnight trip to Monterey where his friend was closing a business transaction. On the appointed Friday, Edward was walking back from taking the children to school when he spotted Morgan's new Packard 443 Roadster parked in front of his flat, a half hour early. He found his friend sitting at the kitchen table, cooing to Baby Audrey in her highchair while Angela brewed a pot of tea.

'Why, here's Daddy now!' Morgan said to the delight of the baby. 'Such a silly old man in his Southwick suit and high-collar shirt. For goodness sake, Edward,' he chided, 'it's an outing to the seaside, not an audience with the Duke of Windsor!' He was dressed in blue seersucker with a cardinal red bowtie.

'But it's tropical weight gabardine,' Edward said, pretending to look hurt.

'Well, I hope it won't fade, for it's a top-down day!'

'Good grief,' Angela said from the counter, 'you two are like a couple of peacocks.'

Morgan laughed. 'It's only to make us more appealing to you ladies!' he said, dabbing the baby's nose with his finger, eliciting giggles.

Angela rolled her eyes. 'You lechers better behave yourselves down there...'

With the fog burning off as they drove passed Playland, Edward and Morgan laughed at the sight of two street sweepers vying with a flock of seagulls for spillover trash from the night before. The two friends were as carefree as schoolboys as they sped down the Great Highway, exhilarated by sight of whitecaps racing to the shore of Ocean Beach. As they drove passed McCloskey's Castle, Rockaway Beach, and Princeton-by-the-Sea, Edward was reminded of his fateful outing with Constance when he returned from the war, but he kept these thoughts to himself. Instead, he preferred to listen to his friend wax on about the new John Barrymore picture, *A Bill of Divorcement* (Morgan opined that granting women a divorce on account of their husbands' insanity would render most marriages null and void).

Ninety minutes later they stopped at the beach resort of Capitola, where they got ham sandwiches and root beers from a vendor, then found a spot to eat in the shade of a cypress tree. Sitting side-by-side on the running board of the roadster, they watched the young sunbathers on the beach below and talked about how much times had changed.

'I remember the day we first met,' Morgan said with satisfaction, '—Homeroom, freshman year, Brother Sorensen droning on with the roll call – "Doherty, Donegal, Dooley…" Oh, but you were a cool customer, Edward – no one dared push you around.'

'That was only because of Colm.'

'No, it wasn't just that. You were more at ease compared to everyone else.'

'Nah, not really…' Edward took a bite of his sandwich. 'I do remember how self-assured you were right from the start, strolling through the Fairmont like you owned the place!'

Morgan smiled at the memory of their youthful daring. 'Remember at The Palace Hotel when a chauffeur mistook us for the sons of some titan of industry? "Hurry now, boys," he said, holding open the door to the Cadillac, "your father wouldn't want you missing the train!"'

Edward chuckled. 'Funny he thought we were brothers…'

'Yeah,' Morgan said, 'what with me always looking up to you!'

Later that afternoon they checked into The Monterey, a luxury hotel in the Belle Époque style, located in the heart of the charming seaside town of the same name. Morgan had reserved two rooms with private baths, and before going off to his appointment at Cannery Row, he told Edward to meet him in the lobby at six. Edward had never been to Monterey, so he took a walk down the old streets lined with jacaranda trees and venerable Mexican adobe villas with scarlet bougainvillea spilling over whitewashed garden walls. Eventually he strolled into the Old Presidio where he sat on a bench among the majestic coastal oaks and took in the splendor of the broad bay.

He was back in the lobby at six, reading an article about street skirmishes in Cologne and Munich sparked by a group calling themselves the Nazis, when he heard the horn of the Packard outside. No sooner had he dropped into the passenger seat than Morgan lurched off toward Point Cabrillo, cheerfully recounting his successful business meeting.

He stopped at a three-story, dragon-roofed hotel on Ocean View Drive, which he explained was the entrepreneurial venture of a Chinaman he'd gotten to know on previous trips. The man himself escorted Morgan and Edward through the crowded restaurant to a table by the window, and, in lieu of menus, recommended a dinner of won ton soup, chop suey, scallops and sand dabs in hoisin sauce. With Morgan's nodded assent, the man bowed deferentially before departing, and moments later a teapot was delivered to the table. Morgan poured a warm liquid into small ceramic cups – not tea, but rice wine – while describing in self-deprecating terms that his broker role for Matson Lines amounted to nothing more than finding ingenious ways to pack sardines into tramp steamers already bound for the Orient.

'Here's to diminished expectations,' he said with a grin as he handed one of the cups to Edward, '—from pushing porcelain toilet fixtures to packing sardines for me, and, for you, from promoting sartorial elegance to peddling aprons in variety stores!'

'Gee, thanks, Old Chum,' Edward said, grimacing at the unexpected taste.

'Actually,' Morgan went on brightly as he lit a cigarette, 'my real aim is to start booking passenger liners so as to get to those exotic ports-of-call like Honolulu, Hong Kong, and Sydney. The dollar still goes a long way in those places, you know...'

Edward held out his cup for a refill, saying glumly, 'At least you have only yourself to worry about...'

'Aw, c'mon, I'll always be there for you!' Morgan said as he exhaled, the smoke curling away like a tiny tornado.

Edward offered a wan smile. 'I can't tell you how much that means to me...'

After dinner Morgan drove unsteadily up into the Santa Lucia

Mountains where they watched the sunset from the side of the road. Morgan said the night was young and suggested they visit a card room he knew; with Edward at the wheel, they made it over the mountains and down to the valley floor in about an hour. As they pulled into downtown Salinas, Edward was reminded of Stockton, only instead of stopping, Morgan directed him to the seedier Chinatown quarter a few blocks further east.

An old grange at the end of Soledad Street had been turned into a gambling hall, featuring gaming rooms in the front and a small arena for cockfights in the back. The clientele was mostly farm workers of Asian descent, along with the sons of some of the growers in the area. In the room where Morgan and Edward played, a heavyset white man sat off to the side nursing a whiskey, his eyes inscrutable eyes beneath a scuffed Panama hat. The only drink served the card players was tequila, but the men around the table were friendly enough. After Morgan primed Edward in the basics of pai gow poker, the two played for a couple of hours – until Edward managed to win back what he'd lost in the first thirty minutes and then some.

Stepping outside into the cool night air that smelled strongly of agriculture, they made their way to the roadster, unmolested by the half-dozen pickers smoking cigarettes under a street-lamp. Morgan got in on the passenger side, and as Edward started the engine Morgan said he knew a place where they could have a proper nightcap before heading back to Monterey.

Despite the hour, jazz music was blaring from the open windows of the two-story house on Abbot Street as Morgan pushed open the low gate and led Edward through the front yard. The people at the party were well-dressed – two couples conversing in the front parlor, another pair dancing in the foyer, and a big man demonstrating card tricks to two girls in the dining room. Morgan proceeded through the room to the kitchen in back where they came upon a middle-age woman seated at a table, smoking a cigarette and reading the newspaper. 'Help yourself,' she said, barely looking up, '—there's an ice box out back if the bucket's empty.'

Edward had sized up the situation by the time they returned to the dining room, cocktails in hand. No sooner did they sit down at the far end of the table than the card trick man left the room and the two girls he'd been entertaining came over. The sassier of the two, a short brunette with a coquettish grin, sat next to Morgan, while a willowy girl with an unnatural red tint to her bobbed hair sat beside Edward.

Morgan got the conversation started by describing the latest Spencer Tracy picture to great comic effect – about a hardened inmate at Sing Sing who is persuaded by the fatherly warden to see the error of his ways before being sent off to the electric chair. In turn, the brunette insisted that the electric chair would be too good for the creeps who'd kidnapped the Lindbergh baby earlier that year. Morgan managed to steer the conversation to lighter subjects while twice refreshing everyone's drinks.

Edward asked to use the facilities and was directed upstairs. When he came out of the water closet, the redhead who went by the name Lucy was waiting for him. His head spinning, he'd already rationalized that his worries about things at home, at work, and with regard to Fitz, had rendered him incapable of resisting temptation. The compunction that had saved him from the divorcée landlady had vanished – he simply didn't give a damn anymore.

Lucy led him to her room where without preamble they undressed each other. He was dizzily aroused to see a woman other than Angela in the nude, his heart pounding at the sight of the pert nipples and pink areolae of the girl's small breasts. She pulled him onto the bed where he carelessly groped her young flesh and smothered her with sloppy kisses. The force of his erection built until he was on top of her, thrusting and moaning while an odd array images ran through his mind – of Constance, pinned in the back seat of her father's Maxwell; of Pitowski, cut down in the first charge; of Angela, describing Fitz pulling the hair of the whore; of Stagby saying, *Lieutenant, I wouldn't go any fur*— before he passed out.

When he opened his eyes – had it been minutes or hours? – he found himself on his stomach, covered by a sheet, a lamp on the nightstand casting the only light in the room. His head was throbbing, his mouth was dry. He closed his eyes a moment and was pinching the bridge of his nose to get his bearings when he became aware that the sheet was being lifted. He felt a hand inserted between his buttocks, and fingers gently caressing his scrotum. Clearing his throat, he tried recalling the girl's name as he started to turn over when—'Morgan!' he cried out, seeing his friend on the bed in his underwear, 'What in the hell's going on?!'

'*Shhh!*' Morgan whispered, pulling his hand away, 'You'll wake the whole house!' Edward's twisting had left him bound up in the sheet with Morgan straddling him, when from the hallway came the sounds of voices and a man's footsteps on the stairs. 'They'll always pull you under, Edward,' Morgan said urgently as he pushed him down by the shoulders, '—your family, Angela, the children – but I care about you, I always have. *I'm* the one who loves you!' Lunging forward, he savagely kissed Edward on the lips just as the bedroom door burst open.

The card trick man rushed in and viciously yanked Morgan off the bed, sending him sprawling to the floor. 'Get outta here, you goddam faggot!' he growled, 'We don't go for that kind of shit here!' With Lucy and the brunette screaming in the doorway, he grabbed Morgan like a sack of potatoes and shoved him into the hall. 'Get your things and get the hell out!'

The brunette led Morgan back to her room where she'd fallen asleep, while Lucy rushed to Edward, sitting on the edge of the bed now, his head in his hands, his lip bleeding. She dabbed at the wound as he began to dress, while downstairs the card trick man could be heard moments later throwing Morgan out onto the porch and slamming the front door. Edward pulled the wad of cash from his trousers pocket and pressed it into Lucy's hand, then with a sidelong glance he snatched his jacket from the post of a chair and crept down the stairs. Hearing sounds in the kitchen, he slipped out the front door and through the garden gate but found the Packard empty. In the pre-dawn light, he went to both sides of the house, hoarsely whispering for Morgan to no avail. Fearing the big man had spotted him from the kitchen window, he returned to the roadster, started it up with a roar, and raced off in search of his friend.

He was overwhelmed with thoughts not of anger or revulsion, but of pity. As he drove through the sinister-looking neighborhood, peering between buildings and across vacant lots, he tried getting his head around the truth that had been hidden all these years. He felt terribly sorry for Morgan and was desperate to find him and forgive him. In hopes of finding his way back to the center of town, he gradually widened the circumference of his search, but drawn to the pink glow over the Gabilan Range he veered further and further east until he was surrounded by artichoke fields. At a T intersection along the Old Stage Road, he panicked at the thought of the men he'd seen smoking under the streetlamp the night before coming across a dandy wandering the country roads in a sullied seersucker suit. *Right or left? Right or left?!*

Frantically grinding the gears, he tore off to the left and careened ahead with scenes from the night before racing through his mind – scallops smothering in a sticky brown sauce, the fat man in the scuffed Panama hat, pert nipples and pink areolae – before giving way to more frightful images – of Miller bashing in the head of the German soldier, of Clara blubbering in the backseat after seeing Fitz, of Laffing Sal bobbing back and forth with her frizzy red hair and thick red lips. Through the reflection of the headlights in the early morning fog he could make out a silhouette ahead, someone walking on the side of the road swinging something – *Was that a suitcase? Did Morgan have a suitcase?* As he desperately jerked the car to the shoulder he could hear gravel spewing violently from beneath the tires before losing traction altogether in a culvert…then spinning, spinning as though in slow motion, until the headlights caught the frightened eyes of a girl…seconds, hours, eons before the inevitable impact…like the magnetic pull of tectonic plates, the destiny of opposing forces hurled at one another – the sorry mess in the natural order of things…

Chapter 46

Like his father, the sheriff before him, George Quinn was a methodical, unflappable man. As Monterey County's chief law enforcement officer, he was familiar with grisly scenes and tangled stories, with unreliable witnesses, the occasional gushing confession, even the unexpected double-cross. But above all, Sheriff Quinn was a pragmatist. He had no problem with the private consumption of alcohol, and mostly turned a blind eye to the gambling and prostitution going on in Chinatown as long as it was kept behind closed doors.

He considered these vices as necessary relief valves for the young men upon whom the local agricultural economy depended. Falling commodity prices had increased the friction between pickers and growers in recent years, and old prejudices (directed originally at Chinese laborers, then at the Japanese who replaced them) were rekindled as pickers from the Philippines, granted a special exception under the 1924 Asian Exclusion Act, faced growing antagonism. The sheriff had his hands full with altercations in front of hiring halls, as well as rising crime in the squalid barrios east of Salinas.

What irked him more than any of this, however, was the arrogance of men from up north who deigned to use Salinas as a toilet – to raise hell, lose their heads, and then leave a mess in their wake.

It was half-passed eleven Saturday morning when Sheriff

Quinn walked back to the cell block of the county jail. Edward was sitting in a cell on the edge of a thin mattress, his elbows on his knees. His head had been pounding for the longest time as he'd tried to recall how he came to have a poultice on his forehead and thick bandage over his right hand. He looked up glassy-eyed when he heard the words, 'Had a high time last night, eh, Doherty?'

Edward winced at a pain in his rib cage as he sat up. 'My name's Dooley, sir, Edward Dooley…of San Francisco,' he croaked to the pudgy man with the steely gaze. 'I do have a friend, Morgan Doherty, who was with me last night. Do you know where he is?'

'You had no wallet,' the sheriff said, 'so I ID'd you from the license plates…'

'Oh, no, you see, the car belongs to Morgan,' Edward explained. 'I was out searching for him when, well…when I guess I crashed…'

'—and put a girl in the hospital,' Quinn said. When Edward blinked hard, not comprehending, the sheriff crossed his arms. 'Why don't you tell me about last night, huh?'

Edward recounted what he could remember: the Chinese dinner in Monterey, the card room, a party at some house. He omitted details of the last stop, hoping the worst he might be in for was driving under the influence. 'You said something about a girl?'

'A Filipino girl – twelve, maybe thirteen years of age. You struck her with your car before plowing into a telephone poll…'

'Oh, God! Is she alright?'

'She'll live,' Quinn offered, then after a moment, 'So you're a Stanford grad…'

'What? No, my name's Dooley. Officer, listen, please let me telephone my wife and—'

'Called Sacramento to run your registration,' Quinn continued. 'Unmarried businessman, posh San Francisco address, nice ride. So what're you doing down here, then?'

Edward again tried to clarify his identity, then explained that he had accompanied Morgan on a trip to Monterey to sign a contract with a cannery concern. 'Please, you ought to be looking for my friend' he implored the inscrutable man, '—somehow we got separated last night and I'm worried he might get roughed up...'

'Yeah, we're pretty rough around the edges down here,' Sheriff Quinn said dryly. 'Sit tight, Doherty, while I figure out what I'm gonna do with you...'

In the course of the afternoon, as the heat in the cell block rose steadily, Edward was unable to get a look at his neighbors. At one point he thought he heard someone eating in the cell next to him; from the other cell, he made out the sound of snoring, or was it whimpering? He gulped down the water brought to him with lunch, but had no appetite, and was gradually overcome with anxiety knowing that Angela had expected him by mid-afternoon. He was nearly frantic by the time Sheriff Quinn reappeared shortly after 5pm.

'Lucky for you, Dooley, you made quite an impression over at the Abbot House last night,' the man with the steely gaze began. 'One of the girls turned your wallet in a little while ago,' he explained, causing Edward to grimace at the memory of Lucy with the bobbed hair. 'A policy of Faye's,' Quinn drawled, bringing to Edward's mind the middle-age woman reading the paper in the kitchen, '—johns try skipping out all the time…'

'Well then they'd have Morgan's wallet, too!' Edward said hopefully.

Sheriff Quinn shook his head. ''Fraid not. Faye says it was just you over there last night, along with a rancher's son and a seed salesman from Fresno.'

'But that can't be,' Edward insisted. 'Morgan was with me – he's the one who brought me there after we left the card room.'

'Checked that out, too,' Quinn said mildly, wiping perspiration from his brow with a handkerchief, 'but Carny – you might remember him, big fellow, wears a Panama hat? – he only remembers someone fitting your description…'

'Oh, no, now please, I—'

'You mentioned you were married, Dooley,' the sheriff cut in. 'Why don't we let your wife know where you ended up, huh?'

He led Edward by the arm to a small room with a telephone and had an operator get Angela on the line. After announcing a call from the Monterey County sheriff's department, he handed the receiver to Edward, who said sheepishly, 'Hello, dear – I'm afraid there's a bit of a problem…' Quinn rolled his eyes and left the room.

'Edward, where *are* you? I've been so worried!' Angela spoke in a low whisper from the telephone alcove in the hallway of their flat.

'Well, actually…I've been arrested.'

'Arrested?! For what? Where are you?'

'Salinas. 'Been here since last night…'

'Salinas? But I thought you two were staying in Monterey.'

'We are, I mean we were…Listen, have you heard from

401

Morgan at all?'

'Why, isn't he with you? What's going on?' Angela waved off Katherine who'd come out from the kitchen to check on her.

'We went a little crazy last night, see,' Edward began hesitantly. 'He took me to a card room in Salinas…there was some drinking, and then one thing led to another…'

'And?'

'Well, I was driving his car, looking for him afterward – we got separated, see – and, anyway, I ended up driving off the road and—'

'Oh my God, are you okay?'

'—hitting a girl, sometime this morning before dawn…out on a country road.'

'A girl? What girl? Is she alright?'

'The sheriff says she's in the hospital…' Hearing Angela gasp, what little composure he had left evaporated. He winced and felt the wound on his lip tear open again. 'Aw, Angela I've made a mess of things,' he said, his voice cracking, 'and now Morgan's gone missing, and it's not the friendliest place down here…'

He could hear Angela assuring his sister in the background that everything was fine, that there'd been a car accident but that everyone was okay. When Katherine had returned to the kitchen, Angela spoke in a low murmur, 'How'd you two get separated? Where were you?'

'Aw, it's kind of a long story…We were leaving a place, see—'

'The card room?'

'…Yeah, that's right, the card room…only, he left before I did and because I had the key to his car he must've started walking…Maybe he was upset for being thrown out…'

'Thrown out? Was there a fight?'

'No, no, nothing like that. Maybe he insulted somebody, I don't really know…'

'Oh, boy…But you, Edward, *you're* alright?'

'Sure, I'm okay, a little banged up, I guess. I don't really remember the accident, but a doctor's looked me over – a few bruises, got my hand bandaged up…'

'My God…' Angela said, bringing her hand to her forehead. 'And when will we know more about the girl?'

'Tomorrow, I guess, and there'll be an arraignment Monday…' Edward said, sounding defeated, then, as an after-thought, 'How're things at home?'

'Never mind about that – get some sleep, Edward, and pull yourself together…'

Late the following afternoon Edward was awakened from a deep sleep by the sounds of a nightstick drawn across the bars of his cell. Rolling over, he found the sheriff looking down on him with a smirk on his lips. 'Well, you'll be happy to know that Mr. Doherty is alive and well,' the lawman said, '—in San Francisco.'

'San Francisco?' Edward propped himself up on his elbows. 'Have you talked to him?'

'I have – and he's awfully sorry to hear about the scrape you're in,' Quinn said blithely. 'Seems he took the train back when you didn't return with the car – I called the hotel and they confirm that he checked out yesterday morning…'

'Huh?' Edward said, swinging his legs over the side of the bed, dizzy as he sat up.

'Yep, Doherty says you dropped him at the hotel Friday when he wasn't feeling well after dinner – that squares with

Chan at the Ocean View Restaurant, by the way – and that you asked to take the Packard for a spin...'

'Yeah, we drove up into the hills to see the sunset,' Edward said, pinching his brow to clear his head, 'but I don't recall going back to—'

'You're not gonna deny being in Carny's card room, are you?' Quinn snapped.

'Well, no, I don't deny it, but—'

'And Faye can verify that you were with a girl at her place 'till the wee hours...'

'Yes, okay, but Morgan was with me the whole time!' Edward protested.

'Hotel manager tells me he never saw you return,' Sheriff Quinn said, balancing the nightstick between his palms. 'Look, Dooley, you better work on your story if you're going to sound convincing before the judge tomorrow morning...'

'My story?' Edward wondered, not for the first time, whether he was in a bad dream. 'Please, Sheriff, let me call Mr. Doherty. I'm sure we can sort all this out.'

''Fraid not,' the sheriff said, '—can only call kin in cases like this.'

'But I'm telling you, it was Morgan who brought me here to Salinas...'

The pudgy man regarded Edward steadily a moment, then the look in his eyes changed to something like pity. 'You been friends with this Doherty a while now?'

'Sure, since we were boys. Why?'

'But you didn't go to college, am I right?'

'Well, no,' Edward said, flustered, 'but what's that got to do with anything?'

The lawman looked down, shook his head, and muttered, 'So earnest,' as if to himself. Then with a weary sigh, he said, 'I'm afraid your buddy's taken the run-out on you, Dooley…'

'What? How do you mean?'

George Quinn pursed his lips. 'Something like this happened back in '15, when my father was sheriff. Some frat boys and a couple of pledges came to town to horse around, busted up a whorehouse…' When Edward looked up quizzically, the man whose doughy exterior belied a shrewd intelligence raised his eyebrows, and quipped, 'Let's just say I have a hunch this Doherty knows how to spread money around…'

Edward stared at the floor trying to make sense of it all, while Quinn said, 'The good news is that he's wiring your bail in the morning. Now let's get your wife on the line. She'll have to get somebody down here to accompany you home after the arraignment…'

Edward stood up and took a deep breath. 'What about the girl?'

'She's gonna make it,' the sheriff said as he led Edward out of the cell. 'Turns out she was bringing lunch to her father yesterday – he's an asparagus picker, and being that it's hotter 'n hell these days, they get started real early…'

The next morning Edward felt acutely self-conscious in his rumpled suit, sitting at the defendant's table in the old Victorian-era courthouse. He'd been permitted to shave earlier – 'I can trust you with a razor, right, Dooley?' Quinn had said – but it had been a lackluster effort with his left hand and no styptic pencil to staunch the nicks. Gilbert Dean, the public defender, sat next to him, his face lined and leathery like a prune from pulling on Lucky Strikes for years. He'd introduced himself in a raspy baritone, saying, 'Luckily, Doyle, hitting somebody with an automobile while drunk is still only a misdemeanor – but it's gonna cost you…'

'It's Dooley,' Edward replied apprehensively, 'Edward Dooley, San Francisco?'

'Uh huh,' the wrinkled man said as he sifted through his stuffed briefcase. 'You'll be pleading "No Contest," see? You don't contest the charges, do you?' When Edward bowed his head and sighed, Dean continued, 'You're not admitting guilt, mind you, only conceding the charges in order to have a chance to explain the circumstances of the accident.'

Several other parties now entered the courtroom, a handful of locals from the rear, and from the front, a burly bailiff. Murmured conversations halted abruptly when Judge Horace Spenger, a large, white-haired, bespectacled man, emerged from his chambers and took his seat on the high bench, his annoyance with Monday morning arraignments palpable. No sooner had the bailiff declared the court in session than an officious representative from the district attorney's office came up to the plaintiff's table from the rear. He gave Edward a withering stare as he passed and was joined at the table by a tall Filipino man who looked straight ahead.

The bailiff read off the charges of "The People of Monterey County v. Edward Dooley: Driving a Motor Vehicle While Intoxicated, Reckless Endangerment Resulting in Personal Injury (to fourteen-year-old girl) and Property Damage (to a telephone pole and a county guardrail), Illegal Gambling, Engaging in Prostitution." When the bailiff had finished, the DA's representative identified the man beside him as the father of the injured girl in the hospital.

'Good thing he's not throwing in a Volstead charge,' Dean mumbled as Edward strained to hear the prosecutor listing the girl's injuries, '—that'll save you a few bucks.'

'And the defendant's plea?' the judge intoned drearily from the bench.

Edward got to his feet quickly but froze when he met the judge's hard stare. To Edward's dismay the public defender remained seated, tallying the various fines on the back of a manila folder. Bracing himself with the fingers of his left hand on the table, Edward stammered, 'Uh, good morning, Your Honor...I-I'd like to say, I mean I'd like to plea "No—'

'"Nolo contendere," Judge,' the public defender cut in, standing slowly.

'To all charges?'

'Yes, Judge,' Dean said, tapping the edge of the folder against the tabletop impatiently.

'And bail's been posted?' Judge Spenger asked, glancing enigmatically to the public defender. Satisfied with a nod, he said, 'Very well, sentencing on the twenty-ninth – that's in two weeks' time,' and with a crisp rap of his gavel, he barked, 'Next!'

Out in the lobby Edward was anxious to know more about the girl's condition, but Gilbert Dean dismissed the concern with a wave, explaining that Edward would be responsible for her medical bills in addition to the various fines he ticked off. 'You'll have to work out the car repairs and the county's impound fee with your friend...' he said before hurrying off.

Colm arrived an hour later to bring Edward home, and over coffee and sandwiches while waiting for the train at the SP

Depot, he said, 'Gotta hand it to you, Eddie – when you let yourself go, you go all the way…' When this didn't get a rise out of Edward, he took a more serious tone. 'Listen, brother, everyone's entitled to a few mistakes.'

'Not maiming a girl,' Edward said, looking glumly out to the tracks.

'Aw, c'mon, you can't think of it that way – she shoulda had a flashlight.'

'I was out of my gourd, Colm. I'm responsible for what's happened to her.'

His brother grunted, not convinced.

After a minute, Edward observed, 'It's like I'm getting a pass – and I'm sure that's not the way it would be if the girl was white…' At this Colm pursed his lips and looked down. 'It doesn't make me feel any less responsible,' Edward added, pushing away his half-eaten food, '—if anything, it makes me feel worse…'

Later that evening, after a tearful reunion with the family and a dinner marked by manic exuberance, Angela was anxious for some privacy and suggested that she and Edward get some air. Katharine had agreed to stay the night, and after putting the children to bed, Angela and Edward set off down Fulton Street toward the beach. Through a high cloud cover the moon cast an anemic light on the world.

Edward had difficulty keeping up with Angela's deliberately brisk pace, and in short order he confessed everything to her (but for the matter of finding Morgan in his bed). Angela said nothing as they passed a shuttered Playland and crossed the Great Highway. They sat on a bench overlooking the seawall, with the Cliff House looming above them on the right like a haunted mansion. The wind had picked up and over the roar of the surf Angela suddenly turned to Edward and in a fit of rage began striking him repeatedly on the side of his head. 'Are you out of your mind?' she screamed furiously. 'You'd risk everything we've got – everything we've worked so hard for? What were you thinking?!'

'I know, I know,' Edward said meekly, trying to fend off the blows with his hands.

'I just can't get over how *stupid* you were!' Angela said, turning to look out to the waves now, her hands balled up into fists on her knees. 'I never figured you'd for reckless and indifferent. The stock market fiasco was one thing, but Jesus, this really takes the cake…' She turned back and gave him a hard look. 'Do you understand that you could have killed somebody? Do you have any idea? Can you picture yourself in prison, Edward?'

'Believe me, I got my fill at the county jail…' Edward replied sheepishly.

'That's a country club compared to a penitentiary!' Angela sneered. 'Somehow I don't see you lasting long among rapists and murderers…'

'Please, Angela…'

She shook her head, seething now. 'I've never been anything but loyal to you, Edward, devoted to you no matter what – only I don't think you fully appreciate that.' Then with a contemptuous shudder, 'Maybe it wasn't your idea, but, boy, are you impressionable!'

'I don't blame Morgan for my behavior,' Edward offered. 'It wasn't all his doing…'

'He's a bad actor – I've never trusted him,' Angela hissed,

then turning to Edward, 'But you're a sucker, that's for sure, and now that son-of-a-bitch leaves it for you to take the fall... He and his precious social standing!' she scoffed. 'People like that only think about themselves – what they can get out of things, and, when necessary, *how* they can get out of things...'

They didn't speak for a few moments, until Edward, thinking about what he hadn't told her, said, 'Maybe you're right. Maybe I've never really understood him...'

Angela cursed into the wind. 'You go lose yourself in drink, give yourself over to some *whore*,' she spat out the word, 'and then have the audacity to come crawling back for a tearful homecoming with the children...and your mother! God forbid she ever know how far her prince has fallen – "Just a car accident, Mother, it could have been worse."' Angela shook her head in disgust. 'Christ, you've got no shame!'

'All true, all true...'

She slapped him again, harder this time. 'That hangdog act won't work with me, Edward, do you hear? I'm not playing the shrew to your hen-pecked husband. That might elicit sympathy for children,' she jeered, having endured his stories of his mother laying into his father when he was a boy, 'but not from me. I'm stronger than that and you better know it.'

'I do, Angela. I do...'

'You didn't marry your mother, you married *me* – and I get no satisfaction in belittling people. You'll take responsibility for this and try to re-earn my trust or I'll take the children and make my own way. It'd be damn hard, but at least I'd have my self-respect...' With Edward looking on warily, she continued, 'I'm not lighting candles hoping you overcome your foibles, either. You're on your own here, and if you can't do it for me, then do it for the children!'

Edward hung his head and placed his left hand on her shoulder. 'Oh, Angela, I'm sorry…I'm so sorry…' he muttered, before breaking down in tears.

She didn't touch his hand on her shoulder, but she didn't shrug it off either. When he was all cried out and had composed himself, she looked out over the seawall, saying, 'You begin by confronting Morgan. It'll be you and me bearing this burden – particularly with respect to the poor girl – but he's not getting a pass. He needs to know that he's failed you as a friend…'

Chapter 47

B ut Edward was unable to reach Morgan that week – telephone messages he left at the Matson Lines offices went unanswered, and he chose not to go by Morgan's Russian Hill apartment, fearing that a personal confrontation might provoke an ugly reaction. Then the following Wednesday, Edward returned from lunch to find an envelope waiting for him on his desk. It contained ten ten-dollar bills and a note in Morgan's hand which read:

Alas, Old Chum, I've relinquished the roadster to an acquaintance in Monterey – here's hoping the enclosed helps take the sting out of our youthful indiscretion...

Sweet, simple Edward, how tragic your blindness to my devotion over the years. Nary a bone tossed my way, forever neglected, passed over, taken for granted...

What you've always lacked, dear boy, is a modicum of mirth, so, with business beckoning abroad, I bid you adieu with these words from the inimitable Housman:

> *Oh, 'tis jesting, dancing, drinking*
> *Spins the heavy world around.*
> *If young hearts were not so clever,*
> *Oh, they would be young forever:*
> *Think no more; 'tis only thinking*
> *Lays lads underground.*

Edward sat there stunned – lately it seemed as if the ground were shifting beneath his feet – and after reading it a second time, he let the note fall from his hands. Mr. Breslin happened to come out of his office just then, and said, 'Everything alright, Eddie? You look confused...'

'Oh, sure,' Edward replied mechanically, 'Just thinking about who I'll be calling on down in San Jose tomorrow ...'

Breslin twisted the cigar in his mouth, and with a doubtful nod he headed down the hall.

The previous Monday Edward had telephoned his boss to explain that he'd been in an automobile accident in Monterey; when he showed up at work the next day with a black eye, split lip, and bandaged right hand, Breslin suspected there was more to the story than his one-time protégé let on. The following afternoon, seeing Edward just going through the motions, he took him out for coffee. Grateful for the chance to talk, Edward confided that the accident had actually occurred outside Salinas, and that he'd injured a Filipino girl.

When Breslin raised his eyebrows, Edward went on to explain that he and a friend had tied one on on Friday night, that they'd gotten separated somehow, and that he was out in his friend's roadster before dawn looking for him. 'Maybe I was going too fast,' Edward said, twirling the sugar pourer with the fingers of his left hand, 'but before I knew it, there she was and there I was, slamming on the breaks and spinning off the shoulder of the road...'

'Before dawn, you say? So you had the headlights on?' Edward nodded, vividly recalling for the first time the lights reflected in the girl's eyes. 'Well, listen, anybody walking on a country road in the dark…' his boss said, shaking his head.

But Edward sighed, knowing there was really no excuse for the accident. He explained that the girl had apparently been bringing lunch to her father, an asparagus picker. 'They get an early start, I guess – given the heat…'

Breslin lit a cigarette. 'Just another way we take care of our little brown brothers…' he said, and seeing that his cynical tone irked Edward, he added, 'That's what Taft called 'em when I was serving in the Philippines – when things were still pretty ugly…'

'You spent how long there?' Edward asked.

'Two years, starting in '03. Funston had captured Aguinaldo the year before. The kid swore allegiance to America and called on his fellow revolutionaries to quit the fight – only not all of 'em did.' Breslin paused to tap the ash from his cigarette, then remarked, 'I suppose it's understandable some resistance would remain across, what, seven thousand islands?'

Edward recognized this was the conversation his mentor had in mind after he'd returned home from France, and now he just let the man talk. Breslin explained that he'd been part of a campaign to put down bandits and religious fanatics in Samar and Mindanao; he described a battle in Siranaya against several thousand Moros as the heaviest combat that he'd ever experienced, before casually remarking that they had it "wrapped up" in a couple of days.

Having read newspaper accounts of the so-called Philippine insurrection as a schoolboy, Edward told his boss about a report he'd done in high school about the backlash at home. As much as Americans wanted to think they had little at stake when the conflict erupted among the imperial powers in 1914,

America had declared imperial ambitions of her own a generation earlier when Admiral Dewey steamed into Manila Bay. Edward mentioned how he'd cited William Jennings Bryan, Mark Twain, and Andrew Carnegie in his report, cautioning against American colonialism.

'Sure, I remember all that,' Breslin said, hailing the waitress for more coffee, 'But what were we supposed to do? Spain's empire had collapsed and we weren't about to let the other European powers swoop in – not in our own backyard, not with the Panama Canal underway. We had our national interest to protect!'

When their coffee cups were refilled, he went on, 'Besides, after three hundred years of feudal subjugation, the place was backwards, let me tell you – and the Catholic Church didn't have its hands clean, either. At least now we're bringing the Philippines into the 20th Century with electricity, health care, schools...'

'...and letting them come here to work,' Edward put in.

'Suits our needs and theirs,' Breslin agreed, then with a chuckle, 'It's what Christians do for Christians!'

Seeing Edward wasn't laughing, the bulldog of a man grew serious. 'Ah, now look, Eddie, it's too bad about the girl. Bad luck for Filipinos in general these days, as a matter of fact – what with growers now recruiting Mexicans 'cause they'll work even cheaper. But that's just the way things are. The point is, she shouldn't have been out there without a flashlight...'

'Yeah, I guess you're right,' Edward said distractedly.

But Breslin knew he didn't mean it. He sensed there was more to the escapade than Edward was willing to talk about – and there was nothing worse than a guilty idealist. He'd long felt that that Edward was in need of a wake-up call and the circumstances at hand offered an excellent lesson on life's gray areas. Stubbing out his cigarette, he said with fatherly resignation, 'You know, Eddie, maybe my war wasn't as noble as yours was, but our intentions haven't been altogether bad. Nothing in life's perfect – but we do the best we can...'

That the sentencing hearing would be held on the twenty-ninth only heightened Edward's anxiety – for some reason it was the reckless advance and subsequent retreat from Gesnes that loomed large in his consciousness now. When he confided these misgivings to Angela during the train ride to Salinas the day before the hearing, she was reminded of her time at Letterman when so many of the men had returned from the war steeped in such superstitions. Standing beside him in the courtroom the next afternoon, it wasn't hard to imagine what was going through his mind as he stared into the middle distance.

Having spent the morning arraigning another sorry collection of scoundrels, inebriants, and sex deviants, Judge Spenger now braced his left arm against the edge of the rostrum and sighed at the backlog of sentencing cases ahead of him. Standing beside Edward and reeking of tobacco, Gilbert Dean didn't bother looking over to the plaintiffs as they assembled at the table to his right. Edward recognized the tall Filipino man coming up the aisle, with a serious boy of perhaps ten years of age in tow, followed by the boy's older sister, being pushed in wheelchair by a white woman dressed in a plain cotton shift. The girl had high cheekbones and her father's square jaw line; her downcast eyes drew Edward's attention to the ominous void where her left calf should have been. Bringing up the rear was a short, solemn Filipino man, wearing an incongruously loud McIntosh suit and wide silk necktie.

Angela surreptitiously studied the girl in the wheelchair, intrigued by her unusual coloring and full lips, closed demurely. She had thick, dark hair done up in two braids, and wore a cornflower blue shirtwaist dress. Daring another glance at the woman who had escorted her, Angela surmised that she was not a nurse, but the girl's mother; before Angela could apprise Edward of this, however, the judge brought down his gavel in a call to order.

Determined to get on with things, Judge Spenger hurried the dapper Filipino attorney through his prepared remarks where the words "recklessness" and "grievous injury" stood out for Edward. The public defender then addressed the court, describing Edward as a responsible family man and a war veteran, never before arrested, who was truly remorseful for what had transpired.

Peering over his spectacles, the judge proceeded to lecture Edward on how careless behavior endangers the community and insisted that proper expiation be made. After confirming that a settlement conference with the Natividad family would immediately follow the sentencing, Judge Spenger levied a collective fine of $100 for the various infractions (equivalent to nearly a month's salary for Edward), ordered that his driver's license be revoked for three years, and that he report to a probation officer in San Francisco County every six months during that period. Seeing Edward bow his head, the judge brought his gavel down, and bellowed, 'Next!'

On their way to the jury room, Angela whispered to Edward

that she thought the woman pushing the wheelchair was the girl's mother. Having suspected this as well, he squeezed her hand. No sooner had the parties assembled across from one another at the long table than Gilbert Dean said brusquely, 'Alright, Reyes, let's hear it…'

Rising to his feet, Fernando Reyes said, 'Mr. Dean, Mr. and Mrs. Dooley, we thank you for the opportunity to sit and discuss this tragic matter with—'

'Yes, yes, get to the point,' the public defender cut in, '— these people have a train to catch.'

'No, Mr. Dean,' Edward countered, glancing sharply at the man, 'we're in no hurry here.' Looking across the table, he nervously cleared his throat. 'I would like to tell the Natividad family how sorry I am,' he said, succeeding in making eye contact only with Mr. Natividad and his serious son, 'and I assure you that I will make amends…'

'Thank you for saying this, Mr. Dooley, sir,' Mr. Reyes replied, still on his feet. 'We place our trust in the hands of Jesus because the Lord watches over us all…'

Gilbert Dean grimaced at his counterpart, and said, 'Let's get on with it…'

'Well, Mr. Dean, the Natividads are hard-working people – there are three more children at home – and while the family can never be made completely whole in this unfortunate matter, they hope that the Dooleys will consent to reimburse them for the medical expenses incurred for the care of Miss Florencia,' eliciting murmurs of agreement from Edward and Angela, 'and for the purchase of a prosthetic device of high quality for her use in the future…'

The words hung in the air a moment before Angela looked

across and addressed the girl with the large, dolorous eyes. 'You're how old, dear?'

After first looking to her mother, the girl said shyly, 'Fourteen, Ma'am.'

'Flora is our eldest,' her mother said without rancor, '—she'll be starting high school in the fall.' Mrs. Natividad was a fair-haired woman in her mid-thirties with high cheekbones and a mouth which was slightly askew, suggestive of a tendency to worry.

'I'm sure you're very bright,' Angela said to the girl with a kind smile. Dean bristled.

'A very good student, yes, Mrs. Dooley, Ma'am,' Mr. Reyes put in.

Angela nodded, then asked the girl, 'Do you have an idea what you might want to do in the future? After school I mean...'

The girl glanced at her mother again before responding. 'I would like to help support my family, Ma'am, maybe finding work at a cannery...'

The public defender had begun to impatiently ruffle through folders in his brief case when Edward broke the awkward silence. 'Again, Mr. and Mrs. Natividad, I want to express how sorry I am,' he said. This time he managed to look each of them in the eye, then addressed their daughter. 'I made a terrible mistake and very much regret the pain that I've caused you.'

Looking to her parents again, he said, 'My wife and I have three children ourselves – nine, five, and a newborn – and we would never want any harm to come to them. We're hard-working people, too, Mr. and Mrs. Natividad. We don't come from a lot of money, but we'll take care of your expenses, of course...I only wish I could do more,' he added contritely.

Mr. Natividad placed his hand over his wife's, and said, 'Thank you, Sir.'

'Alright, that's it, then,' Dean broke in, noisily coming to his feet. 'Send me the bill, Reyes, and I'll see that Mr. Dooley takes care of it,' he said as he prepared to leave the room. Edward and Angela stood up, and as the table was too wide to reach across, they nodded timidly to the Natividads, and Edward gave a clumsy wave as they followed the public defender out.

As soon as he'd shut the door to his office down the hall, Dean snapped at Edward, 'You shoulda let me do the talking in there – you coulda opened yourself to a whole lot of bother…' He took a seat behind his desk and looked up at Edward and Angela like a peeved grade school principal. 'You don't get it, do you? These people come to this country for work and they get paid fair wages – but they're not entitled to the same rights as citizens…'

'They're people though, Mr. Dean,' Angela said, 'and if the situation had been reversed—'

'If the situation had been reversed,' the old man interrupted irritably, 'I'd have nothing to do with this case, I can tell you!'

'But you're the public defender…'

'Not for those people, I'm not,' he said, eyeing Angela warily. When this clearly didn't sit well with her, he sneered, 'You're not from around here, Mrs. Dooley, but I represent *citizens* – not low-class itinerant pickers…'

Though Edward abhorred confrontations, he braced himself against the chair that he stood behind, and said, 'But Mrs. Natividad's American – and I imagine that gives their daughter certain rights…'

The public defender snorted. 'You clearly don't understand the law, Mr. Dooley. Any American woman who marries an Asian alien automatically loses her citizenship,' adding, with evident disgust, '—for the life of me I can't figure why any woman in her right mind would do something like that…'

'Leaving love out of it for the moment, Mr. Dean,' Angela said, bringing her hands across the back of the chair in front of her, 'maybe it has something to do with restricting Filipino migration to men only. I'm from Stockton, you see, with the biggest Filipino bachelor community outside of Manila – and it's not by choice, I can assure you.'

'From Stockton, eh?' the man drawled. 'And *you* can't see the trouble they cause? Let 'em make their money and go back home – nobody invited 'em to settle down…'

'Get rid of them, just like the Japanese and the Chinese?' Angela asked mildly.

'God, this is rich, Dooley!' Dean said with a rasp to Edward. 'You have your little romp down here, injure this Filipino girl and – whaddya know? – your wife's her champion!'

'She's right, though, Mr. Dean,' Edward said, suddenly very tired. 'It seems to me that allowing Filipino women to migrate might not be such a bad idea…'

'Jesus Christ!' Dean exclaimed. 'Already one in ten Californians is non-white. You're a veteran – what the hell did we fight for, anyhow?!' When this merely prompted Edward and Angela to look at each other, he began sifting through his inbox, and not looking up, said, 'So glad I could help you out of your jam, Mr. Dooley – I'll be in touch…'

Edward muttered a few words of appreciation, and as he

and Angela turned to leave they heard Dean say derisively, 'Come to think of it, Mrs. Dooley, I believe Natividad's wife might be from Stockton – you and her people probably have a lot in common...'

Chapter 49

A peculiar frenzy swept the country that fall. With frustrations running high over Hoover's austerity measures, people took to throwing fruit and heckling him at campaign stops; meanwhile, with support for temperance on the wane, Democratic leaders were emboldened to make ending prohibition part of the party's platform. On the second Tuesday in November, a resounding call for change was heard around the country when, behind a "new deal" coalition of urban dwellers, organized labor, northern blacks, and southern whites, Franklin Roosevelt won the presidential election in a landslide. Edward wasn't the only Republican to vote Democrat for the first time – for many the election marked the juncture between an inexorable slide under the old guard and a fresh start with vigorous leadership.

Paradoxically, Edward's enthusiasm for the new direction the country was taking happened to be in marked contrast to his new asceticism: he'd sworn off alcohol entirely. He also switched to a cheaper brand of cigarettes and brought a lunch from home three days a week in order to be able to wire the equivalent of ten percent of his salary to Frank Natividad on the first of every month. Determined to be more attentive to Angela and the children, he made sure to be home by six every evening, and after dinner helped Clara with her homework and gave James his bath; he still took the children on Saturdays, but now also insisted that they join him on Sundays after church with Honora, so that Angela had time to rest with the baby. He applied himself assiduously to his accounts at work, and even helped the new sales managers in Los Angeles and Seattle who were struggling to keep their heads above water.

It seemed the more relaxed the mood around the country became, the more abstemious Edward grew. As promised, in February the new Democrat-controlled congress proposed a constitutional amendment to repeal prohibition; in March the newly inaugurated president signed legislation allowing the sale of low-alcohol beer and wine for the first time since 1920; and though it would be another eight months before 21st Amendment was ratified, downtown speakeasies began converting to lunch and dinner clubs, and bottles of booze exchanged hands in broad daylight. When Edward got wind that colleagues at work had placed bets on how long his newfound sobriety would last, he doubled down and gave up rock candy, a lifelong indulgence, as well. By June he'd become insufferable.

For months he'd been especially solicitous of Fitz and made a point of taking him to lunch on Thursdays where he would go on at length about the Roosevelt Administration's latest initiatives. In April it had been about the President's sympathetic response to a second wave of Bonus Marchers in Washington – unemployed veterans were offered jobs with the newly formed Civilian Conservation Corps and train fare home; in May it was the National Recovery Act giving labor the right to organize and improving working conditions. In early June, Edward and Fitz were hunched over the lunch counter at a Foster's

Cafeteria on Market Street when Edward started in about the new Agricultural Adjustment Administration.

'Listen, Eddie,' Fitz broke in, 'I don't really give a shit about farm production quotas. I'm glad Roosevelt's shaking things up and all, but Christ, can't you give it a rest?'

'It's just that all this change has been a long time coming,' Edward said, trying not to sound defensive. 'You tune in his "fireside chats" on Sunday evenings, don't you?' When the big man pursed his lips and nodded, Edward went on, 'Every week or so he makes a big deal about announcing another program that just might make a difference...'

'Sure, I know,' Fitz said, backing off a bit so as not to offend his friend (Edward had helped him with applications for assistance from Catholic Charities and the local American Legion post so that he could find a better place to live.) 'It's just, you're all wound up these days and it's giving me the heebie-jeebies... Maybe it's all the Coca-Cola you're drinking...'

Edward looked at his half-empty fountain glass, his third, and grimaced.

'Why not have a beer with me sometime?' Fitz asked, twirling a bottle of Acme 3.2 beer in the fingers of his left hand. 'It'll help you relax.'

'No thanks,' Edward said, shaking his head, '—it's a slippery slope...'

Fitz shifted on his stool. 'So you fucked up – once,' he said, leaning into Edward. 'Jesus, you're a responsible family man – you know your limit. And God knows you feel bad enough about that crash down in Salinas...'

Edward glanced at his friend, then looked away. 'The thing is, Fitz, I don't know if I can trust myself, see? I was all too

426

willing to lose myself the once and—'

'I'll let you in on a little secret, Eddie,' the big man cut in, pausing to take another sip of his beer. 'There's another side to our buddy Morgan, see – kinky stuff…with girls, maybe boys, too, for all I know,' he added, shaking his head. 'You can get just about anything you want here in the Tenderloin, and you see some of the nicest-looking folks doing it, too. Now maybe it's human nature or maybe it's a sickness – who knows? But I'll tell you something…' and here he turned and met Edward's eyes, 'you don't have that sickness.'

Edward shifted his gaze and absently watched the short-order cook behind the counter as Fitz went on, 'You've got a fully functioning conscience, Eddie, and no matter how foolish you might feel sometimes, it's what I like best about you. It's what I like about you and Angela both, and I don't see you screwing that up. I'm in your corner, Eddie, believe me – but loosen up a little 'cause nobody likes a pain in the ass…'

Mr. Breslin may have been feeling much the same way because he encouraged Edward to take some time off that summer to relax with the family. (Edward still wasn't touching liquor, but he had dialed back the Cokes, and was taking long walks at lunch to improve his sleep.) Knowing Angela and the children were getting on each other's nerves at home, Edward suggested the family go to Stockton for a couple of weeks in July. The children were delighted by the train trip, and as hot as the San Joaquin Valley could be, it was a welcome relief to the dreary fog out in the avenues.

Gemma was overjoyed to have the whole family with her. Despite a bad hip, she had no trouble with all the cooking and cleaning, thanks to the help of her faithful next-door neighbor, Rose Cappaciola. Rose was tall and somewhat homely like her brother, Joe, who lived at the Veterans' Home in the Napa Valley, and she too had become an American citizen in 1917. Now she looked after the shoe shop Joe had started years before in downtown Stockton; she and Gemma were in the habit of going to daily mass together and sharing the main meal of the day.

Angela, Clara, and Baby Audrey adapted easily to the older women's routine, which consisted of spending the hottest part of the day in the cool of the back porch, chatting, sewing, and thumbing through the *Saturday Evening Post*, with the radio in the background tuned to a program of Paul Robeson singing Negro spirituals.

Early one afternoon, when Edward and James walked downtown for haircuts, the three women left Clara to read stories to the baby on the porch and returned to the kitchen to make gnocchi. As she set a pot of steaming potatoes on the kitchen table, Angela said, 'I hear from Giancarlo that people over there are complaining more than ever, now that the government is running the movie business!'

Gemma smiled. 'He tells me that, too. Ever since the talkies, the censorship, it gets worse – along with everything else the Fascisti touch…'

Peeling a potato, Rose said, 'Mussolini thinks he knows everything.'

The three worked in silence a minute, until Angela said, 'Tell me, Mama, does Papa think Roosevelt can turn around this Depression that we've brought on the world?'

'He doesn't say,' Gemma replied, ignoring the sarcasm, 'but

he thinks the execution of Zangara was a frame-up,' referring to the Italian anarchist who had tried to shoot the president-elect in February. Dropping a peeled potato into a ceramic bowl, she added, 'I bet he thinks Roosevelt will be the same as Hoover...'

'Hah!' Angela scoffed. 'Hoover would never appoint a woman to be secretary of labor – now that takes guts...'

'Speaking of which,' Rose said to Angela after a moment, 'the new emergency relief agency just opened an office on Lafayette, across from the shoe store.'

'Really? Why there, I wonder?'

'With all the out-of-work pickers, I guess Little Manila has the most need,' Rose replied as she started mashing the potatoes. 'Of course, there are people who think Americans should be helped first, so they're carrying picket signs and protesting on the sidewalk...'

Angela poured a whisked egg into the bowl, and her mother dusted the mashed potatoes with flour. Gemma was deftly blending the mixture into a light crumble with a fork when she in passing, she remarked, 'As bad as Mrs. McGrath's funeral...'

'Oh, yes, that was awful!' Rose exclaimed, and seeing Angela's curiosity was piqued, she said, 'Your mother and I were leaving St. Mary's after mass a couple of months ago, just as the funeral was about to start. Mr. McGrath is a mean man, you know, and he insisted that no Filipinos mourners be let into church...'

'Not even his own daughter,' Gemma said, kneading the dough into rolls.

A shiver flashed down Angela's spine. 'Beverly McGrath,' Rose explained, 'the girl who married the Filipino man...'

'You went to school with her sister,' Gemma said. 'You and Alice were friends...'

Angela's mind raced back to her school days. She could picture Alice McGrath, remembered that they'd grown apart in high school, and dimly recalled an older sister. 'But I thought her sister moved away to take care of an old relative somewhere,' she said now.

Cutting the dough into one-inch segments, Rose glanced at Gemma, who said at length, 'No, Angela, that was just a story...'

In the nine months since Edward's accident, Angela had told her mother no more than they'd told Honora – nothing about the debauchery leading up to it, nothing about Edward's injuring a girl. Now, at the risk of sounding suspicious, Angela simply said, 'Oh...'

While her mother pressed the doughy segments into the tines of a fork, Angela returned to the sink and filled the pot with water. Recalling Beverly Natividad at the sentencing hearing, her mouth slightly askew, she was keen to know the truth about her ostracism.

The family was leaving church Sunday morning when Rose squeezed Angela's arm and with a nod pointed out Alice McGrath up ahead. Angela barely recognized her. She'd aged badly, with a scowl on her lips and hair like straw. Two sullen teenagers, presumably her children, were half-heartedly guiding their cantankerous grandfather down the steps to the sidewalk. Angela wasn't at all interested in approaching her.

Instead, the next day she went over to Stockton High School to see Harriet Wheeler, a girlhood friend whom she hadn't spoken to in six years. Harriet went by the name Trueblood now – she'd married an older man during her stint at teachers' college – and had a son. This much Angela knew when she telephoned the school Monday morning to inquire as to whether Mrs. Trueblood still taught history there. Learning that she did, Angela asked the receptionist to pass along a message that she would stop by that afternoon after summer school classes let out.

Old, unpleasant feelings churned in Angela as she made her way down the familiar wide hallways lined with lockers. She knocked lightly on the door to Room 210, and caught the attention of Harriet, seated at her desk. Angela gave a little wave and entered the empty classroom that smelled of chalk, the walls festooned with maps of the world and quotations of America's Founding Fathers. Harriet stood to greet her. She was a frumpy brunette who wore eyeglasses and no make-up, but what she lacked in appearance she always made up for in sarcasm. 'Well, my heavens, to what do we owe the honor?' she said, returning Angela's peck on the cheek, 'I thought you'd given up on us after the ten-year reunion...'

They held hands a moment and exchanged awkward smiles before Harriet broke away and suggested they have tea. Angela followed her to a cubby by the cloak closet in the back of the room where Harriet plugged in an electric kettle and set out two mugs. She reported that she'd been widowed two years now, and that her son would be starting Berkeley in September. 'We simply weren't able to challenge him enough here at Stockton High,' she said with obvious pride, '—he breezed through his coursework in three years!'

'My, that's tremendous, Harriet,' Angela said, relieved that her old friend had something cheery to follow up the news of her husband's passing. 'He must take after you.'

'Oh, his father was no slouch,' Harriet replied, handing Angela a mug of tea. 'He was a journalist, you know, with the *Sacramento Bee*.'

'Yes, I remember you mentioning that,' Angela said as they made their way back up to the head of the classroom. Harriet took her seat behind her desk and beckoned Angela to bring a chair up alongside. As soon as Angela sat down she looked at her old friend and said with genuine remorse, 'Oh, but Harriet, I'm so sorry for your loss...'

'Well, thank you,' the woman said primly, clearing away a stack of folders from her desk blotter. 'Naturally you'd have no way of your knowing – I don't think any of us has heard a peep from you in ages.' She looked up admonishingly, which caused Angela to grimace. 'If memory serves, I believe you were pregnant with your second child at the time...'

Angela looked down apologetically. She felt guilty for having succumbed to curiosity in 1927 to attend her high school reunion; it was an underwhelming affair and Angela had returned to Los Angeles with renewed satisfaction for her life there. 'That's right, James was born the following February,' she said, before adding, "We have another daughter now, too – Audrey arrived just about a year ago...'

'Audrey?! You don't say!' Harriet peered over the steam of her tea, a wry grin on her lips. 'I seem to recall you were pretty smitten by a movie of that name back in high school,' she said, referring to a melodrama about a mistreated orphan girl in Colonial Virginia who is eventually redeemed by a British estate owner who comes to recognize her good character. 'I never understood what you saw in that story...' Harriet ventured, sipping her tea.

Angela gave a self-deprecating laugh. 'I suppose Pauline Frederick made quite an impression on me,' she said of the actress who had played the heroine.

'No, no, you always were one with "great expectations," Angela Luchetti,' Harriet Trueblood said provocatively. 'So after all this time, what can I do for you?'

'Well, it's just gossip, I'm afraid,' Angela began, feigning more shame than she was feeling. 'I happened to see Alice McGrath at mass yesterday...only I couldn't bring myself to go up to her.' When Harriet raised her eyebrows, Angela explained, 'You see, last fall my husband and I were driving through Salinas on our way down to Santa Barbara, and we stopped at a soda fountain with the children to get ice cream cones. Anyhow, I did a double-take when I saw a rather tall woman standing at the cash register with several children – hers, I imagined, though they looked Filipino – but for the life of me I couldn't remember her name. I just let it go...until a few days ago, that is, when my mother happened to mention Mrs. McGrath's funeral.'

'I heard about it,' Harriet said, shaking her head. 'Poor Mable McGrath, with that hot-tempered SOB for a husband. He made her life hell, and Alice's, too. Yes, I'm sure it was Beverly you bumped into, Alice's older sister,' Harriet said, putting down her tea. 'Never comes to Stockton anymore, not since her father threw her out...'

'For marrying a Filipino?'

Harriet nodded. 'Supposedly her mother went to see her from time to time, even though her husband didn't approve. Alice's younger brother, Jim, is just like his father...'

Looking down at the mug in her lap, Angela said, 'I always

thought Alice's sister had gone away after high school to take care of a relative.'

'Oh, that's what everybody was told,' Harriet said mildly. 'You were gone yourself by the time the real story came out – it was after the war, anyway...'

'Did you ever know Beverly's husband?'

'Oh, I saw him around. Nice enough fellow. Quiet – unusually tall for a Filipino. Quite a bit older than we were, if memory serves...'

The two reminisced a while longer, and Angela came away assured of one thing and floored by another – though she maintained a detached equanimity throughout the remainder of their visit so as not to arouse any suspicions. Over the years she'd managed to put memories of her home town behind her; but for the curiosity that got the better of her six years earlier, she preferred to keep it that way.

After putting the children to bed, Angela and Edward took a stroll in the cool evening air on their last night in Stockton. The sound of a train whistle in the distance prompted Edward to say that getting a taste of small town life had done him good – that he found the people were friendlier than those in the city, that an established order provided a sense of security.

'You can also feel trapped by all the conformity,' Angela remarked as they walked along the treelined sidewalks, passed houses with lights on, curtains drawn. 'Believe me, you don't want to stand out in a small town...'

Edward looked over. 'I guess I hadn't thought of it like that.'

'It's true that city life can be overwhelming,' Angela continued, 'but, then again, it's ironic the privacy you can find in anonymity.' They walked on in silence a minute, then Angela said, 'You know, Edward, I went to see my old school chum the other day...'

Edward had been concerned how quiet Angela was after her visit with Harriet Trueblood, and now looked at her with interest. 'Yes, I remember.'

'I wanted to confirm something I've had a hunch about,' she said, looking ahead deliberately. 'You remember that fellow Dean last summer saying that he thought Mrs. Natividad was from Stockton?'

Edward nodded, then put his hands in his pocket, as if to promise he wouldn't interrupt.

'Well, it turns out her name is – or was – Beverly McGrath. I didn't know her, but I was friends with her younger sister, Alice, from the time we were in kindergarten. Something changed in high school, though – Alice became a different person, she was very quiet after her sister moved away, supposedly to take care of a sick relative. Only now I find out it was because her father had disowned her sister for falling in love with a Filipino...'

'Mr. Natividad...' Edward said.

They'd reached the grammar school when Angela suggested they turn around. Retracing their steps she explained that even though Beverly's mother had longed for a reconciliation, at her funeral in May her husband had turned away Beverly, her husband, and his people. Edward muttered how terrible it all was, and they were halfway down the next block when Angela added, 'To think that nothing's changed after all these years...'

Chapter 50

The subject came up again unexpectedly at the end of August when Edward took Angela to dinner at a new café in their neighborhood. Such an outing was all but unheard of, but that morning Edward had prevailed upon his sister to look after the children and stay the night. By the time Edward and Angela placed their dinner orders that evening, Angela was beside herself – imagining that he'd been fired, arrested again, or, worse, that he would propose that they take in Colm and Katherine now, too. His fidgeting at the table, and his outsized interest in everything about the café – from the Moroccan decor to their mustachioed waiter – only heightened her anxiety until finally she blurted, 'For goodness sake, Edward, is something the matter?'

'Oh, aren't you having a good time?' he asked innocently, 'I thought you'd like this place...'

She gave him a hard look, and he settled down. 'Oh, all right,' he said, folding his hands on the table, 'there's something I've been thinking about – something I want to ask you...'

'Okay...' she said equivocally.

The waiter interrupted to refill their water glasses, which caused Edward to grit his teeth. When at last the man had gone, Edward took a sip of water and leaned forward. 'It's like this, see – I made the last installment on the settlement this month, right? And now I've got the court document saying that I've met all my obligations...'

'Yes, I know – you showed me.'

'Right, I know...but then, see, I telephoned the public defender a couple of days ago to ask for the Natividad's mailing address. He thought I was nuts, of course, and urged me not to contact them, but Angela, I feel more certain about this than I have about anything in quite a while.'

Angela shifted in her seat. 'Why do you want to contact them? To say what exactly?'

Edward glanced around the dining room, took another sip of water, and said with a sigh, 'I want to keep sending them the same amount, every month, just like we've been doing – for them to use however they see fit...' He pursed his lips and waited for Angela's response.

'You feel guilty,' she said evenly.

'Well, sure, that's part of it,' he said, crossing his arms, his brow furrowed. 'I mean, I'll always feel bad for their daughter... and then after what you told me about Mrs. Natividad – how her family abandoned her...' He shook his head, 'She and her husband have, what, five children? What we give them isn't much, but it could help a lot in these tough times...'

Angela added a lemon wedge to her iced water but didn't look up.

'I know it sounds foolish,' Edward continued in a whisper, 'what with all that we have to manage ourselves. We need a bigger place, for one – it's not fair Clara has to share a room with her brother, and it's not easy having Baby Audrey in our bedroom...' Looking down, he fiddled with his spoon. 'I know you think Walter could be doing more to help, and I'm not likely to see a raise anytime soon, but my suits were made to last, and if I cut back on cigarettes and...'

He stopped abruptly when Angela's hand covered his, and looking across he was surprised to see her face was flushed and that she was tearing up.

'Clara will be fine, we'll all be fine...' she said, squeezing his fingers. 'It won't be easy,' she went on, her voice cracking, 'but we'll manage, Edward. We always do!'

'So you think we ought to do it?' he asked earnestly.

She mustered a fragile, heartfelt smile. 'I think it's an excellent idea and I'm proud of you for suggesting it...' she said, before reaching into her handbag for a handkerchief.

After dinner they walked out Geary Boulevard to Sutro Heights Park. Cloudcover obscured the moon like a veil as they made their way along the wide paths lined with replicas of Greek and Roman statuary, passed parterres and hedge mazes, the gazebo and the glass-paned conservatory. A few other couples lingered at the railing of the expansive terrace overlooking the Cliff House and Ocean Beach. Angela retied her headscarf against the light breeze and nestled up against Edward, taking his arm in hers. He was feeling very fortunate and was just starting to recount something funny that had happened at work when Angela stopped him.

'Now I need to tell *you* something, Edward,' she said, gazing into the distance.

'Oh? What's that, dear?'

'It's something I've never told anyone. It's hard to talk about...but I want to tell you...'

Alarmed, he tried turning to face her but she only gripped his arm tighter, compelling him to look out to the ocean as she spoke.

'I've told you that I left Stockton after finishing high school because I wanted to do my part – because so many young men I knew were being called up in the draft. But that's not the whole reason I left...' Looking down at her feet now, she said, 'Beverly McGrath was disowned by her family and forced to leave home. Well, my leaving was my own doing – but all the same, I didn't feel like I had a choice...'

Watching the moonlight flicker on the surface of the water, Edward was reminded of the conversation he'd overheard between Angela and her father in the toolshed. 'You were in love with a boy?' he asked.

'There *was* a boy,' Angela acknowledged, '—the son of a prominent grower in the area, someone my father did business for. In those days we were at the Clayton farm a lot. Papa and Mr. Clayton would discuss leasing arrangements, and Daryl, the son, would take me with him when he drove around checking that the gates were locked and the water troughs were full. He was a few years older than me...'

Edward recalled the inconclusive conversation he'd had with Gemma about the Clayton boy, and though he'd long suspected something was amiss, he'd chosen not to press Angela about it. Now by way of encouraging her to let it out, he guided her to a bench where they sat down and he wrapped his arm around her to keep her warm.

After a minute, Angela said with a hardness in her voice, 'One time he took me out to the bluffs to watch the sunset... and he got fresh with me. He slapped me, and when I tried to push him away he punched me...He held me down, forced himself on me...'

Edward sighed. At length, she said, 'My father wouldn't believe me when I told him. He didn't want to hear it, he wanted to think that somehow I'd provoked it – the last thing he wanted was to confront Mr. Clayton...'

'I'm so sorry, Angela,' Edward said softly.

She acknowledged his sympathy with a sidelong glance, then went on to explain that she never went to the Clayton farm again, that she took to wearing sweaters at school to hide the bruises on her arms, that whenever she saw the boy around town he just ignored her.

'I felt horrible,' she said, quietly crying now, 'but then a few weeks went by and I started to worry that it was more than just shame and guilt. I felt physically sick. When I finally got up the courage to tell my father about it, he didn't want to hear it. He knew I wouldn't want Mama to know that I might be pregnant because she was religious and it would break her heart, so instead he took me to a man downtown who gave me a bitter parsley tonic to drink. Only I didn't get better, I got worse – I was feverish and started throwing up a lot. Mama wanted to take me to the doctor but my father insisted that I just needed rest...'

Edward stroked her back, knowing what was coming would be awful. He recalled Angela's first miscarriage, rushing home to their Westlake apartment and finding her with that terrible little bundle in her hands. He remembered the obstetrician pulling him aside after Clara was born, saying something about uterine scarring, and then the second miscarriage on the trip to San Francisco at Christmas – for all he knew, there may have been others. Now he listened uncomfortably as Angela described the night her father took her to see another man somewhere out in the country, with her mother and Rose off at a church function; that the man had given her another kind of medicine and she'd woken up on the ride home with excruciating pains in her stomach; that over the years she became convinced the man had probably been a horse doctor.

'I hated my father for the whole terrible ordeal,' Angela said now, blowing her nose, '—for not confronting Mr. Clayton, for keeping it from Mama and sweeping it all under the rug. Then the more time that went by, the worse I felt about myself – that maybe somehow I'd led the boy on, maybe my manner was too frank and forward for a girl, maybe I deserved what I got...I was going crazy, Edward, and it was all I could do to get away from Stockton...'

'Dear heart,' Edward said now, wiping a tear from her cheek, 'I feel terrible to think you've kept this to yourself all these years.'

'I know you love me, Edward,' she said, shaking her head with regret, 'but I just couldn't bring myself to talk about it – not after we were married, not even after the miscarriages. It was just too painful...Then what I learned from Harriet Wheeler hit me like a baseball bat.'

'About Beverly McGrath, you mean...'

'No, there's more to it, you see,' Angela said, bringing her clasped hands to her chin and taking a deep breath. 'I'd already left Stockton when the truth about Beverly came out, but now I learn from Harriet that, of all people, Daryl Clayton once had feelings for Beverly, too. Oh, Edward, I couldn't believe it!' she said with an odd cackle. 'He was a year or two ahead of her at Stockton High – good-looking, blue-eyed, flaxen-haired, very popular – but when she put him off he evidently didn't take it well, and then when she fell for Frank Natividad – a grown man, and a Filipino, no less – he became downright nasty. Harriet didn't get the full story until years later – how supposedly he'd intimidated Natividad and his family and threatened to embarrass the McGraths. Even after Beverly and Frank left he wouldn't give it a rest – Harriet says he's the biggest bigot around and to this day is still hated in certain circles...'

Edward shook his head, not knowing what to say. They were alone on the terrace now, and no longer burdened with her secret, Angela stood up and led Edward to the railing. They looked out to the ocean, and at length she said with a weary sigh, 'I guess I was just an easy target for him to take out his frustrations...'

'Oh, Angela...'

She turned and looked up to him now with a resigned smile. 'From the first time I met you, Edward, I saw you had an uncommon empathy, the way you were with Fitz...'

'Oh, I don't know...' Edward demurred.

'In the beginning I found your noble idealism admirable,' she continued frankly, 'but you also seemed a bit tragic – taking to heart all that high-mindedness that got us into the war in the first place. You've changed some since then, though – ambition and even a certain amount of greed have made you less agreeable at times—'

'That could be said of a lot of people...' Edward put in, thinking of Nathan Leopold, then adding, 'only some can't accept their comeuppance – as if they've been cheated out of what was rightfully theirs.' He leaned forward and rested his elbows on the railing. 'But then I suppose nobody's hands are clean...'

'No, Edward, that's just it – nobody's hands *are* clean. Everybody is complicit in this world to some degree, and you're the better man for admitting it.' Now she leaned against the railing, and mused, 'You know, it's strange to think that your coming to terms with what happened in Salinas is forcing me to do the same myself – it's helped me to let go of something that I've held onto so tightly all these years.'

'I'm sorry for that,' Edward said, looking over to her. 'It had to be terrible, hiding the truth, worrying what others might think.'

She met his eyes, and said, 'Don't you worry about me, Edward – I'll always manage to take care of myself...On the other hand, it's only since you came into my life that I've found the strength to let my guard down – to receive love as well as give it.' Looking out to the horizon again, she added, 'Your desire to do the right thing has always meant the world to me. To do it now, out of sight and off the record, well...I love you for caring, Edward.'

He felt an exhilaration in his chest unlike anything he'd ever experienced. 'I love you, too, Angela,' he said, before he kissed her and wrapped her up in his arms. With his face nuzzled into the crook of her neck, he added, 'You make me a better man.'

Chapter 51

Edward caught Angela's eye and offered a faint smile as he stood to carve the Christmas turkey, communicating everything and nothing in particular in that moment. The flat on 41st Avenue was steamy from the day's cooking, their bed was piled high with coats, hats, and purses, and two extra leaves had been added to the dining table. The living room had been rearranged to make way for a five-foot-tall Scotch Pine, adorned with an eclectic assortment of glass ornaments, a string of lights, and garlands made of popcorn and cranberries. The small collection of wrapped presents beneath the tree was a reminder that it was a time of needs trumping wants: a new hairbrush and mirror for Clara, a pair of Keds for James, a stuffed Koala bear for Audrey, walking shoes for Angela, and two Arrow Shirts for Edward.

The one gift Edward and Angela cherished most of all was having their loved ones together for the holidays. While they'd be taking the children to Stockton to celebrate Epiphany with Gemma (she no longer traveled long distances on account of a bad hip), and Colm had begged off saying he'd be busy volunteering at a soup kitchen, the Sonoma clan had come down for a few days, which made for an especially festive gathering.

Angela sat at one end of the table, nearest the swinging door to the kitchen, to keep an eye on Clara and James who were charged with looking after Baby Audrey and the Hoagland twins in their highchairs. Katherine was to Angela's left beside Honora, who took her usual spot against the built-in buffet. Opposite Honora and Katherine sat Aunt Hildie and Hildie's eldest daughter, Cora, widowed since '29, when her husband had succumbed to tuberculosis. Edward presided over the other end of the table, with Deirdre and her husband, Tom Hoagland, to his left facing Bro. Michael and Fitz seated against the buffet. Fitz was at the end to afford him the unimpeded use of his left arm, having given up on his prosthetic right arm altogether.

No sooner had Bro. Michael finished saying grace than Honora promptly returned to the subject at hand before they'd sat down to dinner, namely the problem with progress.

'As I say, Hildie, I'll stick with ferries and trains,' Honora repeated, rebutting her sister-in-law's claim that the bridge planned over the Golden Gate would make the trip to Sonoma easier. 'For all the talk about automobiles being the measure of freedom, I daresay Edward does just fine without one, don't you, Edward? I for one prefer a leisurely pace, without the steep grades and all the stop and go – to say nothing of the terrible traffic jams you read about!'

'Well, to each his own,' Hildie said, hoping to drop the subject as she passed the potatoes. The fact was, Honora hadn't been up to Sonoma in years.

'For that matter,' Honora continued, 'I don't know what's so wonderful about all these modern appliances – mechanical dishwashers now, too?! Giving us more leisure time to do what? Worry about whether we're any happier?'

'There's plenty one can do with extra time,' Angela said, careful to not sound resentful, 'Like read a good book or see friends more often…'

'Only most people go to the pictures,' Honora countered, 'to distract themselves…'

'That's freedom for you,' Bro. Michael chimed in brightly, taking the cranberry relish, '—we can do something worthwhile or simply fritter our time away…'

Dede found this amusing and giggled.

Honora smirked at her daughter's delight, then winked at Hildie. She was grateful for her sister-in-law's devotion to Deirdre over the years, certain that country life suited her better than the city. Acknowledging Honora's gratitude with a smile, Hildie said, 'Progress is no panacea, I'll grant you that, Honora. Too much of anything isn't good for you…'

'You can say that again, Hildie,' Tom Hoagland put in, alert to little exchanges between the older women, particularly when they involved Dede. Always anxious to please his insufferable mother-in-law, and because as a farmer he shared her wariness of progress, he said, 'You know, Honora, all this over-mechanized farming is a risky business. After the war everybody in the Midwest was buying tractors like crazy, thinking they could do better with feed crops… Well, they tripled the acreage of pasture and farmland in ten years, alright,' he explained as he served himself from the platter of sliced turkey, 'but now with the drought, they're liable to see all that good top soil just blow away…'

With an emphatic nod to her son-in-law, Honora declared, 'You reap what you sow.'

Talk of farming made Hildie nostalgic, and she said to Honora, 'Remember how James and Aidan used to go on about the old homesteads in the Bluegrass Country?'

446

'Spirit of a bygone era,' Honora said, with more fondness than she'd felt at the time.

'Funny how that story still resonates, even though more and more Americans live in cities now,' Angela remarked. Passing the basket of rolls, she looked down to the other end of the table, and said, 'Take the book you got for Clara last year, Fitz, *Little House in the Big Woods*. How she enjoyed learning about homesteading and raising farm animals...' Laura Ingalls Wilder's book had been Angela's suggestion, part of an effort to revise her daughter's view of Uncle Fitz (after explaining that he suffered from epileptic seizures, that the woman Clara had seen him with the day of Audrey's baptism was a nurse helping him.)

'Got the latest one for her birthday coming up, Ange, just like you asked me,' Fitz said, 'though I'm told there's still no mention of anything bad, like floods or fires or disease.'

Glancing from Fitz to Angela, Edward ventured, 'I'm glad Clara likes the stories, but growing up in the city like Fitz and I did, it's hard to imagine times were ever that simple...'

'It *is* harder to mobilize people around the common good nowadays,' Angela acknowledged, '—as opposed to when neighbors would help with the harvest or with raising a barn. In any case, that's why I like the president's idea of putting men back to work through government programs – fixing roads and bridges and taking care of our national parks.'

'We'll never dig ourselves out of this depression that way,' Honora said bluntly. While pleased to finally have a Democrat in the White House again, Roosevelt was turning out to be not at all what she'd expected. 'At best it'll employ a few million men – young men, at that, who can afford to be away for months at a time. But what about the men with families?' Looking to Edward, she said, 'Thank heavens there'll always be demand for clothes, because without private enterprise we're sunk...'

'True, Mother, I'm lucky to have a job, but what Roosevelt's doing will help in the long run.' Looking around the table, he added, 'Level the playing field, put us on a sounder footing.'

'That man's dangerous, if you ask me,' Honora sniffed as she helped herself to more turkey dressing. 'All this talk about social responsibility – we'll be creating an idle, dependent class if we're not careful.' Reaching for the potatoes, she proclaimed, 'Individual initiative is what really counts – we're responsible for ourselves and our immediate family. Beyond that, it's all just wishful thinking...'

'Oh, but that's not very Christian!' Cora said, pretending to be offended. Hildie bowed her head and grinned, for if her sister-in-law envied her having a man of the cloth for a son, she could only imagine Honora's reaction to the news that Cora was thinking of becoming a nun.

'Show me a missionary feeding the hungry in China and I'll show you a rice Christian or two,' Honora quipped. 'God loves us more when we take care of ourselves...'

Bro. Michael laughed. He'd always enjoyed his aunt's cynical take on things but wasn't about to let her have the last word on the subject. Turning to his left, he said, 'Tell me, Fitz, how do you see the question of individual initiative versus community benefit? Baseball being a team sport, for instance, but so dependent on personal performance...'

'It's a game of ebbs and flows, but mostly ebbs,' the big man began glumly, his beloved Seals having ended the season in the cellar; despite promising performances from the DiMaggio brothers, he was crestfallen when Frankie Crosetti went to the Yankees. 'The best teams are more than just a collection of great players,' he observed, '—the best teams are made up of guys who've learned how to face setbacks together…'

When this elicited nods around the table, Fitz went on, 'Take that "All Star" game they played back in July,' referring to the first mid-summer classic, '—the best of the best, maybe, but not really two *teams*. Now I don't deny that Gehrig, Lazzeri, Dykes, and Cronin make a dream infield, but they don't play together day in and day out. They're individual players putting on a show, only you'll never win a championship by going it alone…'

'Individually accountable, collectively responsible,' Bro. Michael affirmed, as if on cue, 'That's the moral imperative if we're going to work our way out of this depression…'

'You're absolutely right, Michael,' Edward said with enthusiasm. 'We're all in this together and working for the common good is the right thing to do. I mean, isn't it about time government stood for something more than just the bottom line?'

While she appreciated her nephew's optimism, Aunt Hildie was less sanguine about American politics. 'If you're suggesting government has a moral imperative, Edward,' she said, 'you'd better count Prohibition as a failure because you can't legislate morality.'

'No, you can't,' Honora agreed, dabbing her lips with her napkin.

Though Edward continued to abstain from alcohol, he agreed with those who saw the recent ratification of the 21st Amendment as a repudiation of government interference with personal liberties. 'Sure, I'd like to think we're more enlightened on that score twelve years later,' he conceded now, 'but then I can't help thinking that it's all just economic – that making and distributing liquor puts men back to work, and means more tax revenue, too.'

Bro. Michael smiled wryly. 'You make it sound duplicitous, Edward…'

Edward welcomed the chance to challenge his cousin here. 'Come now, Michael, wasn't it hypocritical of the Christian Brothers to buy a vineyard in Napa in order to get into the winemaking business?'

Michael paused to gather his thoughts. 'We live in the real world, Edward, with temptation all around us,' he began, 'but like anything else, used in moderation alcohol can be enjoyable and even salutary – just ask the Italians and the French,' he added, casting a friendly glace to Angela. 'No, if we've learned anything over the last twelve years it's that restricting access isn't conducive to improving behavior – quite the contrary, in fact.'

'People are like children,' Honora declared. 'They behave badly when they're told they can't be trusted to make up their own minds. It breeds a scofflaw mentality…'

'Well put, Honora,' Bro. Michael said with a deferential nod.

'And look where it's gotten us,' she went on, 'We make heroes out of common criminals – people can't get their fill of stories about gangsters like Dillinger and Barrow,' before adding derisively, '…couched as Robin Hoods, no less!'

Edward chuckled. 'That's why they're making make Alcatraz a penitentiary, Mother – so we can lock the crooks up and throw away the key!'

'Now there's the hypocrisy, Edward,' Bro. Michael said,

'—appeasing our consciences when for twelve years we've hidden the truth of Prohibition behind closed doors...'

Honora nodded vigorously. She didn't particularly want to know the reasons why Edward had been refraining from alcohol, though she was certain he shared none of his father's proclivities for overindulgence. 'Good people are responsible for their own behavior,' she declared now, daring to catch his eye, before adding for the benefit of all at the table, 'and I think it's high time we had more taxes to pay down the national debt and get this country back on its feet. Not for any more of that man's *programs*, mind you, or we run the risk of turning into a socialist country!'

This provoked laughter around the table, and as Angela, Katherine, and Cora cleared away the dinner plates, Angela quipped, 'The fascists in Italy do get the trains to run on time...'

'Economic desperation is giving rise to extremists these days,' Aunt Hildie remarked, as she refolded her napkin. 'That German dictator is fomenting all sorts of hatred...'

'First he bans opposition parties and trade unions,' Michael said, 'and now he's trying to scapegoat the Jews, which is the purest form of evil...'

'That's absolutely true, Michael,' Edward agreed, reminded of the night Nathan Leopold warned of the Germans blaming "the enemy within." 'Let's hope the sane majority in that country snuffs out that sort of thing...'

'Let's hope,' Tom repeated.

'Evil can influence even reasonable men,' Michael said ominously, just as Angela and Katherine emerged from the kitchen with a plum pudding and pumpkin pie.

After dinner everyone retired to the living room to sing Christmas carols and watch the children open their presents; Edward served cordials but did not partake himself.

Eventually a cab was hailed for Fitz, and the O'Sheas and Hoaglands left for Old Man McCormick's (despite his senility, his niece insisted the O'Sheas stay with them whenever they were in San Francisco.) Honora bid the family goodnight, and with Angela and Katherine putting the children to bed, Bro. Michael insisted on helping Edward with the dishes.

As they worked side by side at the kitchen sink, Edward washing and Michael drying, Edward returned to the subject of evil, harkening back to their boyhood discussions of *The Sea Wolf*. 'So, are you really more inclined to see things like Wolf Larsen these days, Michael?' he asked. 'You sounded rather pessimistic at dinner...'

'Evil amounts to a corruption of one's being,' Michael observed, adding a dry plate to the stack on the counter. 'It originates from our own free will – which God grants us, of course, but which we've allowed to become diseased.'

'That makes sense,' Edward said. 'I can only hope that what we fought for in the war will stop the spread of the disease...'

'And I share your hope, Edward,' Michael assured his cousin, 'though I've always doubted how effective the League can be when the U.S. isn't a part of it.'

'We can't be the world's policeman,' Edward insisted, then, eager to return to the exchange between the idealist and the cynic in *The Sea Wolf*, he tried to draw out his cousin on St. Augustin describing the redemptive power of Jesus Christ in countering evil. But Michael wouldn't bite, and instead changed the subject altogether.

'Listen, Edward, I hope you won't take this the wrong way,' he began, wiping drinking glasses now, 'but I get the sense that you fear alcohol may have a certain power over you...'

Edward was less affronted than relieved, and as he finished rinsing a glass pitcher, he said, without making eye contact, 'What if I told you that I lost my way a year ago?'

'In your case, Edward,' Michael said, taking hold of the pitcher, 'I'd say it was probably something other than the alcohol that made you do it...'

Edward glanced at his cousin. 'How do you mean?'

'Don't get me wrong, addiction is a serious matter,' Michael said evenly as he concentrated on wiping the pitcher. 'At root, it suggests a low self-worth which could be the result of any number of things. It could stem from childhood, where one judges himself unworthy or lacking in some way. In any case, self-doubt in a mature adult is natural – but I'd venture to say that your doubts have always been about something other than your ability to control yourself.'

Edward didn't look over but continued to rinse glassware and listen intently as Michael continued, 'You've always had a high sense of responsibility and moral integrity, Edward. From the first time I met you, when you all came up to Sonoma after the earthquake, you've been preoccupied with holding your family together. Much was coming your way and you doubted your ability to handle it all – yet that's just what you've been doing all these years.'

Edward stopped and leaned against the sink to consider what his cousin was saying.

'You've been the rock your family has needed, Edward – from the time your father started to slip, then going off to the war,' through Colm's troubles, and with Walter going back east. Yet despite your mother's shrillness you've managed to forge ahead on your own terms.' He wiped his hands with the dishtowel and compelled Edward to look him in the eye. 'I've been privileged to look at life from a more philosophical perspective, Edward, but *you're* the one who's been living in the real world. You've had to get your hands dirty, to fall down and get back up, to recognize your failings and hubris.'

Placing his hand on Edward's shoulder, Michael said, 'It's time you learned to trust yourself, cousin, because you're stronger than you think...'

Angela insisted that her sister-in-law deserved a good night's sleep after all her help with the holiday, and Michael gladly agreed to drop Katherine at her apartment on his way downtown. When the two of them had departed and the flat was quiet again, Edward and Angela returned to the living room, which was dark, but for the lights on the Christmas tree. They sat on the couch, her hand in his lap, and looked out the bay window where a light rain had begun to fall.

'So, what were you and Michael talking about?' Angela asked. 'It sounded serious...'

'He says I need to learn to trust myself,' Edward said after a moment. 'That no matter what pitfalls and temptations are put before me, God loves me...'

'My goodness...'

'That I have to learn to love myself as God loves me...'

'And how did this conversation start exactly?'

'Well, believe it or not, Michael thinks I'm afraid that alcohol has a power over me, though as he sees it, it's more about a deep-seated insecurity I've had all my life.' Angela looked to Edward skeptically, and he explained, 'We've known each other since we were boys, see, and ever since things started falling apart after the earthquake, he thinks I've been worried that I wouldn't be able to hold my family together...'

Angela grimaced and shook her head. 'Well, I can't say I approve of his audacity, but I suppose there's some truth in what he says...'

'He says I'm stronger than I think, that I've done a remarkable job, all things considered...'

'Well, you have done good by your family,' Angela said, taking his hand in hers. 'Look, Edward, for too long you've been concerned about how other people see you, only it's not right because it gives them influence over you. It begins with your mother, of course, but I've also seen how your brothers take advantage of you sometimes, and even in the way your sisters count on you like a father. At work you crave Mr. Breslin's approval, when actually he's the one who should be grateful to you. As for me, we've had our ups and downs, but for the most part you've been my champion because you're a thinking, caring man, and not one set in his ways.'

Edward touched his forehead to hers and squeezed her hand. 'Thank you for saying that.'

'The truth is you shouldn't care so much about how other people see you, Edward, because you're a fine man...Not that many people really care, anyway – most of them are are too caught up in getting what they want to genuinely care about you. You only really matter to the people who love you, Edward,' Angela said, looking him in the eye. 'You matter to me.'

Edward's eyes brimmed with tears and he embraced her a long time before they kissed.

They settled back against the couch, holding hands and looking out to the rain, prepared to face the uncertain future together. For the first time Edward felt content simply sitting beside the person he loved the most and who knew him best, contemplating the raindrops on the windowpane, as resigned to adversity as he was knowing there would always be rainstorms ahead. He was guardedly optimistic about the future, in fact, if for no other reason than he felt a part of life, that in the grand scheme of things, he mattered.

Acknowledgements

The genesis of this novel was my desire to better understand the life and times of my maternal grandfather, an American veteran of the Great War who died when I was five years old, his last years tinged by still more tragedy. Too much was asked of his generation, and I've long wondered what it must have felt like for them to see their sacrifice was in vain when the war to end all wars was resumed just a generation later, with even more disastrous consequences. How sad it is to recognize the forces that threatened to undermine America's great promise in my grandfather's time still resonate today; how ironic that we should find ourselves again in the grips of a global pandemic as we were a century ago, humbled once more by our own hubris.

That we are more interconnected and interdependent than we realize may be our best hope, after all. And in that spirit, I wish to convey my gratitude to a host of people without whom this book would not have come to fruition.

First are those who have long since passed, but who once put pen to paper to leave a record of their experiences, from the mundane to the horrific. "A History of the 362nd Infantry," preserved by the Bancroft Library at the University of California, Berkeley, recounts the trajectory of my grandfather's regiment from the hastily formed training camp in the Pacific Northwest to the cauldron of the Meuse-Argonne Campaign fifteen months later. While this novel is a work of fiction and all of the central characters are imagined, this regimental history helped contextualize the life-altering impact for a young man drafted into military service at the tender age of twenty-one.

Second, I want to acknowledge several writers who have influenced this project, including Vera Brittain and Pat Barker, whose depiction of the impacts of war brought home moved me greatly; A.E. Housman, who captured the pathos faced by more than one "lost generation" of young people; and Sinclair Lewis and John Steinbeck for their depictions of the less glamorous side of America in the 1920s. As for non-fiction, I am awed by the work of Barbara Tuchman, Stanley Karnow, Kevin Starr, Hew Strachan, and Steven Kinzer for their clear vision and rigorous scholarship.

Getting down to the business of producing a novel, there is a special group of fellow readers and writers who generously agreed to my sending them a couple of chapters each month over a two year period, including Elizabeth Ardzrooni, Dave Chambers, Heather Clague, Nicole Clemens, Tom Clyde, C.A. Collier, Thomas Crockett, Brad Dickason, Paul d'Orleans, Dr. Barbara Galligan, Cort Gross, Anne Jones, Glen Lindwall, Al Luongo, Mimi Melodia, Loren Partridge, Kelly Evans Pfeifer, and Terry Thomas. These people sustained me with their thoughtful feedback, constructive criticism, and consistent support.

As an architect I have witnessed a complete transformation of the profession across the past four decades; a similar upheaval in the publishing industry has resulted in market forces driving a worrisome consolidation among traditional publishers, while at the same time unprecedented opportunities for self-publishing have emerged. Having personally chosen a middle path, I have appreciated the encouragement of published authors, including Annie Barrows, Ona Russell, and Helen Simonson; of literary agents Paula Munier and Jaida Temperly; and of a mentor, Tom Jenks, founder and co-editor of www.NarrativeMagazine.com. I was also fortunate to have found New York editor Laurie Chittenden, who encouraged me to clarify the feelings, motivations and emotional stakes of the central characters and stressed the careful weaving of detail to bind the narrative across diverse timeframes and story lines.

Lastly, by way of affirming that there are no coincidences, after extensive outreach to literary agents, traditional publishers, and independent presses in the U.S. and the UK, in the end it was serendipity led me to James Essinger, the founder and indomitable force behind The Conrad Press. I am so pleased to be joining such a supportive community of writers.

Ultimately, I am especially grateful to my wife Eileen. She enabled me to pursue this creative endeavor and her faith in my efforts never wavered. Our respective ancestors came to San Francisco in the late 1800s, and moved in the same cultural and religious orbits within that 49-square mile melting pot for the next hundred years – until we finally connected, quite by chance, at the beginning of this new century. I often wonder if larger forces are at work in all of this – what I know is that were it not for Eileen, this novel would not exist.

Jeffrey J. Lousteau
Berkeley, CA – June 2020
www.jeffreyjlousteau.com

Bibliography

Barker, Pat. *Regeneration*. New York: Penguin Books, 1991.

Barrows, Annie (w/ Mary Ann Shaffer). *The Guernsey Literary and Potato Peel Society*. New York: The Dial Press, 2008.

Barry, Sebastian. *The Whereabouts of Eneas McNulty*. Great Britain: Picador, 1998.

Bellow, Saul. *The Adventures of Augie March*. New York: The Viking Press, 1953.

Brittain, Vera. *Testament to Youth: An Autobiographical Study of the Years 1900-1925*. New York: The Macmillan Company, 1933.

Bruno, Lee. *Panorama: Tales from San Francisco's 1915 Pan-Pacific International Exposition*. Petaluma, CA: Cameron + Company, 2014.

Connell, Evan S. *Son of the Morning Star*. San Francisco: North Point Press, 1984.

Doctorow, E.L. *Ragtime*. New York: Random House, 1975.

Duffy, P.S. *The Cartographer of No Man's Land*. New York: Liveright Publishing, 2013.

Faulkner, William. *Soldiers' Pay*. New York: Boni & Liveright, Inc., 1926.

Goldstein, Gabriel & Greenberg, Elizabeth. *A Perfect Fit: The Garment Industry and American Jewry, 1860-1960.* Texas Tech University Press for Yeshiva University, 2012.

Hallas, James H., Editor. *Doughboy War: The American Expeditionary Force in WWI.* Colorado: Lynne Rienner Publishers, Inc., 2000.

Housman, A.E. *A Shropshire Lad.* New York, John Lane Company 1906; (self-published London, 1896).

Joselit, Jenna Weissman. *A Perfect Fit: Clothes, Character, and the Promise of America.* New York: Henry Holt and Co., 2001.

Karnow, Stanley. *In Our Image: America's Empire in the Philippines.* New York: Ballantine Books, 1989.

Keneally, Thomas. *The Daughters of Mars.* New York: Atria Books, 2012.

Kinzer, Stephen. *The True Flag: Theodore Roosevelt, Mark Twain, and the Birth of American Empire.* New York: Henry Holt and Company, 2017.

Lewis, Sinclair. *Babbitt.* New York: Harcourt, Brace & World, 1922.

London, Jack. *The Sea Wolf.* New York: The Macmillan Company, 1904.

Lukas, J. Anthony. *Big Trouble.* New York: Simon & Schuster, 1997.

Mailer, Norman. *The Naked and the Dead.* New York: Rinehart and Company, 1948.